HOMICIDE
IN THE
INDIAN
HILLS

Books by Erica Ruth Neubauer

MURDER AT THE MENA HOUSE

MURDER AT WEDGEFIELD MANOR

DANGER ON THE ATLANTIC

INTRIGUE IN ISTANBUL

SECRETS OF A SCOTTISH ISLE

HOMICIDE IN THE INDIAN HILLS

Novellas

MURDER UNDER THE MISTLETOE

Published by Kensington Publishing Corp.

ERICA RUTH NEUBAUER

HOMICIDE IN THE INDIAN HILLS

KENSINGTON
PUBLISHING CORP.

kensingtonbooks.com

KENSINGTON BOOKS are published by

Kensington Publishing Corp.
900 Third Ave.
New York, NY 10022

Library of Congress Control Number: 2024949554

KENSINGTON and the K with book logo Reg. US Pat. & TM Off.

ISBN: 978-1-4967-4121-9
First Kensington Hardcover Edition: April 2025

ISBN: 978-1-4967-4123-3 (ebook)

10 9 8 7 6 5 4 3 2 1

Printed in the United States of America

For Ann Collette, a dear friend who got me here.

HOMICIDE
IN THE
INDIAN
HILLS

CHAPTER ONE

It was a good thing that I wasn't afraid of heights, only enclosed spaces, since the steam train we were on was clacking up an incredibly narrow track along the side of a mountain. I still did my best to keep my attention focused inside our car instead of looking out the window at the sheer drop down the mountainside, despite the lovely countryside. Much as I would have liked to enjoy the views of verdant green valley and misty peaks, the path was rather panic-inducing—especially the narrow stone bridges we occasionally crossed over, with dramatic drop-offs on either side that made one feel rather faint. I could only hope the train continued to hug the side of the mountain as it carried us farther into the lush mountains of India.

"Not exactly the honeymoon you had anticipated, is it?" my new husband asked from his seat across the table. Normally I liked to be quite close to him, but the heat of India's plains was such that I didn't want to be too near anyone, Redvers included. The inside of the train car was stifling, even with the windows open. We were fortunate to find ourselves in first class where there were far fewer people. I'd had a look inside the lower-class train cars when we boarded, and people were packed in tightly, not to mention the occasional goat. I couldn't imagine enduring that sort of ride for the long hours it would take us to get to our destination.

"Not particularly, but I never intended to marry again, so I never anticipated a honeymoon at all," I told him as I fanned myself with the ornate but practical hand fan I'd purchased in Chennai. "And I will make the best of things, as you well know. I enjoy exploring a new place."

Redvers' assignment to India was a political one and had come right on the heels of our trip to Scotland, where we'd decided to progress our relationship from an engaged couple to a married one. I'd hoped for a bit of time to settle into married life, but that wasn't to be. Not terribly surprising, given the man I'd married. And it was how I found myself on a steam train headed into the mountains of southern India, toward the hill station of Ootacamund, or Ooty, as it was affectionately called.

I'd been promised that the weather was much more temperate in Ooty. I sincerely hoped that I hadn't been misled: the heat in India was like nothing I'd ever experienced, even in Egypt, and I'd thought *that* would be the end of me. The heat of an Egyptian desert had been child's play, as it turned out.

"Can you give me a rundown of the players we'll be dealing with here?" I asked.

Redvers lifted an amused eyebrow. "That *I'll* be dealing with. I'm sorry that you won't have anything you can assist with on this assignment. The trip will probably be quite boring for you, unless you find some sort of trouble to get yourself into." His eyes always sparkled when he teased me, as they did now.

I wrinkled my nose at him. I wasn't going to dignify any of that with a response.

Redvers chuckled but then grew serious. "Truly, I am sorry that we seem to be hopping from place to place in service of my employer instead of settling down."

I cocked my head and considered that. I appreciated the apology, since we had just come off another assignment from the Crown, but I also understood when I agreed to marry him that this was what our life would look like, even if I hadn't acknowledged it consciously. I also hadn't the faintest idea what "settling down" would be like for us, or whether that was something I even wanted. It sounded quite boring, honestly.

"I knew what I was getting into," I said, and left it at that.

"Very well," Redvers said, going back to my original question. "Lord Goshen is the governor of Madras; he'll be staying in the governor's mansion."

"As one would think," I said.

"Indeed. I will also be meeting with Paramasivan Subbarayan, who is the Indian premier for this area, and one of his cabinet members, Ranganatha Mudaliar."

I liked how the names of the local people were long and musical. "And will that be all?"

Redvers shook his head. "No, the British secretary of state for India will also be joining us, Mr. Feodore Smith."

"And how does he fit in?" I asked.

"Smith headed up the charge for putting together the Simon Commission." Redvers had already explained that the purpose of the Simon Commission was to look at reforming Indian law. Doing so was a promise that had been made by the British government, which had ruled this country for centuries. But the people were interested in having more autonomy, and the commission was meant to look into that. The part I didn't understand was why the commission was entirely made up of British citizens. "Smith is afraid there will be protests, even riots, when the commission arrives next year, so I've been tasked with helping to smooth things over with the dissenters so there will be no trouble when the commission does arrive."

"Are there a lot of protests here?"

"In India as a whole? A fair number. Some of them can get violent, I'm sorry to say."

I grimaced. "I hope it won't come to that."

Redvers eyed me up. "And I hope you'll be able to find something to occupy your time while I sit through meetings."

I had opened my mouth to assure him that I would be perfectly fine without him when the door to our car opened and an older woman strode in. She was dressed in a brightly colored, loose-fitting tunic with flowing white pants beneath, her hair in a short gray bob. She had to be close to my Aunt Millie's age, but her haircut was very stylish and sleek, and despite her short stature she somehow projected height—or perhaps it was simply that she carried herself as a much taller person. The woman gazed around our car, her eyes finally landing on us, and she made her way over.

The other scattered occupants of our car eyed her warily, but I was interested to see what happened next. She had a youthful energy and a slight smirk on her face, as well as no problem sitting herself down next to a pair of strangers, as it turned out. She'd taken a seat next to me but as close to the aisle as possible, which I appreciated for the sake of air flow. The temperature in the car was dropping, but I was still overly warm.

"My compartment is full of fuddy-duddies, and I couldn't tolerate the boredom any longer," she said, adjusting the small pair of wire-rimmed glasses perched on her pert nose. "Who might you be?"

I wanted to ask why she'd chosen us out of the rest of the travelers, but glancing around, I could rather see why she had. The other occupants of our car were mostly older British men, sitting quietly and reading newspapers or sheaves of papers plucked from satchels. They were undoubtably civil servants, relocating along with the rest of the British government to the mountains for the summer. The British might rule India, but I'd quickly learned they didn't care at all for the climate. I wished that I could blame them, but I also wondered why they'd bothered to colonize a place where they couldn't tolerate the heat.

I also knew what answer I would get if I voiced the question out loud: resources. It was always about resources.

Our interloper was staring openly at the two of us, so I smiled and held out a hand. "Jane Wunderly," I said.

She nodded, shook my hand with a firm grip, and turned to Redvers expectantly.

"Redvers," was all he replied, although he reached across and shook her hand also.

When no further name was forthcoming, the woman gave him an odd look but offered her own name in reply. "Gretchen Beetner," she said. "A pleasure to meet you both." Her pale green eyes narrowed a bit in assessment. "Newlyweds?"

I could feel the surprise on my face, but looking over, I saw something like recognition on my husband's. *Husband*—I kept using the term so that I could get used to the idea that I'd married again. It was certainly a more comfortable fit than the first time around but still caught me by surprise when I said it, even to myself. "How did you know?" I asked.

"I can just tell about these things," Gretchen said confidently.

Redvers had a speculative look on his face. "I've heard about you."

Gretchen chuckled. "I'll bet you have."

I looked back and forth between the two, waiting for a story. When Redvers didn't say anything else, Gretchen shrugged. "I have a bit of a reputation," she said in a modest tone.

I saw Redvers' lips twitch before he tipped his head toward her. "Miss Beetner was a member of the Indian National Congress."

Surprise pulled my eyebrows up. "But you're British. And a woman."

Gretchen gave another hearty laugh. "You're quite observant, Mrs. Wunderly. I am indeed both of those things. But I'm quite popular with the Indians, since I believe we should get out of their country and leave them to rule themselves." She smoothed her tunic. "And please, call me Gretchen."

I murmured that she should call me Jane, but my mind was racing. This was the first time I'd heard such an opinion, and I wanted to know not only how she'd arrived at such a belief but how she had managed to become part of the Indian government as well. Wasn't that contrary to that very same belief system? But Gretchen and Redvers had already moved on to less political topics, so I tucked away my questions for the time being.

Gretchen sat with us for the rest of our ride up the mountain to Ooty, occasionally leaning over to point out some interesting feature we passed, like a strikingly green terraced tea plantation unfurling down a mountain slope or a troop of monkeys in the treetops. She finally excused herself to go collect her things once we were pulling into the station. I'd very much enjoyed the older woman's company. She had a quick wit and was very opinionated in a way that reminded me of my Aunt Millie but was otherwise warm and humorous in ways that my aunt was not, at least not when I was around. Redvers and I had learned that we were staying in the same building as Miss Beetner, and I was both pleased and hopeful that I might have the opportunity to spend more time with her during our stay.

The station platform was chaotic and crowded, with what felt like the entire British government attempting to direct its bags to the correct destination, and Indian porters attempting to assist by shouting over the heads of the crowd. For once, though, I found myself unbothered by the noise and activity. I took a deep breath, grateful that thick, wet air wasn't clogging my lungs anymore; the temperature was much lower here on the mountain than in the cities below. In fact, it was downright pleasant, warm but not hot. Redvers had warned me that I would need some warm clothing in the evenings, and for the first time, I believed it might be true.

Eventually our luggage was retrieved, and both it and ourselves were loaded into the back of a small carriage with large wooden wheels pulled by a horse. I intended to offer a ride to Gretchen, but I'd lost sight of her in the chaotic crush as soon as we'd stepped down from the train.

I'd considered opting to walk, but once we were on our way, I quickly realized that everything in this town was going to be either up a hill or down a hill, and in this case, it seemed mostly upward. I was pleased that I'd opted for the ride—we could stretch our legs with a stroll through town once we were settled into our quarters.

I'd developed a light sheen of sweat on my face by the time we reached our destination, despite having been carried there, and was grateful for the light straw hat I was wearing that protected my dark hair from the sun overhead. The temperatures might be cooler here, but the sun refused to relent in ferocity, even at this higher elevation.

We were not staying at the governor's mansion, as I'd assumed since I'd been told that complex was sprawling and accommodated many of the civil workers. Instead, we were staying at a charming house some distance away. The façade was entirely made of stone, with three gabled roofs and a series of red chimneys reaching toward the blue sky, reminiscent of many of the buildings I was accustomed to seeing back in England. I wrinkled my nose in disappointment. I'd been hoping for charming, traditional Indian style, but from what I'd seen of Ooty so far, I was simply going to see more traditional British architecture.

We were shown to our quarters by a man in a white, loose-fitting tunic and pants and leather sandals. "I will be your servant during your stay. Please let me know if there is anything that you need. My name is Sasmit."

I wasn't comfortable with the term "servant," but I smiled and thanked Sasmit, before repeating his name silently to myself several times so that I would remember it correctly. Sasmit gave explanations of where we would find everything we needed, including the location of the breakfast room.

I thought I might take a walk in the mornings while Redvers was occupied with meetings and asked Sasmit about the best place to do that. "Memsahib, you can walk through the city on what they call the mall. It is a path that many people use for walking. Or you can walk to the edge of the city and enjoy the forests and the hills around us. But," his thin face became very grave. "You mustn't walk there at night, even when it becomes dusk. Especially not by yourself. It is a very bad idea."

I frowned. Was this admonishment because I was a woman? That always managed to get my back up, so I wasn't able to keep the edge out of my voice when I replied. "Why is that, Sasmit?"

The porter either didn't catch my tone or chose to ignore it, answering me pleasantly. "Because of the tigers," Sasmit said.

CHAPTER TWO

A shiver went down my spine at Sasmit's pronouncement, and I hugged my arms against my chest. "Tigers?"

His head bobbed side to side in a manner I'd come to associate with Indian people but couldn't begin to interpret. "We haven't had trouble in many years, but recently a tiger has been seen near to the city. They are most active at dawn and dusk, so it is wise to stay indoors during those times."

I didn't have to be told twice. It had never once occurred to me that a wild tiger was something I had to be concerned about. I had a lot more questions about the tigers, and anything else that might kill me, but Sasmit bowed and left us on our own before I could begin my interrogation. When I turned to Redvers, he looked amused.

"Is he serious?" I asked.

Redvers nodded. "I would think so. Tigers are common throughout the country."

All I had seen on our journey into the mountains had been lush green forests, much like the ones I saw at home or in England. This seemed a surprising habitat for a tiger—I had somehow always imagined them living in a jungle rather than stalking through a forest of pine trees.

My mind was still churning with questions, but I turned and took in what would be our living quarters for this stay.

How long we would be here I hadn't the faintest idea, since Redvers hadn't been able to give me a better estimate than "as long as it takes." It was maddeningly vague, but as much as he liked to tease me, I felt certain he was being as truthful as he could be. Well, fairly certain. The man had the devil in him sometimes, which sparked that twinkle in his eyes. It was so charming that I could never be truly mad at him.

The sitting room where we stood had simple but tasteful wood furniture covered with silky red upholstery, elaborately embroidered with gold thread. A large set of glass doors led to a small patio facing a garden, which I thought might be a nice place to enjoy a cup of coffee. There was also a bedroom, simply furnished, as well as a small bathroom.

"I'm surprised we have a bathroom to ourselves," Redvers remarked. "I wonder if the building was updated recently."

"Well, I'm quite pleased that we do, and I'm going to take advantage of it now," I said, leaving Redvers in the sitting room to wait for our luggage. The dust and grit from a morning of travel, topped off by the dried sweat from our open carriage ride, felt like a second skin laid over my own, and I wanted to wash up before I did any further exploration. I ran a lukewarm bath for myself, grateful that the building even had indoor plumbing. I'd already learned that was a luxury here in India, one that I'd always taken for granted before.

By the time I emerged from the bathroom, feeling much refreshed and dressed in a linen skirt and simple green blouse with a wide collar, Redvers had a full tea service waiting with some small finger sandwiches and a bowl of exotic-looking fruits. I'd half expected him to be reading something, but he was sipping a cup of tea while he gazed out at the garden instead. I eyed the tray warily, wondering if tea was all that would be available here.

Redvers caught my look and chuckled. "Don't worry, there's plenty of coffee to be had." He gestured to one of the pots on the tray.

I sank into the chair opposite him with relief. "Gretchen pointed out all the tea plantations, and I became concerned that would be the only choice."

"Do you want a cup?"

"Of coffee? Need you even ask?"

Redvers smiled and fixed me a cup, precisely the way I liked it, and passed it over to me. I decided it was early enough in the afternoon that the coffee wouldn't give me any trouble sleeping that night but would instead power me through a brief exploration of Ooty—queen of the hill stations, as it was known.

Redvers agreed to accompany me since he didn't have any pressing matters to attend to and wasn't expected to be anywhere until dinner. Hand in hand, we strolled out of the complex we were staying in and headed west into town.

Ooty was much larger than I expected it would be— much more like a city, with a racetrack for horses, a botanical garden filled with trees and plants from England, steepled churches, a library, and a large man-made lake. The roads were packed dirt, but the architecture throughout was largely British in nature. At least the local bazaar was full of color and local flavor: reams of flowers; colorful fabrics; spices and sacks of lentils; wooden cages with small, colorful birds chirping noisily; vendors selling hot food. It was chaotic and busy and loud, and I soaked it up with enthusiasm.

The British influence over the rest of the city troubled me, though. "Why bother making the trip if you're just going to import all of England here?" I mused. "Wouldn't you want the experience of foreign plants and foods?"

Redvers smiled. "Not everyone is as fond of adventure as you are, my dear."

I sighed. I found it disappointing to see much of what I'd already seen in England planted and built everywhere on the side of this mountain, cascading toward the valley. It meant I would have to venture farther afield to get a better sense of what the area had been like before the British had taken over, but given Sasmit's warning about wild tigers, I had a great deal of trepidation about venturing anywhere outside of the city.

"Is there anything besides tigers that I should be aware of?" I asked as we passed a group of women in brightly colored saris with cropped blouses and bared sides traveling in the opposite direction. I did my best not to stare, but the colors were so bold and beautiful that it was hard not to admire them. Greens and yellows and blues and purples—all colors of the rainbow seemed to be represented in the clothing here. Several of the women had part of the sari draped over their heads to protect their scalps, and I admired the utility of the thing, even if it was a mystery to me how they tied one long piece of fabric on as a dress.

"Are you asking if there are other animals that you should avoid?" Redvers asked, eyes crinkled at the edges in amusement. "Well, there are wild elephants in the region, as well as some very large and ornery buffalo." He tapped his lip, pretending to think. "I would think it's best to avoid those. Some poisonous snakes, and of course there are leopards, as well as . . ." I gave his arm a light smack, and he laughed. "You'll be fine, my dear. Just stick to well-traveled paths, and I imagine the wildlife will leave you well alone."

"You're very helpful," I said darkly.

Our stroll had filled the afternoon, and by the time we made it back, it was time to dress for dinner. Redvers changed into a dark suit, and I almost asked if he wouldn't rather wear one of the lightweight suits he'd brought along, when I remembered another admonishment I'd received about Ooty; it could get downright chilly at night. I grabbed a black shawl with lace trim that nicely accented the dark green silk dress I'd put on for the evening, although I had my doubts about whether the shawl was something I would need.

It was nearly a half-hour walk to the governor's mansion, a winding track that led us through the botanical gardens and up a long, sloping path.

"Why aren't we staying closer to the mansion?" I asked. "Or *at* the mansion, for that matter?"

"You're not enjoying the view?" Redvers asked, nodding his head to the lush green bushes filled with fragrant flowers.

"When you answer a question with a question, I know you're hiding something," I said. I wasn't sure that was always true, but in this instance, I could tell there was something he wasn't telling me.

He gave a casual shrug. "I like the exercise." I was about to call him out on this white lie when he chuckled and gave in. "And I would rather not stay where everyone in the government can see us. Or keep track of my whereabouts."

That I believed, but there was clearly more to his answer. I opened my mouth to ask, but we had come upon the governor's mansion, a large and imposing green building with columns flanking the front entrance, located beneath one of the architectural bump-outs. I would have to ask later if there was some other reason he wanted distance from the crowd we were about to encounter. We climbed the stairs and stepped through the open door. I could immediately see that the interior of this grand building was entirely British— portraits of British people and paintings of British scenes, tapestries and carpets that could have been found in any country estate in England.

I stifled a sigh.

We came to the dining hall, a pale yellow room, stretched long with a row of columned arches running along the windows. The ceiling was ornately carved, set off by a wide swath of equally ornate carving that had been painted gold. It somehow felt heavy overhead. Two beautifully polished, long wood tables had been set up for the meal, set with what I could only assume was the governor's best porcelain.

There were a number of people present, mostly men, although there was a good mix of both British and Indian, all dressed for the occasion of welcoming the governor and his cabinet to the hills for the summer. It seemed Governor Goshen had arrived only a few days before, and we were in time for the formal arrival dinner. I was relieved when I saw Gretchen pushing through the crowd toward us, and I welcomed her with a little more enthusiasm than was probably necessary.

"They're just as boring as they look, too," Gretchen said, not even bothering to lower her voice. "I'm sorry that he had to drag you here." She tipped her head toward Redvers.

I couldn't help the grin that split my face. "Well, I do have to eat."

Gretchen smiled in return. "The food in this country cannot be topped. Makes even the heat worth it."

I wasn't certain that I would go that far, but I was looking forward to dinner. So far, everything I had tasted since our arrival in India had been absolutely delicious, with flavors and spices that I hadn't experienced before.

"Do you know where you're seated?" Gretchen asked Redvers, who shook his head, clearly bemused by the woman. "I'm sitting with you. Let's go find out."

We were herded to a table near the front where the governor and his immediate associates were seated. Our table was the one just to the right, and Gretchen planted herself in a chair and waved me into the one beside her. While I sat, Redvers excused himself to say hello to people.

"I'll fill you in while he's gone," Gretchen said. With a sweep of her hand, she dismissed most of the people in the room. "Mostly clerks, assistants, and civil servants are what you see here. There are only a few key players that you'll need to know." She gestured with her head toward a slight Indian man sporting a bushy moustache but lacking the elaborately wrapped head scarf that many of the local men wore. His suit was dark and understated but clearly well-tailored. "That's Paramasivan Subbarayan." She then indicated a few other people in the crowd, explaining who they were while I mentally matched them up with what Redvers had told me about each one. After a bit, I interrupted her, curious. "What are your thoughts about the Simon Commission?"

"It's nonsense," she said, her voice passionate. "Electing a bunch of British men to make decisions for a country that many of them haven't even set foot in. Disgraceful." She blew out a breath so forcefully it was nearly a snort. "The Indian people should be able to determine their own laws and how they run their country."

I thought that was an interesting position, given that she'd been on the Indian National Congress. She was British herself, after all. But I kept that to myself, waiting until she had run out of steam before I asked my next question. "You're clearly very passionate about the subject. How did you come to this opinion?" Her eyes narrowed at me, and I hurried to explain. "I don't disagree with you. It's just so different from what everyone else thinks."

Gretchen had opened her mouth to answer when something else caught her attention, and she paused. "That's interesting," she muttered.

I glanced around. "What is?"

She gestured to my right with a subtle chin movement. "The governor's wife is here. Virginia Goshen."

I looked in the direction she'd indicated and saw a petite woman in a silvery beaded gown, her gray hair pinned in an elaborate knot at the back of her head. Her mouth was slightly pursed as she nodded at the men greeting her. There weren't many women in the room; that had been apparent from the moment I walked in. But she seemed especially uncomfortable here. I wondered why.

"Is it unusual that she's here?"

Gretchen nodded. "She usually returns to England for the summer." Her face had taken on a speculative look. "I wonder how Goshen is going to manage both his wife and his mistress taking up residence in Ooty."

CHAPTER THREE

M y eyes widened, and Gretchen chuckled. "Oh, it's common practice for the Brits stationed here to keep a native mistress. But it becomes quite awkward when the wife actually shows up."

My lips pressed together in a moue of disgust, and Gretchen nodded. "I quite agree. It's a despicable practice. Not least because the mistress is tossed aside—usually with a child or two—when the man returns to England. It's another thing I'd dearly love to see changed. Of course, it wouldn't be so much of an issue if the British government got out of India entirely and quit interfering on other continents."

We were quiet for a moment before Gretchen returned to explaining who people were. She often had a little anecdote about each, far more entertaining than the explanations I'd gotten from Redvers, and I found that against all odds, I was enjoying myself immensely.

Redvers returned from his rounds, and we settled in at our table as the waiters began bringing out plate after plate of food. I was excited until I realized that we were being served English specialties and nothing else. Yorkshire pudding and shepherd's pie, roast lamb and mushy peas—all things that would make the Brits feel right at home but were nothing but a disappointment to someone who enjoyed exotic food. I stifled my groan of despair and let the waitstaff fill my plate.

I ate quietly and without enthusiasm while Gretchen and Redvers had a lively conversation about local politics, which seemed to entertain both of them, but I tuned out and let my mind drift to other matters, such as what I might do with myself the following day.

Once my plate was clean, I found it difficult to keep my eyes open and repeatedly had to straighten up in my chair, since my body dearly wanted to slump toward the table. The combination of a long day of travel and a stomach full of mediocre food was clearly taking its toll, and I could no longer hide how tired I was.

"Are you ready to retire?" Redvers asked as my face split nearly in two with a jaw-cracking yawn that I only just managed to cover with a hand.

"I'm ready whenever you are," I replied. "But if that was sooner rather than later, I wouldn't be upset."

"We can go." Redvers glanced around. "The party is breaking up anyway."

I stood and collected my shawl, and Gretchen stood as well. "I'll walk back with you. We could try to get a carriage, but it will take a while, and I would not mind walking off this heavy food. With a small group, we'll be fine. I won't walk anywhere at night by myself."

"That's wise," I said, thinking about what I'd been told by Sasmit. It was quite a long walk back, some of it through uninhabited gardens, and who knew what might be lurking there? I opened my mouth to comment further when Redvers stopped abruptly in front of me, causing me to collide with his firm back. We had been about to pass through a doorway into the garden, and peering around his shoulder I could see the cause of our delay. Two men stood beneath a dimly lit lantern on the path, and they were clearly arguing. They both wore the long dark coats with buttons up the center that I'd noticed many Indian men wearing, with slim-fitting cotton pants beneath. I turned to warn Gretchen that we should be quiet, but her sharp eyes were already trained on the men.

I watched for a moment, but I couldn't remember who it was that I was seeing. A number of people had been pointed out to me, and even with the amusing anecdotes, I was having trouble keeping names and roles straight. I was pleased when Gretchen leaned in to explain without my having to ask. "That's Subbarayan and his cabinet member Ranganatha Mudaliar," she murmured. I smiled my thanks and turned back to the men, but something in the garden coming from a different direction appeared to have startled them, and they broke apart, hurrying away down opposite paths.

We waited a few more beats before continuing on our way through the gently rose-scented courtyard and out onto the path that would eventually take us back to our quarters. "What do you think that was about?" I asked my companions quietly.

Both shrugged. "Could be any number of things," Redvers said.

That was a most unhelpful answer, but I let it go with a shrug. It seemed there was quite a bit of tension in both the state and local government these days, and it was probably nothing more than that.

Redvers was up bright and early the following morning but was kind enough to leave me sleeping soundly in bed. He had given Sasmit instructions to bring me a full pot of coffee once I woke up, and I was eternally grateful to the man for knowing me as well as he did. I wasn't sure how Sasmit managed it, but as soon as I made my way into the sitting room, he came hurrying in with a fresh pot of coffee. At least it tasted fresh, and that was all that really mattered.

He opened the windows and doors now that I was awake and left as quickly as he'd arrived.

I sipped my coffee and sighed happily, melting into the cushions of the couch. I'd been distracted by Redvers' nearness as soon as we'd returned to our rooms, so I'd forgotten to ask him about how he felt about his current assignment and the other various questions I'd assembled the night before. He really was quite skilled at directing my energies to . . . other activities. I wasn't complaining, of course. I hoped the electric attraction between us never diminished. It was something new and wonderful for me, and I wanted to savor every moment of it.

I smiled dreamily for a few moments before shaking myself and turning my mind to what I wanted to do with my day. It had been many months since I had been without a direct purpose, and I decided that I would try to enjoy the feeling. I had been told the botanical gardens were quite lovely and stretched far beyond what I'd seen on our walk the evening before. Unfortunately, it sounded as though the acres were full of plants native to England, which I was not terribly interested in seeing. I'd already seen the plants England had to offer. But it might be worth strolling through, if it came down to a choice between staring at a wall or getting some fresh air.

I was still suspicious of the weather here, the choking heat of the plains still fresh in my mind, but our quarters were quite comfortable this morning, even as I drank hot coffee. A pleasantly warm breeze blew through the open doors, carrying the faint smell of camphor from the numerous eucalyptus trees as well as the musical chatter of birds. It couldn't be that much warmer outside, so I was actually looking forward to spending some time outdoors.

Sasmit returned after a time to see if I needed anything else, and I asked him about the best sights in the area. He listed off a series of things that sounded more suited to someone who wanted to see the British interpretation of Ooty, but I wanted to see the Indian version of it, and I told him as much.

Sasmit beamed. "I could arrange a tour of a tea plantation for you, memsahib. Many Indian people work there, and it is quite interesting to see how our local tea is cultivated."

"You don't have to call me memsahib, Sasmit. Jane is fine," I said. The honorific that the locals used made me a little uncomfortable. "But a tour would be lovely. Thank you." I didn't care for tea, but Gretchen had pointed out the terraced hills on our train ride up the mountain. It might be nice to see a plantation up close, even if I had no interest in the product. I had concerns about walking into the surrounding countryside by myself, but it was daytime, so I tamped down my nerves about the local wildlife population. I couldn't hide inside or even keep to the city paths during my entire stay. It wasn't reasonable, nor was it in my nature—I was compelled to explore.

Sasmit hurried away to arrange a tour for me, and I set about getting ready for the day. I decided on a lightweight blouse with a subtle floral design in shades of yellow and blue with a wide neck above a row of buttons down the front. I paired it with a calf-length khaki-colored skirt and a slim white belt at my waist. I grabbed a pair of low-heeled brown shoes that were sturdy and perfect for walking.

I'd hoped that Gretchen would be available to spend time with me, but she was attending the same meetings that Redvers was, so I was truly on my own. I decided a trip to the library would be in order during my stay, sooner rather than later; hopefully I could find a novel to occupy some of my time. We were in a city perched on the side of a mountain, and I suspected there was a limited amount of sightseeing I could do.

Now that I was dressed, I returned to the sitting room

and poured myself a cup of coffee that was lukewarm but still drinkable. Sasmit came hurrying back.

"Memsahib, I have hired a palanquin that will take you to the plantation, and someone there who speaks English will give you a tour."

"Jane," I corrected, then paused. I'd never heard of the conveyance he'd mentioned. "What exactly is that?"

"It is a box that you sit in, and strong men carry you on their shoulders. It is very comfortable."

My eyes widened in shock, and I sputtered for a moment. "I'm very sorry, but there's no way I can have someone carry me to the plantation." I couldn't believe this was even an option.

Sasmit frowned. "It is no trouble, I assure you. It is their job."

That might well be the case, but I simply couldn't imagine allowing two men to carry me somewhere as though I were a member of ancient royalty. It felt more like something one would see in ancient Egypt than in modern-day India. I simply couldn't do it. "Can I get a carriage? Or is there someone who can simply accompany me there? On a walk?"

Sasmit's frown deepened. "It is several miles along dirt roads. Surely you do not want to walk there; you will gather dust on your fine clothing, memsahib. I could get a carriage for one; it is also pulled by a man, but these men have already been hired."

Having someone pull me in a carriage wasn't much better, as far as I was concerned. "I am quite happy to walk." My voice was firm.

Sasmit was still frowning, but he hurried away again, returning moments later. "The men will walk with you there and back."

I was relieved that at least I wouldn't be carried to my destination and thanked Sasmit for his help. He left the room, bobbing his head slightly, and I hoped he wasn't too frustrated with me. I didn't want to be difficult, but I simply wasn't going to let two men carry me where I needed to go. I'd spent weeks in Scotland, hiking back and forth across a rocky island—I was more than capable of walking a few miles through what promised to be beautiful countryside. Of course, I was a little relieved that two strong men were going to accompany me on the walk. Perhaps they would scare away any predatory cats lurking in the grass. I just didn't want them to carry me there.

I went to the front of the building and found four men waiting for me, not two. The palanquin was on the ground, and they picked it up, the long poles over their shoulders with the wooden box perched in the center. I pointed to it and shook my head, but they shook theirs in return. One of the men in front, thin and wiry, said something to me in Tamil, and I realized that there wasn't going to be any conversation on this countryside trek, not for me anyway. It also appeared they were set on bringing the conveyance with them, whether I rode in it or not. It felt silly, but with a shrug I gestured for them to lead the way.

We headed north, through town and in the general direction of the governor's mansion, where Redvers and Gretchen were attending meetings all day. I did my best to ignore the curious stares we were attracting, the American trailing behind four strong men carrying a conveyance meant to be ridden in. We passed near the botanical garden, turning right instead of continuing toward the mansion, and the sweet scent of blooming flowers lightened my steps. I glanced around, looking for the exact source and saw Gretchen standing on the path with a beautiful Indian woman. She was petite with long black hair, wearing a gorgeous orange and pink sari that looked stunning on her. I could never wear such colors, but she wore them extremely well. Gretchen had her hand on the other woman's arm, and they were talking with their heads bent close together. The woman shook her head violently and wrenched her arm away from Gretchen before swiping at her face. Was she crying? From this distance it was hard to tell, but it certainly seemed to be the case.

I dearly wanted to know who the beautiful Indian woman was and what was happening between the two, but I'd already paused for too long—my escorts were well ahead of me, and I would have to hustle to catch up to them. I would have called out to them to wait for me, but it was quite clear they didn't speak English, so I took off at a trot, hoping they might realize they'd lost me and slow their pace.

They didn't, and I was out of breath by the time I caught up, which made the man in back finally pause and glance over his shoulder. He said something to his companion, and they stopped, speaking to me and nodding toward the box. I was still breathing heavily, but I shook my head, hands on knees while I caught my breath. We might look ridiculous, but I couldn't bear to have these men carry me on their shoulders to our destination. Once I'd regained my composure, they set off again, and I fell into step beside them, enjoying the warm sun on my face and the fresh air. It was warm, bordering on hot now that the sun was up, but it was nothing in comparison to how thick with moisture the heat in Madras had been during the few days we had spent there.

I enjoyed the weather for a while, but my mind kept turning back to the tableau I'd seen in the garden. Gretchen had obviously known the woman and, if I had to guess, liked her quite a bit, based on the body language I had seen. But who was the woman, and why was she meeting Gretchen in the botanical garden? Was she the governor's mistress? And why had she been crying?

Chapter Four

There was not a lot of foot traffic once we got outside of Ooty, and I quickly found that I was grateful for the wide-brimmed straw hat I'd put on—it kept the sun off my head and face. I was also grateful for my companions, despite the language barrier. I kept looking for any sign of a large predatory cat lurking in the long grass, even though I'd been told that tigers were primarily active at dawn and dusk. It was unlikely one was lying in wait for us, but I was on high alert all the same and thankful that I had the men with me, even if it provided nothing but a false sense of security.

The fact that they could probably run faster than me was something I also chose to ignore.

The views were stunning when the trees opened up, allowing me to glimpse sloped green mountains stacked against one another in the distance, still misty at the peaks, with a backdrop of bright blue sky. I'd become accustomed to the chirps and trills of the numerous birds, but a sudden racket from the upper branches of nearby trees startled me, and I shrieked.

The men paused in their steady march, two of them laughing at my reaction, the others merely smiling at me. The man nearest me pointed overhead and said something in Tamil, which I clearly didn't understand. But I peered into the treetops just the same, trusting I wasn't about to see something dangerous, since they seemed so unconcerned.

Monkeys. It was a troop of monkeys swinging from branch to branch, calling to one another and generally creating a fuss. I was immediately charmed. I'd never seen monkeys in the wild before, and I enjoyed their athletic antics for several minutes before nodding that we should continue on.

There was enough of a breeze that I wasn't becoming overheated, and I was almost disappointed when we turned off the main road onto a smaller dirt track leading up an incline. I walked behind the men now as we followed the narrow path cutting between tall trees. Suddenly the trees opened up again, and I was able to see the plantation. Slopes of waist-high green bushes reached before me, terraced downward in places to match the pitch of the mountain, with small, evenly spaced red dirt tracks breaking up the otherwise unrelenting sea of shiny green leaves. A few workers were spotted here and there with large woven baskets strapped to their backs, harvesting the bounty, although how they could tell which ones were ready to pick was beyond me. It all looked the same from where we stood.

My escorts led me to a large white building with a red tile roof where they set down their palanquin, bowed to me, and then disappeared. I would have asked how to find them when I was finished, but they wouldn't have understood me if I tried.

"Mrs. Wunderly?" A man wearing a mustard-colored tunic over a pair of flowing white yellow pants greeted me.

I told him that I was, and he smiled warmly. "I am Hasnan. I will be your guide today."

We exchanged pleasantries, and he gestured for me to follow him as he began walking toward the nearest terrace of tea plants, presumably to show me the leaves. "Do you enjoy tea, Mrs. Wunderly?"

My step stuttered a bit as I tried to think of the politest way to answer his question. "Um, well . . ."

Hasnan laughed, a musical sound. "It is fine if you do not. I will attempt to change your mind."

I laughed too. "I wish you luck. Coffee has always been my preference."

"You simply haven't met the right tea yet," Hasnan insisted. "I think you will find something to your satisfaction here."

I smiled and shook my head. I sincerely doubted he could change my mind on the topic, but I wouldn't stop him from trying.

More than an hour later, I was tasting the different types of tea grown on this particular hillside, and while Hasnan—despite his best efforts—hadn't turned me into a tea enthusiast, he'd found at least one that I didn't mind drinking. During my tour of the grounds, I'd purposely pushed all thoughts of intrigue from my mind. There was none to be found here, and I needed to simply enjoy my time in Ooty, not look for trouble where there was none. Whatever was transpiring between Gretchen and the Indian woman was none of my concern, and I was determined to leave it that way for once.

My tour drew to a close, and Hasnan summoned my palanquin bearers to escort me back to Ooty. As I waited near the conveyance I refused to ride in, a small carriage was just coming up the road. I watched as the man pulling it came to a stop not far from me and very gently lowered the long wooden arms to their resting place. A woman alighted from the seat perched over the two large wheels, and I recognized her face, although it took a moment for me to place her. It was the governor's wife, Virginia Goshen.

Lady Goshen looked around and spotted me. Her face looked puzzled for a moment, then she came forward. "Do I know you from somewhere?"

I smiled. "We haven't met, although I saw you at a distance at the welcome dinner last night."

Her face cleared. "Ah, that must be it. There weren't many women in attendance, so it is little wonder I recognize you." She looked around. "I was informed that this plantation puts out some of the best tea in the area. Did you find that to be true?"

I once again tried to figure out the most diplomatic way to address this issue. "There seem to be a number of very good teas here." Curiosity got the better of me, so I asked what I'd been wondering. "Is this your first time in Ooty?"

She nodded but narrowed her eyes slightly. "I'm sorry, I didn't catch your name."

"Miss . . . erm, Mrs. Wunderly." It was taking some time to remember that I was married now and was no longer a "miss." I was glad Redvers didn't mind my keeping the Wunderly surname, unconventional though that was. I'd fought to have it restored to me after my first husband died, and I didn't want to lose it again.

Lady Goshen's smile was back. "Newly married? I remember those days fondly." Then her smile faded, and she cleared her throat awkwardly. "How are you liking Ooty?"

"I only arrived yesterday, but so far, it's quite lovely. The mountains are beautiful, and the temperatures are much easier to tolerate than in Madras."

I wondered if her abrupt change of subject had to do with the fact that her husband openly kept a mistress here in town. It was quite a leap, but I didn't think it was outside the realm of possibility. Did she know? Or was she simply thinking of better times in her marriage? Either way, the memory seemed to make her uncomfortable.

"I agree. I'm sorry that I haven't been before." She paused, then continued on with an airy wave of her hand. "I usually go back to England to see my mother, but she passed away last year, and there was no reason to make the long journey. Charles tried to tell me that the children would want to see me, but they're grown and living their own lives. I'm certain they'll be pleased to go about their affairs uninterrupted for a while." She stopped abruptly, but I couldn't tell if it was because she'd dropped the word "affair," and it reminded her of her husband's own, or because she realized how much she'd been relating to me about her personal life. "It was nice to meet you, Mrs. Wunderly. I'm sure we'll be seeing each other again."

I smiled politely and nodded as Hasnan, who'd been standing quietly to the side with his hands clasped, came forward to greet Lady Goshen. "Enjoy your tour," I called to her as I followed my escorts down the red dirt road.

That had been an interesting encounter. It sounded as though Governor Goshen had tried to convince his wife to go back to England for the summer, but she'd made the trip to Ooty anyway. The governor would have quite a task ahead to keep the two women apart in a place as small as this.

CHAPTER FIVE

By the time I returned to our rooms, it was afternoon, and I was delighted to find that not only were Redvers and Gretchen in our sitting room, but they had a full afternoon tea before them. I had a plate with crustless finger sandwiches in my hand before my greetings had finished passing through my lips.

"Hungry?" Redvers asked with a sparkle in his eyes.

I wrinkled my nose at him in lieu of a response before taking a seat on the sofa next to him. I finished chewing my bite of cucumber sandwich before offering an apology for interrupting their conversation.

"Not at all," Gretchen said. "We were just discussing the tensions between the various factions."

"Anything of note?" What I was really asking was whether there was anything interesting, but I was doing my best to be polite in front of our guest.

"It seems there is some extra tension between Subbarayan and his cabinet, especially Mudaliar—" Redvers started to say, but Gretchen broke in.

"Those two have never really seen eye to eye, but it's been especially noticeable lately." Gretchen refilled her cup, holding it aloft in question. I shook my head as I was already sloshing inside with tea, and she continued. "I wonder if Mudaliar might be planning to push Subbarayan out."

This was vaguely interesting gossip, especially given that we'd seen them arguing in the garden the night before, but what I really wanted to know was who Gretchen had been speaking with in the garden that morning. So I asked her, much to Redvers' amusement.

"Oh, that is the governor's mistress, Savithri Kumari," Gretchen said. "Lovely woman."

I murmured my agreement that she had indeed appeared quite lovely. "It looked as though she was upset about something."

Gretchen didn't seem surprised that they'd been spotted in the garden, simply nodding her agreement. "She was."

I waited, but it quickly became obvious that Gretchen wasn't going to expound upon that. I was about to ask a follow-up question when Redvers redirected the conversation. "How was your tour of the plantation, my dear?"

I briefly narrowed my eyes at him—he knew exactly why, based on his answering grin—but I filled them in on my trip into the countryside.

"How was the ride? It can be very bumpy, as much as they try not to jostle you about," Gretchen said. "Especially once you get outside the city."

"Oh, I walked behind them. I couldn't possibly let someone carry me to where I'm going."

Gretchen laughed, an infectious belly laugh that brought a smile to my face. "I suppose it takes some getting used to, being carried about, but heavens. What those men must have thought, with you trailing along behind them," she said, still chuckling.

There was a moment's quiet, punctuated by Gretchen's amusement as we all pictured the scene. "I saw Lady Goshen there. We only spoke for a brief moment."

Gretchen raised her eyebrows. "I suppose she's taking in the sights, since she's never been to Ooty before."

I hoped this would spark Gretchen to comment further on what had upset Savithri that morning—something to the tune of the governor's wife taking up residence in Ooty, perhaps—but instead she turned the conversation back to Redvers and the thorny political issues that were afoot.

I poured myself a glass of water and settled back in my seat, prepared to tune out while they chatted.

"I'm sorry you didn't get any better gossip," Redvers said once Gretchen had taken her leave. We would see her again that evening at supper, which pleased me, although I was hopeful that they'd run their course on political talk.

"I wasn't looking for gossip," I said indignantly. Redvers' eyebrows quirked, and I sighed. "Very well, perhaps I was. I'm not used to being at such loose ends, so I may have been looking for a mystery of any sort to occupy my mind."

Redvers nodded. "I'm sorry that there isn't much for you to do on this assignment. I promise that I'll make it up to you."

I stepped close to him, playing with one of the buttons on his white shirt. "I have some ideas about how you could do that."

We occupied ourselves as newlyweds do until it was time to dress for dinner. I pulled a sleeveless cream-colored dress with black accents and a wide black waist tie from the wardrobe, despite the danger of staining something nearly white by dropping my supper onto it, and paired it with my black kitten-heeled shoes. I set my black lace-edged shawl next to my beaded clutch as a reminder to take the shawl with me when we left. I would be cold without it after supper had finished.

While I dressed, I again resolved to find a better way to occupy my time than trying to root out a story where there was none. Perhaps it was time to take up a new hobby, especially if more of our future travels were going to be based on Redvers' work assignments. I'd done some thinking about how I felt about this aspect of our marriage and found that while I didn't mind traveling for his work, since it allowed me to see new and exciting parts of the world, I did need to figure out how I would occupy myself.

Supper was a much less formal affair this time. It was held in the same beautiful room, but there were only a few tables' worth of people instead of the warm human crush of the evening before. I assumed many of the men present were government officials who had no family in Ooty to dine with, a fact that was confirmed by Gretchen when she joined us.

"These are the ones who send their wives back to England for the summer," Gretchen said as she looked around. "Which I don't understand. It's a torturous journey, as you know. I'd rather stay put once I was here, but that's just me, I suppose."

"When did you first come here?" I asked. The waiters were already bringing out the first courses, and I was disappointed to see that it was some version of a roast—much like what we'd been served the night before, and precisely what one would eat for supper back in England. "We aren't having Indian food?"

Gretchen heard the disappointment in my voice and summoned a member of the waitstaff over to us. "We would like Indian food. Is that something you can do without a great deal of trouble?" The waiter bobbed his head in a way that I couldn't tell whether it was a yes or a no, but he hurried away into the back.

"We'll be having Indian food," she said with a satisfied nod. "British food is terrible; who are we kidding? I can't understand why these men wouldn't take advantage of the delicious food available and opt for overdone roast instead."

She shook her head. "Nostalgia, I suppose? But I digress. What were you asking? Oh, yes, when did I first come here?" Gretchen considered for a moment. "In 1898, and it's probably been about five years since I've even traveled back to England for a visit." She shrugged casually. "No great loss, if you ask me."

I was shocked that she had been living in India for so long. If my math was correct, she had been here for nearly thirty years. But she'd been elected to the Indian National Congress, so that made sense; she'd been on the scene here for a long time. Our food started coming from the kitchen, and I was distracted for a long moment by the delicious smells wafting past my nose. Fluffy rice pancakes, chicken chettinad, crispy crepe-like dosas, bowls of a lentil stew called sambar, a vegetable dish called poriyal—the table was suddenly a cornucopia of aromatic dishes served in silver bowls. I was determined to try a little bit of everything and set about doing exactly that, filling my plate with a little bit of each dish. Glancing around, I noticed that the Indian civil servants—seated in little enclaves by themselves—were also eating traditional Indian food, and I felt some relief that the kitchen hadn't had to go to extra lengths just for us.

Once I was able to concentrate on conversation instead of savoring every bite of food that went into my mouth, I prompted Gretchen to continue explaining what had brought her to India.

"I started preaching contraception in the late 1800s, which didn't make me popular in England." She shook her head. "A shame for women. But it led me to becoming interested in matters of politics and the idea of Indian self-rule." She speared Redvers with a look. "What do you think about self-rule, Mr. Redvers?"

Redvers shifted in his seat, the only outward sign that he was uncomfortable. Looking at his carefully neutral face, I realized that I had no idea what his answer would be. We'd spent the majority of our free time since our hasty wedding in . . . other pursuits, and we hadn't really discussed his assignment here, beyond the basics of why he'd been sent halfway across the globe.

"Oh, the usual thing that a loyal subject of the Crown thinks." It was very obviously not an answer, and we all knew it. Gretchen shook her head in disappointment and looked as though she was going to needle him about it further, but Redvers quickly directed the conversation away from politics, asking Gretchen how she liked coming to the hills as opposed to the hot plains of India. She cocked an eyebrow at him, letting him know that she knew precisely what he was doing but was willing to go along with it for the moment, and answered his question.

While they discussed the weather, I sat back and reflected on how nice it was to meet an older woman so opposed to adhering to the social norms. It was a quality that I very much admired, even aspired to.

I should have asked her more questions while I had the chance.

CHAPTER SIX

With supper finished and our tolerance for making small talk at an end, Redvers and I prepared to walk back to our quarters. We invited Gretchen to return with us, but she'd caught sight of the Indian secretary of state, Feodore Smith, and said we should go on without her because she wanted to "corner the man and have a chat." I nearly felt sorry for Smith, but he likely deserved whatever Gretchen was going to "chat" with him about. I realized that I already felt a great deal of affection for Gretchen Beetner and was only sorry that she wasn't available to spend more time with me during the day.

"How will you get back?" I asked.

Gretchen airily waved a hand, already stalking her quarry. "I'll get a carriage."

Our walk back to our quarters was quiet, not to mention tension-filled, since it was now fully dark. There were plenty of other people about, but I still felt the darkness pressing against my peripherals, hiding unseen danger. I was certainly being overly dramatic, but telling myself that did nothing to soothe my nerves.

I held my questions for Redvers until we were back in our rooms—I wanted to concentrate on our surroundings, and I also wanted to make sure that there was no one around to overhear us. The door to our quarters had barely shut behind us before the man was nibbling at my neck, but I steeled my melting nerves and asked my question. "Redvers, darling, how *do* you feel about Indian self-rule?"

I felt more than heard the puff of air that burst from his mouth. "Not you, too?"

I nodded and gently pushed him into a chair. "Me, too, I'm afraid." I sat down opposite him so that he couldn't distract me further. I genuinely wanted to know the answer. I'd never pressed for much information about my husband's profession, and it was time to change that. "All I really know is that you work in some mysterious capacity for the Crown. And I presume that they pay you in a currency that isn't, say, sheep."

"I think ewe would know if I owned a sheep farm."

I paused, blinking. "Did you say ewe?"

He nodded, that now-familiar twinkle in his eyes.

I blinked at him several more times before he chuckled and answered me more seriously. "Yes, I'm compensated for my time in pounds sterling."

"Well, I'm pleased about that at least. I know nothing about sheep."

"I know ewe don't."

This time I couldn't keep a straight face, and I giggled. "That's terrible."

"It is." But he looked pleased with himself at getting me to laugh.

I smiled and shook my head before becoming serious again. "So what do you think about Indian self-rule? I'm not letting you off the hook with terrible puns about sheep."

Redvers sighed. "I know you're not." He paused to actually consider the question, long fingers scratching his jaw. "I think this is the first time I've been given an assignment that I didn't necessarily agree with."

My face must have registered my shock, because he nodded before continuing on. "I'm here to smooth the way between Indians—the ones in local government, anyway—and the Simon Commission, in an attempt to keep the peace when the commission arrives. They want me here to broker discussions and to try to convince those in Congress that the commission will have their best interests at heart. But I'm afraid that I tend to agree with Miss Beetner. The Indian people should be allowed to run their own country. Or at the very least, they should have representation on the committees that run their country so that they can cast votes on matters that affect them and their people." He leaned back in his seat. "Am I making sense?"

"You are. I'm just surprised to hear it, I suppose." We'd never discussed much politics before, and I had to admit that I was a bit surprised at his progressive leanings since he was employed by the British government, although I was far from disappointed by his dissension from his employers. Quite the opposite.

"My only concern is that if protests break out, they could become violent, and someone—most likely a local—will be killed. It's happened frequently enough in the past." He paused. "I'm meeting with some of the leaders of the resistance movement this week, hopefully without anyone else becoming aware of it."

I gasped. "Isn't that dangerous?"

"Only for my employment," Redvers said wryly. "Although I'm sure I can come up with a reasonable excuse for it. I'm not terribly worried." He kicked his shoes off, his fingers moving to his shirt buttons. "It is why we're staying at such a distance from the governor's mansion, though."

I wondered if he should be more concerned. I wouldn't for a moment suggest that he shouldn't do what he was doing, since I thought it was the right thing to do. But could Redvers suddenly find himself without employment? What would he do? As it was, I had no idea how much money my husband had, or where we would live once we settled. Of course, that raised the further question of whether I even *wanted* to settle somewhere? I had to admit that I was quite enjoying our globe-trotting, exhausting though it could be. Would that come to an end if Redvers no longer worked for the Crown? It wasn't as though I had the means to take us gallivanting around the world.

But instead of any of those questions, what came out of my mouth was something entirely different, although something I'd been wondering since Gretchen had brought it up. "And what is your stance on contraception for women?" The question had popped out before I'd had time to fully consider how to ask it. "I suppose I mean in general. Since I use a diaphragm and you're aware of that, you must be fine with it in at least some instances."

"Truthfully, I'm all for it. I'd have to be, wouldn't I, since, as you said, we don't plan on having our own children, and we've taken steps to prevent it." He paused thoughtfully. "But I also think it should be available to all women, especially those of lower classes who can't afford the children they already have. It's a burden to expect them to keep having more."

All this talk was making Redvers even more attractive to me than he'd been before, if such a thing were possible. I decided to demonstrate that, immediately, putting all thoughts of politics and intrigue far from my mind.

The next morning, I awoke and stretched, thinking about what Redvers had revealed to me the night before. I was still surprised that he didn't agree with his assignment here in Ooty, and given that, I was rather astonished that he'd agreed to take it. Of course, it could be that he didn't have a choice in the matter. I wanted to understand my new husband, and that included what he might want to do if his current occupation were no longer available to him. I assumed he had a backup plan, especially since he was making the risky choice of meeting with local resistance leaders.

I wondered if I could convince him to let me tag along. Most likely not, but it was worth a try.

I set aside last night's dress in the hopes that Sasmit could send it out to be cleaned. It had not, as expected, come away from dinner unscathed, and there were the telltale marks of fallen sauce on my skirt. I hoped they could work some kind of magic on the delicate fabric. I shook my head as I gazed at it. I knew better than to wear something so nearly white.

I got dressed in a much more practical blue cotton dress and took a seat facing the windows where I had a view of the garden. Sasmit was there almost immediately with a pot of coffee and fresh milk, and I thanked him enthusiastically while I tried to plan out my day. My first stop needed to be the library, so that I could look for something to keep my mind occupied. I could also take a turn through the botanical gardens, maybe find a shaded bench to sit and read for a bit.

Sasmit soon returned with a breakfast tray full of South Indian specialties, just as I'd requested. He explained what each item was before leaving—pongal, a sweet rice dish, and sambar vada, doughnut-shaped savory delights served with coconut chutney, as well as a selection of fresh fruit. I was just tucking in when Redvers came back into the room. I was surprised to see him—I'd assumed he'd been gone for at least an hour and was deep into his meetings for the day. But his face was grave, and I felt my stomach drop. I set my fork and knife down; I had the feeling that whatever came next was going to rob me of my appetite.

Redvers took a seat next to me and took my hand in his. "I have terrible news."

My mind flashed to my father, then to my Aunt Millie and her husband and my cousin Lillian. I found myself fervently wishing this news didn't have to do with any of them.

"It's about Gretchen," Redvers said.

My eyes filled with tears. It wasn't a member of my immediate family, but it was still heartbreaking news—I'd become quite fond of her in the short period of time we'd known her. Gretchen had been getting on in years, but it had seemed that she was in the peak of health. Could it have been a sudden heart episode?

"What happened?" I asked, tears quietly streaming down my face.

Redvers squeezed my hand and took a deep breath. "She was killed by a tiger."

CHAPTER SEVEN

My blood ran cold. "She what?" I shook my head and raised a hand. "You don't need to repeat that. But how?"

Redvers' brows pulled together. "They're saying that the beast found her while she was strolling around Ooty last night. Apparently, she decided to walk back from the governor's mansion alone instead of hiring a carriage to bring her back to her room, and she left the main path to walk along the outskirts of town to take in the air." His fingers made air quotes around this last part.

"No," I said, grabbing his hand back. I'd never felt more certain of anything than I did about this. "She never would have walked that path at night. She told us as much at the governor's party." I realized I was squeezing his fingers in my indignation and released my vice-like grip on him. "Gretchen wouldn't have walked back here alone without someone coming with her. No, something else happened to her."

Redvers sighed and leaned back in his seat. "I'm afraid I was thinking the same thing."

I shuddered. "You're going to have to look at her body."

He pressed his lips together briefly. "I was afraid of that as well."

* * *

I decided to accompany Redvers to the local hospital where Gretchen's body had been taken. I didn't want to see her, but I also didn't want to be left alone with my racing thoughts, so I elected to go with him and stay in the hallway. I also wanted to be on-site so that I could learn what he discovered as soon as he left the room. That way we could figure out what to do next. Together.

The hospital was near the busiest part of Ooty, located in a long white building with numerous cross-hatched windows and a red tile roof. The open interior was chaotic, as I'd come to expect in India, locals and Brits rushing here and there, sick patients and nurses with their uniforms and white caps weaving among them, doing their best to determine who most needed attention—or so I assumed. Redvers managed to locate someone with a clipboard who directed us to the morgue, located at the back of the building. As we neared the area, we were stopped by a clerk who looked distinctly shifty once we told him whose body Redvers was there to see.

"I'm afraid that is not possible," the man said, bobbing his head slightly. I still couldn't tell what the bob meant, but in this case, I assumed it was a rather large no.

"And why is that?" Redvers asked with a great deal more patience than I would have been able to muster. "Is the body here?"

The man pursed his lips, clearly unsure whether he should even admit to that much.

Redvers gave a nod and reached into his pocket, pulling out a wad of rupees. I had no concept of how much money it was, but it looked like quite a bit. "Now may I see the body?"

The clerk considered the wad and nodded once, taking the bills and tucking them away in a pocket of his own, before beckoning for Redvers to follow him. My mouth was still agape when Redvers disappeared behind the door leading to the morgue. What had just happened?

That question was fleeting, and soon my mind started conjuring up images of what Redvers must be seeing in the room just beyond the door. I tried to push them from my mind, but my imagination was already running rampant, creating a lump of lead in my stomach. I paced the hallway, trying to focus my attention elsewhere but losing the battle.

After a few minutes, the newly-flush-with-money clerk peered back through the door. "Your husband wishes for you to join him."

The pit in my stomach grew larger, but if Gretchen's body was terribly mangled, Redvers wouldn't be asking me to enter. I'd seen my fair share of bodies since I'd met Redvers, and while I'd never get used to the experience or find it any less horrifying, I was a great deal less squeamish than I once had been.

I took a deep breath, then followed the clerk through the door, where I immediately began breathing through my mouth. I knew the room would not have a pleasant smell. It would be either decaying bodies or antiseptic, and neither was appealing to the senses. Redvers was standing beside a gurney covered with a white sheet. Spots of dried blood dotted a small area, stark against the otherwise pristine covering, and a few tears slipped down my face at the sight. I took another bracing breath and moved forward, although I still kept my distance.

"I know it's unpleasant, but I thought you should see for yourself." Redvers pulled the sheet back from Gretchen's body, and I saw that her clothes were torn in numerous places by something quite sharp. Without thinking, I stepped even closer until I was standing next to the gurney, frowning mightily at what I was seeing.

Redvers spoke to the clerk standing behind me. "Could

you please give us a minute?" I heard the man's footsteps as he left the room, the door closing behind him.

"Her clothes look like they might have been ripped by claws," I said. "But her body hasn't been touched, just surface scratches. These were not made by a tiger, and they certainly wouldn't have killed her."

"Exactly," Redvers said. "A sloppy job, really."

"Sloppy job?" I was still looking at the torn clothing. The silk tunic and pants were what I remembered Gretchen wearing to dinner the night before, so at least that much was consistent with the truth.

"Someone clearly wanted it to appear like a tiger attack, but they didn't do a thorough job. They didn't bother to cut the body, just the clothes. The scratches are surface marks, probably done as they were cutting the clothing."

"How did she die, then?"

Redvers had been careful not to uncover Gretchen's face, and he gestured to her head while leaving the sheet over it. "She was shot from the front. At quite close range."

I grimaced. "Last I heard, tigers can't use guns."

"Exactly right."

I had a lot of questions, but I also wanted to be anywhere else at the moment, so Redvers re-covered Gretchen's body and we left the room. Redvers pulled several more bills from his pocket as we passed the clerk.

"We were never here," Redvers said. The clerk bobbed his head and pocketed the bills without a word.

Once we were outside and I was breathing freely through my nose once again, I let the questions start spilling out. "Do you think that was enough money to buy his silence?"

Redvers shrugged. "Probably not, but I'm hoping no one will think to ask whether anyone came to view the body."

"Why try to make it look like a tiger attack but not follow through on the execution?" I thought I knew the answer, but I wanted to hear Redvers say it.

"I would bet quite a lot of rupees that whoever is behind this hired the job out. Either the execution itself or the cover-up. And whoever was getting paid did the bare minimum with the body."

"It would be gruesome to tear up a body like a tiger would."

Redvers nodded. "It would require a pretty strong stomach. And they would never be able to show her face, since that was where the bullet went in."

The mere thought turned my stomach, and I paused my steps, breathing deeply.

Redvers touched my shoulder. "I'm sorry, my dear. I was just thinking aloud."

"I know you were." I took another deep breath. "I just need a moment." My stomach settled once more, and I started walking again. "Who would have wanted her killed?"

"That's the question of the hour," Redvers said thoughtfully. "And who has enough money to pay for the cover-up?"

CHAPTER EIGHT

"How much money would someone need?"

"You have to consider at least three people have to be paid off: whoever found the body, the morgue attendant, and the police. And possibly more than one person at the morgue and police station, really."

I was shocked to hear the last part. "The police were paid off as well?"

Redvers grimaced. "I'm afraid there is rampant corruption in the police force here. Not just Ooty—the entire country. It's well-known."

I'd had run-ins with the police in foreign countries before and wondered whether they might be corrupt, but this was the first time it was presented as an acknowledged fact. I didn't know what to think or how we would proceed with an investigation faced with corrupt local law enforcement. Clearly, we would be looking into what had really happened to Gretchen Beetner. But how difficult would it be without local support? Or even with possible obstruction from the people who were meant to protect the citizens?

I'd wanted a mystery, but this was truly the worst way I could think of having one delivered to me. I hadn't known Gretchen well, but I'd liked her a great deal and had felt that we were well on our way to becoming fast friends.

Redvers was still musing aloud as we walked. "Gretchen poked quite a few hornet's nests, even in the short time she was here."

"Do we know which ones in particular?" The only issue I was aware of Gretchen being involved in was the governor's wife and mistress residing in Ooty. I'd seen Gretchen with Savithri, but it seemed unlikely either woman would have a reason to kill Gretchen. If anything, they would go after one another, wouldn't they?

"Gretchen stayed behind last night to speak with Feodore Smith, and I'm sure he didn't like what she had to say, although that's hardly enough to kill the woman. There are plenty of people unhappy with the Simon Commission—Gretchen was far from the only one."

"Remind me why Gretchen was against the commission?"

"Because it's a group of white men coming to make decisions for the Indian people. Some of them have never set foot here."

"When you put it like that, I'm not wild about it either," I said.

Redvers inclined his head in acknowledgement.

"If she was no longer a member of Congress, why was she here?" I asked.

"She may not have been officially elected any more, but she was still very active in politics and held a great deal of political sway. Gretchen was here for the talks under her own steam, but she came to advocate for the Indian people. She had no qualms about speaking her mind," Redvers stopped when I snorted and agreed with me. "I suppose that does go without saying."

"What kind of threat could she have posed? If she wasn't even here in an official capacity."

"Quite a bit of one. I'm not saying she would have started a riot, but her influence was still such that she could have caused quite a bit of trouble for any number of people. She could easily have convinced members of congress to split away and make things very difficult for the commission."

"What about the governor?" I asked. "Did he have a reason to be unhappy with Gretchen?"

"I think that's along the same lines as Smith. She disagreed with both men and had enough clout to make things annoying for them. I also saw her speaking with Subbarayan and Mudaliar, and neither of them looked happy either."

I sighed. That was quite a lot of suspects. "We're going to have to do some digging."

Redvers nodded. "The first thing we need to do is to search her rooms and see if she had anything squirreled away there that would point a finger toward her killer."

We walked quietly the rest of the way back to our quarters, each lost in our own thoughts. I found that I was grateful Gretchen had been shot instead of mauled to death by a tiger. At least a shooting death would have been quick. Perhaps so quick that she didn't even know what was happening. Did she have family back home to notify? Would she be buried here in India? These were the questions swirling in my mind when we finally arrived back at our lodgings.

We'd walked Gretchen to her room after the first dinner, so we knew precisely where she was staying—on the second floor, tucked into a corner of the same building as ourselves. The upstairs hallway was deserted, so we didn't bother with any subterfuge, instead striding straight to her door. Putting my hand to the doorknob, I found that it was already unlocked. I shared a knowing look with Redvers before pushing it open.

The room was quite a bit smaller than our own, the sitting room furnished with two wooden chairs, upholstered in brightly colored silk, green and orange and yellow, all mixing in a cheerful way. There was only a bedroom attached; she must have used the community bathroom in the hallway. I took a moment to be grateful that we had our own.

The room smelled vaguely of her perfume, a citrusy scent, but it hung in the space. The windows clearly hadn't been opened today, or even the day before, which was strange. The staff had been very attentive so far, but perhaps Gretchen had asked for less service in her room.

In one glance we could tell that her quarters had already been searched, so we moved through the sitting room into her bedroom. Whoever had done it hadn't trashed the place, but they hadn't been particularly careful either. I'd caught a glimpse inside when we dropped her off, and from what I'd seen, she'd been a very tidy woman. I couldn't imagine that she would have left drawers hanging open with contents spilling from them, which is what we saw now.

"Whoever is responsible was very quick in getting here to do a search. I wonder if she was even cold yet."

I shuddered at that grim possibility. "We should still look around in case they missed something," I said, moving toward the wardrobe. Without a word, we each took a side of Gretchen's bedroom. We'd done this together so many times that we could split the task without speaking, trusting that the other would do a thorough job. There was some comfort in that, although I found myself fervently wishing for the looming boredom of the day before.

As I quickly and carefully searched through Gretchen's clothes, which I was certain she'd left neatly folded in the drawers instead of the utter disarray I now found, my mind flipped through potential suspects. A group of politicians, the governor's wife, and the governor's mistress all topped the list, although the two women were much further toward the bottom. It was hard to see either of them killing Gretchen in such a manner, motive or not.

I still struggled with how commonplace it seemed for the

governor to keep a mistress here. I realized I'd spoken my musings out loud when Redvers answered a moment later.

"I think it's not that uncommon anywhere, really."

I paused my search of Gretchen's unmentionables.

"And no, I've never had one," Redvers said without pausing in his own search. It was sometimes remarkable how he knew exactly what I was thinking. Or perhaps it wasn't that remarkable. It was a pretty logical step for my inquisitive brain to have taken.

He surprised me a moment later, though. "My brother did, though. A series of them."

I completely stopped what I was doing and turned to look at him. He'd finished searching Gretchen's wardrobe and was going over the bed thoroughly. He paused and glanced my way, then shrugged. "He never told me, of course, but I heard my father arguing with him about it plenty of times through closed doors. Percival always did tire of his playthings quickly."

I took offense to calling women "playthings," and I knew that my face reflected my outrage.

"His words, darling. Not mine," Redvers said, shooting me a small smile. His face became serious again as he returned to his search, but my attention was entirely on him now. Redvers rarely spoke about his brother, and I was not going to miss a word. But it seemed he was not going to say any more on the matter, so I turned to the dressing table and resumed my search. It was a long moment before he spoke again, and I once again stopped what I was doing to listen.

"For a while, he simply paid them off, and that seemed to work. Only one or two of them came back and demanded more money for whatever it was that he put them through. My father quietly took care of those."

"Took care of them?" I asked nervously. I was hoping there weren't a series of bodies buried on the family land.

Redvers gave a small chuckle. "Just paid them off. I don't think Father is capable of murder."

That was fair. I'd met the man, and while Humphrey Dibble wasn't a warm person, I also didn't think he was capable of murder. Redvers' deceased brother, Percival, was another story entirely.

"But then Father stopped hearing about them. I'm not sure if Percival simply became more discreet or if he stopped keeping mistresses altogether. And then Percival was killed in the war, taking his secrets and his scandals with him." Redvers' tone was neutral, his feelings about his brother never on display or even close to the surface, although I knew how he privately struggled with the contradiction between caring for family and the type of family Percival had been.

I slowly started going through the few pieces of jewelry on the dressing table while I contemplated what Redvers had just told me. There was a rather large gold piece that looked as though it might be a locket, but the clasp wasn't immediately obvious. I played with it, while letting various scenarios about Percival play out in my head. From the little I'd heard about Redvers' older brother, I wouldn't have been surprised if he'd left a string of bodies in his wake, male and female. But there was no evidence of it—just my overly suspicious mind.

I had conjured up another possibility when two things happened: the locket in my hand popped open, and Redvers spoke again. "But I've often wondered if I have a niece or nephew out there that we don't know about."

I was surprised by both things, and it took me a beat to figure out which one to attend to first. My curiosity about Redvers' statement won out.

"Do you think that's possible?"

He shrugged, his back still to me. "Honestly, I think it's more than possible. Percival was not a careful person as a child or as a man. He would have simply paid the mother some money to go away and not given it another thought."

"I suppose there's no way to find out, either."

He shook his head. "Not unless someone comes forward with a claim. Which hasn't happened yet and at this point I think is unlikely to happen." He was quiet for a beat. "So much time has passed that this is the first I've thought about it in a while."

This was all quite fascinating, but it wasn't what we were here for, and besides, it was nothing more than hypotheticals at the moment. I needed to turn my attention back to the tangible matter at hand—searching the room of a murdered friend. I looked at the locket I was holding and gently cracked it open, revealing two pictures inside. One was clearly Gretchen as a younger woman. Opposite her was an Indian man, who was rather plain-looking but quite strikingly dressed in what appeared to be fancy regalia. "Redvers, look at this."

Redvers stopped rifling through the bedcovers and came to my side. He made a little hmm-ing noise when he saw what I was holding.

"Who is he, do you think?" I asked.

Redvers looked up at me, eyebrow raised. "Based on the way he's dressed, it looks to me like Gretchen was involved with an Indian prince."

CHAPTER NINE

I'm not sure how long my mouth hung open, but it was long enough to make Redvers chuckle at my reaction.

"Couldn't say which province without some research, but I'm nearly positive that's what we're looking at here." He peered at Gretchen's picture. "Although it looks as though this was quite some time ago already. It's probably not useful to our investigation now."

I frowned. "I didn't realize there were still princes in India."

"Depends on the province, but there are still some areas that are ruled by their own royal families. Fewer now, and many are royalty in title only, having made alliances with the British Raj and given their power over."

"That makes me sad, somehow. Giving up their authority to the British."

Redvers nodded. "Me too, actually." He glanced around the room, then tipped his head toward the door. "I think we've found all we're going to find in this room."

I followed him into the sitting room, still holding the locket in my hand. After a moment, I snapped it shut and slipped it into my dress pocket. Redvers was right. It was probably evidence of a long-ago romance, but it still felt significant enough to hang on to. Even if it wasn't worth anything, it had clearly meant something to Gretchen, and that was enough for me to want to keep it. For now, anyway, until we discovered if she had any family to inherit her things.

We split the room once again, searching efficiently but ultimately turning up nothing else of interest. If there had been something here, it was long gone—probably in the hands of Gretchen's killer.

"Do you think the police will come through her rooms?" I asked once we'd finished and were heading back to our own quarters.

Redvers shook his head. "The official report will read that she died by tiger attack. No one will be coming to look at her things in an official capacity."

Which meant that whoever conducted the search was not the police. It also meant there would be no investigation, except what we did ourselves. It was a strange feeling; we usually had to work with or around the authorities when we looked into a case. I hoped we wouldn't be working directly against them this time. It would make things especially difficult if the police decided to deliberately obstruct our investigation. Or if they were ordered to do so, which was the more likely scenario.

"Do you think the police will be told to work against us?"

"I thought of that. It's possible, if anyone gets wind that we're looking into things. We need to be especially careful not to let on."

I nodded, following him out of Gretchen's room and down the stairs to the floor where we were staying.

Back in our room, Redvers glanced at his watch. "I should head back to the governor's mansion. The meetings will still be taking place, murder or no murder."

I nodded. "I'll go with you."

Redvers cocked an eyebrow. "I don't think you'll find the meetings interesting."

"No, I know that I won't. But I want to find Savithri Kumari and see what she and Gretchen were talking about yesterday morning."

"She won't be at the governor's mansion," Redvers said thoughtfully. "Not with Lady Goshen in residence. I wonder where the governor has stashed her."

I'd already realized that Savithri wouldn't be lodging there. But someone at the mansion would likely know, and I told Redvers as much.

We parted ways once we reached the garden of the governor's mansion; Redvers to his meetings and me to find someone who knew where Savithri Kumari was staying. The first few members of the staff that I asked didn't speak any English, and I realized that my task wasn't going to be as easy as I first assumed that it would be. I had just asked a woman in a cotton sari, who bobbed her head at me in that incomprehensible way Indians did, when a voice came from behind me.

"You're looking for Savithri Kumari?" The voice was British and cultured, and I turned slowly to find that Lady Goshen was its owner.

I could feel my face flush with pink. I had no quick answer as to why I was looking for her husband's mistress. Should I say I had a message for her? Or she had a message for me? Or that someone sent me to find her? I pressed my lips together, not sure what I could present as a reasonable excuse when Lady Goshen's mouth quirked into a small, wry smile.

"I'm not offended. I'm sure you have your reasons for wanting to speak with her. I overheard some staff, and I believe she's been removed to the plantation to stay. The one we both visited yesterday." With this, Lady Goshen smiled politely and continued on her way.

I stared after the woman long after she'd turned the corner, my mind turning over a slew of questions. Had Lady Goshen gone to the plantation to see her husband's mistress? That couldn't have been a coincidence. Did she just want to get a look at the other woman, or had she talked with Savithri? Why had she been kind enough to tell me Savithri's location?

I decided to add Lady Goshen to my list of mysteries.

I knew the way to the plantation, so I didn't need an escort this time, but I did spend the long walk there completely on edge. I knew that Gretchen hadn't actually been killed by a tiger, but I couldn't stop scanning the forest for one all the same. Since it was nearly the middle of the day, I thought I was in the clear, but my nerves were strung tight, and I cursed my decision to walk instead of hiring a carriage to take me. At the time, I'd decided not to be cowed into fear by lies about Gretchen's demise, but now I was regretting my moment of boldness. Instead of mulling over the many questions of the day as I'd intended, I was scanning the hills and nearly jumping out of my shoes at every small sound. And there were many: the forest was alive with birds, large red squirrels, and the occasional troop of playful monkeys. The occasional haunting scream of a peacock did nothing to soothe my nerves, either. In fact, I was beginning to curse the fact that the population of those beautiful birds was so robust here. At least the enormous white cows with their drooping necks and sturdy horns were uninterested in anything but the grass they grazed upon when I passed by them.

I breathed a huge sigh of relief once the tea plantation was in sight and there were people around. Not that a few scattered people would scare off a large predatory cat, but it made my shoulders drop back down all the same.

I made my way to the main building and asked a few local people where I might find Savithri. Unfortunately, no one spoke English, and they merely bobbed their heads at me in what seemed an apologetic manner before hurrying along their way. I pressed my lips together in thought. How could I find my guide from the day before? He'd spoken beautiful English.

"Mrs. Wunderly?" I heard a warm voice behind me, and I turned in relief. It was Hasnan, the very man I was looking for. "I heard you had returned. Did you have some further questions for me? Or perhaps you enjoyed our tea so greatly that you want to take some home with you?"

I was grateful to whatever worker had alerted the man to my presence, and I found that I couldn't help a small smile at his gentle ribbing. He knew full well after spending the morning with me that tea was not my preference. "I'm looking for Savithri Kumari, actually. Can you tell me where she is?"

Hasnan gave me a long look without answering, head cocked, clearly trying to discern what my interest in the woman was.

"A friend of hers was killed, and I want to talk to her about it."

A shadow passed over Hasnan's face, and he bobbed his head. "Come this way." He led me along a path that passed by the main building to a smaller one in the back. This was another long, low building with a red roof, but a wide porch stretched in front of the numerous windows and doors, their wooden shutters open to the fresh air. Hasnan gestured to a chair and asked me to wait on the porch while he went inside. After a moment, he returned. "Savithri will be right out."

I smiled and thanked him for his help.

"I will have some tea sent out for you," Hasnan said.

I almost asked him for a cup of coffee instead but held

my tongue, simply thanking him for his kindness instead. It wasn't the end of the world if I had to choke down one more cup out of politeness.

Hasnan disappeared into the shadows of the house, and I readjusted my seat on the small chair. I took a moment to appreciate the beauty of the plantation while I waited, the verdant rows of tea bushes winding lazily down the mountain slopes, so I was quite lost in my own thoughts when Savithri came gliding out of the house.

"Mrs. Wunderly?"

I gave a little start, and she let out a light, musical laugh. "I'm sorry to startle you."

I shook my head. "It's quite alright," I said. "I was just reflecting on how beautiful it is here."

Savithri took a seat next to me, and another woman in a green and yellow cotton sari appeared carrying a tray of tea for us. She set it on the table and Savithri said something to her in what I assumed was Tamil, the language that the people in this part of India spoke.

"Why have you come to see me?" Savithri asked once she'd poured each of us a cup of tea. I took in her unlined skin, dark hair, and large dark eyes framed by long, black lashes. She was a beautiful woman, and I couldn't help but wonder why she hadn't chosen another path in life, one that wasn't serving as a mistress to the governor, a married man. Of course, it was possible that there weren't many other paths available to her as a woman. I made a note to ask Gretchen about women's prospects here, then with a sinking heart remembered the reason for my visit. I wouldn't be asking Gretchen anything ever again.

Savithri adjusted her sari, a gorgeous dark green and yellow with delicate gold embroidered designs running along the edges of the cloth and encircling her arms, the gold threads glinting in the sunlight. It was clearly made of expensive cloth, fine enough that I wondered if the thread was made of actual gold. "You look sad, suddenly," she said.

I nodded, then took a drink of the tea in my hand to clear the lump in my throat. "Have you heard about Gretchen?" I asked.

Savithri gave a solemn nod of her head. "I heard about her unfortunate death. There is talk about hunting down the tiger; we cannot have maneaters left to roam the forest. It is a danger to us all when they get brave enough to kill humans."

Terrified as I was by the prospect of coming face to face with a tiger in the wild, I was horrified by the idea that one might be killed under false pretenses.

"Gretchen wasn't killed by a tiger," I said with authority, setting my cup of tea on the table with enough force that a bit sloshed into the saucer. I hadn't given any thought to the wisdom of sharing that information, but it was too late now. The cat was out of the bag, as it were.

Savithri raised one dark eyebrow. "How do you know this?"

"I saw the body. It was made to look like a tiger attack— or rather it was meant to. They did a poor job of it, really." I paused. "I would appreciate it if you would keep this information to yourself, though."

Both of Savithri's eyebrows were now scaling her forehead, but she still said nothing. I'd hoped this revelation would be enough to start the woman talking, but it clearly wasn't. I stifled a sigh. It would be up to me, then, to continue probing for answers. "I saw you speaking with Gretchen yesterday morning. What were you talking about?" I didn't think that I needed to add that Savithri had seemed upset. I doubted she needed a reminder.

Savithri studied me for a long moment. "What is your interest in this?" she finally asked.

"I want to find out what really happened to Gretchen. I think she was murdered, and I would like to know by whom."

"It would be safer for you to let this lie," Savithri said. "Nothing good will come of you asking questions. You will only put yourself in the same danger that Gretchen did."

CHAPTER TEN

Her answer gave me pause. I didn't think she was threatening me, although it certainly sounded that way at first. No, this was meant to be a warning. "Do you know who did this?"

"I did not mean to give you that impression. I am simply warning you to be careful. These men are willing to do whatever they need to get what they want. And they rarely suffer consequences."

"How do you know it was men that were involved?"

"Isn't it always men in cases like these?"

"It sounds as though you're speaking from experience," I said.

Savithri gave a small, sad smile. "I think that is every woman's experience, is it not?"

It was hard to argue with her on that point. Or any of her points, really.

"Lady Goshen was here yesterday," Savithri said, then took a quiet sip of her tea. Mine was going cold where it sat on the wooden table.

"Was she looking for you?"

Savithri cocked her head to the side a bit. "I believe so, but she did not find me."

I could only imagine how uncomfortable that interaction

would have been. "Lady Goshen told me where to find you. I went to the governor's mansion this morning, and she pointed me in this direction."

Savithri acknowledged this with a bow of her head. "I think she is a kind woman at heart."

It was a strange conversation to be having. I was curious about both women's relationship with Governor Goshen, but I was not going to ask any of the questions I had. Even I wouldn't be so forward.

"I will be staying with my cousin here on the plantation, most likely until the Raj return to Madras."

The Raj was what the British occupiers were called. I nodded, then recalled something else. "Do you know if Gretchen was ever involved with an Indian prince? When she was younger?"

Savithri laughed again. "I have not heard this, but I would also be far from surprised. Gretchen Beetner was a woman who was full of life and full of surprises." Savithri fell quiet, studying her tea. "I will miss her."

I nodded and excused myself. It was clear that Savithri wasn't going to give me any further information. And it hadn't escaped my notice that she had deftly avoided answering my question about what she and Gretchen had been discussing that morning. I would let the issue lie for now, but I would address it again later. There was clearly a reason that Savithri didn't want me to know, and it looked like I would have to gain the woman's trust first.

Or find another way to learn what had made her so upset.

My walk back to Ooty was as solitary as my walk to the plantation, but this time my mind was occupied with thoughts of Savithri and Lady Goshen, and I nearly forgot to be wary of tigers lurking among the trees. It was probably for the best. I likely would be dead before I saw one anyway, and without a weapon, there was little chance of escaping. I had no idea how the locals simply went about their lives with the constant threat of death by a large animal, although I supposed humans could get used to most anything after enough time. We were built to adapt.

When I returned to our quarters, I found Redvers waiting for me. "I'm surprised you're back so soon," I said, giving him a kiss in greeting before taking a seat in one of the cushioned chairs. My legs were immediately grateful for the break.

"I used your grief over Gretchen's loss as an excuse to leave the meetings early."

I wrinkled my nose at him. I didn't particularly like having my genuine feelings used as an excuse with a group of men I didn't know. "The entire delegation thinks I'm very delicate now, do they?"

Redvers gave an apologetic shrug. "I'm certain you can use it to your advantage later."

I narrowed my eyes then changed the subject. "Did you learn anything useful?"

"Perhaps. I learned where Gretchen's body was found. I thought we might take a walk out there and look around."

"Do you think we're likely to learn anything? We already know it wasn't a tiger attack." I felt doubtful about this endeavor. Not to mention the growing blister on my small toe from the long walks to and from the plantation. Once I'd sat down, I could feel it throbbing. Next time I made the trip, I would hire a carriage. A horse-drawn one.

"I thought it might be useful, especially since the police station is out that way," Redvers said. His eyes had a mischievous glint to them; he knew I wouldn't be able to resist accompanying him on a visit to the police.

"You just wait here." I pointed a warning finger at him, in case he had any ideas of heading off without me. "Let me get a plaster for my toe."

A few minutes later, I had changed into my sturdy walking boots. They were a bit heavy for the climate, but better for walking since I'd well and truly broken them in during our recent trip to Scotland. It was trading one discomfort for another, but at least it wasn't as hot here in the hills as it was on the plains.

We stepped to the front stoop of the house, and Redvers looked down at me. "Should we hire a carriage? I don't want to make that blister worse."

I considered the offer. It would be entirely more comfortable—not to mention more practical—to take a ride where we needed to go. But Gretchen's death had left me feeling uneasy, restless, and I thought another long walk might help ease that, not to mention helping me to sleep that night. If I was properly exhausted, my mind should let me sleep instead of spinning, as it had a tendency to do when I was troubled but hadn't worn myself out.

Decision made, I shook my head. "Let's walk. My mind needs the exercise."

Redvers knew better than to argue, and though he was skeptical, he led me up the hill in the direction of the governor's mansion. We came near the botanical gardens, but instead of entering, we veered right and to the north, following a red dirt path.

My spirits were still weighed down by Gretchen's death, but I was doing the only thing I knew how to do—stick my nose into things and try to figure out who was responsible. It always felt good to be doing something when faced with this sort of situation. I wondered if that was how Redvers felt about his occupation.

"How did you get involved with spying for the Crown?" I asked. I realized that I'd never asked him this before and didn't even have a guess as to what his answer might be.

He glanced over at me, amusement on his face, but I noticed that he didn't deny my spying charge. "The opportunity came through my father. He knew a lot of people in high places, once upon a time. Before my brother's death, of course."

I knew that his brother had been killed by his own men during the war for being a traitor. It had brought some scandal down on the family, and his mother had never recovered from it, dying not long after her favorite son. I'd never said as much aloud, but I'd always wondered how the woman could choose a lying, thieving scoundrel as her favorite son over the kind, thoughtful, and steady man that Redvers was.

"One of the men who knew my father approached me while I was at university and offered me an assignment, very hush hush. One thing led to another, and when I graduated, I found myself fully employed by the Crown." He shrugged easily as if it had been precisely that—easy. But I knew many of his assignments put him directly into harm's way and he was no stranger to being shot at.

I was quiet while I absorbed that. "Do you like it?"

Redvers cocked his head. "I do. I'm not sure what else I would be suited for. Certainly not a desk job."

It was my turn to chuckle. I could not imagine my husband stuck behind a desk, even though that had been his claim when we first met. I'd known instinctively that it was a lie, and I'd been as correct then as I was now about what type of person Redvers was.

I would have asked another question, but it looked as though we had arrived at our first destination as Redvers stopped suddenly, fixing his gaze on the ground around us.

"It was here?" I asked.

Redvers' brows were pulled into a frown, but he nodded. "Supposedly." He gestured to a small rounded hut sitting in the open grassy space, wooded hills stretching up behind it. "They say she came to the temple."

"This is a temple?" I asked, regarding it curiously. It appeared to be made of dirt, thatched with layers of straw which composed a roof that stretched from the ground on either side and swept up over the top. Large *x*'s had been painted on the front of the structure, except above the tiny carved door in the center, which formed a near-perfect square. Above the door a more complicated symbol had been painted.

Redvers looked up from his inspection of the ground to take in the temple. "It is a Hindu temple built by the Toda. The Toda tribe inhabited these hills long before the British arrived."

I looked around, seeing nothing that would indicate anything remarkable about where we stood other than the small structure. I already knew there was no chance that Gretchen would have come here by herself at night—we were far off the beaten path, and it would only take a few steps beyond the temple to be swallowed by the forest. Prime hunting ground for a predatory cat, especially given the scattered cows grazing the land here.

"Why wouldn't the tiger grab a cow instead?" I asked. "Surely that's easier hunting than a human." I was horrified by my own line of thought, but it was valid all the same.

"A fair point," Redvers said. "Tigers do tend to avoid human contact, unless they've gone rogue."

A rogue tiger was the story that someone was trying to sell. But who was that someone? "Who told you this was the place?" I took a few cautious steps closer to the forest, shuffling my feet through the grass, looking for anything of interest, but keeping one eye on the looming line of trees.

Redvers was doing the same around the dirt path that had brought us there. "The governor's secretary. He didn't find the body, but he was called to the scene as soon as it was reported."

"Who *did* find the body?"

"Ahh, that's the thing. He couldn't tell me. Or rather, wouldn't tell me."

"Not suspicious in the slightest," I said. "How will we find out?"

Redvers had paused and bent over, peering at something in the grass. "We'll inquire at the police station."

"I hope you have enough money to pay for all our questions," I muttered before asking more loudly, "Did you find something?"

Redvers squatted down to pick something up, holding it up to show me. "I did. It's a casing from a bullet."

CHAPTER ELEVEN

"This is, in fact, where she was killed then," I said, coming to his side.

"Most likely," Redvers agreed. "There's no sign of any tiger tracks, not that we expected there to be." He looked around critically. "But this is a remote spot, close to the forest yet still reasonably close to the city. Quite a good place to kill someone if you don't want to be seen."

Redvers was right. Besides the tiny temple, there were no buildings in sight, which meant it was unlikely anyone saw Gretchen get shot out here. But how had they convinced her to come this far from town in the first place? She'd been adamant about not venturing out by herself at dawn or dusk when the tigers were out stalking their prey. Had she been dragged here against her will? I imagine she would have fought her attacker if that were the case, and we hadn't seen any marks on her body, nor were there any signs of a struggle on the path.

I said as much to Redvers who was thoughtful for a moment. "There was . . . a lot of damage to her head. She might have been knocked out and brought here. If that was the case, I wouldn't have been able to tell."

I grimaced and tried not to think any further about that, scanning the ground around us instead. "It's already been more than twelve hours since she was killed, so it's not likely we'll find anything else here."

Redvers shook his head, pocketing the metal bullet casing and taking my hand, giving it a squeeze. With a final glance around, we started walking again, following the path back toward town. We looped back to the botanical garden, taking a shortcut through it and back onto the mall that would take us into town. I supposed that was another advantage to the place where Gretchen had been killed: notifying the police would have taken quite a long time, giving the killer plenty of time to disappear.

The police headquarters was near the hospital. I almost asked why we hadn't combined the trip with our stop to see Gretchen's body, but I already knew the answer. Redvers wanted to see the scene of the murder before we spoke with the police. I wondered if he would turn over the bullet casing. If the police were corrupt as he'd suggested, my guess was that he would keep it to himself. But it was nice to have a hidden advantage all the same.

The police headquarters building was a two-story affair, although the second story was perched atop the first, roughly half the size of the ground level. The yellow of the second floor was offset by the red roof tiles and the red brick of the first floor. I thought the brick was a strange choice, giving the building an uneven appearance. We entered the police station, and Redvers took the lead, asking the khaki-clad officer behind the counter to point us toward the person in charge of the death investigation. The officer's expression of boredom changed not a bit, but I was grateful that he spoke English and directed us to an office in the back where his superior officer sat.

I was surprised that the man we found inside was British, and immediately chastised myself for thinking that only an Indian police officer would be corrupt. This man, with his overgrown moustache, overlarge belly, and air of indifference was a perfect candidate for pocketing a few extra dollars in exchange for his silence. His tall black boots, perched on his desk, hadn't seen polish in some time, if ever. The rest of his uniform was surprisingly neat—crisp khaki pants tucked into the boots, with the matching khaki shirt, and a black leather belt that went around the waist and also stretched up over the shoulder, where a holstered gun sat, silent and deadly.

There were no seats in his office, which I was certain was by design, so Redvers and I remained standing. "We're here to ask a few questions about Gretchen Beetner's death."

"Mmm, tragic thing," the officer said, not removing his feet from his desk or the toothpick from his mouth. The hum of an electric fan on his desk was loud enough that he had to speak up. The fan was also unnecessary, in my opinion; the temperature was quite pleasant inside the building. "We'll have to get a group together to hunt the tiger down, of course. Can't have a maneater roaming the countryside, picking off people whenever it likes."

He didn't seem in a hurry to do any such thing. I had conflicting feelings about that. On the one hand, I was glad, since I didn't want to see a tiger killed for manufactured reasons. But on the other hand, it was clear that this man didn't care in the slightest that my friend had been killed, and he wasn't going to lift a finger to do anything about it.

Redvers regarded the man for a moment before stepping to the door and calling out a few words in Tamil. I had no idea that he knew a single bit of the language and found myself impressed. When had he picked that up? Would there ever come a time when my new husband didn't surprise me? I genuinely doubted it.

A man appeared in the hallway, and Redvers asked him—in English—for two chairs to be brought in. I looked to the officer sitting behind his desk and noted the immediate displeasure on his face. Well, he might as well get comfortable. We wouldn't be going anywhere until we got the answers we'd come for.

Nothing more was said until the chairs appeared and Redvers and I took a seat. "What is your name?" Redvers asked, crossing one leg easily over the other.

The toothpick bobbed a bit while the officer chewed it, catching some moustache hairs in his mouth for his efforts, and considered whether or not he wanted to answer the question. He finally gave a small shrug of his shoulders—they were strangely narrow for someone with such girth—and smirked. "Inspector Thornycrest."

I stared at the inspector for a long moment, fully expecting Redvers to accuse the man of inventing such a name, but to my surprise, Redvers simply nodded.

"And how much exactly have you been paid to maintain the story about the tiger?" Redvers always did love getting right to the point.

Thornycrest maintained a neutral expression, sizing Redvers up. "What makes you think I've been paid anything?" he finally asked.

"We can sit here all day," Redvers said. "And we will until we have the truth." Redvers' voice was deceptively casual. "The way I see it, you have two options. You can tell us now and get rid of us, or you can bluster for a while and waste everyone's time before I finally give you the proper incentive to tell us the truth."

A grudging look of respect came over Thornycrest's face. But he still didn't say anything, readjusting his feet in their position on the desk instead. A small clump of dirt fell from his boot onto the desktop, and my eyes narrowed, but I didn't comment on it. For a few long moments, there was only the sound of the fan, until Redvers shook his head.

"Tell me how much, and I'll add to it."

"Now we're getting somewhere," Thornycrest said, his dusty boots dropping to the ground with a thud. He swept the clump of dirt from his desktop onto the floor with his hand.

Redvers reached into his pocket and pulled out a small wad of bills, made a show of displaying them, and dropped them on the man's desk.

Thornycrest rifled through them and made a face, before pocketing the amount. "Very well, it was one hundred pounds."

I could feel my eyebrows shoot up. That was quite a bit of money, not to mention it had been paid in pounds instead of rupees.

"Who paid you?" Redvers asked.

"Ahh, that's the tricky part, and not even the money in your wife's pocketbook could get me to tell you, because I don't know. An envelope with instructions was left here anonymously with my name on it." The inspector shrugged.

Redvers made a noise of frustration, giving voice to my own feelings. "Did anyone see who left the envelope?"

"It was early morning, so everyone here was dead asleep."

"Of course." Redvers breathed out, fighting for patience, although to an outside party he appeared as measured as ever. I could only tell how frustrated he was because I knew him so well. "May I see the note?" Redvers asked.

Thornycrest leaned over the side of his desk and fished a piece of paper out of the small waste basket sitting there. It had been crumpled, and he didn't bother smoothing it out before tossing it onto the desk. Redvers laid it on the table and did his best to smooth it with his palm before picking it up and angling it so that we could both read it at the same time.

Inspector: Enclosed should be enough money to ensure that the following story is all you will relate about today's tragedy. Gretchen Beetner's body was found near the forest at the Hindu temple just outside

Ooty. She was mauled by a tiger. That is all you are to say about this unfortunate incident. Signed, a friend.

"Doesn't tell us much," Redvers said, folding the note in half and slipping it into his pocket.

"That is my letter," Thornycrest protested.

"It was in the waste basket," Redvers told him flatly. "I'm not paying extra for your trash."

Thornycrest sniffed but didn't respond.

I slipped my hands under my thighs, sitting on them in the hopes that it would quash my desire to throw something heavy at the inspector's head. I was more than ready to be done here, but Redvers had one more question for Thornycrest. "Do you know who found the body?"

Thornycrest cocked his head but didn't answer. Redvers narrowed his eyes and reached into his pocket, pulling out another small wad of bills. I was impressed that he'd prepared separate little wads of money before we'd come here; he'd known precisely what we would encounter. I also wondered exactly how much this was costing him.

Thornycrest put the wad into his pocket without so much as looking at it first. It cemented my impression that the man could be bought easily. Too easily. The look on my face must have betrayed my thoughts because he gave me an amused look. "They don't pay civil servants much, you know."

I didn't respond to this, but I pressed down on my trapped hands and tried to arrange my face in a neutral expression. I had no idea how successful my efforts were with my face, but at least I was restraining my impulses to cause this man physical harm.

"A local on her way to work at one of the tea plantations found her. From what I could tell, she knew enough to come straight here. I'd just found the envelope with my marching orders and took charge immediately."

Redvers extracted the name of the local woman while I tuned out for a moment, pondering the two things I'd noticed during this infuriating interaction. The first was that even though Thornycrest had been paid a decent amount for his silence, he'd cracked at the first whiff of a bit more money. What Redvers had given him couldn't have been anything close to a hundred pounds, despite handing over two wads of rupees. If anyone else offered the man another pound or two, he would sway like a thin reed in that direction as well. Which meant he couldn't be trusted in the slightest.

The other thing I'd noticed was that the letter he'd received had been typed, and every single *e* dropped just enough to be noticeable. Perhaps we could locate the typewriter and figure out who had access to it.

It was a better lead than anything we were going to learn from Inspector Thornycrest.

CHAPTER TWELVE

We left the police station without speaking to anyone else, both of us heavy with an air of disgust.

"That was disappointing, to say the least," I said once we were out of sight of the building. I gave myself a full body shake, as though to physically toss off the bad feelings left by that interaction.

"Quite the understatement, my dear." Redvers shook his head. "I wish I could say I was surprised, though." We started slowly walking north in the direction of our lodgings, dodging locals with baskets full of goods, carriages waiting for customers, and horse-pulled carts.

"I had no idea things were that bad."

"They are," Redvers said simply, then took a deep, cleansing breath and changed the subject, directing us toward a quieter street where we'd be less likely to be overheard. "I'm assuming you noticed what I did."

I narrowed my eyes at him in mock anger. "I can't believe you would even ask."

Redvers smiled. "Very silly of me."

I became serious. "We need to find the typewriter. I think that's something that you're going to have to handle, though—I can't really be wandering through the governor's mansion demanding to use each typewriter that I come across."

Redvers raised an eyebrow. "It's not going to be particularly easy for me, either, since there are quite a lot of typewriters in that building. I was thinking we could start checking them tonight, when everyone is out of their offices. It will be faster with two of us, and if we want to keep it under wraps that we're looking into Gretchen's death, it's best to do it when no one is around."

This put a spring in my step, despite the terrible events of the day. "I do enjoy a little break-in."

Redvers didn't say anything, but he closed his eyes and gave a shake of his head.

I sobered. "Who else do we need to speak with?"

"It would help to locate the woman who initially found the body and notified Thornycrest. We'll need an interpreter, though, someone we can trust to do it correctly." His brow was furrowed as he considered our options on that front. "I'm coming up short on a name at the moment, I'm afraid. Too much loyalty to one camp or another to trust that they'll be entirely truthful."

My footsteps were measured, but my brain was racing. "Someone independent of it all." The only person I could think of who spoke beautiful English but didn't seem connected in any way was Hasnan, my tour guide at the tea plantation. I said as much to Redvers.

His eyes lit up. "That's a brilliant idea." Redvers glanced at his watch. "Can you ask him if he would be willing to help us? I have a meeting in a bit that I really should try to attend."

"With the governor?" I asked.

"With the resistance, actually."

I had a good understanding of what the Simon Commission was about—they were coming to look at reforming the current laws governing India. I wasn't certain what the resistance hoped to accomplish, however. I was fairly certain I understood which side my husband was on, however, after our earlier discussion about his assignment. "I have a feeling you're far more aligned with the resistance than with the commission."

"I am, although I'm afraid they have little chance of succeeding."

"Succeeding at what?"

"Convincing the Raj that the Indian people have a right to make choices about their own laws and government. The British have ruled here for over a century and have little intention of giving up any power."

I nodded, taking that in. "Who is leading the resistance?" I wouldn't know the names, but I was curious about who was brave enough to go up against the British Raj.

"There are two men that are primarily involved. Mahatma Gandhi is one, but he is occupied elsewhere in the country at the moment. The other is Lala Lajpat Rai, who is the man I'm meeting with today." We were quiet for a few steps before Redvers continued. "Rai and Gandhi have convinced the Indian National Congress to oppose the commission—they're pushing for a constitution that is more acceptable to the Indian people."

"I assume that isn't going over well with the Raj."

"You assume correctly. Both Governor Goshen and Mr. Smith are quite displeased with the entire affair and are trying to convince the local governments to support the Simon Commission."

"That sounds like an uphill battle. Convincing the Indian people to support a commission of white men coming here to make decisions for them."

"It's all a matter of power. Who has some, who wants to hold on to what they have, and who wants more."

"It sounds like a bit of a mess."

Redvers nodded. "And I'm supposed to 'smooth things over' between the factions."

"Is that what you're going to do?"

Redvers' mouth quirked up at the corners. "I haven't made up my mind yet."

"I support whatever you decide," I told him. That included whether he did something that would cause him to lose his employment with the Crown, but I didn't think it necessary to say that much. Hopefully it wouldn't come to that, but if it did, I knew we would figure out what to do next together. I also trusted that he would make the decision based on what was the right thing to do. And I could never argue with that.

As we neared the botanical garden, Redvers gave me a quick kiss, and we parted ways. I watched him go and looked at my feet. We'd already walked quite a bit, and my feet weren't particularly excited at the prospect of walking out to the tea plantation yet again. I couldn't call, as there were no telephones yet in Ootacamund; those were still relatively new to India and relegated to the big cities on the plains. Faced with no other option, I decided it was time to hire a carriage and save my feet.

A wiry Indian man wearing a dusty tunic over the flowing cotton pants that I'd come to recognize as common here gestured for me to step up into the wooden conveyance he pulled. I shook my head, still not comfortable with the idea of a man pulling me anywhere. But he smiled and gestured again, so I bit back both a sigh and my reservations and hoisted myself up onto the black leather seat. A little cloth umbrella shaded my head, and I mused that it wasn't that uncomfortable until he began to pull. It took him a few steps to find his rhythm, and even though he was mindful of the ruts in the road, it was still a bumpy ride. But at least my feet weren't suffering.

We very quickly reached the outskirts of the city, where pedestrian traffic thinned out to nearly nonexistent. I caught sight of someone walking ahead of us, apparently headed in the same direction. Based on the long black hair and stunning sari the woman was wearing, I had a good guess as to who it was.

I called to the man pulling the carriage, and he slowed, looking over his shoulder at me curiously. I motioned for him to stop, and he obliged, setting the wooden bars that he used to pull the cart on the ground, allowing me to get out. I caught up with her quickly, confirming that my suspicion was correct—it was Savithri Kumari. I was surprised that she'd come into Ooty and was already heading back to the plantation—it didn't seem that long ago that I had left her there. I glanced at the sun in the sky and realized it was late afternoon already, and my stomach rumbled, reminding me that I'd been so caught up in the investigation, I'd forgotten to eat lunch.

With any luck, they might have some food at the plantation.

Savithri accepted my sudden appearance with a nod, stopping to talk with me. "I'm surprised you're heading back to the plantation. I didn't think tea was an interest for you."

I smiled. "It's not. I'm definitely a coffee drinker. May I walk with you?"

She looked at me curiously but nodded and waited while I paid my driver and dismissed him. I was a little sorry to see him go, but there wasn't room in the cart for two of us to sit comfortably, and he'd gotten me through a fair amount of the walk. Besides, we were approaching a steady incline toward the plantation, and I would have felt terrible having him pull me uphill. It was bad enough being pulled in the first place.

We set out walking together, enjoying the shade from the trees and the cheerful racket from the birds. I let my mind wander, noting the burn in my legs as we started the upward climb, and was nearly surprised when Savithri interrupted my meditation with her question. "What brings you back to the plantation?"

I threw caution to the wind and told the truth. "I was hoping to speak with Hasnan and convince him to serve as an interpreter for us."

Savithri's dark brows pulled into a frown. "He's quite busy at the plantation with his duties."

"It would only be for a few hours at most. My husband and I would like to speak with the woman who found Gretchen's body."

Savithri's steps slowed until we came to a halt in the middle of the red dirt track. Luckily, this whole stretch of the walk was heavily shaded by large trees, so the sun wasn't beating down on us—for the moment, at least. I wondered how Savithri managed in the sun with her dark hair and no hat—her scalp had to get quite hot. But perhaps she was used to it.

"I'm certain that Hasnan would be willing to help you, but I think that I will do this instead."

I was taken aback that she would offer her services. "You're not . . . too busy?" I wasn't sure exactly what she occupied her time with, especially since the governor's wife was in residence.

Savithri smiled wryly. "I believe that I can spare a few hours." She was quiet for a moment. "I am sorry about what happened to Gretchen, and it seems that you are looking into it."

I didn't say anything, unwilling to either confirm or deny this charge, but I also knew that I wasn't fooling her. Savithri was clever enough to know precisely why I'd been asking questions about her interactions with Gretchen, and why I wanted to speak with the woman that had found her body.

"I expect that you have spoken with the police inspector?" she asked.

The sour look that distorted my face spoke volumes, and Savithri chuckled. "This is not a surprise. He is uncommonly useless, even for the police." Her smile faded, and her head gave a little bob, as though confirming her intentions to herself. "I will help you with this." Her voice was firm, and I couldn't think of a way to refuse her services, so I reluctantly thanked her instead.

"Send word when you want to speak with the woman, and I will meet you at your lodgings," Savithri said.

I nodded, and she continued along the path. I watched her for a moment, admiring her easy, elegant way of moving before my stomach rumbled. I sighed, regretting the decision to dismiss my ride since I would now have to make the long walk back on foot. I turned back toward town to find a meal, keeping to the edge of the path where the shade was heaviest. I was developing a headache from being out in the sun with an empty stomach, so I hurried my feet along the path. My only real consolation was that I was going downhill now, instead of up.

I'd found an interpreter, which was the good news. The bad news was that we couldn't entirely trust Savithri Kumari to give us an accurate translation; she'd been cagey when I'd asked her direct questions before, not to mention that it was difficult to say where her loyalties might lie. With the governor? With someone else? There were any number of reasons not to trust Savithri's translation.

And I wasn't sure there was anything we could do to change that.

Chapter Thirteen

I was determined to find a local restaurant that served Indian food. Real Indian food. Even if I couldn't speak the language to place an order, I would eat whatever was served to me. Or perhaps I would get lucky and could simply point to someone else's meal as what I wanted for myself. The danger, of course, was that the food would be entirely too spicy for me, but it was a risk I was willing to take.

I found a small place on the outskirts of town in a simple concrete building and ducked through the open doorway. As I'd found was common, the wooden doors and windows were open to the outside, the red-painted walls chipping in places. The room was small and simply furnished with wooden tables and chairs, painted in cheerful colors, reds and yellows. These too had seen some wear, but things looked clean and well cared-for despite the age, and I glanced around at the other diners. There were only a few scattered customers at the little wooden tables, one of whom I recognized as Paramasivan Subbarayan, the Indian premier for Madras. I kept an eye on him out of the corner of my eye, but he didn't seem to notice me, too intent on the sheaf of papers stacked beside the banana leaf his meal had been served on.

The proprietor hurried forward and said something to

me in what I assumed was Tamil, and I shook my head sadly, indicating that I couldn't understand him. He bobbed his head, and I smiled, pointing to a table near Subbarayan. The man bobbed his head again. I gave a little nod of thanks and wove my way through the tables toward the one I'd indicated, hoping that his head movement had meant yes.

As I neared his table, Subbarayan finally noticed me and narrowed his eyes slightly, probably trying to figure out where he recognized me from. We hadn't been formally introduced, but we'd come near to one another several times during the welcome dinner. I took my seat and called a greeting over to him.

"Good afternoon, Mr. Subbarayan. I'm Mrs. Jane Wunderly. I'm here with Redvers." I didn't bother using Redvers' last name since he never used it himself, and it would only cause more confusion.

"Ahh, yes, Mrs. Wunderly. I thought that I recognized your face."

Subbarayan was interrupted by the proprietor who asked him a question, looking back at me. "Mr. Dorairaj would like to know what you would like to eat and drink."

"I appreciate your help—I wish that I could speak Tamil. Would you be so kind as to order something for me? Not too spicy, of course, but I would like to try the local cuisine. And a local drink as well."

Subbarayan looked pleasantly surprised at my request and did as I asked. At least I hoped he had. I couldn't be sure until the food arrived and I tasted it. But the man bobbed his head and went away. After a moment, Subbarayan sighed and put his papers into the small brown satchel next to his chair. "Would you care to join me?"

I said that I would be delighted and left my table to join him at his. It was an unexpected opportunity to talk to the man, and I would use it to see what he knew. Cautiously, of course. "What did you have?" I asked, nodding my head at his half-finished meal.

Subbarayan pointed to each item as he described them. "I had poriyal, a delicious vegetable dish, served with plain rice, and kootu. It is made of lentils and vegetables. I ordered something similar for you, but much less spicy."

I thanked him again and paused while the café owner brought a drink and set it before me. I took a sip and made a noise of appreciation. "What is this?" I took another sip; it was a dark brown, almost like coffee, but tasted sweet and delicious.

"Sarbbath." Subbarayan said. "It is made of lemon and the sarsaparilla plant, mixed with milk. Among other things."

"Thank you so much," I said, taking one last sip before deciding to save the rest for when my meal came. I thought the creaminess of the drink might be helpful if the food was a little too spicy for my palate, which I'd quickly learned during my short time in India would likely be the case. Of course, too spicy was better than the alternative, as far as I was concerned.

We chatted about inanities for a little while, and I learned that Subbarayan had a wife and children back in Madras that he left behind every summer. "They don't want to get out of the heat and join you here?"

The man smiled gently, his eyes kind behind his gold-rimmed spectacles. "The heat does not bother us as it does you foreigners."

I could feel my neck grow warm. "I suppose not."

We regarded each other awkwardly. I couldn't think of a single question to ask the man, and it appeared he was having the same trouble. Could I bring up Gretchen's death without it sounding like an interrogation? It felt inappropriate as a topic for conversation, but it was what I most wanted to ask about. No surprise, since it was foremost in my mind.

I was relieved when Subbarayan did it for me.

He cleared his throat. "It's a shame what happened to Miss Beetner."

"I was very sad to hear it. I liked her a great deal," I said.

The premier nodded. "I have known her for a long time. I hope they are able to locate the tiger that was responsible."

His statement sounded genuine, as though he truly believed Gretchen was mauled by a tiger. I decided to prod the issue a little bit. "Does that happen often? Tiger attacks?"

Subbarayan shrugged. "A handful of people are killed every year by either tigers or leopards. With a leopard, you are lucky. They drop on your neck from above, usually from a large tree, and you don't even know what has happened before you are dead."

My face was a mask of horror. "And people just go about their lives, knowing this could happen?"

Subbarayan gave a short, humorless laugh. "If you die in such a manner, the government pays your family a good sum of money to compensate for the loss. It can set a family up for generations, so many believe this is not a bad way to die."

This was a lot to take in, so I was quiet for a moment, turning that over in my mind. Luckily, my food came out from the kitchen, which gave me a moment to regroup. I closed my eyes for a moment, savoring the spicy aromas wafting up from the banana leaf placed before me. Everything looked as good as it smelled, and my mouth began to water. I also appreciated the use of a leaf for a plate; it seemed economical and easy to clean up, not to mention easy to find since they grew everywhere. I tucked in, trying not to appear too eager, but my rumbling stomach betrayed me.

Subbarayan let me eat in silence for a bit before politely asking, "How is your meal?"

"Delicious," I said. It was the truth—the vegetables in the poriyal were still crisp and the lentil dish was equally delicious. My taste buds were in absolute heaven. But our pause in conversation had given me time to think about what I wanted to ask next. "I heard that Gretchen may have been romantically involved with a member of Indian royalty in her youth. Do you think there is any truth to that?"

Subbarayan's eyes widened in surprise. "I'm surprised anyone is still talking about such a thing; it was many years ago."

I looked at him expectantly while I loaded up another bite of food and took a sip of my drink.

He looked at me, considering. "I heard something similar once. I believe it was the prince of Travancore. He is now the maharajah." As if Subbarayan had heard the question in my mind, he continued on. "It would never have been acceptable for the raja to marry a British woman. He was already promised to a woman of his own province, so it could never have been more than a brief affair."

I nodded, feeling sad for Gretchen, who had obviously cared for the prince a great deal if she was still carrying a locket with a picture of him so many years later. I wondered if the raja would want to know of her death or if thoughts of Gretchen Beetner had simply been relegated to his past. I had no idea how to contact the man, however. Perhaps it was something I should ask Redvers about.

"I have never met the man in person, but by all accounts, he is a fair and just ruler of his province," Subbarayan said. "The maharajah had close connections with Governor Goshen, up until recently."

This was surprising information indeed. Perhaps the governor would know how to contact the maharajah to inform him about Gretchen's death. But I was also curious about why the men had had a falling-out. "What happened recently?" I asked.

Subbarayan's face closed down. "I can't remember." Then, seeming to believe that he had to say something, he offered, "Perhaps it has something to do with the governor's ambitions to become viceroy."

Subbarayan not being able to remember was very clearly a lie, and I had no idea whether this tidbit about the governor was as well, but I tucked it all away to discuss with Redvers later. Was there something here beyond politics that had contributed to Gretchen's demise? What would the governor have to gain from Gretchen's death?

Of course, the same could be asked of anyone here in Ooty. What did they have to gain with Gretchen dead?

I finished my meal, and Subbarayan seemed relieved to be excused from making more banal conversation with me. He hurried away as soon as was polite, and I strolled leisurely in his wake back to my quarters. Redvers had yet to return, so I paced around the room for a few minutes before heading back out. If I was going to pace, I might as well do it in a place where there was scenery and fresh air to enjoy, and the botanical garden seemed a good place for that. I could wear a track in the paths there instead of in my sitting room. I left Redvers a quick note telling him where I'd disappeared to, in case he came back and wondered where I'd gone.

I walked to the gardens, turning things over in my mind. It was growing late in the afternoon, but I had enough time before dusk that I thought I could make it back to Stone House without running the risk of becoming a tiger treat. This possibility was never far from my mind now, and it was a disconcerting fear, one I was entirely unused to. I'd faced down traitors and killers and spies in the recent past, but I'd never before had to worry about being killed by a large murderous cat.

I decided I might actually prefer the former, since people were more predictable than wild animals.

I'd been told that the gardens stretched over nearly fifty-five acres, which was rather a mind-boggling plot of land to set aside for gardens on the side of this mountain. There were people scattered about, but I paid them no mind, still ruminating on everything I'd learned that day. I barely saw the beautifully landscaped plants and trees around me, nor did I stop to smell the bushes of lightly scented roses, although I did pause to look when a family of monkeys chattering in a nearby treetop startled me by dropping a piece of fruit on the path.

But I didn't pause for long, my mind itching with the need to keep moving, since movement usually helped me work out thorny issues. I stuck to the main path, one that looped near the entrance so that Redvers could actually find me if he decided to come looking for me here. I was on my second or third time around when I heard my name being called.

"Mrs. Wunderly!"

I stopped in my tracks, glancing around. I spotted Lady Goshen seated on a bench just off the path I'd been stalking in circles, tucked in next to a large green hedgerow. "Lady Goshen, you startled me," I said as I approached her. She scooted over on her bench and gestured for me to join her.

"I'm not surprised," she said. "You seemed quite intent on your walk. I thought you would see me on your last trip around, but then I realized you would never see me if I didn't say something." She paused, adjusting her wide-brimmed hat, long enough for me to wonder why she would want me to see her. "You seemed quite deep in thought."

I nodded but didn't answer the unspoken question.

She made a little hmm-ing noise. "Did you find Savithri?"

This was the second time today the governor's wife had surprised me. "I did." I didn't elaborate further.

But Lady Goshen wasn't going to let that stand. "And did she have the answers you wanted?"

I regarded the woman for a moment, wondering just how much she knew about her husband's paramour but not wanting to ask. "She did. She was very helpful, actually."

Lady Goshen nodded. "George has always chosen well when it comes to his mistresses' personalities. They tend to be kind and quite intelligent." At my sharp look, she chuckled. "Oh, of course I know all about them. And this one wasn't the first, and I'm sure she won't be the last. Although she is quite lovely and seems young, so who knows? Perhaps she'll last longer than the others."

I had a lot of questions, but I had no idea how to go about asking them. I settled for a simple, "Are you alright?"

"Very much so. I quite enjoy my life and my freedom. I only ask that he not have children with any of them, and so far, he seems to have been careful."

I consciously kept my jaw snapped shut even though it wanted very badly to gape at the woman. How she could seem so . . . unaffected by it all was beyond me. Not to mention that her knowledge of his activities didn't excuse the man's behavior in the slightest, but I held my tongue on that front. It wasn't any of my business.

Unless, of course, it had something to do with Gretchen's death.

As though Lady Goshen could read my mind, she continued on. "Gretchen was a terrible busybody, but I will miss her," she said. "I'm sorry you didn't have the opportunity to know her better."

"I genuinely enjoyed what little time we spent together," I said. "I'm sorry it was cut short." I couldn't let her comment on Gretchen pass, however. "Why do you say she was a busybody?"

She waved a hand airily, as though her words had no consequence. "Oh, she just liked to be at the center of gossip."

I glanced at my companion, whose eyes appeared to be

focused on the small greenhouse in the distance, up the terraced hill from where we sat. I didn't think Gretchen gos-
siped simply for the sake of it. It seemed to me that she'd
gathered anything that could be useful politically, which
was a far cry from what most people considered "gossip."

Lady Goshen returned to our conversation from wherever she'd gone in her mind. "I know she thought she was
being helpful, sending me a note about my husband's mistress, but I already knew."

"She sent you a note about it?" I couldn't help the frown
pulling my eyebrows together.

Lady Goshen nodded, then picked up her small handbag
that was tucked on the bench beside her. I was surprised
that she was carrying the note with her, and I said as much.

"I was trying to decide whether or not to destroy it. And
if I do destroy it, I need a place where I can do so without
the servants becoming curious. You should be mindful of
what you say and do around them." She offered this unso-
licited advice as she opened the clasp on her bag and retrieved a small typed note, passing it over to me. I read it
quickly, noting that the letter *e* was dropped.

> *Lady Goshen: Your husband's mistress has been
> moved out to the Dodabetta plantation. Her name is
> Savithri Kumari. It's certain that your husband will
> continue seeing her even though you are here in
> Udhagamandalam.*

"It's not signed," I said. I noticed that the writer had also
used the old name for Ootacamund, the original Indian
spelling that had since been anglicized.

"No, but I can't think of anyone else who would have
tried to warn me. Gretchen liked to stir things up, so it very
much seems like something she would do." Lady Goshen

wrinkled her nose. "And she used the native name for Ooty. Who but Gretchen would do that? Since she was so attached to the people here."

I did my best to memorize the note before passing it back over since there was no chance she was going to let me keep it. I didn't even bother asking. It would only lead to questions that I did not want to answer about why I wanted it and what I would do with it.

But I found that I didn't care for the implication that Gretchen liked to "stir things up." I hadn't known Gretchen well enough to say whether or not that was actually true, but the accusation did not sit well with me. I also didn't care for the contempt in Lady Goshen's voice when she spoke about the Indian people, as though it had been a personal failing of Gretchen's that she'd cared about the people here.

I decided to direct the conversation toward less controversial waters. "Had you known Gretchen long?"

"Oh yes," Lady Goshen said. "We actually ran in some of the same social circles in England before she came here to India. We were all quite shocked when she decided not to return home."

I was surprised that Gretchen ran in a higher social set back in England. She hadn't appeared particularly wealthy or to care at all for material things. Even the way she'd dressed was quite simple, although that could have been from living here in India for so long.

"She never married?" I asked. I knew the answer to this, but I was hoping Lady Goshen would have some insight into Gretchen's affair with the maharajah.

Lady Goshen shook her head. "No, never. I'd heard a rumor that she'd once been involved with an Indian man, something quite inappropriate, but I never did find out the details."

That wasn't helpful, and based on her attitude, I suspected that probing for more information would only incense me. I was going to ask something else entirely when Lady Goshen surprised me again. "I do hope someone is able to figure out who killed her."

"It was a tiger attack," I said slowly.

Lady Goshen cocked her head at me as though disappointed. "I think we both know that isn't the case. But since the police won't be looking into it, I hope that someone else will. For all her faults, Gretchen deserved better than that." With this announcement she checked her watch and stood, gathering her elaborately embroidered clutch. "It's been lovely chatting with you. We should do this again—there aren't that many ladies here I would want to spend time with. But I would enjoy having tea with you some time."

I thanked her and said that would be nice, although I was fairly certain that I didn't mean it, and watched her leave. Lady Goshen had been a wealth of surprises today, although I disagreed with her that Gretchen had sent her the note, not to mention disagreeing with Lady Goshen's attitude toward the Indian people in general. No, if I had to nominate a suspect for the sender of this note, it would be Gretchen's killer, although I had nothing but intuition to back the theory up.

The more I thought about it, the more convinced I became that I was correct. Gretchen wouldn't have sent Lady Goshen that message, especially not about something so personal. Gretchen would have told her the news about her husband's mistress in person, if she'd even been inclined to do so, which I doubted. But then I recalled the scene in the garden between Savithri and Gretchen. Had that been related to this somehow? Was Lady Goshen correct about the sender of the message, and I simply didn't want to admit it? I was feeling fiercely protective of Gretchen since she couldn't defend herself now, so perhaps I wasn't seeing her—and her motives—as clearly as I should.

I sat on the bench, oblivious to the carefully manicured bushes with blooming flowers around me, and considered that for some time but came back to my initial conclusion. My instincts told me that Gretchen would have addressed such a touchy subject in person. She wasn't afraid of confrontation; that was for certain. Which meant that she wouldn't have sent an anonymous note.

The other thing that surprised me during my conversation with Lady Goshen was that she clearly knew Gretchen hadn't been killed by a tiger. I'd only recently revealed that to Savithri, and beyond that, the only person who knew besides myself, Redvers, and the police inspector was the murderer.

CHAPTER FOURTEEN

I was still sitting on the bench when Redvers appeared. I was quite grateful to see him, since the sun had already lowered enough for me to feel uncomfortable walking the path back to our quarters by myself.

"How was your day, my dear?" Redvers asked. He didn't sit but tipped his head toward the path, so I stood and joined him as we walked toward the south exit.

"Interesting. I've quite a lot to report, I'm afraid. Although I'm not certain any of it is useful."

"Sounds quite similar to my own day. Let's wait until we're back in our rooms to discuss it, though." Redvers glanced around, and I wondered who he expected to see listening to us.

I was fine with hurrying back, however, and I breathed an audible sigh of relief once we were safely in our quarters. Redvers' mouth quirked in amusement, but he resisted the urge to tease me for once.

Removing my shoes, I went into the sitting room and took a seat on the chair, adjusting the pillow behind my back. The couch was more comfortable, but I needed to sit across from Redvers so that we could discuss our respective days without being distracted by his nearness. "What did you learn today?" I asked when Redvers had taken his own seat.

"You first," he said, eyes twinkling.

I rolled mine but gave him a breakdown of my day. "Did you know that the governor was interested in becoming viceroy of India?"

Redvers nodded. "It was one of the things that came up today."

"I don't think that gives him a motive to kill Gretchen, though. I would think the opposite, really."

"That's a fair point. I'm not sure who in the government would be willing to risk it, although that's where our most viable suspects are." Redvers tapped his finger against his lips. "You said Lady Goshen had a note?"

I nodded and told him what it said. "She thought it came from Gretchen, because apparently Gretchen liked to stir up trouble." Redvers frowned, and I shook my head emphatically. "Her words—I didn't care for the implication either. Quite honestly, I didn't care for a lot of her implications."

Redvers raised his eyebrows, and I grimaced. There was no need to elaborate on that, even if I had come away with a bad taste in my mouth for Lady Goshen. I turned back to the issue at hand. "The note she showed me was written on the same typewriter as the one that was sent to the inspector. It had the same dropped *e*. But I can't imagine that Gretchen would have sent an anonymous note instead of simply addressing the problem in person."

"Even if she had, I can't imagine that would give Lady Goshen a motive to kill Gretchen."

"I agree. Especially since Lady Goshen didn't seem particularly bothered by the fact that her husband was having an affair."

Redvers' eyes widened, but he didn't comment on that. "I'm sure there is something Lady Goshen isn't telling us."

"I assume that is the case with everyone."

"Except me, of course." Redvers had a devilish look in his eye.

A sly smile crossed my face. "I don't know. Perhaps you should convince me that you're revealing all."

So much for sitting across the room so as not to be distracted by my husband.

Sometime later, we dressed and headed to dinner. "I forgot to mention that Gretchen's funeral service will be held tomorrow," Redvers said.

"That seems fast," I said.

"It does. But since she has no immediate family in England, there's no reason to send her body back there. Since she'll be buried here, I suppose they saw no reason to delay it."

A wave of sadness washed over me, but I did my best to shake it off. We would find her killer; that was the best way I knew to avenge her untimely death. "What will happen to her things?"

"As far as I know, the staff packed up her room. I don't know what they will do with her belongings."

I sighed. It was heartbreaking, all of it.

We were nearly at the governor's mansion when I remembered that I'd forgotten to tell Redvers one of the most important details from my interaction with the governor's wife. "I forgot to mention that Lady Goshen knew Gretchen wasn't killed by a tiger," I said.

This brought Redvers up short, and I stumbled in surprise at how quickly he'd stopped moving. He stared at me, then asked, "What exactly did she say?"

I paused, trying to remember her exact words. "I hope they find out who killed her." I cocked my head, then nodded. "Or something very close to that."

Redvers started walking again. "How could she know that?" he asked, more to himself than to me.

I answered all the same. "I don't know, unless Savithri told her. But I find that to be a very unlikely scenario." I couldn't imagine the two women sharing secrets or even gossip with one another.

"That does seem unlikely." Redvers narrowed his eyes as he let me pass by him through the front door to the mansion. "I can't believe you forgot to tell me that piece."

I wrinkled my nose at him. "Entirely your fault for distracting me."

Redvers gave me a little wink and led me down the hall toward the dining room.

The next morning was overcast and threatening to storm, which should have surprised me, but instead I found it appropriate. It matched my feelings about the day's events. All through breakfast, I couldn't help but think about how Gretchen would be buried that afternoon in the small local cemetery. Having no family in England, I was sure she would have been pleased to be buried in her beloved India, although she might have preferred a location on the plains, where she'd spent the majority of her time.

I dressed that morning in a simple green linen dress with a V-neck and a fabric tie at the bottom of the *v*, nearly covering the buttons that marched up the front. I didn't have any darker clothing along with me, since I hadn't wanted to wear anything that would absorb the hot sun and make me even hotter. I doubted Gretchen would have cared, though.

Redvers looked dashing in his gray linen suit, and once I pinned my straw boater-style hat to my head, I took his arm. The cemetery was on the far side of Ooty, out past the man-made lake, so we hired a carriage to take us there. From my perch in the horse-drawn conveyance, I noticed a number of other officials streaming slowly in the same direction. At least Gretchen would have a nice turnout.

We walked the last half mile or so to the graveyard, climbing the path leading up the gentle incline. The graves were located on a green hill gently sloping upward; at the very top I suspected there would be a stunning view of the surrounding mountains, maybe even of the nearby lake. On another day I would be tempted to climb to the top to find out, but today we followed the others gathering around the newly dug grave. Governor Goshen and his wife stood close to the gaping hole in the ground, with Subbarayan, Feodore Smith, and a few other officials crowded around. The rest of us filled in behind them, waiting for the arrival of the casket.

Two horses pulling a simple wooden cart finally arrived, and a few local men gathered around the back of the cart to grab the simple pine box that Gretchen had been placed in. The grimaces on the men's faces when they hoisted the box up were surprising—Gretchen hadn't been a large woman—and we all watched somberly as they approached the gravesite, the crowd parting to let the men through. In unison the men dropped the box down from their shoulders toward the ropes that had been laid on the ground. Once they had the box positioned over the ropes, the men lifted the casket by hoisting the ropes and began moving in unison toward the open hole. As I watched, I could have sworn that I saw a man's foot come out of the crowd directly in the path of the casket bearer in front, who tripped and fell into the man behind him. This caused a chain reaction, and we all held our breath as the casket dropped abruptly to the side, the top flying open from the sudden weight pressing against it.

There was a collective gasp, but what rolled from the casket now lying on its side were several large bags of rice.

CHAPTER FIFTEEN

There was an immediate cacophony as everyone in the crowd began talking among themselves. My first instinct was to rush forward and look into the casket to see if Gretchen's body was buried beneath the rice bags, but Redvers grabbed hold of my arm and gave his head a little shake. I took this to mean that we shouldn't give ourselves away, so with a great effort I stayed where I was.

The initial shock quickly wore off, and it became quite obvious that Gretchen wasn't inside the casket. Someone had clearly taken her body and replaced the weight with several rice bags, which were now being hoisted onto the shoulders of the locals who'd been carrying the casket. No one seemed entirely sure what to do, least of all the casket bearers, but after a few minutes the crowd dissipated without the service going forward. How could we have a service when there was no body to bury?

"Who do you think has it?" I asked Redvers in a low voice as we joined the crowd making their way back toward Ooty.

"I have some ideas," he said darkly.

"Are you going to share them with me?"

"When we get back."

I huffed in frustration but silently acknowledged that he

was probably right in being cautious. We were surrounded by people without any idea of what they might hear or where their loyalties might lie. Not to mention the fact that someone here was likely responsible for Gretchen's death in the first place.

In any case, a quiet walk gave me an opportunity to eavesdrop on what the crowd around us was saying. Mostly there was speculation on what had happened to Gretchen's body, with some people indicating that they thought she might still be alive. I wished that was the truth, but I'd seen her in the morgue with my own two eyes, so I knew she was really and truly dead.

What I couldn't even begin to fathom, however, was why someone would steal her body. What could anyone gain by doing so?

As we neared the main stretch of Ooty, the crowd of funeral-goers broke up, and we were able to hail a carriage to take us back to our quarters. But even alone and being pulled through the city streets at a decent clip, we held our tongues.

Back in our room, Sasmit was clearing up our breakfast things, so we each took a seat and sat quietly until he'd finished. "Can I bring you something else?" he asked politely.

"Another pot of coffee would be lovely," I said, before realizing that this would only delay our conversation. Redvers looked bemused but didn't contradict my request. I shrugged helplessly. I truly did want a cup.

Sasmit left with our dishes, promising to return shortly with another pot.

"Did you see someone trip the casket bearer?" I figured we had enough time for this piece of the conversation before Sasmit returned.

Redvers frowned and shook his head. "I didn't see anything. But that doesn't mean that it didn't happen."

"I thought I did, but now I'm not so sure."

I closed my eyes and tried to picture what I'd seen—or rather, what I thought I had seen. Even during the course of our short walk back, I'd started to question whether I had actually seen someone trip the men carrying the casket, or whether it had simply been an accident. Memory was a tricky thing, and it was too easy to replace real memories with false ones.

I reopened my eyes and shook my head. "I don't know. But if someone did trip the men on purpose, that means they likely knew about the switch. There's no other reason to try to tip over the casket, is there?" Given the damage to Gretchen's face, it would have been horrifying if her body had actually rolled out. I couldn't imagine someone would be terrible enough to expose that to the crowd, which meant the culprit knew about the rice bags.

"Unless they knew she'd been murdered and wanted to uncover the lie about the tiger attack," Redvers said.

I shuddered. That was an awful thought. I was glad that we'd all been spared the gruesome sight of Gretchen's destroyed visage.

Sasmit came back with my coffee and some fresh fruit, and Redvers and I paused our discussion as he delivered the tray. I thanked him. Once he'd gone, I asked my next question.

"Who do you think took the body?"

"I think Lala Lajpat Rai and his resistance members had something to do with it," Redvers said, his eyes narrowed.

"But why? Why on earth steal the woman's body? Why not just dump her out and show everyone that she'd been shot instead, like you suggested?"

Redvers' mouth turned down into a grimace. "I'm glad they didn't. No one needs to see that."

"I'm sorry that you did," I said.

He nodded and took a breath. While he gave himself a

moment to recover, I realized that I had never stopped to consider how many gruesome things he'd seen during his years working for the Crown and whether he was able to forget them. I thought it was likely difficult to get the images from his mind; once you've seen something terrible, it's difficult to unsee it. Redvers always seemed so strong, so capable, that I never considered how much these things bothered him. It was something I resolved to be more sensitive to in the future.

Redvers continued. "If it was Rai, he wouldn't have subjected the crowd to the sight. But, and this is only a guess, Rai might have wanted Gretchen's body to prove that there's a cover-up surrounding her death, throwing suspicion on the government. Then they might be able to sway some voting members of the government against the Raj and the Simon Commission. And they're holding it as a bargaining chip."

This sounded like a pretty outlandish conspiracy to me, but I couldn't think of a scenario that made even a little bit of sense, so I shrugged. "Very well, how do we find out?"

"Once you've had your coffee"—this was said with a raised brow that I chose to ignore—"we can head out to where they are staying."

"You make it sound as though they aren't in Ooty."

"Oh, they are not." Redvers chuckled, and it was my turn to raise a brow.

Redvers called for another carriage since we were heading further out of town than I'd been before. "Where are they staying, exactly?" I asked while we waited to be picked up.

"Rai and a few of his followers are staying at an estate outside of town," Redvers said. "Near a Toda settlement." As though that cleared things up.

I took this to mean that we were heading out to a part of the hills that was otherwise largely uninhabited.

The horse-pulled carriage took us out into the country-side, easily tackling hills that I was grateful I didn't have to climb. The wooded areas ebbed and flowed with the hills, alive with creatures calling to one another. Luckily, we didn't see a tiger or a leopard, although we did startle a family of small deer, and they bounded away through the trees. There also seemed to be a profusion of peacocks, even more than the day before, and I nearly jumped out of my skin when one screamed at us from the roadside. I would never get used to such a terrible noise, loud and almost human-like. Redvers laughed at my reaction, and I gave his arm a little smack for his impudence.

We had the carriage drop us off on the road seemingly in the middle of nowhere. The driver looked skeptical, but Redvers insisted, and we disembarked and paid the man, then waited while he drove a little way down the road, turned around, and went back to Ooty. We didn't start walking again until he was well out of sight.

"Don't want anyone to know where we're going?" I asked.

Redvers tweaked the end of my nose. "Perceptive as always, my dear."

It was a short walk along the road until we came to a path leading through the woods off to our right. The trees finally opened up into a clearing, delivering us to a rather grand-looking manor house, yellow stucco with white columns gracing the lower level. A servant in white tunic and pants hurried forward to greet us and directed us to a small grouping of chairs on the porch, tucked beneath the balcony and out of the sun. I'd barely had time to get comfortable in my chair before Rai and two other men joined us. We stood and were immediately gestured back into our cushioned seats.

Redvers exchanged some pleasantries with the men, then got down to business. "Rai, did you and your men take the body?"

Rai's look of innocence was entirely overdone, and I knew immediately that Redvers' instincts had been correct.

"To what end?" Redvers asked.

Rai became serious. "We wanted to prove that the Raj was responsible for her death and is spreading lies about how it happened. But once we took the body, we now have other concerns."

"What do you mean?"

"Did you see the body?" Rai asked.

"Yes, my wife and I both took a look at the body when it was at the hospital. It wasn't a tiger attack. She'd clearly been shot," Redvers said firmly.

"Yes, of course. But her . . ." Rai shot a quick glance at me and then looked meaningfully at Redvers.

"You can say whatever you need to in front of my wife."

Rai looked back and forth between the two of us before continuing with what he wanted to say. "I am not sure that the body belongs to Gretchen."

Redvers looked shocked, and I was certain that my expression mirrored his. "What do you mean it doesn't belong to Gretchen?"

"There was not enough left of her face to be sure it was really her," Rai said, then looked to me. "I am sorry to be so blunt."

My stomach felt queasy, but I assured him that I was fine all the same. Of course, fine or not, my mind was already quickly flicking through different possibilities. Could he be correct? I hadn't seen anything above Gretchen's neck, Redvers had been careful to keep that covered. And she'd been fully clothed when I saw her, wearing the same outfit from the night before, although the pieces had been quite torn. It seemed quite unlikely that the body had belonged to anyone else, but could I, or even my clever husband, say that for certain, especially if there had been little left of her identifying features?

Could the body belong to someone else?

Chapter Sixteen

R edvers and I looked at one another. I could feel the frown creasing my forehead as I thought this theory through. "What is the likelihood of finding a person that looks so much like Gretchen here in Ooty?" The natural extension of that question was, If there was someone who looked like Gretchen, were they killed simply to perpetuate the hoax of Gretchen's death? I couldn't imagine Gretchen being involved in such a thing—and to what end? Even thinking through these questions made the idea hard to believe. A hoax of that scale would involve too many people and be too difficult to pull off without word leaking out about it. A secret could only be kept between two people if one of them were dead.

"I was wondering the same thing," Redvers said, turning back to Rai. "It's true there are quite a lot of British citizens here, but it's unlikely to find another foreign woman that so closely resembles Gretchen here in India, let alone Ooty. I think the body has to belong to Gretchen Beetner."

Everyone was quiet, and I readjusted in my seat, taking a moment to gaze out over the lush green garden lying just beyond the porch. It was beautiful here, a backdrop of thick forest on the hills behind us, and lush flowers in a profusion of colors, red and purple and pink. I wondered briefly who owned the place and why it was located so far from town.

"You have the word of both my wife and myself that Gretchen was shot and the Raj is lying about the tiger attack, so will you put the body back?" Redvers asked.

Rai thought about that for a second, then nodded. "We will do that. Although I think if the body belongs to Miss Beetner, she would have wanted a traditional funeral, not a British one."

I was a little afraid to ask what a traditional funeral called for, but my curiosity won out. "What does that look like?"

"We cremate our dead on funeral pyres," Rai said simply. "That is, the Hindus do, although some Hindus of lower caste choose to bury their dead. There is also a Muslim population here in India, and they prefer to bury their dead as well. But mostly we celebrate the life of the one who has passed away and then cremate them."

I nodded. It was always fascinating to me how cultures around the world handled their dead, and this method was not uncommon. I also thought that Rai was correct about Gretchen preferring cremation to being buried, but I didn't say anything. There was now just enough doubt in my mind that the body belonged to Gretchen Beetner that I thought it best to bury the body in the hole that had already been dug in the cemetery.

Just in case.

Redvers and Rai discussed the logistics of returning Gretchen's body to its casket, and I took the opportunity to walk around the garden since I didn't necessarily need or want to hear the details of that. I could only imagine where they currently had her stashed, and I didn't want to examine those details either. Instead, I enjoyed the views, strolling along a landscaped path, where blooming flowers and gorgeous green plants flourished in the warm sunshine, and peered up at the cheeky green parakeets that made such a ruckus wherever they perched. When I thought they'd had enough time, I wandered back to the men and heard Rai invite us for a meal, which we politely declined.

"I'm afraid we must be getting back, although I'll return to discuss the commission with you at a later time," Redvers said.

Rai nodded. "I look forward to our reunion."

With that, we said our goodbyes and started the trek back to Ooty. "We still need to speak with the woman who found the body," I reminded Redvers once we were back on the main road. "Savithri volunteered her services as translator, and I could hardly say no, even though I absolutely do not trust her."

"Why not?" Redvers asked. "I think that's wise, of course, but I'm curious about your reasons."

I shrugged. "No reason in particular, just that she has been cagey about other topics and avoided giving me answers to direct questions. It's also impossible to tell where her loyalties might lie." I looked at him. "If there's one thing I've learned, it's that you can't trust anyone in a murder investigation."

"True enough," Redvers said. He was quiet for a few steps, and I could tell he was thinking something over, so I let him ponder without interrupting him. "What if we did something of an experiment?" he finally said.

"I'm listening."

"What if you interview the local woman with Savithri and see what she translates for you. Then I will go with Rai and one of his people and see what they translate for us. Afterward, we'll come back and compare notes. If the stories are vastly different, we'll know that someone is lying."

"It's a good plan, but how will we know which of them is telling the truth?"

"That's the only kink I haven't managed to work out yet," Redvers said.

We came to a split in the road where I turned off for the tea plantation to find Savithri. I was hoping she was free right now so that we could interview the local woman and put Redvers' plan into motion. When I got to the main building, however, Hasnan informed me that Savithri was in town. I thanked him before sighing and trudging off toward Ooty. Even if I hurried, there was no way I'd be able to catch up with Redvers, so I walked at a reasonable pace, although I found that my body was now on high alert for anything lurking in the forest.

I didn't meet anyone on the path, and as I neared town, I decided to take a detour to the market in the hopes of finding Savithri there, although I knew it would be challenging in the crush of people I'd learned to expect.

Fortune favored me, though. As I neared the market, I saw Savithri coming my way, carrying a covered basket. I smiled and greeted her. "Is now a convenient time for you?"

"Convenient time for what?" she asked.

"To interview the woman who found Gretchen's body," I said. "You said that you would translate for me."

Savithri's face cleared as she recalled our conversation. "Oh, of course." She thought for a moment, glanced down at her basket, then gave a little head bob. "Now would be fine. Do you know where the woman lives?"

I did, since Redvers had given me very specific instructions on how to find the woman's home. She lived on the outskirts of Ooty, where a majority of the Indian people were relegated.

We headed in that direction, both of us quiet. Savithri finally broke the silence. "I heard what happened at the service this morning. It is very shocking."

I nodded but cocked my head. "You weren't there?" I quickly realized that was a silly question since I had seen the governor and his wife there. Savithri wouldn't be there as well; it was unlikely that the two women would be found in the same place unless by complete accident. I started to retract my question, but Savithri gave a little laugh.

"It's quite alright," she said. "It was only partly because of Lady Goshen that I did not attend."

"What was the other reason?"

"I had some personal matters to take care of."

I considered asking what those "personal matters" might be, but I knew in my gut that she wasn't going to answer that truthfully. And to be fair, if the roles were reversed, I wouldn't either.

I was still thinking about Savithri and her mysteries when we arrived at the Indian woman's house. It was moving well into the afternoon now, and we were lucky to find her at home. She was a tiny woman with gray threading liberally through her dark hair, wearing a simple cotton sari in green and yellow. Savithri asked her something in Tamil, and the woman bobbed her head and motioned for us to come inside.

It was a simple building, the doors open and wooden window shutters thrown open as well, as I'd noticed was common. The dirt floor was neatly swept, and the few items inside the house were obviously clean and in their places. It was a single room, with a mat in the corner where the woman slept and a carved wooden chest where I assumed she kept her clothing.

"She says we are most welcome. She and her husband live here with their son. She would like to know if we want to sit down and have some tea."

I did my best not to look around. Three people lived here? I glanced down at my slim-fitting skirt. It was definitely a hindrance to accepting this woman's kind hospitality, since it would be impossible for me to get down on the ground while wearing it.

"Please thank her for me and ask what her name is," I said. "And tell her not to trouble herself with tea."

Savithri relayed the information and reported back that the woman's name was Sudha.

"This is a lovely home," I said. It was well cared for, but it was also clear that this woman and her family were quite poor based on the simple nature of the single room and its lack of furniture or personal possessions. The items on display were functional, like pots and cooking utensils, not decorative. "Please ask her if we may ask some questions about how she found Gretchen's body."

Savithri paused for a long moment, then ran off a long string of words. Sudha bobbed her head, then spoke back. She spoke for long enough that I started to become nervous, but I held my tongue and let the woman finish.

"Sudha says that she was on her way to the other side of Ooty, where she works in one of the big houses as a maid. One of the estates near the governor's mansion. She sometimes walks with a friend, but on that day, she was alone; her friend was not feeling well. When she came to the part of the path that is near the forest, she saw something lying in the grass. When she got close, she realized it was the body of a woman, and there was blood all over the head." Savithri took a breath before continuing on. "Sudha went to report what she had found to the police station and led the inspector to the site before she went to work."

"Did she see anyone else in the area? In the forest maybe?"

Savithri relayed the question, which Sudha thought about for only a moment before answering. "No, she saw no one." Sudha spoke again, and Savithri listened with her head cocked, then turned to me. "She thought it was strange that the police told her to say it was a tiger attack."

"Why isn't she saying that now?" I asked, a frown tugging my brows together.

Savithri asked the question, then laughed at Sudha's response. "She does not like the inspector. Her brother had some trouble with the police, and the inspector treated him very poorly." Sudha shrugged but had a wicked gleam in her eye while Savithri translated, and I believed that Savithri was relaying at least this part correctly.

"Please thank her for her help and ask if there is anything I can do for her in return for her information."

Savithri did as I asked but shook her head. "Sudha is happy to have told her story. She insists that she does not want anything from us."

I thanked her again in English, even though she was unlikely to understand me, and Savithri and I took our leave. I still wanted to do something for the woman—give her some rupees, perhaps—but I also didn't want to offend her sense of dignity.

Now all I could do was go back to my quarters and see if Redvers returned with the same story.

CHAPTER SEVENTEEN

Savithri and I quickly parted ways after leaving Sudha's house. I thanked her for her help, but as I walked away, I reflected that every interaction I'd had with the woman so far had left me with far more questions than answers.

And while Lala Rai might think otherwise, I still believed that Gretchen was dead, despite wishing that it weren't true. But wishing wouldn't change the facts: a body had been found, a murder had been committed, there was an attempt to cover it up, and it was incredibly unlikely that the murdered woman was anyone but Gretchen. I kept reminding myself of these facts while I paced around the sitting room, waiting for Redvers to return.

I was tempted to pace the garden in the courtyard just beyond the patio doors that I'd thrown open on my return, but I didn't want to wait an extra moment while Redvers tried to find me. I'd finally dropped in a chair to wait when Redvers came through the door and I sat bolt upright, anticipating his news. "Well?" I asked impatiently. "What did Sudha tell you?"

Redvers looked amused and took a seat across from me, casually crossing one leg over the other, catching an ankle on his knee and leaning back in the chair, hands behind his head. "How was your afternoon?" he asked, in what could only be an attempt to vex me. I gave him my most annoyed face, but it made him laugh.

With a sigh, I gave in and reported what Sudha had told me about finding Gretchen's body, as translated by Savithri. Once I had finished, Redvers nodded and looked thoughtful. "That's nearly exactly what we learned as well, down to Sudha's brother having been in trouble with the law once upon a time."

I thought through those implications. "Which means it's likely that both Savithri and Rai are telling the truth. As far as this goes, anyway."

"It's highly unlikely that Rai and Savithri would have conspired to tell us the same story. I'm nearly certain they don't know one another."

It was too bad that when Sudha found Gretchen, she hadn't seen anyone lurking around the scene or even fleeing into the forest, although it was better for her safety that she hadn't. Whoever had shot Gretchen wouldn't have thought twice about silencing a witness. I had no doubts about that, and I said as much.

We both pondered what we'd learned. "What next?" I finally asked.

"There's still the matter of the notes that were sent to Lady Goshen and the inspector. We need to find the typewriter that was used to write them, and I think our best bet is to try the offices at the governor's mansion. After dark, of course."

"Although that won't narrow things down a whole lot, will it?"

"It will hopefully give us an idea of who had access to it." Redvers glanced at his watch. "We can do that tonight, once the building is empty and most people are in bed."

I liked a good after-hours search, but I was nervous about walking that far in the dark. I told Redvers this, and he looked amused. "We'll be fine. I have my pistol."

I didn't think that would have much stopping power against a tiger, but it was better than nothing.

It was well and truly dark when we made our way to the governor's mansion. To cover my nerves, I chatted as I scanned the brush along the walking path as well as the trees above us—I recalled what I'd been told about the leopards dropping from the sky.

"I don't know why Lady Goshen would think Gretchen sent her a note informing her of her husband's affair," I said.

"I don't know why, either," Redvers said.

A breeze moved the branches above us, and I grabbed his arm, stifling a shriek.

"Just the wind, dear." Redvers had to practically peel my fingers from his arm. "I think that's going to leave a mark," he muttered, although I could tell he wasn't angry, just bemused. "I don't think I've ever seen you so jumpy."

"I've never had to worry about being attacked by a large and hungry cat before."

"That's a fair point. But it would be over before you knew what hit you."

I scowled. "That is not as comforting as you think it is."

Redvers chuckled, and I heaved an enormous sigh of relief when we made it to the mansion a few minutes later. The walk hadn't taken very long at all since I'd been moving my feet at quite a clip, but I was already dreading the return trip.

"Maybe we could find a closet to hide out in until morning," I muttered.

Redvers just shook his head and put his finger to his lips. We stood behind a lush green bush, peering around the branches. Two guards in khaki were posted at the front of the mansion, lounging in wooden chairs, smoking and chatting. Redvers tipped his head, indicating we would continue skulking through the brush until we reached the side of the building nearest the garden. Here too was a khaki-clad guard, sitting on the steps near the open door. We crouched at the outskirts of the garden, hidden in the shadows, and waited. This was the door that Redvers had staked out as the easiest for us to get through. If we could just get past the guard, we would be in excellent shape—the door behind the young man was open. I supposed they figured they didn't need to close up since they had guards posted.

We hunkered there in the dark for some time, and when my feet began to tingle from crouching, I slipped to the ground to sit and wait. The ground was damp and cool beneath me, but I'd endured worse for longer. A quarter hour stretched to a half, and I was considering lying down fully when the young man finally stood and stretched, then wandered off toward the front of the mansion after giving the garden we were hiding in a quick scan.

Once he was out of sight, we hurried along the garden path, up the stairs, and through the door. We moved away from the open entrance in case the guard returned, then waited for a moment, listening for the sound of anyone moving around. When we heard nothing but the peculiar silence of an empty space, Redvers led me further inside.

The second floor of the building was as deserted as the first, and there were no other guards—they were only posted outside. We did the same thing on the second floor—listening quietly to ensure there was no one working late. When we heard nothing, we moved to the first office space.

We'd been so quiet up till that point that I nearly had a heart attack at the first typewriter we tested out. The sound of the keys clacking was so loud in the deadly stillness that I was certain one of the guards would hear and come to investigate. By the third typewriter, however, I'd become more immune, especially since we only needed to type a few words to check the letter *e* on any given machine.

I lost track of how many rooms we went through, although we'd found far fewer typewriters than I had initially anticipated. Toward the end of our search, we came to the governor's office suite and uncovered yet another machine sitting on his secretary's desk. Redvers rolled the paper in and typed the words, then shined a flashlight beam on what he had typed.

"Aha!" he crowed softly.

"Found it?"

"We certainly did." Redvers folded the piece of paper he'd been typing on and slipped it into his pocket, clicking off his flashlight. "Time to go."

After giving our eyes time to adjust to the darkness, Redvers led me back down to the first floor. He went first down the hallway leading to the garden entrance we had slipped in through, and in the moonlight streaming through the windows I could see him gesture for me to join him. I did, and we escaped into the garden, which was lit here and there with oil torches that cast long and dancing shadows.

We'd become a little too cocky that the guards were occupied elsewhere, so we were both startled by the sound of someone walking on the gravel path. We froze, trying to determine if they were coming toward us or going away. Before we could choose an escape route, a figure came out of the darkness and spotted us immediately.

It was an Indian man that I didn't recognize. He was

wearing a dark kurta that blended with the shadows on the path. "Redvers? What are you doing out here so late?" He glanced at me, clearly curious as to who I was.

"This is my wife, Jane Wunderly," Redvers said. "I'm surprised you're still at the mansion this late, Mr. Kandiyar." He was obviously stalling for time in order to come up with a convincing story as to why we were here at this time of night.

"I could say the same about you," Kandiyar said. His tone was neutral, but I knew we needed a story, and fast.

I jumped in. "We were looking for my shawl. I think I left it out here this evening." I mentally crossed my fingers that the man wouldn't know that I had been nowhere near the governor's mansion that day.

He looked at me strangely. "It could not have waited until tomorrow?"

I shook my head, mind rapidly searching for a story that made sense. "It was my late mother's shawl. And with all the monkeys around—" I gestured a bit wildly at the silent trees. "I was afraid if we didn't come tonight that they might steal it and then we would never get it back."

Mr. Kandiyar smiled kindly at me and gave Redvers a knowing look that irritated me greatly, but I bit my tongue. If I had to play the part of the foolish wife dragging her husband to a garden in the dead of night, so be it. But I would have something to say about it later.

Redvers exchanged some pleasantries with Kandiyar while I pretended to continue my search for the fictitious shawl, finally wailing, "I don't see it anywhere."

Redvers patted my back. "Perhaps someone found it and is keeping it safe. I'll be sure to ask around the mansion tomorrow."

I pretended great worry but after some exaggerated dithering agreed to his plan. We said our goodbyes to Kandiyar and left the garden, walking at a much more measured pace than I would have liked.

"Quick thinking," Redvers said once we were well out of earshot of the building. Even so, he kept his voice quite low.

His praise warmed me from the inside out, and I couldn't help but beam. "Thank you. But who was that?"

"The owner of the typewriter," Redvers said.

CHAPTER EIGHTEEN

I gasped at this revelation, and Redvers continued. "Vihan Kandiyar is the governor's personal secretary, and it was the typewriter at his desk that those notes were written on."

"What do we know about him?" I asked.

"Not much, which of course I will rectify first thing in the morning. It's not a given that he wrote the notes, but that office is locked after hours." It was true. Redvers had needed his lockpick set to get us through that door. It wasn't the only lock he'd had to pick, but many more typewriters had been out in the open than not, which made it feel that much more significant for the letters to have been typed on Kandiyar's machine.

"Either someone would have to know how to pick a lock, or they would have needed to gain access while Kandiyar was away from his desk." Redvers was quiet for a moment, clearly thinking through that scenario. "I imagine it would be difficult for someone to explain why they were using the desk of the governor's secretary to type something up. And doing it while the office is unoccupied is unlikely—there are nearly always people in that office. Or it is locked, like it was tonight."

It was interesting that someone would use a typewriter in such a high-traffic area, and go to great lengths to do so.

"Unless someone is trying to frame Kandiyar for the notes? I would think a frame-up would make the effort worthwhile."

"An interesting possibility," Redvers said. "Let's leave the rest for the morning, though."

"Do you have any guesses as to why he was out so late?"

Redvers shook his head. "I caught a whiff of smoke, so perhaps he'd stepped out for a cigarette. The quarters where some of the civil servants are housed are not too far from the garden. But I'll still make inquiries about that as well."

We crossed the threshold to the Stone House, and I could feel my shoulders drop now that we were safely inside once more. Once out of sight of the mansion, I'd set the pace, which had been just short of a trot. As a result, we'd reached our quarters in record time.

I had no issue with tabling our discussion about the governor's secretary. There were far more pleasant ways to spend what was left of our evening than speculating about Vihan Kandiyar.

Redvers waited to have breakfast with me the next day instead of disappearing like the morning mist to attend the meetings he'd been tasked with sitting through. I thought it sounded more like he'd been tasked with suffering through these meetings, since every one he detailed sounded boring enough that I stopped listening halfway through his description. From what I could tell, it was a group of men who liked to hear themselves talk, dragging out meetings far longer than they needed to be and accomplishing less than nothing while doing so. I was glad it was him and not me, since I would have fallen asleep and hit my head on a table during any one of them.

Instead, I enjoyed my coffee and my husband's company while we batted quite a bit of speculation back and forth, but we didn't have any concrete answers—not even about whether or not Gretchen was actually alive, although we both agreed that the most likely scenario was that Gretchen had been killed, and it was truly her body that Rai had absconded with.

"When is Rai returning her body?"

"They had to arrange transportation to bring her to town, but I believe Gretchen will be back in her casket this morning," Redvers said.

I was quiet for a few beats, overcome with sadness for Gretchen and her fate, but then I had another question. "No one else will be there to see her interred? Just Rai and his men?"

Redvers nodded, and I quickly made a decision. "I'll go. It won't be a formal service like last time, but I could still say a few words."

"I'm not sure Gretchen would have cared about that type of formality."

He was right, of course. "That may be true, but I still think that someone who cared about her should be there. And since she had no family here..." I trailed off. It sounded as though Gretchen had no family anywhere, and that made me even sadder on her account.

Redvers nodded and leaned over to kiss my cheek. "Your kindness does you credit, my dear."

I shrugged. It was the least I could do for the poor woman, and I could only hope that someone would do the same for me if I were in her shoes. It was a sobering thought; I had a family, small though it was, but Redvers and I were now on the other side of the world from them. If something happened to me, it would be a long time before they heard the news, and it was unlikely they would ever be able to see my grave, since I couldn't imagine having my body sent back over the wide ocean just to be interred in the ground. I shuddered to think about the length of that trip and what would happen to a body in that length of time, even one that had been preserved.

I resolved to be very careful. Of both tigers and humans with murderous intent.

Once our breakfast was finished and I'd drained every last drop from the coffee pot, Sasmit tidied up our dishes while we both got dressed. Redvers headed off to the governor's mansion, and I was headed to the cemetery. It was still quite early—the birds were nothing short of cacophonous and looking out the window, I could tell that the mist would still be hanging low over the hills. It was a long walk, but I refused Redvers' offer to escort me.

"You have work to do, and I can always hail a ride. But don't forget to look for my shawl," I said with a wink. "I'd be devastated to lose such an heirloom."

Redvers chuckled and left me, and I cautiously started my walk in the other direction. The morning mist that hung over the hills like a soft white veil was just beginning to lift, but I was still nervous about what might be lurking in the long grass that danced on the hills between the thick swaths of forest. Even though I'd just resolved to be careful, I was also too proud to admit that I didn't want to take a simple walk by myself. Instead, I hurried my steps toward town where I'd be able to find a carriage to take me out to the cemetery.

The sounds of the everyday birds and the occasional monkey were becoming commonplace enough that they blended into the scenery now, but the haunting shrieks of a peacock echoing through the trees were still unsettling—I didn't think I would ever get used to the sound. I was nearing the crossroads that led into the heart of Ooty, which would leave this short but deserted strip of forested path behind, and I was looking forward to breathing a sigh of relief once I reached a more highly trafficked area. Even just a few more pedestrians would make me feel better, less alone out here on the road, a slowly moving target.

I hailed the first horse-drawn carriage that I saw, and I was still rolling all our questions over in my mind when the carriage dropped me off at the cemetery. The area was totally abandoned except for a small group gathered around the site where Gretchen's grave had been dug. I had the horrible impulse to ask if they could open the pine box just so I could make certain that Gretchen was in there, but I restrained myself. I'd seen the body in the morgue with my own two eyes. I had to trust that it was the same body these men were about to lower into the ground.

There was a sudden murmur among the handful of bystanders at the grave side, their attention focused on something behind me. I turned to see what had drawn their attention and saw a splendidly dressed man coming straight for us. He wore the traditional dhoti kurta that I had seen other Indian men wear, but his had exquisite gold embroidery thick along the front of the jacket-like top. Even at a distance, I could tell it was made of the highest-quality fabric, and I couldn't imagine how long that embroidery had taken someone to complete. The man also wore a white cap, embellished with a few scattered jewels and a large white feather extending from the side, bobbing gently as he walked. I looked to Rai, who stood at the head of the casket, directing his men. "Who is that?" I asked in a lowered voice.

Rai looked surprised but pleased to see this newcomer. "It's the maharajah of Travancore, Ayil Thirunal."

I had a lot more questions, but the maharajah had nearly reached us, so I tucked my queries away for later. The man came to stand with me at Gretchen's gravesite, and we all stood quietly, not sure what to say. I was staring at the man quite openly, although I noticed that no one else seemed willing to make eye contact with him; the men around me were studying their feet or the ground where they stood. I was glad when the maharajah spoke first, breaking the awkward silence.

"Mrs. Wunderly?" he asked. His English was quite precise.

"Yes, I am." I was certain my face showed my surprise, asking the question of how he could possibly know who I was.

"Your husband told me you would be here."

I nodded. This made sense, although I couldn't imagine why a maharajah would be looking for me, an American with no official purpose here in Ooty. Which meant that he had to be in this cemetery for another reason entirely.

The maharajah gestured to the box that the men had set to the side of the hole. "I was already traveling here when I received word about Gretchen . . . Miss Beetner's death."

The sadness in his voice was palpable. I studied him while he spoke and realized that he did resemble the picture I'd seen in Gretchen's locket, although he was obviously many years older now. The maharajah wasn't traditionally handsome, but there was both keen intelligence and kindness in his eyes. I thought it very likely that he possessed some other hidden qualities as well that had made him so irresistible to Gretchen. Whatever their personal past, I was touched that this member of Indian royalty had not only come to her grave but was clearly moved by her death.

I wondered if he knew what had really happened to her.

The maharajah looked at the men. "I would like to see her one last time. I understand that you have only just put her in this box."

The men looked at each other but didn't say anything, instead looking to Rai for instructions. Rai's brow was furrowed. "Respectfully, raja, I do not know if you want to do that. It is an unpleasant sight."

The maharajah considered that for a moment before bobbing his head in what I took as a decisive motion. "Please open it."

Rai paused, likely giving the maharajah time to reconsider, but then gestured for the men to do as the maharajah asked. A tall thin man took a metal implement and, with surprisingly little difficulty, cracked open the top of the wooden casket. I glanced inside involuntarily before taking a large step back. I didn't need to see Gretchen's body again, especially now that she'd been dead for a few days.

I turned toward the hills, trying to concentrate on the gorgeous view. A pale mist covered only the very tops of the mountains now, the sun quickly burning the veil away as the morning went on. I sensed that the maharajah had moved to the side of the casket and heard the sigh that gusted from him. I heard the sound of fabric rustling, then a noise of surprise. "This was clearly not a tiger attack," he said.

Neither Rai nor his men said anything, so I filled the silence. "It was not, but we are trying to keep that quiet until we can figure out what happened to her." I still had my back to the coffin, so I couldn't see what the maharajah's reaction to this was.

"Very well," he said at length.

I impulsively spoke again. "Can you be sure that is actually Gretchen?" I asked.

The maharajah made a little noise of surprise, and I turned back toward him slightly. I could see his back at the coffin, and he made a motion as though moving aside a piece of clothing.

"This is her," the maharajah said before stepping away from the casket. Once the top had been replaced, I turned around to face the man.

"Are you certain?"

He pressed his lips together, clearly annoyed with my interrogation, but he answered me. "She had a beauty mark on her stomach, just here." He pointed to a place on his own abdomen. "I assume this is an important question," he said with impatience. Given his station in life, he was probably not accustomed to being questioned.

I nodded. "It is."

He looked at me for a long moment before giving me his own nod. "Very well."

Rai looked between the two of us. "Are you ready?" We both nodded, and he directed his men to start lowering the coffin. Once that was done, the men started shoveling dirt onto the pine box, each shovelful landing with a thud of finality. The maharajah and I stood quietly with our hands folded in front of us until the men had finished.

In the end, no words were spoken over Gretchen's body, not out loud anyway, but before I left the cemetery, I made a silent promise to the woman that we would find her killer.

Chapter Nineteen

I made my way back to our rooms, thinking about the maharajah's arrival and feeling grateful that someone else who had cared about Gretchen had made the trip to the cemetery.

It was also something of a relief to have confirmation from the maharajah that Gretchen was actually dead. It made the investigation entirely more straightforward, at least from my perspective. There had been a seed of doubt that we should be investigating when there was a chance that she was still alive, but with a definitive answer I had a definitive direction. Of course, I longed for that first day of boredom. I would trade any comfort for Gretchen to still be alive, but since she wasn't, I would do my best to find out what happened to her. Not to mention that there was still the question of motive and why someone would want her out of the way in the first place.

Redvers had agreed to return and eat lunch with me, so I was at loose ends until then. Sasmit came in and found me wandering aimlessly around the sitting room. "Would you like something, Mrs. Wunderly? Perhaps a pot of coffee?"

I nodded. "Thank you, that would be wonderful, Sasmit." A cup of coffee—or two—would at least give me something to do while I waited for Redvers, and sipping at the black brew often helped me think.

Redvers returned an hour later and found me twitching slightly from the extra pot of coffee. "Redvers, I'm so glad you're back." The words tumbled from my mouth, falling over each other like rocks tumbling in a stream. "The maharajah came to the grave, you must have told him that he would find me there because he knew who I was and he looked at the body and said it was definitely Gretchen that was in there because she had a beauty mark . . ."

I could easily have kept going, but Redvers put a finger over my lips with a little laugh, tilting his head toward the coffee pot that I'd nearly emptied. "One cup too many, perhaps?" At my chagrined nod he dropped his finger. "Let's get some food into you."

We made our way toward the center of Ooty in no time at all, since my feet were moving at quite a good clip, and ended up at a small restaurant that a local had recommended to Redvers. I was happy wherever we landed since I'd already come to believe it was impossible to have a bad meal in India as long as one was eating local cuisine. I never would understand the British who came and colonized this country only to never once try the food. It seemed a wasted opportunity, especially when one considered traditional English food.

The restaurant was off the main road, down a crowded side street on the ground floor of a two-story building. The doors and windows were thrown open to the breeze, the interior dotted with small rustic tables. We took a table at the back of the restaurant where we were far enough from other diners that we were unlikely to be heard. Redvers ordered for both of us after asking what I would like to eat. I told him I was happy with whatever he was having. Once the waiter had left our table, I bounced in my seat, anxious to hear what Redvers had learned that morning. The walk had helped burn off some of the excess caffeine, but I was still wound up and a little shaky.

"I don't think I've ever seen someone with so much pent-up energy," Redvers mused.

"Redvers! What did you learn?" From the look on his face, I was afraid that he would continue torturing me just for sport, but he finally started to answer my question.

"From what I can tell, the governor's secretary—"

"Vihan Kandiyar," I interrupted.

"Are you going to let me tell it?" Redvers asked, but his tone was teasing. I made a motion as though I were buttoning my lip and he continued on, amused. "From all reports, and I mean all, Vihan Kandiyar is quite devoted to the governor. It sounds as though he would do nearly anything the governor asked of him."

"How many people did you ask?"

His mouth quirked up in amusement. "Plenty."

I bounced a little in my seat, wanting to ask if "anything" included murder, but managed to keep my mouth firmly shut this time.

Redvers chuckled. "I can see you have a question, and I can guess what it is." He sobered. "I'm not sure if Kandiyar would be willing to go as far as murder. He has taken care of Goshen's mistresses in the past—" My eyes got wide, and he raised a hand. "Only paying them off. Not burying them in the forest or faking a tiger attack."

"How many mistresses has the man had?" I asked incredulously.

"A few," Redvers said, shaking his head. "In any case, it sounds as though Kandiyar has some political aspirations of his own, far more than being the governor's secretary. I think he's hoping that if the governor becomes viceroy, Kandiyar will be promoted to some plum position in the government. I've also heard that he has appealed—more than once—to Mudaliar for political support."

"Which one is Mudaliar?"

"He's a cabinet member. Working for Subbarayan. We saw them arguing in the garden."

"Ah, yes."

The waiter delivered our food, and I took a moment to inhale the delicious spicy aromas wafting up from the banana leaf. It looked delicious, similar to what I'd had when I'd dined with Subbarayan. Once the young man left, I asked my next question.

"What kind of political support would Kandiyar be looking for?"

Redvers shrugged. "If Mudaliar is trying to push out Subbarayan . . ." He trailed off, and I filled in the rest.

"Then Kandiyar could fill the position that Mudaliar currently holds."

Redvers nodded, and I sighed. "Killing off an old woman doesn't seem to fit in with those sorts of plans," I said. "For either of them."

"Unless there was some reason that Gretchen was standing in their way, but I can't see how that would be. She's no longer part of the government machine and hasn't been for several years."

Gretchen still had influence, though, which was why she was here in the first place. She was taking part in the same discussions as Redvers, indicative of the sway she still held. Of course, Redvers would have a much better sense of how much sway she had and how she would have been able to use it. And if he didn't think either man had a motive based on her clout, then I needed to trust that he was correct.

Instead of continuing down that path, I turned my mind to more tangible things and the search we had conducted. We hadn't found anything in Gretchen's rooms, but that didn't mean that there hadn't been something to find, since someone had beaten us there.

"It's a shame there's no way to tell who searched Gretchen's rooms before us."

"I agree," Redvers said. "But we can't search the quarters of every person who knew her."

I looked speculative, and Redvers chuckled. "There's not enough time in the day to search fifty or so rooms."

"You're making that number up," I said, even though I knew he was absolutely correct. There was no way we could search the rooms of every single person who'd interacted with Gretchen.

"I know how much you like a search, my dear, but perhaps let's narrow the field down a bit."

I gave a gusty, theatrical sigh. "Very well. How about we just search Vihan Kandiyar's quarters," I said.

Redvers sobered. "Now that is a very good idea."

We needed to lure Kandiyar out of his lodgings long enough for one of us to conduct a search. Going through his belongings would take a little longer, too, since we didn't exactly know what we were looking for—just something suspicious, whatever that might be—so we needed to keep him occupied for some time. We bandied about a series of ideas about the best way to do that, everything from faking a medical emergency to staging a monkey coup.

Very well, I was the one bandying about ideas. Redvers had a boring but ultimately reasonable plan already in mind.

It was decided that immediately following our meal we would head to the governor's office and see if Kandiyar was there. If he was, as we expected him to be since the man was rarely far from his desk while the governor was in, Redvers would stay and occupy him with detailed questions regarding the logistics of the Simon Commission's upcoming visit. Meanwhile, I would break into Kandiyar's room, located nearby in an adjacent building where the civil servants quartered at the mansion, and give it a thorough search.

"A monkey coup would be more fun," I said.

"But much more difficult to arrange," Redvers said. "Now be sure to leave everything exactly where it was," he reminded me. "We don't want him to think he's come under suspicion."

"This is far from my first search." I thought for a moment. "I would like to borrow your lockpicks though." Even with the right tools, I was still much slower than Redvers at getting through a locked door, but there wasn't a reasonable way for me to detain Kandiyar long enough to conduct a search—it had to be Redvers who did the detaining. We'd already stretched credulity a little thin with the story of my shawl the other night. Kandiyar had bought it, but it had seemed a close thing.

Redvers chuckled and slipped the pouch from his jacket pocket, handing it to me. I slipped it into my clutch, grateful that I wasn't in the habit of carrying much with me in the little bag. The lockpick kit fit inside easily.

We finished our meal and headed back toward the governor's mansion. The food had balanced me out quite a bit, and I was no longer shaking from the excess of coffee, which was a relief since I needed to pick a lock. Shaky hands would be nothing but a detriment, especially since picking a lock in the middle of the day without being seen was going to be the trickiest part of this operation.

My mind drifted from the matter at hand to what Redvers and I had discussed about his family and his beliefs about sovereignty for the Indian people. That had been before Gretchen's murder and seemed an age ago already. "Why did you accept this assignment if you don't agree with it?"

Redvers' eyebrows shot up. "Where did that come from?"

I shrugged. "Just something I've been wondering but haven't had an opportunity to ask."

We were walking along the path leading through the western corner of the botanical garden, and there was no one else within hearing distance, although Redvers did check behind us before answering my question. "I never really feel as though I have a choice. They give the assignments, and I do them." He looked thoughtful. "It has never really bothered me in the past, but I also didn't have anyone else to worry about before."

I knew that Redvers and I had both been surprised at falling in love and getting married. He never expected to wed, and after my first husband, I'd been quite keen never to marry again. But I supposed that was precisely what happened when you tempted fate with absolutes.

"This assignment obviously goes against what I personally think is right, and I suppose there has been a part of me that hoped I could sway some individuals in the direction of the resistance." He was quiet for a moment. "But I think in the future, I don't want to accept assignments that will either take me away from you or are too personally dangerous."

"Will those in charge be alright with that decision?"

"I really don't know the answer to that," Redvers said.

We walked a few steps before I asked my next question. "What would you do instead? If they weren't happy with your decisions and decided to . . . well, I don't know, fire you?" I didn't know if someone could be fired from what Redvers did. Could you fire a spy? Or did you simply eliminate them? That was a frightening thought, one I tucked away to worry about later.

He shrugged. "As I said before, I'm not sure what else I'm fit to do. Not at this point. I've been doing this for far too long."

"No sheep farming for you, then," I said, trying to lighten the mood, which had become quite heavy.

Redvers winked at me. "You'd never run out of wool, though."

We arrived at the governor's mansion, which temporarily put an end to our conversation, but I didn't think we were finished discussing the topic.

Inside the mansion, Redvers nodded at a few of the men scattered about. We made our way upstairs, but then I let him go ahead while I hung back a little. Redvers poked his head around the door leading to the governor's office suite and greeted someone, then came back to give me a brief kiss on the cheek. I smiled and said goodbye, then headed out of the building and through the garden, toward the place where Kandiyar was staying.

The garden path wound a bit but led me to a pair of buildings where civil servants were housed. It was the same path that Kandiyar had found us on the night before, when I'd claimed to be searching for my shawl. Since the path led to his quarters, it made sense that he'd been on it, although it didn't explain why he'd been out walking so late at night, not to mention in the opposite direction of his bed. I hadn't caught the whiff of cigarette smoke that Redvers had, and though I didn't disbelieve my husband, I thought it was an unusual time of night to decide to head outside for a cigarette. There had to be another reason Kandiyar was out wandering so late.

The building was painted the same pale green as the mansion, although this had a much simpler layout. The front door was wide open, which was not surprising, and I walked inside. The ground floor appeared deserted, and I hurried up the stairs to the second floor. I paused on the landing, holding my breath to listen while I stood just out of sight behind a wall. Hearing nothing, I moved around the corner and started down the hall. As I neared number eighteen, where Redvers told me that Kandiyar was staying, the door directly next to me opened, and a woman with a bucket stepped into the hall. I startled and smiled nervously at the tiny woman. She looked at me a little strangely but smiled in return and said something that I did not understand. I shook my head with a shrug, and she smiled and patted my arm before walking down the hall to let herself into another room.

She closed the door behind her, and I breathed a small sigh of relief. At least she hadn't let herself into Kandiyar's room, but her presence on this floor meant that I had only a limited amount of time to get done what I needed to. It also greatly increased the chances that I might get caught, so I needed to work quickly.

I turned my attention to Kandiyar's door, and I was frustrated that the extra stress of being so close to discovery was making it even more difficult to get the lockpicks to work. The adrenaline coursing through my veins was making my hands shake, and I cursed a host of things while I worked, breathing an enormous sigh of relief when the lock finally gave and I was able to slip through the door. I locked it behind me, hoping it would give me enough time to hide if I heard the cleaning woman at the door.

I cast a glance around. Or maybe there would be no hiding after all. This was a simple room with only a bed, a desk, and a wardrobe to speak of for furniture, but at least the sparse furnishings meant my search shouldn't take too long. I dismissed the bed for the time being and went straight for the desk. There were some stacks of papers, but rifling through them, I found that they were all in Tamil, so I couldn't tell what any of them said or were even about. I continued my search but found nothing else of interest, at least nothing that I could read.

Increasingly frustrated, I moved to the wardrobe. There was an upper shelf with some clothing, and I went through everything there first but found nothing even remotely interesting. I then went through the clothes that were hanging neatly, even checking all the pockets of his kurtas, and found nothing. I huffed a quiet noise of frustration before making sure everything looked as it had when I found it. Then I turned and surveyed the room, hands on hips. I moved toward the bed, then swiveled my head to the right. Aha! There was a small garbage can that I had missed earlier, tucked close between the desk and the wall.

I walked over and bent in half, peering inside. There were papers in the bottom, but I was becoming nervous about the cleaning woman. How much time had I spent in this room already? Would she be coming in here next? I made a quick decision and stuffed all the papers from the trash can down my shirt, glad that I was wearing a belt, which should hold the papers in place. I checked the desk once more to make sure it looked as though it hadn't been rifled, cracked the door open, and slipped into the hall. I hurried toward the landing as quickly as I could while keeping my steps light, breathing a sigh of relief when I hit the stairs. I heard a door somewhere down the hall behind me opening, and I nearly tripped in my hurry to get to the first floor and out the door without being seen again.

CHAPTER TWENTY

I scurried back to our rooms, the crinkling of the papers in my shirt distracting me from my surroundings. I made it past the governor's mansion and into the botanical gardens, but I was so intent on the path that I nearly jumped out of my skin when someone just behind me called my name.

"Mrs. Wunderly!"

I stopped in my tracks and, with one hand to my heart and the other to the crinkly bulge around my midsection, I turned around to find Maharajah Ayil Thirunal coming up behind me. He stopped beside me, giving me a strange look that I attributed to my bulging shirt, then gestured for me to continue walking. I did, at a much slower pace now, although my heart was still pounding in my chest.

"Did you know Gretchen well?" he asked. I appreciated that he got right to the heart of the matter instead of bothering with small talk.

I shook my head. "I only knew her for a few days. But she made quite the impression, and I will miss her."

Thirunal looked surprised. "Since you were the only foreigner there this morning, I'd assumed you were acquainted much longer."

"I wish I had been," I replied simply.

Thirunal nodded. "Understandable. She was extraordinary."

We were quiet for a bit, and I recalled that I had Gretchen's locket in my possession. I wondered if he would like to have it, especially since it held a photo of him. "I have something of Gretchen's that I think she would want you to have." I didn't think this was overstepping, since from all accounts she didn't have family to give the locket to, and I truly believed that she would have liked the maharajah to have it.

He looked surprised but thanked me and agreed to accompany me to my quarters to retrieve it. We arrived at the cottage, and I left him in the sitting room while I darted into our bedroom. I removed all the papers from my shirt, leaving them in a crumpled little pile on the desk, then found the locket sitting right where I'd left it and returned to the sitting room. I handed the maharajah the locket, and he looked at it curiously before gently opening it. I took a seat across from him while he sighed quietly.

"We were so young then." He gazed at the photo for a long moment before clicking the locket shut and slipping it into his pocket. "Thank you for this. I will treasure it, and your kindness."

I assured him it was no trouble and walked him to the door. It might have been my imagination, but his shoulders appeared a little more stooped as he headed down the path toward the walking mall. But I may have been seeing what I wanted to see.

With a small shake of my head, I returned to my sitting room, only to find the door leading to the terrace wide open, a curtain blowing gently through the opening. I quickly cast my gaze around. Nothing appeared to be disturbed or even rifled through. I walked to the bedroom and stood in the doorway, looking around here too.

This time something was missing—the papers I'd taken from Kandiyar's room.

With a breathy curse, I shot across the room and out the terrace door, trying to catch a glimpse of who might have stolen the papers, but there was no one to be seen. How had they managed to get in and out of our rooms so quickly? I had walked the maharajah to the door and said goodbye; it couldn't have taken more than a few minutes.

Feeling panicked, I stepped outside and did a quick circuit of the area, but with the same result. Whoever had been in our room and taken the papers had done so with lightning speed. They must have known that I had them, or they wouldn't have broken in and stolen them without bothering to rifle through anything else. Did someone see me go into Kandiyar's room? Someone other than the cleaning woman? Had they followed me here? I cursed myself for not paying closer attention to my surroundings during my walk, for a variety of reasons including both tigers and thieves.

Wait. Could the culprit have been a monkey? They were known to have sticky fingers, grabbing anything that caught their fancy. My eyes swept the treetops, but I quickly deflated. Not only was there not a monkey in sight, but the animals would have likely taken food, not a stack of stolen papers.

I paced around the garden, then went back to my sitting room and thought for a moment, before ringing for Sasmit. He arrived a few minutes later, which gave me enough time to decide exactly how much I wanted to tell him.

"Can I help you, memsahib? Do you need some coffee?" Sasmit asked.

I did have to smile; he had caught on quite quickly to

what made me tick. "No, but thank you. I need to ask you something." I paused, then forged ahead. "Have you seen anyone here today that seemed out of place?"

Sasmit frowned. "I am not sure what you mean."

I tried to think of another way to say it without coming right out with it. "Maybe you saw someone that looked suspicious, someone hanging around the building that shouldn't be here?"

This time Sasmit shook his head firmly. "No, I have not seen anyone like this."

"Could you ask the other workers? Perhaps someone saw something unusual."

Sasmit's frown deepened. "Is something wrong, memsahib?"

I debated how much to tell the man while he waited with the utmost patience. I finally landed on the truth. "I had a stack of papers on the desk in the bedroom, and now they're gone. I wasn't away for very long, but it seems that someone came in through the patio," I gestured at the open door, "and took the papers."

Sasmit looked shocked. "Who would do such a thing?" Sasmit thought for a moment, then bobbed his head. "It must have been Vasinth."

"Vasinth?" I asked.

"Yes, he collects the trash every day. He is a little . . . simple, so we give him this to do in exchange for some food and a little money."

I stared at Sasmit. "What about the open terrace door?"

Sasmit tilted his head. "I opened that this morning to let some fresh air into the room."

Had it already been open when I came in to get the locket? I tried to visualize this, but I couldn't. Of course, I'd been in a hurry to return to the maharajah, so perhaps

I simply hadn't noticed. Or could Sasmit be lying about the door? I couldn't imagine a reason why he would, unless he had been assigned to us by someone with nefarious intent.

I shook my head. I was starting to see conspiracies where there were none.

"Come, let us find Vasinth, memsahib." Sasmit stepped out the terrace door and looked both ways before starting off to the right. At the next small terrace, he called the man's name. There was no response, so we set off again, coming to yet another terrace. Sasmit called out again, but here there was an answer.

"Vasinth!" Sasmit said kindly to the elderly man that stepped out of the room. He was missing quite a few of his teeth and was thin to the point of emaciated with a stooped back. Sasmit asked him something in Tamil.

Vasinth smiled his broken smile and bobbed his head, then said something in return. It was at moments like these in our travels that I dearly wished I was better with languages—I envied Redvers' ability with them. Because while he claimed he didn't know much Tamil, it was impressive to me that he knew any at all.

The men went back and forth a few times, before the old man went back inside the room he'd come out of and returned with a large woven bucket. It was easy to see that it was full of trash the man had been collecting from each room.

I looked at Sasmit. "Is my trash in there?"

Sasmit asked a question, and Vasinth nodded, then tipped the trash can over before either Sasmit or I could stop him. It was rather horrifying, watching that trash spill out onto a meticulously tidy space in this lovely garden, but it was already done. I pursed my lips and stepped forward, then gingerly started poking through the pile of trash.

"Memsahib! No, I will do that." Sasmit tried to physically stop me from what I was doing, coming between me and the trash and blocking me with his person. "What did the papers look like?"

I paused, but I had no intention of letting this poor man dig through the trash on my account. "It was a stack of papers that were all crumpled. I suppose they already looked like trash," I said. I didn't want to explain that I didn't actually know what they looked like, because I'd stolen them from someone else's room without looking at them first. "I can do this," I insisted. I didn't want anyone to have to do my dirty work for me. And I couldn't really blame Vasinth—the papers had looked like trash, crumpled as they were, even though they weren't in the trash can.

Sasmit's lips flattened into a thin line at my pronouncement, and he said something to Vasinth in Tamil, continuing to stand between me and the trash pile. I quickly figured out that the men were not going to let me poke through the mess on the lawn, as much as I'd tried to insist.

I stood back and rubbed my temples. What a disaster. I could only hope I would walk away from this with everything I'd taken from Kandiyar's room, but looking at the mess on the ground, it seemed highly unlikely.

Sasmit and Vasinth were now sifting through the trash, which consisted of a lot of tissue, remnants of fruit and banana leaves, and some personal items that appeared broken or used up. The men pulled every piece of paper that was even slightly crumpled from the pile and held each one up to me for confirmation. I nodded each time, my stomach dropping at the growing pile of papers that was gathering at my feet. When it looked as though they'd finally finished, I thanked them both profusely, silently promising each man that I would have Redvers tip them very well.

Not only was the stack of papers crumpled, but many of

the sheets were also sticky with food remnants. I wasn't pleased to be touching them, and as soon as I returned to my sitting room, I put the stack on the coffee table and stalked into the bathroom to scrub my hands thoroughly before coming back out and glaring at the messy stack, hands on hips.

Redvers found me like this a few moments later. "I was coming to see if you wanted to have lunch, but it appears you are locked in a battle of wills with these papers. Please don't let me interrupt."

I stuck my tongue out at him, and he chuckled. "They're winning, are they?" His tone was quite amused.

I sighed and explained how the papers that I had taken from Kandiyar's room had wound up in the trash and now we had even more papers than before, all of which were quite disgusting.

"I was right, then. They *are* winning." Redvers thought for a moment, then rifled through his luggage, returning a moment later with a pair of leather gloves. I hadn't even bothered to pack a pair, since I didn't think I would need them in so hot a country.

"My darling, you should always pack a pair of gloves. Fingerprints, you know."

I wrinkled my nose, wanting to toss back a devastating retort but also knowing he was correct. Even the most innocent of excursions seemed to wind up with us needing to break in somewhere.

Redvers donned his gloves and started sifting through the sticky stack of papers. As I watched, he began sorting them into two piles. One was papers that clearly weren't important. The other was papers that might have come from Kandiyar's room.

"Aha!" Redvers crowed when he was nearly halfway through the stack.

"What is it?" I asked and crowded in behind him. I was put off by the pungent mixture of smells wafting up from the stacks, but I peered over Redvers' shoulder, pressing my nose into his linen jacket, which smelled deliciously like Redvers himself. It was quite an improvement.

He held a typewritten note, and it had the same dropped *e* as the other notes we'd come across.

> *The police are not holding up their end of the bargain. Take care of the issue.*

But once again, the note wasn't signed.

Chapter Twenty-one

"It's to the point," I said. "But not much for us to work with."

"No and unfortunately, we can't say that it definitely came from Kandiyar's room. It's crumpled, as the papers you found in his trash can were, but that doesn't mean this didn't come from one of the other rooms here."

"Who else is staying here?" I asked. I hadn't seen anyone about except for Gretchen.

"Feodore Smith is staying here, and so is Mudaliar."

"Interesting that they aren't staying closer to the governor's mansion. Or at the mansion itself," I mused. He'd listed two people that we hadn't really considered before for any part in what was going on. Or at least I hadn't.

"It's unlikely that either of those men would receive such a message, though, isn't it? I can't imagine anyone ordering either of them to do anything," I said.

"A fair point about Smith," Redvers said. "And possibly even Mudaliar, although he is lower on the food chain." He sighed. "I don't think we can completely rule either of them out, but it does seem more likely that this note was sent to Kandiyar."

Redvers finished going through the stack of papers, sorting them into their respective piles. One he put into our wastebasket. The other stack he put in a drawer of the desk. "I'll have someone translate the ones in Tamil to see if there's anything of interest here," Redvers said before moving across the room and taking a seat on the sofa. He peeled off his gloves and set them on the table.

I joined him, taking a seat in the chair next to him. "Who can we trust to translate them?"

"That's an excellent question. I'll have to think that over, but there's certain to be someone who won't talk."

I had my doubts about that but decided to let the issue go. He would find someone that could be trusted enough to get the job done. "What do we know about either Smith or Mudaliar?" I asked.

He considered for a moment. "Smith is the one who set up the Simon Commission, which obviously doesn't make him terribly popular with the locals and especially not with Lala Rai and his resistance group. Smith is a member of the Conservative Party and has been since the time of the pyramids." Redvers shrugged.

I smiled. "What you're telling me is that he's old."

"Ancient," he replied with a grin. Then he sobered. "Mudaliar is on the opposite side of the political spectrum and is quite clever. I think he's quite against the commission, although he hasn't said as much publicly. He wouldn't, of course. It would be political suicide."

I grimaced, and Redvers cocked a questioning eyebrow. "I hate that politics always seems to be about jockeying for power instead of telling the truth," I said.

"You're not wrong." He recrossed his legs. "I haven't specifically asked Rai, but I wouldn't be surprised if those two—Rai and Mudaliar—were working together behind the scenes."

I recalled that we'd seen Mudaliar and Subbarayan arguing in the garden and said as much.

"From what I've heard, that's not unusual," he replied.

"I suppose not, if one is trying to overthrow the other," I said, slightly deflated. "I wonder if Subbarayan knows about Mudaliar's agenda."

"Most likely. He's no fool either, but he is quite wishy-washy."

"In what way?" I thought that Redvers had mentioned something about this earlier, but I hadn't been paying as close attention as I should have been. I tended to tune out where the finer details of politics were concerned, but I clearly needed to pay attention to those points now.

"He's gone back and forth on whether he supports the commission. The Indian National Congress is against it, and that charge is being led by Gandhi and Lala Rai. Subbarayan initially sided with them but then changed his tune and decided to support Smith. It's why Congress held the vote to see if Subbarayan would continue in his post."

"I see." I wasn't sure that I actually did. My head was swimming a bit with allegiances and the changing of them, not to mention who was who in this political game. I could write out a chart to help myself keep track, but given that I'd already lost a stack of important papers, I was wary of writing anything down and having it fall into someone else's hands.

I decided to leave it up to my husband. Hopefully, Redvers would keep track of it all, and I could focus on the investigation. Such as who that note might belong to.

I leaned back in my chair and pondered that, tapping my fingers on the arm, before remembering something odd that had happened earlier. "When I spoke with Subbarayan at lunch the other day, he mentioned that the governor and the maharajah used to be closely aligned but something happened between them recently. When I asked what that was, he shut down and said he couldn't remember."

"Interesting," Redvers said. "I wonder what that could be about. And why Subbarayan didn't want to talk about it."

"Especially if he wasn't involved." I shrugged. "But perhaps he simply isn't the type to gossip with a stranger."

Redvers inclined his head, acknowledging my point.

I rubbed my temples again, feeling a slight ache there threatening to take hold. "This is all well and good, but who had a motive for killing Gretchen? And who was the recipient of that note about dealing with the police? Can you think of a motive for Smith or Mudaliar to have killed Gretchen?"

"Not really," Redvers said. "Smith created the commission, and its visit is already scheduled. And from everything I know about Mudaliar, he and Gretchen were on the same side of this issue, the side of independence."

I tapped my fingers on the arm of my chair. "So if the note really did come from Kandiyar's room, it's likely that he typed it. Or that he's being framed."

"That seems most likely. I don't see someone sending Smith a note telling him to do anything related to the police."

I was inclined to agree. It was highly unlikely that the secretary of state for the entire country of India would be getting his hands dirty cleaning up a mess, which is what the note instructed. Which meant it was unlikely to have come from his trash. Or Mudaliar's, for that matter, since he and Gretchen both sided with the resistance.

I sighed. "This hasn't gotten us much of anywhere. We still don't have a good motive for why someone wanted Gretchen dead. Or for who is framing Kandiyar."

Redvers shook his head. "She had to have known something. It's just a matter of finding out what."

"Who will you get to translate these papers?" I asked, frustrated that we had more questions than answers about anything. It would be nice to know even one thing for certain, beyond the fact that Gretchen was dead.

"I had been thinking about asking Sasmit," Redvers said.

I pressed my lips together and turned to ensure that Sasmit wasn't coming through the door as we spoke. We were alone, but I dropped my voice all the same. "I have some reservations about Sasmit. What if someone placed him here to keep an eye on us?"

"And report back to them?" Redvers ran an elegant finger along his jaw, thinking. "It's not outside the realm of possibility, but it doesn't leave us with a lot of other options. I can't ask someone in the government."

That was true. There was no way we could ask anyone who worked for either the Raj or for the local government. It had just been illustrated for me how many different political and personal allegiances there were. No one could be trusted, especially since no one's true feelings could be known on any given matter.

The list of people that I knew who read Tamil was even shorter, but one friendly face did pop to mind. "What if I ask Hasnan?"

"The guide from the tea plantation?" Redvers asked. He thought that over and then spoke slowly, "It's not a bad idea, if he can read."

That was something I hadn't considered, but I thought it was worth finding out. "He might have close ties with Savithri, but that isn't likely to be colored by politics."

"It's worth a try," Redvers said. "He's about as neutral as we're likely to find at this point."

After lunch, Redvers headed back to his government meetings, and I pondered how I wanted to return to the tea plantation to find Hasnan. I didn't relish the long walk and decided to take a carriage—I'd already had plenty of exercise for the day. I would need to get to a more highly trafficked area to hire a ride, so I walked in the direction of the botanical garden. The headache that had threatened before lunch still lingered at the edges of my consciousness, and between that and the tumble of thoughts surrounding Gretchen's death, I was quite lost in thought. So much so that it took me a long moment to realize that the strange noise I heard wasn't one of the noisy parakeets in the trees, but someone calling my name. I turned to find Lady Goshen strolling toward me. I was amused that she wasn't hurrying to meet me; she had simply bellowed until I noticed.

"I called several times, but you didn't hear me. For a second time," Lady Goshen said when she reached my side. "I wonder if you need to have your hearing checked." I didn't have an answer to that, but I didn't need one because the woman continued on with barely a pause. "I'm going riding. Would you care to join me?"

I didn't have to give that any thought at all, shaking my head before her sentence was finished. "I'm afraid I'm not a horsewoman, although I'd be happy to accompany you there. I've heard the grounds are lovely." I'd heard no such thing, but I thought it was a good idea to talk with her while I had the chance; I could head to the plantation afterward. "We can hail a ride up ahead, I believe." I nodded my chin toward the entrance to the garden, where a horse-drawn carriage was letting off a mother and son, clearly a British wife and child who'd agreed to come to the hill station for the summer. The boy bounded off toward the gardens, while his mother trailed behind.

Lady Goshen easily agreed. We fell into step, despite my having quite a few inches of height on the older woman. She had a strong stride and was obviously fit.

"Shocking about Gretchen's body," Lady Goshen said, giving me a start that her thoughts had been so close to my own. "I can't imagine who would do such a thing—steal a dead body right out of the casket. Shocking, absolutely shocking. I only hope someone has recovered it. The poor woman deserves a proper burial."

"I believe she has since been recovered and buried," I said, then quickly moved on before I had to give any more details as to how I knew that. "How did you hear that it wasn't a tiger attack?"

"What do you mean?" my companion asked. "Of course, it was a tiger attack."

I could feel my eyes narrow, and I worked to keep my expression neutral. "The other day you told me that it wasn't a tiger attack and that you hoped they found whoever was responsible for Gretchen's murder."

"Oh, my dear, you must have been confused. I'm sure I said that I hoped that they found the tiger responsible. It's quite dangerous to have a man-eating tiger on the loose. They have to hunt them down and kill them once they get the taste for human flesh." Her tone was casual, and she raised a hand to the carriage driver, indicating that he should wait for us.

I could examine how morbid that statement was at another time. Right now, I was focused on why Lady Goshen had completely changed her story. If I had been anyone else, I might have been convinced by this act, but I knew what I'd heard the other day. Lady Goshen had clearly known that Gretchen was killed by a person, and now she was claiming quite the opposite.

What—or who—had changed her story?

CHAPTER TWENTY-TWO

Screaming in exasperation felt like an excellent plan at the moment, but I held my frustration in. Perhaps later I could scream into a pillow about the lies and stories and hidden motives that swirled around this small town. Ooty was nothing but muddy waters, and I wanted—no, needed—some clarity. Unfortunately, clarity seemed more and more impossible to find.

We reached the stables near the racetrack and dismounted from the wooden carriage. I paid the driver while Lady Goshen strode toward the long white building, the otherwise dull façade broken up by a series of columns. There were a series of smaller white buildings to the left, and I assumed one of these held the stables. I scurried to catch up with Lady Goshen, reaching her just as she gave a cursory greeting to the stable hand waiting with a horse, ready for Lady Goshen to mount. She'd clearly sent a servant ahead so that she wasn't obliged to wait while a horse was readied for her.

"Since you can't ride with me, perhaps we can have tea sometime this week," Lady Goshen said as she put her foot in the stirrup and hoisted herself up to sit sidesaddle.

"Of course," I said politely, not meaning it for a moment. There seemed little point to drinking a beverage I disliked with a woman I was also learning to dislike. Unless a compelling reason turned up for me to interview her again, I would be avoiding any further invitations from the governor's wife.

Lady Goshen trotted off, and even though I was not terribly familiar with the world of horses and riding, I could tell that she was an accomplished rider. She looked completely at ease and in control of the large animal beneath her.

Well, bully for her.

I was fully prepared to head back in the direction I'd come and then out to the Dodabetta plantation to find Hasnan, but our conversation on the way over forced me to reconsider what I was going to do next. Lady Goshen had completely changed her story about Gretchen's cause of death, which was beyond suspicious. I hadn't misunderstood what she'd said to me the first time around—she'd called it a murder. But who would have convinced her to change her tune? Her husband? Or someone else entirely?

I realized I was standing aimlessly near the entrance staring into space while I considered the governor's wife and was beginning to attract some strange looks. Regardless of who had convinced the woman to change her story, I had changed my mind about Lady Goshen's innocence. I didn't know what possible motive she could have for killing Gretchen, but I now needed to give the governor's wife a very hard look. There was little doubt in my mind that Lady Goshen was involved; I just needed to figure out the how and why.

We were surrounded by open fields where people like Lady Goshen could ride their horses in the sun, but I found a shady spot beneath a stand of trees to conceal myself and settled in to wait until Lady Goshen had finished her afternoon ride. It took quite a while, and I was fighting heavy eyelids by the time I saw her reemerge from the stables. She looked very little the worse for wear, and I was a bit envious. There was no way I could have gone for a ride under this warm sun and not wound up red-faced and sweat-stained. But Lady Goshen looked as though she'd done nothing more than gone for a leisurely stroll, not a hair out of place from her tidy gray bun.

I followed her at a distance, frowning. Could Lady Goshen be behind the notes? She likely had access to her husband's keys and therefore to the typewriter used to write the letters. But why would she do that? It seemed completely out of character, especially since she'd claimed to receive one. But then, it was more than suspicious that she'd changed her story about Gretchen's murder, so something was certainly going on there. I wondered if it was worth searching her quarters to see if there was anything incriminating to be found.

The trick, of course, would be getting into her room to search it. I could only assume that the governor and his wife had a host of servants, so how would I get in and out without being seen?

I sighed. I knew exactly how I would get in. I would have to take tea with the blasted woman.

Lady Goshen took a carriage back toward the governor's mansion—a carriage that was already waiting for her. There were no other carriages in sight, but there was a man pulling a passenger cart with a little black umbrella-like shade over the rider's seat. I sighed, then signaled to him that I would like a ride, giving in to the fact that this was how things were done here, and I needed to get over my discomfort with having humans pull me around. My driver smiled and waited until I had climbed into the little cart and taken a seat. He then turned his head, waiting for a destination. I simply said, "follow that woman." He turned around further, the long wooden poles he held dipping as he twisted to look at me. I smiled apologetically and pointed at Lady

Goshen's horse-drawn carriage disappearing down the road. "Where she goes."

This time he seemed to understand what I meant. He picked up the wooden handles and leaned forward with a sharp pull to get us started, then pulled me along after Lady Goshen. I was hoping that she would go somewhere out of the ordinary, perhaps meet someone in a tryst, but it soon became apparent that she was simply returning to the governor's mansion. I was disappointed—I'd come back to where I'd started with no new information for the trouble. I had my driver stop near the botanical garden, and I stepped down to pay him. He smiled and nodded before trotting away to join the little line of other cart pullers.

At least I was closer to my quarters than I'd been fifteen minutes ago. I didn't think it would pay to stake out the governor's mansion. I would no doubt be seen by someone who would wonder what I was doing, lurking outside the building instead of going in. Except for the gardens in the back, there weren't many good hiding places nearby, and if Lady Goshen were to leave again, she would likely leave from the front door, where there was nothing but an expanse of sloping lawn—no bushes or trees nearby to hide behind.

I walked back to my quarters and went straight to the desk, sitting down and pulling out a piece of stationery, quickly penning my missive.

Dear Lady Goshen, it has been such a pleasure see-ing you these past few days and I would dearly love to take tea with you, as you suggested. Would tomor-row afternoon be convenient? Sincerely, Jane Wunderly.

It was not sincere, but I was the only one who knew that, and I hoped that it would do the trick, winning me an invitation to tea. Once I was inside her quarters, I could claim that I needed to use the bathroom and conduct a quick search. I hoped that the layout of the governor's quarters was conducive to this, but I wouldn't know until I went. I sealed the note and then rang for Sasmit, who came so quickly I wondered if he waited just outside our door in case we decided to summon him. Could he be a spy for someone? Hovering and listening and reporting back to someone else? Or was paranoia simply getting the best of me?

It was likely the latter.

"Can you please get this to Lady Goshen?" I asked, handing him the note. Even if he read it, it wouldn't have anything of interest.

"Of course," Sasmit said, and disappeared just as quickly as he had appeared.

That done, I crossed the room and flopped onto the couch. I hated the idea that we couldn't even trust our friendly steward, but was there some proof that he was untrustworthy? Something I was missing? I closed my eyes for a moment— merely to think—and was jolted awake sometime later when the couch cushion beside me moved. I looked over to find Redvers seated beside me, looking quite amused.

"How was your nap?"

I sat up, a little groggy. "I didn't mean to take one. The sun must have gotten the best of me." I blinked a few times.

"Even though we're in the mountains, it still gets warm during the day and the sun takes a toll," Redvers agreed. "I'm going to assume you were outdoors, then?"

I nodded. "I intended to drive out to the plantation— again—but I ran into Lady Goshen. She was going riding at the racetrack, so I walked with her." I paused, recalling our conversation. "She brought up Gretchen's death but then claimed that it was in fact a tiger attack. When I asked her about her earlier statement that it hadn't been, she tried to claim that I was mistaken."

"Interesting," Redvers said.

"Very. Why on earth would she change her story so completely? And pretend that she'd never said otherwise, when she so clearly had?"

Redvers looked thoughtful. "If I had to guess, I would say that she was told she wasn't supposed to let that information out. But who would be able to convince her to change her story?"

"Her husband?"

"He's a logical choice, but what motive would he have to kill Gretchen? It seems a risky endeavor for someone that wants to become viceroy of the entire country," Redvers said.

"What is a viceroy again?" I asked. I wanted to be clear on the importance of the position, and I wasn't entirely sure that I grasped it fully. There were a lot of titles bandied about, and it was hard to keep track of who was in charge of what.

"It's one step below the monarch himself. They are essentially the king's representative here in India."

An important post, then. "What are his chances of actually becoming viceroy?" I asked.

Redvers shrugged. "Not terribly good. Lord Irwin is the current viceroy and a favorite of the king, so he's unlikely to lose the position any time soon."

"Even so, it doesn't seem likely Goshen would risk killing someone and lose any chance he does have."

"I wouldn't think so," Redvers said. "Unless that person stood directly in the way of him becoming viceroy. But Gretchen was hardly doing that."

"Who else would have enough sway with Lady Goshen to convince her to abruptly change her story?"

"That's the question," Redvers said. "I'm not sure who else Lady Goshen is friendly with in the current government. I've never seen her outside of the welcome dinner or Gretchen's initial burial ceremony, such as it was."

I thought about the additional times I'd had contact with her, but she'd been alone each time. So who was she close with?

"I'd initially ruled her out for impersonating Gretchen by writing those notes, but since she changed her story about Gretchen's murder, I'm now convinced that she has to be the one doing it," I said. Before Redvers could comment, I continued. "I sent a note and invited myself to tea. I want to search her rooms to see if there's anything incriminating."

Redvers looked skeptical. "What will you look for? And how will you do that?"

"I'll tell her I need to use the restroom."

His only response was a cocked eyebrow.

"You don't think I can do it?" I asked, affronted.

"It's not that, my dear; you're quite good at conducting a search." He grinned. "You've come quite far in a short amount of time."

I gasped in mock outrage and tossed a decorative pillow at him. He chuckled, then continued on, thoughtful. "I'm not certain you'll be able to make the restroom excuse last long enough to get the job done. Nor that you'll find anything worthwhile. The woman is obviously lying, but it doesn't necessarily mean that she's directly involved in anything. I can't begin to imagine what you might find that would make a search worthwhile."

I took this as a personal challenge, which I suspected Redvers very well knew by the gleam in his eye. Well, we would just see who was right. "What did you learn today?" I asked, changing the subject. He'd gone back to his meetings, but I knew he wouldn't waste any opportunity to ask questions about our wide range of suspects.

"Not much," Redvers said ruefully. "I asked around

about the governor's secretary, but from all accounts Kandiyar is quite loyal to the governor."

We were interrupted by Sasmit's return. We fell silent as
he entered the room, both of us looking at him expectantly.
I noticed that he held something in his hand, and he came
forward and handed it to Redvers, then looked between the
two of us.

"I delivered your note to the governor's mansion, memsahib, but as I left, one of the staff handed me this and said
that I was to give it directly to you, Mr. Wunderly."

Neither of us corrected Sasmit on the use of my surname
as Redvers' own. He had his own surname but used it so
rarely that people assumed we shared the name Wunderly.

"Thank you, Sasmit." Redvers glanced down at the envelope, then looked back at Sasmit. "Who gave this to you?"

"It was Naveen," the steward said. "He has worked at
the governor's mansion for many years."

"But you don't know where he got it from?"

Sasmit shook his head. "I didn't ask, sahib."

"Thank you. We'll let you know if we need anything
else," Redvers said, politely dismissing our steward. As soon
as Sasmit had left the room, Redvers gently tore open the
envelope to find a note. I crowded in behind him to read it.

*If you know what is good for you and your posi-
tion with the Crown, you'll stop looking into the
death of Gretchen Beetner immediately.*

CHAPTER TWENTY-THREE

I gasped out loud, but Redvers seemed much more non-plussed by the message. I took it from his hand and studied it, immediately spotting the dropped *e* we'd seen in the other notes. Which meant that this had been typed on the same typewriter as the other threatening messages, and likely by the same sender. We were obviously getting too close for our culprit's comfort.

I was quiet for a long moment, contemplating the implications of this threat for my husband. We'd already discussed how Redvers didn't think he was fit for another job. What would happen if he no longer worked for the Crown? And did the sender actually have the political clout to carry through with this threat?

Either way, I was deeply uncomfortable with the note, but Redvers seemed rather nonchalant about it.

"Well, we've certainly poked a hornet's nest," he said thoughtfully, taking the note from my clenched fist and putting it on the low table. He sat in one of the chairs and leaned back, hands clasped loosely behind his head.

I wasn't nearly so relaxed. I certainly couldn't sit quietly, so I paced in front of my husband instead. "This doesn't make you nervous that they'll carry through with their threat?

That perhaps we should stop looking into things so you don't lose your job?"

"All it means is that we're getting close to something." He gave me a curious look. "I'm surprised you of all people would be willing to give up on a murder investigation over an idle threat."

"No one has ever threatened your livelihood before," I said, stopping long enough to give him an incredulous look.

"Only your life."

I recognized his dry tone for what it was and stuck my tongue out at him. "You're truly not concerned?"

Redvers shook his head. "I'm not. I'm quite well liked at all levels, so I think it's highly unlikely I'll be dismissed for it, regardless of who is making the threat. Reassigned maybe, but not dismissed."

This was reassuring enough that I dropped onto the couch opposite him and studied his face. He seemed sincere, and I was confident that he wasn't saying this simply to placate my fears—I would be able to tell. I knew him well enough for that, even if his nonchalance just now had surprised me. I also trusted that he would be honest with me, regardless of the upset it might cause. We'd faced plenty in the time we'd known one another, and I believed we could face nearly anything together. Redvers believed that also, so there was no reason for him to lie to me about this—or anything, really.

Which meant that if he wasn't concerned, I shouldn't be either. At least I would try not to be. "Very well. If we won't be frightened off, then what's our next step?"

"I think it's time to speak with Kandiyar directly."

I agreed. "And after that, I'll find Hasnan and see if we can get these papers translated. Hopefully there's something there that will be useful, and we can put this all to rest."

*   *   *

We walked to the governor's mansion and went directly up the stairs to where the government offices were located. I wasn't sure we would still find Kandiyar here, since it was late in the afternoon and this section of the building seemed deserted, but as we approached the governor's suite, we could hear the distinct sound of keys clacking at the infamous typewriter. We passed through the open doorway and found the governor's secretary busily tapping something out. He barely paused when we entered.

"We have a few questions for you, Mr. Kandiyar," Redvers said.

"I hope it can wait," Kandiyar said, not bothering to look up at us. "I am very busy."

Redvers ignored this, grabbing two of the wooden chairs from along the far wall and dropping them directly in front of the man's desk before taking a leisurely seat in one. I sat in the other, much less leisurely. Even the brisk walk to the mansion hadn't been able to burn off my nervous tension.

Kandiyar must have realized that his unwanted visitors were going nowhere soon, because he finally stopped typing and gave us both a long, assessing look. "I have quite a bit of work to do this afternoon."

"I'm sure you do," Redvers replied. "But it will wait. Have you been sending threatening messages?" His question was completely at odds with his pose, ankle crossed over knee as he leaned back and relaxed.

Kandiyar's dark eyebrows pulled into a confused frown. "What are you talking about? Threatening messages? Who would I send such a thing to?"

"I received one this afternoon threatening my job if I didn't stop nosing into Gretchen Beetner's death."

The secretary's head did a bob. "Miss Beetner was killed by a tiger. It is tragic, yes, but why would you be looking into that?" He continued on, seeming to answer his own question. "Is it because her body went missing? I have it on good authority that she was recovered."

"You're correct. Her body was found," Redvers said. "She's been properly laid to rest."

Kandiyar nodded as though that closed the matter. "That is good to hear. It is best for her spirit that her body is properly taken care of." He paused. "If you will excuse me, I need to get back to work." Kandiyar gestured to the half-typed letter rolled into his machine.

I believed that he accepted the story about the tiger attack as truth—his confusion had felt quite genuine. But there were other messages to address. "Did you send a note informing Lady Goshen that her husband's mistress had been relocated to the tea plantation?" I asked.

At this, Kandiyar looked horrified. "Why would I do such a thing? It would bring shame on everyone involved."

I had to bite my tongue to keep myself from saying what I really thought about his reaction. Because it was apparently fine to have the mistress as long as it wasn't talked about; that was the shameful part, as far as I could tell. My objections were numerous, but with an effort, I moved on to my next question. "But you do know the governor's mistress? Savithri Kumari?"

Kandiyar shifted in his seat. "These are things that are known but not spoken of," he finally said, avoiding eye contact with me.

I bit my tongue again, but I was certain my face reflected my thoughts.

"The note Lady Goshen received was written on your typewriter," Redvers said.

Kandiyar's thick brows furrowed once more. "How can that be? No one uses this machine besides myself. The governor himself does not use it. I do not think he even knows how to type." He looked down at the typewriter. "And how can you know it was this machine?"

Redvers got up and went to look at the letter that Kandiyar was typing, pointing to a spot on the paper. "See here? Your machine drops the letter *e*, which is the same as the letters that have been sent to several people making threats against them."

Kandiyar stood out of his chair slightly to look at what Redvers was pointing to. "That is very strange," he muttered.

"What is strange?" Redvers asked.

Kandiyar sat back down slowly. "Not long ago, I noticed that my typewriter felt different. One of the keys always stuck, the letter *r*, but suddenly it didn't. I did not think much of it. I thought perhaps someone had come and oiled the machine."

"You didn't notice the dropped *e*?"

Kandiyar shook his head. "Not until you pointed it out."

Redvers and I looked at each other. I wondered if it was worth going back through what Kandiyar had typed over the past few weeks to see if we could pinpoint exactly when the typewriter had been switched out but dismissed it as a last resort. I suspected Redvers was thinking along the same lines, because he glanced down at the files on the secretary's desk, then gave a little shake of his head.

"Do you know exactly how long ago it started to feel different?" Redvers asked.

Kandiyar thought about that, then shook his head. "I couldn't say. It is all very strange, though. Why would someone go to the trouble of switching my typewriter with another?" The secretary pressed his lips together and regarded us. "Do you suppose that someone is trying to make it look as though I sent those notes?"

"It's possible," Redvers said. I would have said it was very likely, since I couldn't think of another reason to make the switch, so I was glad Redvers had answered instead of me. It was best not to alarm the man too much.

"Are they trying to make it look as though I'm responsible for Gretchen's death?" His voice was indignant. "Even though it was an unfortunate accident?"

Redvers and I glanced at each other, then looked back at the secretary, who was now tapping his fingers on the top of his desk. Our questions had obviously agitated him, and I hoped that it might spur him to tell us something useful. But the silence stretched out until it was apparent that Kandiyar wasn't going to offer up anything more without a direct question.

"I've heard rumors that you're interested in becoming more than the governor's secretary," Redvers said. "Perhaps looking for a position in Congress."

Kandiyar's previously open face closed down immediately, as fast as a slammed door. "I am entirely loyal to the governor." His mouth moved as though he was biting the inside of his lip. "Of course, if Governor Goshen were to accept a higher position, I would be happy to follow him."

"And that's all?" I asked. "Secretary to the viceroy is your only ambition?"

"The governor values my services highly," Kandiyar said, his voice taking on a stubborn edge.

It was clear that the man wasn't telling us the whole truth here—that last answer hadn't been an answer at all. Just a statement meant to shut down our line of questioning. It was obvious we wouldn't get anything else useful from Kandiyar, so we left him to his work, punching the keys a little more vigorously than he had been before we appeared.

Before we left the mansion, we needed to look for Naveen, the servant who had given our own threatening note to Sasmit. Redvers asked the first servant he saw on the first floor, and he directed us to the back of the building. We made our way there and found a group of men gathered in the garden just outside the kitchen, smoking and relaxing for a moment before the hustle and bustle of the evening meal.

"I hate to interrupt, but does anyone speak some English?" Redvers asked. Two hands went up, and Redvers addressed the man nearest us. He was on the short side, and rather round, his stomach pushing his kurta to its straining point. "Is Naveen here?" Redvers asked. Our translator pointed at a tall, thin man in the group, who looked alarmed at being outed.

"Can you ask him where he got this note?" Redvers pulled the envelope from the inner pocket of his linen jacket, holding it up to show Naveen what he referred to.

Naveen said something rapidly in Tamil, and the English-speaker shrugged. "It was left on the table, sahib. Naveen saw that there was a name on it and asked many people who knew the name. He learned that Sasmit was your servant and gave it to him." He took a long drag on the rustic cigarette in his hand, blowing smoke to the sky.

A dead end, then. Someone was being very clever to cover their tracks, both while typing the notes and in delivering them.

When were they using that blasted typewriter, though? It had to be after dark, when Kandiyar was out of the office. The governor's secretary worked long hours from everything I'd heard, much longer than anyone else in the building, so the window of time that his typewriter was unattended had to be quite short. Were we going to have to do some overnight surveillance of the office? The thought was entirely unappealing, especially since we couldn't know when the next note would be written. And now that we'd confronted Kandiyar about his machine, I suspected the threats would no longer have the dropped *e*.

But not because Kandiyar had written them. I believed that Kandiyar hadn't sent the notes and didn't know who had; that much had been genuine, as had his story about the typewriters being switched out. Whoever was using that typewriter was doing it when the secretary wasn't around and framing him for the threats.

Redvers thanked the group of men, assuring them that there was no trouble, and we left them to their moment of leisure. We were quiet on the walk back to the Stone House.

"Do you think Kandiyar was telling the truth?" I asked once we were back in our room. I had my own answer, but I wanted confirmation from Redvers.

"I do. His confusion was genuine."

I agreed with him. "Which leads me to believe—"

Redvers cut in. "That Kandiyar is correct. Someone is framing him."

"Why make it look like Kandiyar is responsible?" I asked.

"They might be trying to make the governor himself look responsible for the notes, through Kandiyar, since he's so loyal to the governor. Outwardly loyal, at least. I don't believe anyone with political aspirations is entirely loyal to their boss."

"Why would they try to cast suspicion on the governor or his secretary? And for a murder that is supposed to be a tiger attack?"

"I'm guessing it's in case the police weren't able to hold up their end of the bargain and keep the real cause of death a secret, just like the last note said. Although I don't know why someone would decide to frame such a high-ranking member of the Raj. The only reason I can come up with is that it has political ramifications."

I thought about that. "It makes sense that they would want to be prepared, especially since it looked as though someone tripped a casket bearer at the ceremony. If Gretchen's body had been in the casket, it would have been obvious that she wasn't killed by a tiger, and everyone would have seen it."

Redvers cocked his head at me. "Did you see someone trip them?"

"I could have sworn that someone stuck their foot out in front of the lead man, but I couldn't say who did it or even whether it was intentional." I sighed. "And as soon as it happened, my mind started questioning whether or not I'd actually seen anything."

"Memory is a funny thing," Redvers said. "But I would trust your first instinct."

I smiled at him, but the smile quickly faded from my face. I was frustrated that we hadn't been able to fully eliminate a single person for Gretchen's murder, nor for the other suspicious happenings. Who tripped the casket bearer? Who was sending threatening notes? Who was impersonating Gretchen? Who was aligned with whom? Who had reason to frame Governor Goshen or his secretary?

The "whos" were making my head swim.

Redvers was thoughtful. "I think the only person we can really eliminate for any of this is Lala Rai."

"Why can we eliminate him?" I asked.

"Because he and Gretchen were on the same side. I truly can't see what reason he would have had to kill her. And he certainly wouldn't have tripped a casket bearer, knowing it would out him for having stolen Gretchen's body."

I shook my head. "I disagree. I think it's entirely too likely that we just don't know his motive, but he could still have one. You may take him off your list, but he's still on mine until he's proven absolutely innocent."

Redvers looked amused. "He hardly has access to the governor's suite to use the typewriter."

I narrowed my eyes at him. "Perhaps he's just very good at picking locks."

Redvers put his hands up in surrender. "Point to you, Mrs. Wunderly." His amusement turned to something else entirely as he leaned over to nibble at my ear.

"Are you trying to distract me?" I asked with a great deal of false indignation.

"Is it working?" He murmured against my neck.

I didn't need words to answer that.

Sometime later, we dressed for supper. We had decided that we would take our meal at the governor's mansion with the rest of the group, although I would have much preferred a quiet meal with just the two of us. But Redvers had pointed out that we needed to observe a number of people and they would most likely be at dinner.

Since it cooled so well at night in Ooty, Redvers traded his light linen suit for a traditional black one, and I couldn't help but admire how well it set off his dark good looks. I decided on a blue silk dress with long flowing sleeves. The dress was slim-fitting and not particularly heavy, so I made sure I had my shawl with me, and we set off.

But as we approached the mansion, a buzz of activity on the lawn outside alerted us that something was amiss. Redvers spotted Mudaliar in the growing crowd of both locals and Brits, and we pushed toward him.

"What is going on?" Redvers asked.

"We aren't being allowed back inside the building," Mudaliar said, only sparing us a glance, his attention fixed on the front entrance as was everyone else's. A moment later, I saw Inspector Thornycrest step onto the porch outside.

The crowd that had gathered fell quiet as Thornycrest

began speaking. "This building is off limits for the moment. You'll be allowed to come back to work in the morning, but for now, please find somewhere else to be."

"What happened?" someone in the crowd shouted.

"There was a death," Thornycrest answered.

"A death?" I muttered to Redvers. "Or is it another murder?"

CHAPTER TWENTY-FOUR

Redvers murmured a curse beneath his breath, and I couldn't help but agree.

"What do you want to wager that it's Kandiyar?" The question may have sounded flippant, but I was deadly serious.

Redvers took my hand, and we threaded back through the crowd to stand by ourselves at the edge of the gathering. "That's my guess as well," Redvers said to me in a low voice. "And I doubt it was natural causes. We saw him only a few hours ago, and he was in the peak of health."

Despite the announcement, people had yet to disperse, murmuring speculation among themselves about what had happened and to whom. We moved around the edges of the crowd to the front and approached the porch just as Thornycrest was about to go back inside, but Redvers called out to him, and we trotted up the steps to meet the inspector.

"Oh, it's you two," Thornycrest said without enthusiasm.

"It will be worth your while to let us in," Redvers said.

Thornycrest considered for a moment. I couldn't help the look of disgust that crossed my face, but I managed to wipe it off by the time the police inspector even glanced at me. "Fine," he said. "But go around to the back. I don't want these ghouls to get any ideas. The last thing I need is a parade through here."

I bit my lip to keep myself from letting out the tart response that was my initial impulse. Instead, I paused and took a deep breath before Redvers walked around the building to the courtyard as Inspector Thornycrest had instructed.

"Despicable," I muttered.

"At least he's predictable," Redvers said. "And I've been carrying extra rupees for occasions such as these."

I growled something unintelligible as we rounded the corner of the building. We found ourselves in the back garden and went to the entrance we'd used recently to enter the building and sneak around, finding the door closed this time but still unlocked. Thornycrest was at the base of the stairs, waiting for us and his bonus payday.

I followed the men to the second floor but elected to stay in the hallway. I didn't need to see another dead body; I'd seen quite enough for one lifetime. But I did note that we had stopped outside the governor's office, so our initial suspicion was likely the correct one. A wave of sadness for Kandiyar passed over me; he'd clearly been a hardworking man who'd done little to nothing to deserve the fate that had befallen him.

"Just waiting for someone to come collect the fellow," Thornycrest was saying. "Cut and dried case of suicide, really. A note on his typewriter and everything."

"Were you paid to tell that story, or is it what you truly believe?" Redvers asked.

Thornycrest didn't reply; he merely gave a little shrug of his shoulders. I could feel Redvers' frustration as he and Thornycrest stepped into the office. They were only inside for a few moments before Redvers came back out.

"Is it Kandiyar?" I asked.

Redvers nodded. "It is. And there is a note—" He stopped himself from saying more, gesturing with his head for us to head back downstairs as the inspector joined us. Neither of us acknowledged the man as we hurried away.

"Nice doing business with you," Thornycrest called after us. It took everything I had not to growl in return.

"I can't remember the last time I've disliked someone so intensely," I said once we'd reached the ground floor.

"A natural reaction," Redvers said. "He's immensely un-likeable."

We paused at the bottom of the stairs, and I could see my husband's mind working quickly. Without a word, he headed toward the kitchen where the servants gathered, and I followed close on his heels.

The room was deserted. Redvers huffed in frustration, and we went back out the same way we'd come in. "We need to talk to the staff and see who was in the building," he muttered as he stalked along the garden path.

Unfortunately, the staff had been sent away as well and had most likely scattered to their own homes—I had only seen a few standing in the crowd at the front, a crowd that had mostly dispersed by now. My stomach rumbled, and I put a hand over it to silence it. It was not the most appropriate timing given what Redvers was trying to accomplish and what we'd just learned about poor Vihan Kandiyar.

But the stomach wants what the stomach wants, and it rumbled again, even more loudly this time. Redvers took my hand and started us on the path toward town. "Let's find somewhere to get some supper."

We found ourselves in a quiet local restaurant and took a table near the back, where we could keep an eye on anyone else who came in. It was currently empty of anyone we recognized, but that was likely to change at any moment, since everyone from the governor's mansion was now on their own for dinner and we were within a reasonable walking distance of the governor's mansion and the civil servants' quarters. The owner greeted us, and Redvers ordered food for us in halting Tamil.

"What did you get us?"

"I'm hoping it's curry, but we'll have to see. It's a bit of a gamble since my Tamil is not good."

"It's better than mine."

Redvers conceded the point but turned back to the issue at hand—a little sooner than I would have liked, frankly. "That wasn't a suicide."

I sighed. There were moments such as these when I wished we didn't have so many murders to discuss and could have a normal dinner conversation. I wasn't entirely sure what that would look like, but it seemed like a nice thing to wish for. "How do you know?"

"I can't think of a single case of suicide where they shot themselves right in the forehead. It's an uncomfortable way to hold a gun, at that angle."

I didn't want to think through the logistics of any of that, so I decided to take his word for it.

"Plus the suicide letter was on a clean sheet of paper. It had clearly been rolled in and typed after he had been shot."

"If it had been done beforehand, it would have had blood on it," I said as my stomach roiled. Was I going to be able to eat my dinner after this conversation?

"Exactly," Redvers said.

I swallowed back some nausea and took a few deep breaths, thick with the spicy aromas wafting from the kitchen. Garlic and ginger, turmeric, and something else I couldn't quite put my finger on. I focused on identifying the other spices, trying to settle my stomach. After a few more deep breaths, it seemed to work.

I refocused my gaze on Redvers, who looked slightly concerned. "I'm fine." I nearly believed that to be true, too, even if he still looked skeptical.

"Do you think he was eliminated because we spoke to him?" I asked. The idea that we might have caused the man's death weighed heavily on me.

Redvers shook his head. "Based on the fact that Kandiyar was clearly being framed, he was always a target for elimination. It's even possible that he thought about what we told him, and then confronted someone after we left. Either way, I think he knew more than he was admitting to us."

That made me feel only a tiny bit better. "That poor man," I said. "He just wanted to do his job. I don't think he knew he was being framed for someone's murder until we showed up."

"We'll talk with the staff tomorrow and see if someone knows who was in the building before Kandiyar was shot. Perhaps someone heard something." Redvers then reached into his pocket and set something small and brass onto the table. I picked it up and peered at it, rolling it in my fingers.

"Another shell casing?" I set it back down.

"Another shell casing," Redvers confirmed, reaching into his other pocket and pulling out another small piece of metal and setting it on the table next to the first. "I'll have to compare the two, but it looks the same as the one I picked up from where Gretchen was killed. I wanted to see if I could tell whether they came from the same weapon."

"Is there a way to do that?" I asked.

"There is, although I think it might need to be done with a more powerful device, like a microscope, which I don't have with me." He closely examined one casing, then the other, and sighed. "I can't see anything here. The only thing I can tell is that they are the same caliber."

"I'd already assumed this was done by the same person, but it's nice to have proof, I suppose." I thought for a moment. "How could someone have shot Kandiyar in his office without being seen? There are people all over that building."

"It was good timing if everyone was dressing for dinner. Most of the office workers would have already left for the day, and the servants that were still in the building would have been either in the kitchen or preparing the dining room."

"What did the suicide note say?" My tone put the term "suicide" in quotation marks.

"It claimed responsibility for Gretchen's death and said that he couldn't live with the guilt."

I was about to say something else when our food arrived from the kitchen. It was indeed a curry, and I congratulated Redvers on managing the order.

But then I put a spoonful into my mouth and began coughing. "I've swallowed the sun," I gasped. The curry was so spicy that my lips went numb, but my mouth was absolutely aflame, and my eyes immediately began releasing streams of water down my face. Redvers' eyes were doing the same, and if my own mouth hadn't been in so much pain, I would have chuckled at the sight.

The owner saw our distress and came over, tsking and taking away our plates before returning with a pair of creamy drinks. They had milk in them, and after sucking down more than half of mine, I thought the fire in my mouth was moving toward tolerable. I was still hungry, though.

"Do you think he'll bring more food?" I asked now that I could speak again.

Redvers shrugged, sipping enthusiastically on his own drink. We were quiet for a little while, each lost in thought about everything that had happened, as well as our scorched mouths.

Despite what Redvers had said, I couldn't quite lose the crushing sense of guilt over Kandiyar's death. We had just spoken with the man, and it had been clear that he didn't know he was being framed for the threatening notes and possibly even Gretchen's death. I kept replaying our conversation, over and over, and I wasn't convinced that he'd been hiding anything other than some political ambitions, as Redvers believed.

My husband had obviously been thinking along the same path, but he'd come up with a practical next step. "We should be able to ask for alibis for this murder, at least. We have a much smaller window of when it could have been done."

"That's something, I suppose." I was happy to see that the owner was bringing out new banana leaves of food. It looked like more curry, and he said something when he set the leaves down that neither I nor Redvers understood. "You first," I said. I'd learned my lesson.

Redvers took a tentative bite, then made an appreciative noise and thanked the owner in Tamil. I eyed my own plate suspiciously but took a bite myself and found that while it was quite tasty, the fire was gone. I thanked the man profusely, whether or not he understood English, and he smiled and left us to our meal.

I was quiet as I happily shoveled the very mildly spiced curry into my mouth. It was a bit indecorous, but I was hungry. Once I'd cleaned my plate with the delicious flat naan bread, I leaned back in my chair and looked at Redvers. He was watching me with a great deal of amusement on his face.

"Better?" he asked.

I smiled and nodded.

The excitement of nearly setting my face on fire had distracted me from observing the rest of the restaurant, and I'd missed a couple of newcomers who'd entered and taken a seat behind me. I understood why Redvers always liked to sit facing forward, with his back as close to a wall as possible and a clear view of any room he found himself in.

"Is that Mudaliar sitting with Subbarayan?" I whispered to my husband. He nodded, and I frowned. "When did they come in?"

"Oh, a while ago," he said casually.

I sighed—I hated it when I missed the obvious—but then considered the implications. "I'm surprised they're dining together since Mudaliar is trying to push Subbarayan out of office."

"Politics are always complicated," Redvers said, "with too many currents flowing beneath the dark waters."

I quirked an eyebrow. "That was quite poetic, dear. Perhaps a new line of work to consider."

"I'm glad you think so, but I will stick with my current occupation all the same."

His tone was playful, but I sincerely hoped that he'd be able to hold on to his employment. The threat he'd received was not far from my mind, and I kept worrying over whether the sender had the power to back it up.

Unaware of my thoughts, Redvers stood and paid the owner for our meal, and we made our way over to Mudaliar and Subbarayan's table. Their conversation halted abruptly as we neared. I would have loved to know what they'd been discussing, because it was clearly something they didn't want us to hear.

"Gentlemen," Redvers said. "Have you met my wife, Jane?"

Both men murmured something polite, although I found it strange that Subbarayan didn't acknowledge that we had met in a restaurant similar to this one only a few days prior. Perhaps he didn't remember me. I wouldn't flatter myself that I was terribly memorable, although I couldn't imagine there were that many Americans wandering around Ooty, dining with politicians. Even so, there was little reason to find it suspicious.

"Terrible about Kandiyar," Redvers continued. Mudaliar

and Subbarayan exchanged a brief look but then agreed with Redvers. I was given the distinct impression they knew something that they were obviously going to keep to themselves. Could they know that the secretary's death hadn't been a suicide as Inspector Thornycrest insisted? And had Thornycrest been instructed to say as much? Or was he really that bad of an investigator?

"He was a good man," Subbarayan said, interrupting my thoughts. "Very loyal."

I found it interesting that Kandiyar's loyalty was what everyone remarked on when his name was brought up.

"I spoke with him just hours before he died," Redvers said sadly. "When was the last time you both saw him?"

I appreciated this smooth questioning of the men's alibis.

Mudaliar seemed stricken and cleared his throat but didn't say anything. I was watching both men carefully and saw Subbarayan give his compatriot a strange look before he answered Redvers' question. "I believe I saw him just before teatime. I met with the governor for tea and then returned to my office. I went back to my quarters to take care of some things without seeing either him or the governor again."

I almost interrupted and asked what time it was that Subbarayan had left, but I held my tongue and let Redvers keep charge of the conversation.

"I believe I saw the secretary sometime in the morning," Mudaliar said vaguely, barely pausing before he hurried on. "Did you hear that Inspector Thornycrest has been reassigned?" Mudaliar asked.

It was clearly a distraction, but the news set us both back on our heels all the same. "When did this happen?" Redvers asked.

Mudaliar bobbed his head. "The governor said he was very grateful to the inspector for handling his secretary's death so well and was reassigning him to a cushy position

in the north, effective immediately. It seems that Thornycrest had been hoping to relocate there, and he is being rewarded for his service."

I didn't have to look at Redvers to know that we were
both thinking the same thing. There was no way the police
inspector was being sent away for doing a good job with
Kandiyar's death, since it was clearly not a suicide as
Thornycrest so adamantly claimed. Which begged the question of whether the governor was covering up his secretary's
murder.

We excused ourselves soon after Mudaliar dropped that
news and started the walk back to our cottage. It was just
dark now, which set me on edge. I had other questions for
Redvers, but I didn't want to ask them until we were safely
indoors. Right then, I wanted to concentrate on making certain we weren't being stalked for someone else's supper.

"I doubt there are even tigers in the area," Redvers said
in a clear attempt to reassure me.

"We don't know that, though." I looked up into the trees
overhead as well, squinting my eyes to try to see if there
were any leopards lurking overhead.

Redvers simply squeezed my hand and hurried his pace
to match my own, easy for him, since his legs were much
longer than mine and ate up the ground at a faster rate. As
was the new usual, I breathed a sigh of relief when we
reached the safety of our quarters, until I took a closer look
and realized that our rooms had been thoroughly searched.

Things in the sitting room were just slightly out of
place—books moved and restacked, the papers on the desk
rearranged. Whoever had done the job had made a passing
attempt to make it look as though our things hadn't been
gone through, but it was still quite obvious, to us anyway.
Our bedroom was another story entirely. There hadn't been

clothes tossed on the floor and drawers upended when we'd left, and now there were.

"A terrible job," Redvers said, glancing around, hands on hips.

"They tried to cover their tracks a bit in the sitting room, but they shouldn't have even bothered," I said as I walked into the bedroom and pushed a dresser drawer closed with my hip. "Not if they were going to leave our bedroom like this."

Redvers made a hmm-ing noise. "Perhaps they were interrupted."

"That's possible. Maybe by Sasmit?" The wardrobe door was hanging open, and I looked in, noting that the clothes hanging inside had clearly been searched. A few things were askew, and the hangers were bunched up in a way that neither of us would have left them.

I suddenly remembered the papers and went to the desk, frantically looking for them.

"Don't worry, I put those somewhere safe."

I breathed a sigh of relief. I was fortunate my husband was always thinking one step ahead. "Is that what they were looking for, do you think?"

Redvers pulled the shell casings from his pocket, letting them roll in his palm for a moment. "I would imagine they were looking for these." He replaced them in his pocket, and I was grateful that he'd been carrying them with him instead of stashing them somewhere in the room. If he had, they would certainly be gone now.

I frowned, and returned to the sitting room and took a seat in one of the chairs. I was trying to ignore the feeling of violation that came with our things being pawed through by an unknown person. It was an uncomfortable feeling, especially given how many times in recent memory I had searched someone else's belongings. I didn't enjoy the shoe being on the other foot, but I also knew that I would continue to search what needed to be searched. I would simply do a better job of concealing it than whoever had been here.

I was distracted from this rumination by a strange movement on the couch opposite me. I froze when I realized what it was.

A very large, brown, patterned snake. And it was slowly leaving its coiled position on the couch and slithering right toward me, tongue flicking.

CHAPTER TWENTY-FIVE

I didn't even have time to scream before Redvers was there, pulling me out of my chair and behind him, putting himself between me and the threat. The snake's body caught up with the head, and it paused and made a hissing noise as the two of us backed up slowly toward the bedroom.

"I hate snakes," Redvers muttered quietly. I was pressed to his back and could feel his body trembling against me.

We were about to close ourselves in our bedroom when there was a knock at our outer door, and Sasmit came inside. He immediately assessed what was happening, which wasn't hard since Redvers was walking slowly backward with me behind him, both of us fixated on the angry snake in the middle of our living room.

"Keep its attention, sahib," Sasmit said, then quickly left. Moments later, he reappeared at our terrace, quietly opening the door and coming inside, padding softly in bare feet across the floor to come up behind the snake. With very little noise, he swung one leg and then another over the back of the couch, then crouched down, hands out. The snake must have sensed the movement and seemed about to turn around, so I shouted a nonsense word and stepped out from behind Redvers. The snake refocused on me, and in one quick movement Sasmit grabbed the snake right behind the head, his other hand grasping the body. The snake had so much girth that Sasmit's fingers didn't even meet around the thing.

"It is okay now, sahib." Sasmit held the large snake aloft. It seemed irritated, although it was truly hard to tell with a snake. "It is not poisonous; it is a python." He glanced around, brow furrowed. "I wonder how it came to be here."

I already had a good idea of how and why the snake was here in our room, and it hadn't gotten in on its own. What I was wondering was why our terrace door was unlocked—I distinctly remembered locking it when we left the room. "The terrace door was unlocked, Sasmit?"

He nodded. "I was hoping that it would be, memsahib. It worked out well." He was moving toward the door with the snake grasped firmly in his hands.

"Where will you take that?" I asked. I wasn't interested in its well-being, merely in whether or not it would be able to return. Poisonous or not, I didn't want to see it ever again, and I was certain my husband had even stronger feelings to that effect.

"I will release it in the woods later. For now, I will put it in a sack, and then we will take it far enough away that it won't be able to find its way back here."

Redvers was still clear on the other side of the room; he hadn't moved a muscle since Sasmit had entered, and it was only once our steward had left with the snake that the tension started to ease from his body.

"I learn something new about you every day, my dear," I said once Sasmit and the snake had gone.

"What's that?" Redvers said. It sounded as though he was trying for nonchalance, but he was also carefully peering beneath every cushion in the living room, using only a tip of a finger to lift each and standing as far back as physically possible. If there had been a stick or a cane handy, he doubtless would have used that for this operation, but we had nothing of the like in our quarters.

"You're afraid of snakes," I said gently. I was touched that despite his obvious fear, he'd put himself between me and the python, because there was no doubt in my mind that the man was petrified of them—I'd felt his physical reaction to the creature.

"I don't know what you're talking about," he said, finally taking a cautious seat on a chair he'd inspected closely, his eyes still darting around the room, feet twitching slightly as though they expected to encounter another serpent at any moment. I was a little surprised Redvers didn't pull his legs up onto the chair with him, as indecorous as it might be, but he kept his feet where they were, unprotected.

I wondered if he would be able to sleep that night. Something told me the answer was no.

"Do you want me to check the bed?" I asked.

He pursed his lips, then admitted, "Maybe."

I smiled gently and went to do that, searching our entire bedroom carefully to ensure there were no other surprises waiting for us. I found nothing and returned to the living room. "There's nothing there." I took a seat on the couch without ceremony, and Redvers visibly flinched, causing me to smile a little, but I held my teasing. For once. "Since it wasn't poisonous, it was just a warning," I said.

"I'd prefer they leave a strongly worded note next time."

That was fair, and preferable to me as well. "Whoever searched the place left the snake." I was stating the obvious, but I felt that it needed to be said aloud all the same. It sometimes seemed that naming a thing could dispel the negative energy around it, bringing it into the light.

Redvers nodded, finally leaning his back against the chair cushion but still looking tense. Apparently, the negative energy left by the python would be much more difficult to dispel for my husband.

I eyed him with concern. "Will you be able to sleep to-night?"

"Of course," he said, but there was little conviction in his tone. I'd never seen him so unsettled, and by a reptile—a slithering, mildly dangerous one, but still. I never would have guessed my husband could be so undone by anything if I hadn't seen it firsthand.

I shook my head and went back to the matter at hand. "How are we going to figure out who is behind all this?" I waved a vague hand at "all this." There was a lot to en-compass.

"They clearly want us to stop looking into things and let everyone accept that Gretchen was killed by a tiger, Kandiyar killed himself, the Simon Commission is coming to Madras, and everything will be just grand. No protests, no angry Indian people, nothing to upset the Raj."

"Who has the most to gain from such a rosy view of things?" I asked.

Redvers sighed. "Any one of these government fellows, I suppose. The governor, Feodore Smith, Mudaliar, Subbarayan . . . I think any one of them has sufficient motive. Either their positions or their political power could be affected by the truth." Redvers frowned. "I would think Smith has the least to lose if the truth comes out, though. And possibly the governor as well—I'm not sure the murders could have any effect on his aspirations to viceroy one way or another."

Names rolled in my mind, pebbles rubbed smooth by my constantly rushing thoughts. "You're sure Rai and his people aren't involved in any way?"

Redvers shook his head. "It wouldn't help the resistance to kill off one of their strongest advocates."

"Unless they didn't like how Gretchen was going about things?" I asked thoughtfully. "You said she was poking all the hornets' nests she could." And it sounded like there were a lot of them.

"She was, but I can't see any other way she could have gone about it. Not only that, but stirring up trouble was how Gretchen operated, and that was well known."

It didn't seem like a sound argument in favor of Rai, and I thought we should still keep him on our suspect list, but I kept that to myself for the time being. "Mudaliar was clearly avoiding your question of where he'd been at the time Kandiyar was killed. I'm sure he thought his information about Thornycrest would distract us."

"Yes, I did make a note of that."

"Do you think he's capable of it?"

Redvers shrugged. "It's hard to know what anyone is capable of until they are backed into a corner."

That was true. I'd learned quite a lot about myself by being backed into a corner before, not all of it flattering. But I thought about how that related to our suspects. It didn't feel as though the governor or Smith were backed into a corner, but what about the Indian politicians? "Do you think Mudaliar is backed into a corner? I thought he simply wanted Subbarayan's position in Congress, and that is why he was trying to push Subbarayan out. The vote of confidence and all that. Why would either have a motive for this?"

"Subbarayan's back and forth on whether he is for or against the Simon Commission is what nearly got him voted out of Congress. I imagine he is desperate to hold onto his position. Mudaliar is tougher to read. He is secretly working with the resistance but seems to be only serving his own best interests, not acting out of genuine belief. It's hard to say what he might be willing to do to advance his career and power." Redvers rubbed his forehead. "There is something else going on there that we need to look into, too—

perhaps related to the arguments they've been having. I'll talk with Rai to see what he knows about either of the men. Hopefully he'll have some further insights."

I didn't think that would be especially fruitful, since Rai clearly had his own agenda, but I let it go and tried to lighten the mood. "I think we can rule out snake charmer from your list of alternative professions. Which only leaves us with poet or sheep farmer—it's not a very long list."

A sparkle finally lit his eyes, the first I'd seen since we'd encountered the python. "Are you afraid I'll start writing poetry about the sheep instead of you?" Redvers asked.

I tossed a silky decorative pillow from the chair at him, and he easily blocked it from hitting him. It was a much-needed moment of levity, but I did hope the threat against his employment wasn't a real one. He obviously wasn't concerned about it, though—which meant I would have to do my best to let my worries go.

The next morning, I looked at my normally immaculate husband over the top of my coffee cup as we had a quiet breakfast together. He looked quite the worse for wear, as though he'd barely slept a wink, but I decided not to give him a hard time about it. This was the second time in a row that I'd passed on the opportunity to tease him, and I mused I should get some kind of award for my efforts—a ribbon perhaps, like they presented at a fair.

"You sure you don't want the good stuff?" I asked, holding my cup up.

Redvers shook his head, although he grimaced as he took a sip from his own cup. "I'll stick with my tea."

"Suit yourself," I said, although I'm certain both my tone and my face reflected my doubt in the soundness of his choice. "What is our plan of attack for today?"

"I've had some time to think about that," he said. I didn't mention that it looked like he'd thought about it all night long based on the dark circles under his bloodshot eyes, holding my tongue yet again. "I think we should lie low for today. Lull whoever it is into a false sense of security that we're heeding their warning," Redvers said.

I frowned. "Are you certain? I was thinking quite the opposite: we should start checking alibis for the time that Kandiyar was killed." Mudaliar had deliberately avoided giving us one the day before; he was at the top of my list to investigate today.

"Let's leave that for a day or two," Redvers said, refilling his cup with more tepid-looking tea.

My frown was still furrowing my brow. I had the uncharitable thought that Redvers was backing down because he was afraid of another snake—a less friendly and more venomous one—being left as a gift in our room, and that was why he wanted us to back off.

But after giving it more thought, I wondered if he was actually nervous about losing his employment with the Crown. He might lose sleep over a snake, but I didn't think he would back down from an investigation over one. Besides, it was understandable to be wary of losing one's employment, especially when you hadn't trained to do anything else and had a new wife to take care of.

Although I had learned to be incredibly resourceful over the years and was perfectly capable of taking care of myself. But men, even good ones like Redvers, seemed to forget that.

I willed my brow to clear and agreed, saying that I might take the opportunity to check out the local library or perhaps head to the man-made lake and stroll along the banks while the sun was up and glistening on the waters.

Of course, I had no intention of doing either of those things, but the poor man was so tired that he took my word for it.

Once the teapot was empty, Redvers and his dark eye bags left for the governor's mansion. I gave him a kiss on his way out the door, as well as an assurance that I would find a way to keep myself busy and out of trouble.

I gave him a ten-minute head start before I left as well, strapping my sturdy walking boots onto my feet. As much as I wanted to chat with Mudaliar or the staff at the governor's mansion about alibis, it was entirely too risky to be seen there if I didn't want Redvers to know that I was still investigating.

My trip to the tea plantation to find Hasnan had been interrupted the day before, and now was an excellent time to make that trip. I could ask Hasnan if he read Tamil and whether he would be willing to tell me what my sticky stack of recovered documents said. I was especially curious now that Kandiyar had been killed what I'd managed to recover from his room before his death.

I could also have a chat with Savithri. As the governor's mistress, it was likely that she heard quite a bit of behind-the-scenes gossip, and I was hoping she might finally be ready to reveal what she knew about the goings-on. She certainly knew much more than she'd been willing to share with me, and I hoped I could convince her that it was time.

The trick was going to be whether I could figure out where Redvers had put those papers. He'd told me the night before that he'd put them "somewhere safe"; it was up to me to figure out where that somewhere might be. I truly hoped that they were still here in the room somewhere, or I would be quite out of luck.

I stood in the bedroom for a long moment, tapping my finger against my mouth and attempting to think like my husband. If Redvers had something to hide, where would he put it? It had to be somewhere that wasn't obvious. Or conversely, somewhere obvious but with a sneaky trick to it. I smacked my hand against my forehead—of course, his suitcase. Redvers had long ago had a false bottom built into it, for situations precisely like this one.

I rang for Sasmit and asked where our suitcases had been stored. There was nowhere in our quarters where they could be stowed away, so I assumed they'd been removed to a storage area somewhere in the building.

"Memsahib, just tell me what you are looking for, and I can fetch it for you," Sasmit responded to my request.

I shook my head firmly. "No, I must do this myself. If you could just show me where the luggage is kept, I will be fine."

Sasmit looked as though he wanted to argue with me some more, but he pursed his lips. "Very well, memsahib. This way." He led me to a small shed in the back of the garden, opened the door, and gestured inside. "This is where we keep the luggage for our guests." I passed by him, and he paused in the doorway. "Shall I wait for you, memsahib?"

"No, no, that won't be necessary," I told him with a smile. "I've got it from here."

Sasmit stood in the doorway for a moment longer before giving a little bob of his head and leaving me to it. I didn't move an inch until I was certain he'd gone. He may have helped me to recover this stack of papers from the trash, but I also didn't trust him, not any longer. I didn't think I could trust anyone at this point.

I quickly located Redvers' suitcase and popped the false bottom open, muffling a crow of victory when I found the papers inside. I replaced the panel in the suitcase and tidied everything away before returning to my room with my treasure.

Redvers would probably regret showing me his trick suitcase once he realized what I'd done. But it was for the best. We needed to know what these were about, and if they were related to Kandiyar's murder.

I didn't want to carry the papers as they were, so I searched the desk, finding an empty folder in the desk drawer. I put the papers inside, grateful to have a way to carry them without displaying to the world what I had. I was also pleased that I wouldn't have to carry them with my bare fingers—being trapped in Redvers' suitcase had done nothing to air them out. I wrinkled my nose at the aroma wafting from them, but I was resolved to take them with me. It would be fine once I was out in the open air—the breeze would work in my favor.

I decided to walk to the tea plantation instead of hiring a ride, hoping that the exercise would help me to think things over. There was quite a lot to consider, and my mind was busy as my feet trudged along, tumbling theories this way and that to see if any of the pieces fell into place. I considered Governor Goshen. We'd ruled him out earlier, but was that wise? Goshen had both easy access to the typewriter that was used to write the threatening notes and the political clout to actually carry through with the threat against Redvers. Lady Goshen's sudden change of story was incredibly suspicious, as was Thornycrest's sudden relocation elsewhere.

The governor had high political ambitions, which could be used to argue either for or against his being responsible. What would he do to realize those dreams? Plus it was his loyal secretary that was killed, a man who would have done anything for the governor. Could that include killing a nosy woman? The note left in Kandiyar's typewriter had been written after his death, but could it be based on reality? Could Kandiyar have killed Gretchen? It was more than a little suspicious that the governor had immediately reassigned the police inspector once Thornycrest had announced Kandiyar's death as a suicide. Had the governor orchestrated everything, then eliminated Kandiyar once the secretary had carried out the governor's dirty work?

I was fully aware that my speculations were wild and highly unlikely to be correct. Plus this scenario ignored the fact that Kandiyar had seemed legitimately convinced Gretchen was killed by a tiger. It also ignored the fact that the threats against Redvers' employment may have been just that—threats, without any political teeth—but it felt good to have a suspect and a purpose, so I ignored those little details for the moment and made mental plans to further my investigation into Governor Goshen.

Without Redvers knowing, of course. That would be the tricky part.

I was so focused on my own thoughts that I barely registered the man walking in front of me until I had pulled up alongside him. Even then, I offered a vague greeting without fully registering who I was speaking to, barely looking at the man. But his greeting in return finally snapped me into the present, and I realized I was walking with the maharajah. He looked amused at my inattention to his presence.

"You appear to be deep in thought, Mrs. Wunderly," he said.

"I was," I agreed before looking at him curiously. "Where are you headed?"

"I imagine to the same place that you are. There isn't much else this way that a person would want to visit."

I was rather surprised to see the man on foot instead of being carried on a palanquin or riding in a carriage, but I thought it might be a rude question, so I focused on another. "I'm going to see Savithri Kumari, and she's staying out this way. Who are you looking for?"

"I'm looking for her as well," the maharajah said, but he didn't elaborate further.

We walked in silence for a few moments while I wondered whether I should come clean about my intentions to interview Savithri. It looked as though the maharajah had been thinking along the same lines, because we both suddenly started to speak at the same time.

"You go first," he said.

I paused, then spoke slowly. "I was just going to say that I have questions about what Savithri might know about the deaths of both Gretchen and the governor's secretary."

Maharajah Thirunal nodded. "I have those same questions."

I wasn't excited at the prospect of speaking with Savithri at the same time as the maharajah, but it looked as though I had no other choice. I couldn't exactly ask to speak with the woman alone, although perhaps I could wait until the maharajah finished his questions and stay behind to speak with her by myself. I frowned in frustration. I couldn't imagine that Savithri would be forthcoming about what she knew when faced with both of us.

Of course, it was hard to say whether she would be honest at all, regardless of who spoke with her. Savithri Kumari had secrets, that was for certain, and she kept them quite close to her chest.

As we came near the plantation buildings, a man was carried past us by two local men with the palanquin balanced on their shoulders between them. The man in the litter was wearing a light-colored suit and hat and gave us a brief nod as they passed; the maharajah and I had to stand to the side of the path to let them by. I'd never spoken with the man, but I recognized Feodore Smith, and I couldn't help but wonder what the man was doing all the way out here.

Savithri was already on the porch when we arrived at the plantation, looking beautiful in a blue and pink sari, embroidered in silver and wrapped elegantly around her. She was sipping what looked to be a milky tea, her face troubled, although it cleared once she caught sight of us. "Maharajah Thirunal, Mrs. Wunderly, how lovely to see you both." The words sounded wooden, but she gestured for the servant hovering in the door to bring one more chair. "Can I offer you some chai?" There was an empty cup on the table that the servant quickly cleared away before disappearing into the building. I surmised that Smith was Savithri's previous guest, though I couldn't begin to guess what they would have to discuss. She appeared troubled by it, though, whatever it was.

The maharajah immediately accepted Savithri's offer, and I did the same a beat later, hoping that chai would be better than the British tea I was used to being offered—the same tea that they grew on this plantation. I'd already tasted everything they served here, and none of it was coffee-flavored. An extra chair appeared a moment later, and the maharajah and I took seats next to each other, facing Savithri, who hovered nervously before settling herself into her own chair again.

"How may I be of service to you both?" Savithri asked.

I was hoping that Maharajah Thirunal would take the lead and ask his questions so that I could ask mine once he'd gone, but he leaned back in his chair and gestured for me to go ahead. I suppressed a sigh and lobbed my first question. "Have you heard about Mr. Kandiyar's death?"

Savithri's face clouded, her dark eyes sad. "It is devastating. He was a good man, always very kind to me. And he was very loyal to George—I mean, Governor Goshen."

"Do you believe that he took his own life?" I asked. Out of the corner of my eye I saw Thirunal shift in his seat.

Savithri looked between the two of us, then her eyes flicked to something behind me. I whirled quickly and was relieved to see the young man from before coming through the doorway. He was carrying a tray with two more cups of piping hot chai, and he deposited them on the table, bowed, and hurried back inside. I mentally chastised myself for being so jumpy. Savithri had just ordered tea, after all.

We were all quiet for a long moment, and I was beginning to think I would have to prompt her again, but Savithri finally raised her large eyes to meet mine and started to speak. "I was not honest with you before, Mrs. Wunderly, at least not entirely so. There is much happening here in Ooty, and it is dangerous. I do not believe that Kandiyar took his own life; the governor received a note warning him to announce the death as a suicide, but neither of us believe this to be true."

If I was to believe the woman—which I was reluctant to do, at least fully—then I thought it was safe to assume that the note had a dropped *e* like the other threatening notes that had come before. My next question, setting aside whether this story was even true, was whether the governor had sent the note to himself to throw off suspicion, but I kept that to myself. His mistress seemed as loyal as Kandiyar had been and was unlikely to receive such a question well. It would shut our conversation down immediately.

Before I could decide what to ask next, Savithri frowned and held up a finger before getting up and disappearing into the building. The maharajah and I shared a speculative look, but we both held our tongues, sipping our tea and sitting with our thoughts.

Savithri returned a moment later, carrying a small wooden box inlaid with what looked like marble. "It is a puzzle box," she said, setting it on the table next to her cup of tea. "It belonged to Gretchen."

CHAPTER TWENTY-SIX

Maharajah Thirunal gestured toward the puzzle box, and when Savithri inclined her head, he picked it up, turning it this way and that, his surprisingly short fingers probing the edges of the wood, searching for the trigger to open it.

I looked at Savithri expectantly, eyebrows raised, waiting for the story of how she'd come to have this in her possession.

Savithri's face was a perfect mask of sadness, but whether it was real or contrived was difficult to say. "Gretchen gave it to me the day before she died and asked me to keep it safe for her," Savithri said. "It is what she asked of me that day you saw us in the garden. I was upset that she seemed so concerned for her own safety and felt that she needed to take this measure." She shook her head. "But she'd been right to be so concerned."

"Why didn't you tell me about this before?" I asked, doing my best to keep the frustration from my tone.

Savithri bobbed her head. "I didn't know whether I could trust you."

That was fair, I supposed, although I wasn't sure what

had changed now besides Kandiyar's death and a supposed note threatening the governor. "Do you have any idea what might be inside it?" I asked, watching Thirunal examine it. It was a sizable piece, just short of a foot long, so any number of things might be found inside. Perhaps even the reason that Gretchen had been killed.

Savithri shook her head. "I do not, nor have I been able to figure out how to open it."

The maharajah gave it a small shake, but there was no noise from within as we had both clearly expected. Maharajah Thirunal put it back on the table, his brows deeply furrowed as he gazed at it.

"You haven't seen it before?" I asked him.

He shook his head. "Why give it to *you*?" he asked Savithri.

She bobbed her head. "I do not know. We were friendly but not particularly close. Perhaps because I am staying outside of town? She did say something about how it was safer to have it somewhere other than her room."

Which led me to believe that Gretchen knew she was in trouble. Either that or that her rooms could be searched at any time. And the only reason someone would be so suspicious was if she had something to hide.

I removed my straw hat, dropping it in my lap, and raked my hands through my hair as I surveyed the box. I didn't have the patience for this particular type of puzzle, and I briefly thought about cracking it open with a hammer just so I could see what was inside with the hopes that Gretchen's secrets might point to her killer.

"If you give me some time, I think I can open it," the maharajah said, giving me a bemused look. My violent thoughts toward the box must have been written on my face.

I smiled sheepishly. "Of course." I turned back to our hostess. "Why was Smith here?"

Something flashed across Savithri's face but was gone before I could identify it. "He wanted to know if I had typed some note and sent it to Lady Goshen," she said shortly.

I looked at her, brow furrowed. "Why is that his concern? And why did he think it was you?"

She bobbed her head with clear indignation. "He said because of my relationship with the governor, I had easy access to the typewriter. I told him I knew nothing about any notes, but he didn't believe me. Why would I send a note to Lady Goshen about myself?"

I couldn't think of a single reason why Smith would blame Savithri for the note sent to Lady Goshen, other than the weak one he presented. I nearly asked if Savithri could even read English in order to type a note, but decided it was too indelicate a question. I also couldn't imagine why Smith would be overly concerned with Lady Goshen's sensibilities, which as far as I'd been able to tell were far from delicate. Why travel out here to make some weak accusations?

But I also couldn't help but think there was still more that Savithri wasn't telling us. She had clearly been hiding something each time I'd spoken with her, and I would bet money that that something wasn't simply this puzzle box. She knew much more than she was saying—she'd dodged too many of my questions now and in the past for anything else to be true. And who could say whether she was telling the truth now, or only a sliver of the truth? I felt the latter was likely, even now, when she appeared to be making an effort to share some of the secrets she'd been holding. My guess was that she was revealing just enough to hope that we might go away, satisfied with the puzzle box and a handful of half-truths.

I wanted to growl in frustration, but I didn't think that would be helpful. Instead, I sipped at my tea for a moment, which was quite delicious. If I'd been in a better frame of mind, I would have thoroughly enjoyed it—it had just enough sweetness to enhance the melody of spices on my tongue but wasn't sickly sweet. I thought I tasted nutmeg and cinnamon and something else, something I couldn't quite name. Clove, maybe?

I pushed the tea from my thoughts and took a moment to organize all the confusing ties—both political and personal—that were clouding the waters of this investigation. I wished that I had made a chart of some kind on paper before coming here, but I hadn't, and I did my best to map it in my mind so that I could decide on my next question.

Before I could, the maharajah stepped in with a question of his own. "Has the governor mentioned the business between us?"

Savithri considered him over the top of her cup for a moment before setting it down. "He has."

This told me two things. First was that there was in fact an issue between the maharajah and the governor, an issue that Subbarayan had known about, which had caused him to shut down at lunch when I'd asked about it. The second thing was that the governor spoke with Savithri about politics, something I had wondered about but was now confirmed for me.

"He was not surprised that you were unwilling to accept a deal with the government. Disappointed, but not surprised."

Thirunal nodded once, turning his attention back to Gretchen's box. There was a long moment of silence while I tried to decide whether or not to ask what deal Savithri had in mind, but of all the issues swirling around the murders, I decided this was the least likely to be relevant. I also suspected that I could guess what the deal might be; Redvers had said that the British Raj was trying to get all the smaller kingdoms to turn over their power in exchange for some weak voting rights. I suspected that Maharajah Thirunal was a holdout, wanting to keep power over his own kingdom, and I mentally applauded him for it.

Was Governor Goshen a dead end? It was beginning to feel that way. I sighed quietly into my teacup. If I were honest with myself, I'd known all along how wild my speculations had been surrounding the governor. Savithri was hiding plenty, but that didn't mean that the governor had killed Gretchen and his own secretary.

Who else might have motive? There were two people in this whole debacle that I hadn't given enough attention to—Mudaliar and Subbarayan. I wasn't sure what motive either of them might have for killing Gretchen and Kandiyar, but I also hadn't dug into either of them deeply enough to be able to dismiss them. I thought it was less likely that Mudaliar was the culprit, simply because he was purported to be on the side of the resistance, but did we know that for certain? He'd also avoided giving an alibi for the time of Kandiyar's death, so it was still safest to trust no one and suspect everyone.

A glance at the maharajah showed me that his attention was again focused on the puzzle box, which I was frankly glad of since we needed it opened and I preferred to be there when he figured out how to do it. I wasn't ready to trust him either, even though he seemed the least likely to have killed his former lover and hadn't even arrived in Ooty until well after she'd been murdered.

Savithri's head was cocked as she gazed at me, and I had the unnerving thought that the woman could read my thoughts. "You have much on your mind, Mrs. Wunderly."

"Call me Jane," I said automatically, then focused my eyes on her, pausing for a moment before asking my next question. She waited patiently, sipping her chai tea. "What do you know about Misters Mudaliar and Subbarayan?" I asked. Perhaps I would get further with her if I asked about people not related to herself or the governor.

Savithri nodded once, setting her teacup on the table and smoothing down the silk sari draped over her legs before folding her hands in her lap. "Those two men are always at odds, and it is quite well known that Mudaliar would like to push Subbarayan out of government and take his position."

This lined up with what Redvers had said as well.

"Is there any chance of him doing that?" I asked.

Savithri bobbed her head slightly. "I think there is a chance, especially depending on how the commission is received once it arrives."

I frowned. "What do you mean?"

"If it goes well, and the commission is supported without civil unrest, Subbarayan will be vindicated since he currently supports the commission. Although that may change between now and January when the commission arrives."

"And if it goes poorly?"

"They may vote again, and this time Subbarayan could be removed from his position," Savithri said.

I filled in the rest. "And Mudaliar could take over."

She bobbed her head as I processed that. I wondered if Mudaliar actually supported the resistance against the commission and was in favor of voting rights for Indian people or if he was simply using the resistance to create an opening to take over his superior's position. It left a bad taste in my mouth, and I hoped the latter wasn't the case—I found myself hoping that Mudaliar truly believed in the cause. Two people had already lost their lives because of this issue, and I hoped that it wasn't for nothing.

But it also made me wonder if he or Subbarayan could in

fact be responsible. Would it have benefited either of them to get Gretchen out of the way? Perhaps because she'd seen Mudaliar's true motives and was going to make them public? Or maybe she'd decided to help overthrow Subbarayan and push him out? I could only hope whatever was in the puzzle box might answer those questions.

I gave a little sigh. There was a reason I tried to stay out of politics. It seemed to make enemies out of everyone as they jockeyed for power, and every aspect was murky and distasteful to me. No one was who they appeared to be, and everything seemed to be done in the name of holding on to some kind of power instead of doing what was best for the people they oversaw. It was all quite depressing.

But this was the world that Gretchen had been caught up in. She was so involved in local politics she'd even been elected to the Indian National Congress, so the answers to her murder had to lie here somewhere. It did make my head spin, though, trying to figure out everyone's motivations and where they actually stood.

My eyes fell on the folder of papers I'd put next to my chair when we sat down. I picked it up. "I was hoping to speak with Hasnan," I said.

"Is it something I can help you with?" Savithri asked.

I paused, studying her.

She cocked her head. "Anything my cousin learns I will also learn."

She nodded as I sat back in surprise. "I didn't realize he was your cousin." If that was true, there was no way I would ask Hasnan to translate these papers. "No, it was nothing," I said, increasing my grip on the folder as though she might snatch it away from me. I wasn't ready to trust her, which meant I would have to look elsewhere for a translator.

I looked at the maharajah, and he gave me a slight nod,

which I understood to mean that he was ready to take his leave. I stood, thanking Savithri for her time. "If you learn anything that might be useful, will you please let me know?" I asked her.

Maharajah Thirunal was already down the stairs, his fingers still pressing various corners of the box, looking for a solution to its mystery, when Savithri spoke.

"I will. But please be careful, Jane. I would hate to see something happen to you as well."

CHAPTER TWENTY-SEVEN

It didn't feel like a threat against me, but it certainly was ominous, and Savithri's words echoed in my brain far down the path back to Ooty. To shake myself free of the bad feeling they had left in their wake, I turned my attention to the maharajah, who was keeping step with me despite the distraction in his hands.

It seemed that he'd been observing me once again, without my noticing. I really needed to pay more attention to my surroundings.

"You are very distracted by this . . . issue," Maharajah Thirunal said.

"I am," I said. I was quiet for a few steps, deciding how I wanted to explain my interest. "I did not know Gretchen well, but I have some experience in . . . well, poking my nose into murders that strike me as suspicious. I don't like how the police—and whoever is behind this—has tried to make Gretchen's murder look like a tiger attack. And now Kandiyar, they say his death was a suicide, when it was not. It does not sit well with me."

Thirunal nodded. "You seek justice."

"I do," I said simply. "For those who cannot seek it themselves."

He considered me for a moment, then seemed to come to a decision. "What can I do to help you in this quest?" he asked. I looked at him in surprise, and he bobbed his head slightly. "Gretchen and I once cared a great deal about one another. For obvious reasons, this could not last, but I never forgot her." He was quiet. "I will not accept her death being washed away by the Raj."

There was a great deal of bitterness in his voice on that last word. "You don't approve of the Raj?" It was more of a statement than a question.

"They are hungry for power and care not for the people they rule. I do, which is why I refuse to turn over my kingdom to them. Many others have, keeping their titles in name only and surrendering their power, but I will not. No one will care for the people of Travancore the way that I do."

I nodded. I respected his position and his passion for the subject. In fact, since my arrival in Ooty, I had come to realize that I was firmly in the camp of the resistance movement and those who wanted Indian independence. And not simply because Gretchen had most likely been killed in the name of it, but because I believed in my heart that it was what was right for the people of India.

I realized that I hadn't answered the maharajah's question. "I think the best thing you can do for me right now is to get that box open." I nodded at it with my head. "And to tell me as soon as you do."

He bobbed his head. "I give you my word that I will do so." We walked several steps before he spoke again. "And what about your papers?"

I glanced at him out of the corner of my eye. "They need to be translated. I cannot read Tamil." Or speak it, but I thought that went without saying. I considered how much more to reveal, but it turned out I didn't have to say anything else.

The maharajah held out his hand for the folder after

tucking the box carefully under his other arm. "I will do this for you."

I slowly put the folder in his hands, and he tucked it in with the box. My stomach fell as soon it left my hands, but there was little I could do about it now. I could hardly snatch it back and run. Besides, I had to trust someone with the task, and the maharajah had the least motive for Gretchen's murder of anyone here.

At least I hoped that was the case.

I returned to my quarters, sank onto the sofa in the sitting room, and removed my boots. My feet welcomed the release, and I flexed my toes for a moment in relief. Then my eyes fell on the tray that sat on the low table. I put a finger to the coffee pot and smiled when I found it was still warm. Sasmit was a very thoughtful and attentive attendant; I was sorry I had to wonder whether he'd been planted by someone to gather information from us. I poured myself a cup of coffee and added a touch of fresh cow's milk, then took a sip.

I frowned. The coffee didn't taste the same as it usually did. I took a larger sip, then frowned and replaced my cup in its saucer. I stood and went to the door, opening it in the hopes that I might spot Sasmit, but there was no one around. Should I go to the servant's area and see if I could find him? I wanted to ask how long the coffee had sat for, since it tasted strangely bitter. But there was no one about.

I shrugged and returned to the sofa. Sasmit would be by in a few moments. He was never far away, especially when he knew we were in residence. I turned my mind back to the issues at hand, mindlessly taking another sip of the brew before setting it aside for good. Something was not quite right, and I would ask Sasmit to bring a fresh pot.

It wasn't long before my heart was beating in an irregular fashion—too fast and then too slow. Then I put a hand to my stomach where my intestines were now roiling in anger. Was I going to be sick?

With growing horror, I looked at the coffee pot, a small silver contraption with matching cover. I leaned forward, my stomach cramping painfully, but I managed to remove the lid and peer inside. There were two leaves floating in the dark brew, leaves that had no right to be there.

I shot up from the sofa and closeted myself in the bathroom, ready to do what needed to be done in order to make myself sick, but found it wasn't necessary. My body was on top of things.

While I was busy being violently ill in the bathroom, I distantly heard footsteps approach the bathroom door and quickly retreat again. I was otherwise occupied and had no idea how much time was passing until I heard several sets of footsteps approach the door.

"Jane, I've brought the doctor."

I was lying on the floor now, in between bouts of being ill, enjoying the feeling of the cool tile against my cheek. "Check the coffee," I muttered.

The door pushed open, and Redvers stood in the doorway. "I couldn't hear you, what did you say?" It wasn't a large room. Only Redvers could fit inside with me, but I sensed another man standing just outside the door.

"Check the coffee," I said, only moderately more clearly, since my face was pressed into the floor. Redvers left and quickly returned, the leaves carefully sitting atop a plate that he showed to the doctor.

"Oleander," the doctor said. "She has been poisoned with oleander."

Chapter Twenty-eight

"Will I die?" I asked weakly. I hoped I was done getting sick even though the intense discomfort in my guts continued. The discomfort was what had me concerned, and the fact that it hadn't yet subsided—I'd never been ill for such an extended amount of time, and so continuously. My heart was also still skipping the occasional beat, which made me nervous.

"No, you won't die from only two leaves," the doctor said. He had a raspy voice that I would have loved to match with a face, but I couldn't force my head to look in his direction. "And this looks to be from a pink oleander plant instead of yellow. But you will be uncomfortable for some time."

"That's good, I suppose," I mumbled in reply, my cheek still smashed into the tile. "That I won't die."

Redvers made a strangled noise, somewhere between a chuckle and a sob, and this time I managed to turn my head and crack my eyes open enough to see my husband. He had tears in his chocolate brown eyes and looked quite beside himself, as though he didn't know what to do with the emotions roiling in his own gut.

The doctor and Redvers left the bathroom, and although I was relieved that Redvers was here—with a medical professional—I was also pleased to be left alone for a moment. Eyes closed, I concentrated on the coolness of the tile beneath my cheek and counted my breaths, trying to ignore the cramping in my guts and the offbeat rhythm of my heart.

Several hours passed, and I finally improved. I was still vaguely nauseated, but my heart had stopped skipping around and fell back into a regular, steady rhythm. Redvers helped me to bed and insisted that I not get up from it unless it was a trip back to the bathroom. My husband then proceeded to bustle around the room, ensuring that I was comfortable, fluffing pillows and smoothing sheets. I appreciated his worry and care, but I also was beginning to wish he had somewhere else to focus his nervous energy.

"Do you need another pillow?" he asked for what had to be the fourth time.

"No, what I need is for you to come here and stop fussing. Sit next to me," I said, patting the bed next to me.

He looked uncertain but then did as I asked, perching on the end of the bed, holding himself stiffly as though he might crack in two if he let himself relax. This was the most worked-up that I had ever seen him. I had been in plenty of danger before, of course, but I'd never been poisoned. I supposed in his eyes this was the closest I'd ever come to actually dying on an investigation, even though the doctor said I was going to be fine. But Redvers was not handling things with near the same level of equanimity that I was, which was frankly surprising.

"I'm fine, my dear. I'm fine, and I'm going to continue to be fine," I said.

I could still feel the tension radiating off him. "I think we should leave immediately and head back to England. As soon as you're able to travel," Redvers said.

I leaned over far enough to place a finger on his lips. "Not a chance. We are obviously getting close to answers about what happened to Gretchen and Kandiyar, and I'm not going to let whoever is responsible win."

"This isn't a game, Jane. You could have died." His eyes filled with tears again before he blinked them rapidly away.

"I know this isn't a game, but I did not die, nor am I going to. It was clearly just a warning." I said this in my most soothing tones, but to no avail.

"We are going to heed that warning." His voice held more fear than conviction, and I decided that arguing right now was pointless, especially given how late the hour had become.

"Let's just try to get some sleep," I said, letting my eyes drift close. I was utterly wrung-out but finally felt as though I could sleep through the lingering discomfort.

I would pick this argument back up in the morning.

I slept much later than usual—not surprisingly, of course, given what my body had been through the night before. When I cracked open my eyes, I found Redvers quietly packing our things into our luggage, which he'd laid on the floor next to the wardrobe. I sighed and slipped out of bed, padding across the tile floor in my bare feet. I would argue about this with my husband, but not before I'd had some coffee.

"You're awake," he said, giving me a long once-over as though he expected me to collapse on the floor at his feet. "How are you feeling? And how do you want your dresses folded?"

I ignored the questions and passed into the sitting room, happy to find Sasmit coming through the door with a breakfast tray. "Do you have some coffee for me?"

"Are you certain you want to drink coffee, memsahib? I think perhaps some juice would be better for your stomach this morning." Sasmit looked worried.

I sat on the couch and shook my head. "I will have some juice as well, but I need coffee. I'm feeling much better this morning." That much was true; the symptoms had very nearly passed, and I was mostly just tired, in body but also in spirit, since I knew I had a lengthy argument with my husband ahead of me.

Because I wasn't going anywhere until we solved Gretchen's murder and gave her the justice she deserved.

Sasmit gave a little bob of his head and left the room as quickly as he had come. I was both hopeful that he would return shortly with a pot of hot coffee and grateful that he hadn't argued with me. I only had energy for so much, and I was saving my strength for the battle to stay in Ooty.

Redvers must have sensed my morning resolve because he ceased his packing and came to sit across from me on the chair. "Jane," he started to say.

I simply shook my head. "I'm not leaving." I said the words gently but with conviction. I fully expected to carry out a lengthy argument, but he gazed into my eyes for a long time, then simply sighed. "If I had been poisoned, would you still want to stay?" he asked.

"I see where you are coming from, but I truly need to see this through. I will be very careful and do my best to stay out of harm's way. But we are getting close, and I can't pack up and go."

Redvers nodded. "Very well." He went into the other room and returned with two stacks of papers. One was the stack Sasmit and the old man had pulled from the garbage a few days prior. The other stack was much smaller, a few pieces of paper really, with tight, looping handwriting scrawled on it. "Maharajah Thirunal translated the documents for us and dropped them by while you were . . . indisposed." I could tell he was fighting with himself over what to ask me. The questions likely ranged anywhere from how I'd found the papers to how I'd come to ask the maharajah to translate them for me.

I leaned forward eagerly, holding out a hand. "What do they say?"

Redvers passed the crumpled stack to me, placing the other, small stack on the low table between us. "Nothing much different than we had expected. Kandiyar did have political ambitions, and they included taking Mudaliar's job if he was able to move up."

I only glanced at the papers briefly and then placed them on the table next to the other stack. There was a reason I'd given them to the maharajah in the first place—I couldn't read them, so it was silly of me to have asked for another look at them. "Is that all?" It was a disappointing amount of information indeed.

"He also had complaints about his current employer, Governor Goshen, that were expressed in a letter intended for his father back home, then apparently discarded."

I leaned forward in my seat again. "What kind of complaints?"

"He found the governor's series of mistresses to be distasteful. But he also felt strongly against the governor becoming viceroy. Kandiyar didn't seem to think Goshen has the natural ability to do well in such a position."

"Why would he write such things down, even in a letter home?" I mused. "It seems foolish. Anyone could come in and take your papers, just like I did."

Redvers nodded. "It was foolish of him, although it helps us in the end."

At least my efforts hadn't been a total waste—this was the most interesting bit of information we'd gathered about the governor's secretary, not to mention a potential motive for the governor to eliminate Kandiyar in order to achieve his goal of becoming viceroy. Especially if he thought his secretary might do or say something to keep him from being promoted.

"Might he have known something about the governor? Something that Goshen wouldn't want getting out?" This theory neatly dovetailed with the idea that Goshen was covering something up by sending Inspector Thornycrest away immediately following Kandiyar's "suicide," but I'd already considered and ruled the governor out—more than once.

Redvers was about to reply when Sasmit returned with my pot of coffee, setting it carefully on the table and then shifting awkwardly instead of leaving, squeezing his hands in front of him.

Redvers and I both watched him for a moment. "Is there something else, Sasmit?" I asked.

The porter bobbed his head. "I just want to say, memsahib, that I feel responsible for what happened to you yesterday."

I cocked my head at him, curious about where this was going. Redvers was much more on edge and shot off a question before I could, a distinctly unfriendly tone to his voice. "Why do you say that?"

Sasmit swallowed and cleared his throat, eyes shifting between the two of us. "Because I left the pot of coffee here in your room, anticipating Mrs. Wunderly's arrival. I know that memsahib likes to have hot coffee as often as she can during the day."

I smiled at him. Sasmit really had taken care to learn what I liked, and he went out of his way to provide it. Redvers shot me a dark look, no doubt due to my friendly countenance. But sometime during my ordeal, I had decided there was little chance Sasmit had anything to do with my poisoning, at least not directly. He was entirely too earnest, as evidenced here. There was no way he could have tried to poison me and still serve as our porter without us noticing a change in his behavior.

"You didn't put the leaves in there," I said. It was less a question than a statement. I already knew the answer in my gut.

The man looked stricken, a red flush visible at his throat. "Of course not!" His head bobbed vehemently. "But I must have missed something. I checked the doors to ensure they were locked, but someone was able to get in. And I could swear that I locked the door after I left the coffee for you. But if I had done my job properly, no one would have been able to add the poison to your coffee, memsahib. So I must have made a mistake."

Redvers looked as though he had something to say to that, but I shook my head and cut him off. "It is not your fault, Sasmit. I have no doubt that you did your job quite properly. But whoever added the leaves would have done anything to make sure they got into our room—even stealing a key. Is another key to this room kept somewhere?" I gave Redvers a quelling look, and he frowned but sat back in his seat.

Sasmit frowned. "Yes, memsahib, the owner of the cottage keeps copies of all the keys in his office."

That was easy enough, then. The culprit had likely stolen the spare key to our room from there, or even the master key. It was also useful to know that whoever had done this had come straight to our room and hadn't gotten the coffee from the kitchen area, where they would have been spotted by one of the many servants who worked at the cottage. It meant they knew something of our routine and had waited for an opportunity to present itself. I suspected they had seen Sasmit enter our room with the tray and used the stolen key to slip in behind him to administer the oleander leaves.

"You didn't see anyone when you dropped the coffee off?" I asked.

Sasmit thought for a long moment, then finally bobbed his head. "I did not."

I sighed. That would have been entirely too easy, and our villain was too smart to be so readily caught out. If they'd done the deed themselves, of course. Depending on who was responsible, it was entirely possible they were merely giving orders to someone over whom they held power, which could be any number of people.

The thought sent my fingers to my temples. I truly hated politics.

The smell wafting up from the pot of coffee was too appealing, and I poured myself a cup, then looked to Redvers to see if he had any follow-up questions. He shook his head, fingers tapping on the arm of his chair. I dismissed Sasmit with the assurance that we didn't hold him responsible for what had happened. He was nearly through the door when I decided to ask one final question.

"No one sent you here to work for us, did they?"

Sasmit stopped in his tracks, turning back slowly, and his face told me exactly what I needed to know—someone had indeed planted the porter in our room. But which of the men in power had done it?

CHAPTER TWENTY-NINE

Sasmit looked near tears when he finally turned all the way to face us. This time Redvers stepped in, moving to sit beside me on the couch and gesturing to our porter to have a seat in the chair he had just vacated.

"I couldn't sit with you, sahib—" Sasmit started to say, but Redvers interrupted him.

"I insist."

Redvers' tone brooked no argument, so Sasmit came back across the room and sank into the chair, looking miserable.

"Who sent you to spy on us?" Redvers asked. I was pleased that his tone was at least a touch friendlier than it had been earlier. I had no issue with Sasmit, especially since it appeared he was about to spill everything.

"Paramasivan Subbarayan," Sasmit said with zero hesitation. "He specifically asked for me to be posted in your quarters, sahib." Redvers raised a single brow, and Sasmit continued. "I used to work in his summer cottage, but he had me reassigned here. Well, here and anywhere else he needs me."

"And what precisely is Subbarayan trying to learn by having you here?" I asked as I sipped my coffee. I'd anticipated several names, but the government official wasn't at the top of my list.

"He wants to hear what sahib knows about the resistance to the commission that is coming to India next year."

Redvers and I looked at each other and back at our porter. "Is that all?" Redvers asked.

Sasmit nodded, his face earnest. "It is, sahib. I swear on my mother's grave."

The fact that Subbarayan had Sasmit posted here to gather information was not surprising to me—that type of thing had been going on for centuries and would likely continue for centuries more. As a spy, my husband was an information gatherer as well. No, what I was curious about was why Sasmit had given up the information so easily, which is precisely what I asked him.

"Because you both have been very kind to me, and you did not deserve to be poisoned, memsahib." Sasmit took an unsteady breath. "I will not be part of something like that. I tell you the truth, even if it means I will no longer have a job with Subbarayan."

"Do you have any idea who did it?" I asked.

Sasmit shook his head, but I could tell he had something to say on the subject. "But?" I prompted.

"I am worried that Subbarayan is responsible."

Redvers had been frowning throughout this part of the conversation, and he took over. "Even if he is responsible—and I'm not certain that is the case—neither of us believe that *you* are responsible, Sasmit."

It took some assurance, but the man was finally placated and dismissed. I suspected we would have the best service Sasmit was physically capable of for the rest of our stay, despite the fact that he owed us nothing.

"Subbarayan is not who I would have guessed sent a spy," I said once the door had closed firmly behind Sasmit.

Redvers shook his head wearily. "I'm not surprised by anything I hear about political intrigue anymore. Or anyone—they seem to be capable of anything."

"Should we have him reassigned?" I asked.

Redvers considered for a moment before shaking his head. "I don't see the use. We already know who he's working for, and we can't say the same about anyone else they might send in his place. Better to keep the devil we know."

I nodded. "I also think he's unlikely to report anything on the two of us. Not anymore."

"I agree. I think he's rather finished working for Subbarayan."

I was quiet, then offered up something that had occurred to me while Sasmit had been talking. "Could someone in the kitchen have slipped the leaves into the coffee? If Sasmit was planted here, it's more than possible that someone else was as well. Someone less scrupulous and more willing to poison a stranger on command."

"That had occurred to me as well," Redvers said. "I'll make some inquiries."

That sounded too vague for my liking, as though he was simply placating me. "Once you do that, what is our next step? We still need to interview the staff at the governor's mansion to see if anyone was around just before Kandiyar was killed."

"Jane, *we* are not doing anything. You need to stay here and rest," Redvers said. I opened my mouth to argue, but he held up a hand, and I knew I wouldn't win this round. "I will go over and talk to the staff, see what they know."

I conceded his point. "I will stay here while you do that. Perhaps I'll take a nap." My body betrayed me with a huge yawn, and I covered my mouth before giving him a sheepish smile. Despite the coffee I'd just consumed, I really was still exhausted.

Redvers smiled and came over to give me a kiss on top of my head. "Thank you. I'll report back everything I learn." With that assurance, he took his leave as well, grabbing his straw hat and heading out the door.

Only moments later, Sasmit knocked on the door and came back inside, holding a sealed envelope. "This came for you from the governor's mansion," he said. He handed it over and then excused himself again, not quite meeting my eyes during our interaction. I pursed my lips as he left. I truly hoped that he would be able to move past this awkwardness soon and we could get back on a friendly footing.

I turned the letter over in my hands, curious. Redvers had only just left, so it couldn't be from him; he would have come back to tell me if he'd forgotten something. Instead of grabbing a letter opener from the desk, I impatiently slipped a finger beneath the flap and broke the seal open, removing a single piece of heavy white stationery, noting the neat handwriting flowing across the page.

> *Jane, I know it's short notice, but would you be available to take tea with me this afternoon? No need to reply, simply come to the governor's mansion if you're available.*
> *Sincerely, Lady Goshen*

I was barely finished reading the note before I was changing my clothes into something presentable and running a comb through my hair. I was pleased to know that news of my "illness" hadn't left my quarters; it might prove useful later. And since I was feeling quite a bit better, there was no reason I could see to decline this invitation. I still had quite a lot of questions about Lady Goshen and her role in the various mysteries surrounding Gretchen's death, and this was the perfect opportunity to both ask questions and poke around her quarters a bit.

Of course, I would have to be especially careful to avoid my overprotective husband, who would send me home immediately if he caught sight of me. Yes, I was bone-tired, but I could take a nap when I returned. The matter decided, I put on a pair of T-strap shoes and headed out the door to find a carriage.

It occurred to me, as I left the safety of my quarters, that I might be walking into a trap, albeit a nicely packaged one. But I resolved to stay alert, not drink anything before Lady Goshen did so herself, and be aware of my surroundings.

Trap or no, I wouldn't turn down this opportunity to learn something from the governor's wife.

I found a carriage quite quickly for once and had it carry me all the way to the governor's mansion. The fresh air felt good on my face after a long night of being ill. It also did wonders to help wake me up. I would be fine.

At least that was what I kept telling myself.

Once I'd paid my driver, I eyed the front of the mansion warily. I knew that I needed to avoid the servants' area, since that was where Redvers would likely be. There or in the government offices. I crossed over the threshold, taking care to walk lightly even though there was no one in sight. I cautiously climbed to the second floor, looking for someone who knew where I could find Lady Goshen's quarters. The first person I recognized was Subbarayan, the very topic of our last conversation. I was tempted to ask him how his spying was going, but I managed to offer a polite hello in response to his greeting instead.

"Are you looking for your husband?" Subbarayan asked. "I believe he was heading down to the kitchen." His brows were pulled together, leading me to believe he thought this was odd.

"Erm, no, actually." Although I was glad to know precisely where he was. "Do you happen to know where Lady Goshen's quarters are?"

He blinked once, and I hurried to explain. "I'm to take tea with her."

Subbarayan nodded, then gave me precise directions to where I needed to go.

I was able to make my way to the governor's quarters unseen by anyone but the occasional servant, who couldn't possibly know that I should be resting instead of visiting the governor's wife and was unlikely to inform my husband where I was. The governor's quarters were guarded by a pair of young men in khaki uniform, and I showed my invitation to the one standing to the right of the door. He looked at the note, then me, before handing it back and knocking on the door behind him—two loud, ringing knocks. It was quickly opened by a woman in a cotton sari woven with threads of purple and gold.

"I'm here to take tea with Lady Goshen," I said.

The woman said nothing, holding the door open and nodding for me to follow her inside. I did so, finding Lady Goshen already sipping a cup of tea in her sitting room. With the exception of a few silk throw pillows that reflected the gorgeous textiles I'd seen in the country, the room could have been lifted from any estate in England. Tasteful wallpaper was peppered with paintings of rural scenes. There were plenty of horses represented, and I wondered if Lady Goshen had especially requested them. Lady Goshen was seated on a stiff-looking floral love seat, upholstered within an inch of its life.

Lady Goshen set her teacup in its saucer when she spotted me in the doorway. "Mrs. Wunderly! I'm so pleased that you could join me on such short notice."

I smiled graciously and took a seat across from her. "Thank you for the invitation." I didn't mention that I'd sent a note earlier in the week inviting myself to tea or that I'd been quite sick from being poisoned only hours before. I hoped I didn't look as though I'd been up all night—I hadn't done a thorough job of checking the mirror before rushing out the door. "But I must insist you call me Jane."

"Jane, then," Lady Goshen said with a smile, although she didn't offer the use of her own Christian name in response, which I found amusing.

We observed the formalities of small talk while a cup of tea was prepared for me and a tray of sandwiches was requested from the servant who had yet to speak a word. Once she had left the room with the list of requests Lady Goshen had given her, my hostess explained. "She's mute. But she does an excellent job despite that."

"I'm sure she does," I murmured, pretending to take a sip of the tea I was now holding. "I was pleased to get your note. What did you want to discuss with me?" I asked.

Lady Goshen cocked her head, either confused or doing a fair imitation of it. "Why did you think that?" She shook her head. "I was just a bit lonely for conversation with someone who speaks English as their native language." She waved a hand. "As you can see, not everyone here even speaks."

I nearly asked "what about your husband?" but managed to stop myself in time. "Understandable," I said instead. I sought a mundane question I could ask Lady Goshen to keep the small talk going long enough to be polite. All I could really think about was how I was going to excuse myself to conduct a search.

"It's terrible about Mr. Kandiyar," I said, wincing at my own words. This was what my brain came up with for a mundane question? Perhaps I *should* still be resting. "I'm sure your husband is devastated."

Lady Goshen didn't seem to notice my discomfort at my own question. "It's a terrible waste. Vihan was a brilliant secretary and a very kind man. He will be missed."

I noticed that she hadn't spoken about her husband's re-action, only saying Kandiyar would be missed, but not by whom. "Will the governor hire another secretary?"

"Oh, yes," Lady Goshen said. "He is quite useless at typing and such. I believe he's already started the interview process."

"That's quite fast," I said.

She shrugged. "He's a busy man and can't waste too much time on social niceties."

I decided to plunge further into the murky political waters, since we were already swimming in them. "And whoever takes the post will go with him if he becomes viceroy?"

The question didn't even faze the woman. "I would assume so, if George can manage to pull it off. The current viceroy was ill for a short time, and George stepped in as acting viceroy. Only for a few months, but he got a taste of it and wanted more." Lady Goshen rolled her eyes.

Her dismissive attitude toward her husband's ambitions surprised me. In fact, if I thought about all the conversations we'd had so far, it sounded like Lady Goshen was disenchanted with her husband altogether. Could there be someone else for Lady Goshen?

There wasn't a polite way to ask that question, but my intestines took that moment to gurgle unhappily. I put a hand to my stomach and apologized, then asked where the facilities were located. Lady Goshen gave me directions, although she did so with the faint shadow of a frown pulling at her brow. I couldn't blame her, really, for any number of reasons, suspicion being the last on that list.

I followed her instructions down the hall and availed myself of the facilities, but did so in record time—I was grateful that my guts were working with me right now instead of against me. I silently opened the door to the bathroom—leaving the water in the sink running—and, seeing no one, tiptoed to the closed door at the very end of the hall. I was pleased to see that it was her personal bedroom, and I quickly went inside, closing the door behind me. I only had a few short minutes to look around before my absence would be noticed, and I got right to work. I opened the wardrobe and peered inside, seeing nothing out of the ordinary. I then went to her dressing table, pulling open drawers and taking a quick inventory. There were hairpins and combs, but nothing that looked remotely suspicious or even interesting. My eyes lit upon a small piece of paper, folded up, and I grabbed it and unfolded it quickly, then greedily scanned the contents.

It was a love note, and a rather ribald one at that, but contained nothing that would tell me who the sender was, although it clearly wasn't the governor, based on the use of the phrase "should your husband find out."

It meant that I was correct in my assumptions that Lady Goshen was having her own affair, but I wasn't sure this tidbit had been worth the trip.

A knock at the bathroom door came, and I froze, waiting to see if anything was said. I quickly refolded the note and replaced it, then moved stealthily to the bedroom door and put my ear to it. There was another knock, but no one said anything, which I thought was odd. If it was Lady Goshen, she would surely ask if I was alright. Footsteps moved down the hall and as soon as I thought was reasonable, I slipped out of the bedroom and back into the bathroom next door, shutting off the water after splashing a bit on my face.

I was just leaving the bathroom when Lady Goshen appeared from around the corner. "Jane, I was beginning to worry about you. My maid knocked, and when you didn't answer, she became concerned. She indicated something was happening, but I couldn't tell what."

The mute woman stood behind the governor's wife, a curious, knowing expression on her face. I wondered how she'd been able to relay all that information to Lady Goshen without the ability to speak. I also wondered if she suspected where I'd actually been and whether she would be able to let Lady Goshen know.

I supposed I was about to find out whether the woman was really mute, after all.

CHAPTER THIRTY

I excused myself not long after that incident, claiming trouble with my stomach, which explained my lengthy absence. Lady Goshen was sympathetic, tsking and telling me to be more careful about what I ate and drank in this country. "A bite of the wrong food can lay you low for days," she said cheerfully.

I smiled weakly and slipped from her quarters and then from the governor's mansion entirely, deciding a nap was in order. My stomach was mostly fine, but I was truly exhausted. I'd been tired when I went there, but the small talk had taken what reserves I had left. My body was still recovering from my bout with the oleander, and going to see Lady Goshen had probably been overdoing it. I hated to admit when Redvers was right, but he had been in this case. I really did need more time to rest and recuperate.

At the same time, I was glad I'd snooped around Lady Goshen's quarters, even if I had likely been found out by her maid. The note had at least confirmed for me that Lady Goshen was involved with someone else, but who could that someone be? Mudaliar or Subbarayan seemed unlikely choices, especially given how the woman had spoken about the local people, as though she had a bad taste in her mouth. So who then? And was her paramour involved in the murders?

Back in my room, I shucked off my shoes and went straight to bed, lying on top of the covers and closing my eyes for just a moment. I wasn't asleep, but neither was I fully awake when a few minutes later the mattress beside me sank with my husband's weight.

"Well, what did you learn?" he asked.

I cracked one eye open to look at him. "Whatever do you mean?"

Redvers pinned me with his eyes, and I sighed, opening both of mine but remaining as I was, fully reclined on the bed. "Very well, I didn't learn much. I took a brief look around Lady Goshen's bedroom and found a note confirming that she is having an affair, but not with whom. And nothing else incriminating, more the pity."

"And did you learn anything from Lady Goshen herself?"

I gave that a moment's thought before answering. "I don't think she cares much for her husband."

"That's certainly not unusual, especially among her set."

I tilted my head, acknowledging his point. "True, but she was very dismissive of him and his ambitions. Not surprising, I suppose, since she's involved with someone else. It also explains her nonchalance about his mistresses."

"I wonder who it is, though," Redvers mused. "I doubt she would consort with an Indian, so it would have to be someone in the government."

"I couldn't even begin to speculate about that," I said, closing my eyes again.

Redvers gave a quiet chuckle and kissed me on the forehead. "Perhaps when you've had a chance to rest."

I made a mmm-ing noise. "Which is what you suggested in the first place."

"But I'm far too gracious to say I told you so."

*　*　*

I awoke several hours later, thirsty and disoriented. I had obviously slept quite hard, and once I'd taken a moment to remember where I was, I wandered into the sitting room in search of something to drink. The room was empty, although Redvers had left me a note. I read it while I sipped my water.

> *Jane, I've gone to speak with Lala Rai. I'll be back soon, hopefully before you wake. Love, R.*

I couldn't be annoyed with him for doing some investigating while I slept, especially since I had been out cold for a few hours, although I could wish that I were there with him. It was now late afternoon, nearly evening. Did I remember the route to where Rai was staying well enough to get there on my own?

I was pulling on my walking boots before I had any time to think about it. I was feeling much better after my nap, and even if I couldn't find my way to the estate house, some exercise would feel good. Gentle exercise, of course. But a walk to stretch my legs and get the blood moving would be most welcome.

I stepped into the fresh air and took a deep breath, savoring the mountain air. I hadn't had much time to think about how ill I had been, but I was finding myself grateful to be out and about, walking on my own two feet instead of six feet under. The poison had been a warning, although the administrator clearly didn't know me at all—they had merely strengthened my resolve to find Gretchen's killer instead of frightening me off the path.

These musings occupied my mind as I walked in the general direction Redvers and I had taken the morning after Gretchen's botched burial. I walked slowly, taking my time and trying not to push myself too hard and overdo things. It was an unfamiliar feeling, but at least the countryside gave me plenty to enjoy while I walked at what was nearly a me- ander. I stopped entirely and at a very respectful distance when I came across a water buffalo standing in the path— I'd been warned that the creatures were also quite danger- ous and to give them a wide berth. The fellow eventually moved off the path and back into the woods, and I hurried my steps to get past him without inciting the beast's ire.

I paused once or twice more, trying to get my bearings and fervently hoping that I was going in the right direction. I breathed a happy sigh of relief when I spotted the turnoff to the estate, hurrying my steps as the house finally came into view.

I paused in the shadow of a tree, listening for a beat be- fore following the low sound of men's voices along a gravel walkway around the side of the house. As soon as I cleared the side of the building, I could see a small group of men gathered in the garden, seated in chairs pulled into an infor- mal circle. There was chatter, but the closer I crept, the qui- eter the group became until every one of them was looking at me curiously. Except Redvers. Even at a distance I could see him roll his eyes.

The men were silent as I joined them. The gentleman who had assisted me on my last visit fetched a chair for me while my husband assured the group at large that I was his wife and could be trusted. There were perhaps six local men there, at least two of whom I'd never seen before, and they regarded me warily. I couldn't say that I blamed them. I was both an outsider and a woman.

There was a long pause while the men exchanged glances, and then Lala Rai took over. "Mudaliar, I'm glad you could make it. We were discussing the best way to proceed."

This led me to believe that Mudaliar had also just ar- rived. Strange, since I hadn't seen him on my walk, but he'd likely been far ahead of me. I had been moving rather slowly.

It also appeared the men were going to ignore my presence entirely, and for once I was happy to melt into the background. I wanted them to forget I was there and speak freely among themselves.

Mudaliar greeted the group, then addressed Rai. "I'm still working to weaken Subbarayan's position before we hold another vote."

I assumed they were discussing having another vote of confidence and attempting to push Subbarayan out of office so that Mudaliar could take over. I didn't ask any questions, though, instead holding my tongue and absorbing everything that was said. I could ask Redvers for clarification on muddy points later.

But Rai spoke up, asking the very question that I had been wondering. "That's all well and good, but do you believe in independence from the Raj? Or are you simply siding with us to advance your own cause?"

Mudaliar's face remained exactly the same, and I couldn't help but think this was quite a handy skill for a politician—never showing your true emotions. I would be hopeless at this, since my face often betrayed me, no matter how hard I tried to control it.

"Does it matter?" Mudaliar asked.

A glance around showed that a few men looked surprised at the blunt response. Lala Rai, however, was not impressed. "It does matter. Because we are going to do whatever is necessary to stop this commission. I need to know if you're willing to do the same, or if you are merely using us for your own political gain."

Mudaliar regarded Rai for a long moment, clearly weighing his next words. "I do truly believe in independence for our country, but I also am not willing to give my life for it."

Rai met his direct gaze, then bobbed his head, seeming to accept this answer. "Very well."

Redvers and I exchanged a look. It was impossible to say

whether Mudaliar was being entirely truthful, but his answer was unwelcome enough to the group that I suspected it might be. It also made me wonder what the other men here were willing to do in the name of independence. Would they be willing to kill for it?

Of course, Gretchen was on their side, so I couldn't see a reason why any of them would murder her and cover it up. If anything, she would have been a useful ally. And she could only have been useful to them if she were alive.

Mudaliar's answer meant that I was moving him well down my list of suspects. I couldn't remove him entirely, but for now, I thought we needed to look elsewhere for our killer.

Chapter Thirty-one

The discussion between the men continued for some time, although it didn't seem as though they had reached any conclusions by the time Redvers and I took our leave. We were both quiet until the isolated estate was out of eyeshot and, more importantly, earshot. Mudaliar had elected to stay behind, so it was only the two of us making the return trip.

"I should have known you wouldn't stay put. Even though someone poisoned you only yesterday," Redvers said. There was no anger in his voice or even frustration. It was more of a musing on his part.

I just smiled and patted his arm. "Perhaps we should dine at a local restaurant for supper," I suggested.

"Good idea." He glanced at me. "You're feeling well enough to eat?"

I nodded, happy that this was true, but also knowing we were both thinking it was less likely that someone could slip either of us poison at a restaurant where we were unknown as anything other than foreign visitors. I didn't want to avoid eating or drinking anything from the kitchen at our cottage for the rest of our stay, but it felt safer to eat the next few meals somewhere neutral.

"Have you spoken to the staff at the Stone House?" I asked.

He nodded. "No one saw anything."

"Of course not," I sighed. "And they don't work for anyone besides the cottage owner either, I assume."

"Of course not," Redvers said.

I could tell he was equally frustrated with our lack of progress. I decided to change the subject. "I'm inclined to believe Mudaliar, which moves him to the bottom of my list of suspects."

"But not completely removed?" Redvers asked.

"No one can be removed from my list. Except possibly Rai, like you said before."

"You won't like what I tell you next, then," Redvers said.

I stopped in my tracks to look at him. He turned, and his lips quirked at the expression on my face. He tilted his head indicating that we should keep going, and I took a few hasty steps to catch up to him. "Well?" I prodded with both words and a finger in his side.

"Rai said he was the one who tripped the casket bearer at Gretchen's funeral."

I stopped again, my mouth agape, poking finger dropped back to my side. "Why would he admit to such a thing?"

Redvers turned to look at me. "We'll never get to supper if you won't keep going," he said.

"Quit shocking me, then."

He chuckled and took a step back toward me. "He admitted to me that he had done it. He said he wanted the other side to know that the body was missing."

I frowned. "Why would Rai want that?"

"So that when he sent a threatening note—or series of notes—he had proof that her body was missing and he was the one who had it."

I was moving again, although slowly, trying to get Rai's motives to make sense in my head. "I suppose I can see his reasoning." If the pro-commission folks thought Gretchen was buried safely in her grave, they might think Rai's claim that the Raj was responsible for her death was nothing more than a made-up accusation. But if they knew Rai had the body . . . Well, it lent credence to his claims that the resistance knew something damning. I wondered if Rai also thought he might be able to stir up some unrest with Gretchen's body and proof that the Raj had a hand in her murder.

"It seems a convoluted way to go about things, but very well," I finally said, before turning my attention to the threatening notes Redvers had mentioned. "You aren't suggesting that Rai sent the threatening notes on the secretary's typewriter, are you? He had no access to the building."

"No, I think he sent a note to the governor, but it was handwritten. You're correct—Rai has no access to the governor's mansion or the typewriter. I don't think he was responsible for the other notes."

I sighed. Perhaps I shouldn't have been so hasty in taking Rai off my list, though. I was about to say as much when we came upon an intersection leading into the heart of Ooty. We had gone to the left, in search of a restaurant for supper, when I heard someone call my name. Redvers and I both stopped and saw Maharajah Thirunal coming up quickly behind us. While we waited for him to reach us, I reflected that he was dressed in a much less flashy way today, although even from a distance I could tell that his kurta was made from quality material. But he looked less like the ruler of a kingdom and more like just another wealthy man. He was alone, and I wondered if he'd snuck away from his bodyguards and was dressed as he was in an attempt to blend in.

"Mrs. Wunderly, Mr. Wunderly," he greeted us each in turn. "I have learned something that you will want to know."

I dropped my voice to a near-whisper. "Have you opened the box?"

He nodded.

"Let's find a restaurant with a private table before we say anything else," Redvers said.

The maharajah and I both glanced around and agreed—we needed to find somewhere we wouldn't be overheard. We were still on the outskirts of the city, and Redvers led us to a local restaurant off the main road that was nearly deserted. We sat at a table toward the back of the small room, feeling confident that no one would be able to hear our conversation, and if anyone approached, they would be quickly spotted. The windows were open, and the breeze that brushed over my bare arms prickled my skin into goose flesh. Out of the sun, it was almost chilly now.

Redvers and I both looked at the maharajah expectantly, and he produced several tightly folded sheets of paper from his tunic pocket. He put the tight bundle on the table, his hand hovering over it for a second before pushing it across the scratched wood toward the two of us. Redvers picked it up and unwound the sheets, and I stood behind his shoulder to read the top sheet at the same time he did.

I frowned. "What am I looking at here?" It was in English but contained a lot of political jargon that I didn't have the patience to wade through. Redvers continued reading, but I took my seat, deciding that the maharajah could explain the significance of the papers to me.

"The top paper looks like correspondence between Governor Goshen and the current viceroy of India. Goshen is trying to learn whether the viceroy will be retiring. The other sheets are correspondence to various other members of the

Raj indicating that the governor has a plan to push the viceroy out of his position and take over."

There seemed to be a lot of that going around—political ambitions that required usurping someone else. "Why do you think Gretchen had them?"

"Blackmail," Redvers said simply, placing the papers back on the table. The maharajah nodded, and I sat back in my chair.

"You think she was trying to blackmail the governor? To what end?"

"I think it's likely she was trying to get Governor Goshen to disband the commission. Or at least go against it, weaken its authority, and ultimately, hand more power to the people of India."

That made sense. And frankly, I respected that Gretchen was willing to go to such lengths to help the cause she believed in so strongly. Unfortunately, it was probably what got her killed.

"You didn't mention the last sheet there," Maharajah Thirunal said, nodding his head toward the papers. Redvers gestured for the maharajah to go ahead. "The last is a note sent to the governor informing him that his wife is having an affair."

I gasped. "Was it sent to him? Did the governor actually see the note?"

The maharajah bobbed his head. "It's impossible to say, but it seems likely. It looks like Gretchen had collected all the other bits of correspondence after they'd reached their recipients as well."

"She must have had a wide network of people willing to help her in order to collect these," Redvers said. "She couldn't have done it all by herself."

The maharajah nodded. "She would have had much help,

but I think it would have been easy for her. Especially since she was on the side of native independence."

I agreed, but couldn't help wondering how the governor took the news about his wife's affair.

Redvers tapped his fingers on the table. "The question is with whom is Lady Goshen having the affair?"

I frowned. That was the piece I couldn't quite work out.

CHAPTER THIRTY-TWO

While the men speculated on who the object of Lady Goshen's affections may be, I turned my mind to who might have the information. A servant in the home, especially an observant one, usually knew everything that happened. So, who on the governor's household staff might be willing to tell us what they knew about Lady Goshen's activities?

Sasmit was a good resource for this question. The man was still troubled by his perceived part in my being poisoned, and I would present this as a way to make it up to me. It would benefit both parties—I could learn what we needed to, and perhaps he would be able to get past his guilt. I wanted that for both of us.

"I'll ask Sasmit," I said, interrupting the men and their idle speculation.

Redvers looked amused. "You'll ask him what?"

I smiled. "I suppose you couldn't hear my thought process, could you? Very well, I'll spell it out. Household staff usually know what is happening in the house, so I'll ask Sasmit to bring us the staff members most likely to know who Lady Goshen is having an affair with. And we will ask them to talk to us."

I watched as both men thought it through, then nodded.

"It's a good plan," Maharajah Thirunal said. "But why will this Sasmit help you?"

"He feels guilty that I was poisoned."

The shock on the maharajah's face was enough to tell me that he hadn't heard the news. Nor had he been a part of it, not that I'd ever considered him as a suspect. Before he could say anything, I raised a hand. "I think it was just a warning. It wasn't enough to be fatal, clearly, since I'm sitting here."

Beside me, Redvers sighed. "You sound so cavalier about the fact that someone tried to kill you."

I patted his arm. "As I just said, I don't think they were trying to kill me. Just giving me a warning." I could tell both men were about to start an argument about my involvement in our next steps, so I headed them off by signaling to the restaurant owner that we wanted service. "Let's order, shall we?"

After our delicious and poison-free meal, all three of us returned to our cottage in order to locate Sasmit, which was a simple task since he appeared moments after we took seats in the sitting room.

"Sasmit, we need help," I said to him. "And then, I hope you will feel as though you have more than made things right."

"Anything I can do, I will, memsahib," he said solemnly.

I nodded and thanked him. "We need to learn some information about Lady Goshen from her staff. Who would be the best person to ask? Someone that will actually answer our questions."

Sasmit only gave this a moment's thought. "I will bring you someone." He was nearly at the door when he turned. "Do you need any refreshments, memsahib? I apologize that I did not ask."

All three of us shook our heads, and he hurried out the

door. Once he'd left, I couldn't help but speculate about the suspect who'd climbed to the top of my list. "As far as I can tell, everything points to Governor Goshen."

"I'm not convinced that he's responsible, at least not entirely, but I agree that things do point to him," Redvers said.

The maharajah was quiet, stroking his moustache. "Is it possible there are two separate parties that are responsible for the murders?"

It was an angle that I hadn't fully considered before, and I did so now. It seemed that the two murders were connected, but was it possible that they weren't?

Redvers reached a conclusion before I did. "While anything is possible, based on the threats and our having spoken with Kandiyar just before he was killed, I think it's likely that we are looking at the same person for both."

Maharajah Thirunal bobbed his head, then spread his hands. "I'm only offering suggestions that you may not have considered."

"And we truly appreciate that," Redvers assured him.

With the excitement of my poisoning, I'd forgotten to ask Redvers if he had learned anything from the governor's staff about our suspects' whereabouts during the time that Kandiyar was killed. I asked him now, while there was a brief lull in the conversation.

He grimaced. "Nothing useful, I'm afraid. No one could think of anyone that was upstairs during that time, which of course doesn't mean that no one was there, just that no one was seen. It sounds as though the staff was quite busy with supper preparations—their own, as well as supper for the government employees."

I wasn't surprised to hear it, but it was disappointing. I was becoming increasingly frustrated at our inability to narrow the field of suspects or find any evidence that definitively incriminated one person. It wasn't as if we could go accuse the governor of murder—Redvers was likely to actually lose his job if we did that. And that was setting aside the fact that Governor Goshen was never going to admit culpability for murder, even if it were true. The same went for the other suspects on my list; they were highly unlikely to admit to killing two people and covering it up. The staff was really our only hope for retrieving information, and it was frustrating to be at a dead end otherwise.

My internal frustration was mounting, and I was relieved when Sasmit returned with two local women in colorful cotton saris whose faces I recognized from my visit to Lady Goshen's quarters. I raised an eyebrow. "You really do deliver, Sasmit."

He gave a little smile and a bow, then excused himself as we turned our attention to the women. I was surprised to realize one of them was the maid that Lady Goshen had assured me was mute. I almost called Sasmit back to ask why he'd brought her along, but he'd already disappeared out the door.

Both women looked nervous, one playing with the long black-and-gray braid that hung over her shoulder and the other twisting her hands in her orange and pink sari. Redvers invited them to sit down, but they both bobbed their heads in a way that I took to mean a refusal. I couldn't blame them. They probably had no idea why they'd been summoned here, and they were now faced with the three of us, one of whom was an Indian king, even if he wasn't currently dressed for the part.

I decided it was probably best if I took the lead. "Ladies, thank you so much for coming. We need to ask you some questions about Lady Goshen."

Neither woman moved a body part in any sort of acknowledgement. Did they speak English? Sasmit wouldn't have brought them if at least one of them didn't. But I hoped they would answer the questions instead of watching me with wary eyes, as they were now.

"Does Lady Goshen have a friend other than her husband?"

Both women frowned, presumably at the word "friend," and I realized that I was being a little too opaque with my questioning. I decided to try a different tact.

"Is Lady Goshen having an affair?" I asked. "I promise that the reasons why we ask are important. We think someone was killed because of this secret." That wasn't entirely true, but I was hoping the dramatic statement would spark a response to my rather direct question.

The taller woman tugged on her braid but said nothing. The mute woman glanced at her companion, straightened a bit, then in a rusty voice said, "Memsahib is gone at strange hours. But we do not know who she is with. She is careful around the staff."

My mouth fell open in shock. "You're not mute."

CHAPTER THIRTY-THREE

The woman shrugged. "I prefer not to speak." Then she shut her mouth as if that were her quota of words for the week. Her companion picked up for her. "Fatima finds it easier to claim she is mute, then she does not have to make conversation with the British who come here."

I understood why she felt that way. Making small talk was one of my least favorite activities; pretending to be mute was a creative way to avoid it. My eyes narrowed. "Did she—"

Fatima bobbed her head emphatically, and her companion answered for her. "She told no one that you were in Lady Goshen's bedroom instead of the bathroom." She cocked her head. "No one but me, that is."

I supposed at this point it didn't matter much either way, because it seemed the only way we were going to learn the name of Lady Goshen's paramour was to confront the woman herself. And since that was the case, it mattered very little whether she knew that I'd been snooping around her quarters. She'd soon be offended anyway.

We thanked the women for their time and dismissed them. They were eager to leave and rushed from the room. I looked at the maharajah and my husband. "I think we should divide and conquer."

Redvers raised an eyebrow. "And how do you propose we do that?"

"I'll find Lady Goshen and speak with her. Well, confront her. And you should speak with the governor," I said.

"Are you certain you're feeling up to this?"

I nodded, distracted. "I took quite a long nap and feel very well, thank you." I was already considering another topic. "Do you think Lady Goshen could be having an affair with either Mudaliar or Subbarayan? Or even Smith?"

"It's possible," Redvers said. "Perhaps we'll talk with each of them as well."

Maharajah Thirunal nodded. "We'll use Gretchen's blackmail note to . . . entice them to talk."

I was a little disappointed that I wouldn't be there to watch those interviews. I suspected there would be more than a simple enticement involved.

The three of us stood and stepped outside. I was surprised to see that the sun was quite low in the sky. It was nearly dark, which meant I was grateful for the company on the walk over to the governor's mansion. It also meant that I would be waiting for at least one of them to walk back to our quarters as well.

At the mansion, the three of us parted ways, hoping to find the targets of our inquiries. I went to the governor's quarters and was stopped by the guards at the door. I made my case for speaking with Lady Goshen and was informed that she wasn't in but was set to return at any moment. It took some negotiating, but one of the guards recognized me from tea and finally agreed to let me wait inside. I made myself comfortable in the sitting room, refusing the offer of refreshments. It was far too late in the day for coffee, and I was quite sure the taste of English tea would never grow on me. And even though I had enjoyed the chai tea I'd been served at the plantation, I didn't want to bother asking for some. It seemed time-intensive, and I didn't plan on being there long.

While I waited, I hoped that Redvers and Maharajah Thirunal were having better luck than I was. The guard at the door had seemed confident about Lady Goshen's impending return, although as the minutes ticked by, I started to wonder if he had simply been telling me what I wanted to hear. I soon grew restless and wandered around the sitting room, picking up decorative ornaments and setting them back down. I was preparing to make another foray into Lady Goshen's bedroom when the door to the suite finally opened and she stepped inside. Lady Goshen startled when she saw me, obviously surprised that anyone was here.

"Mrs. Wunderly, you gave me a fright!" she said.

"My apologies, I assumed the guard would have told you I was here."

She frowned. "They know better than to speak to me unless spoken to, so how would I have known?"

It was on the tip of my tongue to say "how offensive," but I bit the words back. Neither of us took a seat, staring at each other across the sitting area, instead.

"What can I do for you?" Lady Goshen asked. "I'm in quite a hurry, I'm expected somewhere in a few minutes."

"To see the man you're having an affair with?" I asked. My tone was casual, but my eyes were intent on her face, watching for a reaction.

She pressed her lips together and played with her wedding ring, twisting it around her finger. It was obvious she didn't want to admit to the affair. But I was having none of that—the time for politeness was long over. "I already know you're having an affair with Subbarayan," I said. "So you might as well tell me everything."

At the mention of Subbarayan's name Lady Goshen frowned heavily. "Subbarayan? That Indian man? Heavens, why would I have an affair with him?"

"He's not bad-looking," I said, as though his looks were what she objected to. I'd blurted out his name as a test and her reaction confirmed that she would not take an Indian lover, so it was unlikely to be Mudaliar either, but who else could it be? She didn't seem the type to consort with mere civil servants. No, it would have to be someone with an important post.

"Feodore and I have had an arrangement for a long time now," Lady Goshen said, interrupting my musings.

It took me several beats to realize who Feodore was. "Feodore Smith? The secretary of state?"

"We've known each other for a long time," she said defensively. "And he understands me."

I doubted that was true, but she was going to believe what she wanted to. "Okay," I said slowly. Did that mean Feodore Smith was responsible for the rest of it as well? The notes, the murders, my poisoning? But Lady Goshen continued talking, not giving me time to work anything else out.

"He sent me out to talk with Savithri when I first arrived here." Her lips pursed in distaste. "That's when you saw me at the plantation."

"Why would he send you out there?"

"Feo wanted me to see if the woman knew anything about Gretchen, anything he might be able to use to stop her meddling. I liked Gretchen, I really did, but she did tend to meddle in matters best left to the men."

I could feel my lip curl in distaste. This woman just kept getting more unlikeable. I would be happy to leave and never set eyes on her again.

"Is that why he went to see Savithri also?" I asked before I could think better of it. Gretchen was already dead by that point, so I wondered what reason Smith had had to talk with the governor's mistress. Lady Goshen didn't answer, still twisting her ring, and I sighed.

"And did you try to poison me as well?"

Lady Goshen finally looked shocked. "How gauche. I would never. What makes you think you were poisoned?" She paused. "Although now that I think about it, Feo did say that you'd been unwell. I don't remember when that was, though." She waved a hand. I didn't bother to point out that I'd "been unwell" when she invited me to tea—I suspected she didn't think about anyone but herself, and as soon as others were out of sight, they were out of mind as well. "That was why I wasn't surprised when you needed to leave our tea so abruptly. Otherwise I would have commented on what poor taste that was, to even come in the first place when you were ill."

From what I could tell, Feodore Smith was the only person outside our cottage who knew I'd been ill, which led me to believe that he was the reason for it. I was beginning to think that Smith was in fact our culprit for everything—the murders, the poison, even the notes.

I nearly told her that I'd come in order to search her room just to offend her further but managed to ask another question instead. "You changed your story about what happened to Gretchen. You first told me she had been murdered, but then you said it was a tiger attack. Did Feodore tell you to change your story?"

She looked deeply uncomfortable, and a red flush was working its way up her neck. "That was a mistake that I made. I misunderstood things but corrected myself."

I just looked at her, although she avoided my gaze. I finally shook my head. I knew in my heart that there had been no misunderstanding. Lady Goshen simply didn't want to believe that Smith might be responsible for anything but a little gossip. She didn't want to admit to herself, let alone me, that her lover might be responsible for murder.

*　*　*

After that interaction, I quickly excused myself and left Lady Goshen to her own thoughts. I hoped they were troubled, because mine certainly were. I was now convinced that Feodore Smith was likely responsible for everything, including both murders, although I didn't have the foggiest idea what his motivations might be. I needed to find Redvers and the maharajah so that we could discuss the matter further and then decide how to confront Smith. I didn't think it would be easy since Smith was the secretary of state for the entire country; he held quite a lot of political weight and power. He wasn't likely to cave easily, so we needed a strategic plan on how to approach him. I also had doubts about how much he'd actually done himself. It was likely he had a lackey doing dirty work for him that I hadn't identified yet, so perhaps that was an angle we could explore.

I paced the halls of all three floors in the governor's mansion, but neither my husband nor the maharajah was anywhere to be seen. I stepped outside, taking in how truly dark it had become. I had no intentions of walking back to our quarters alone, and I couldn't imagine that Redvers or Thirunal would have gone back without me; I had been quite clear about walking after dark. Gretchen's death was a murder, but that didn't mean a tiger wasn't still lurking in the grass somewhere nearby.

I stood there for some time, uncertain about my next move. I'd already checked the entirety of the mansion. Where else could they be? I was just working up the courage to either hire a carriage to take me back to my quarters or check the mansion again when I caught sight of a man on a horse in the distance, coming at a near gallop. I quickly recognized the maharajah and realized that he appeared to be carrying something, but I couldn't yet tell what it was.

He was within shouting distance when I realized what the maharajah was carrying in one hand, using the other to handle the reins. It was a rifle.

CHAPTER THIRTY-FOUR

I didn't know why the maharajah had a weapon with him, but my anxiety spiked, knowing that whatever had happened, it wasn't good. I also had a sinking feeling about my husband's whereabouts since he wasn't with Thirunal.

"Have you seen Mr. Wunderly?" the maharajah asked once he'd slowed his mount and pulled it around so that he could speak to me without shouting. The horse danced in place as I shook my head, stomach now roiling. Where could Redvers have gone?

The maharajah must have read the worry on my face because he answered my unspoken question. "We split up once we reached the mansion." He nodded at the building with his head. I realized they must have decided this after I had gone my own way to see Lady Goshen. "Redvers was meant to speak with the governor, and I was set to speak with Mudaliar and Subbarayan."

"You didn't see him after that? Do you know if he found the governor?"

The maharajah bobbed his head. I still didn't know if that was a yes or a no, so I was glad when he also explained his answer. "I do not know. I found Mudaliar, who clearly did not know what I was talking about. And then I went to look for Redvers. I found the governor in his office, working late. I asked the man if he had seen your husband, and he had not."

"Do you think he was telling the truth?" I had little doubt that even though plenty of suspicion had been thrown the governor's way at various times during our investigation, he was being set up by Feodore Smith. As the governor's secretary, Kandiyar, had been—a setup that had ultimately cost Kandiyar his life.

I could only hope it hadn't already cost Redvers his own.

The maharajah considered my question only briefly. "I do think he spoke the truth. But I do not know where Redvers could have gone. I searched that floor and the one below, and I could not find him." He looked at me apologetically.

"It was Feodore Smith, the secretary of state for India," I said, even though Thirunal knew full well who Smith was. "Redvers must have found him first, and something happened. But where would they have gone?" I thought wildly. "Did you check the garden?"

"I did not," Thirunal said, his horse already carrying him in that direction. I moved as quickly as I could, although Thirunal obviously gained quite a lead on me. As the maharajah rounded the corner of the building, he slowed his horse and leapt off, leaving the animal unattended as he hurried into the garden. The garden paths were narrow and would be difficult to navigate on horseback. I kept a respectful distance from the horse as I ran past and into the garden, hopeful that we would find my husband.

The only person we saw, however, was Subbarayan, sitting on a bench. He looked at us, brow furrowed.

"Have you seen Redvers?" I asked breathlessly.

Subbarayan shook his head, still frowning at us.

I looked to the maharajah. His brow was also deeply furrowed, which did nothing to soothe my anxiety. "How long do you think he's been gone?" I asked.

Subbarayan stood. "Can I be of assistance?" He joined us, but I ignored him, waiting for the maharajah's answer.

Thirunal shook his head. "Maybe half an hour?"

I looked about frantically. "Where could Smith have taken him in that amount of time?" I hated to admit that it was long enough that they could be almost anywhere by now. I thought frantically. If Smith was going to kill my husband like he'd killed the rest, where would he take him?

Maybe they would go to where he had murdered Gretchen. It didn't make a whole lot of sense, but it was the best I could come up with. My feet were moving fast in that direction before I even spoke a word to the men who were now trailing in my wake.

"Where do you think Smith took him?" Thirunal had remounted his horse, and he held the reins tight, as though he were about to take off at any moment.

"The edge of the woods. My guess is another tiger attack would be most convenient for him."

"Did you say Smith?" Subbarayan asked.

Maharajah Thirunal had already taken off on the horse, well ahead of us already.

I simply nodded to Subbarayan's question, my feet not slowing for a moment. I was glad the maharajah had thought to retrieve a horse and a rifle, even though I had no idea where he might have gotten the weapon from. I hoped we wouldn't have need of it, but it was better to have it than not.

Subbarayan and I were hurrying along the path in silence, our footsteps and strained breathing the only sound bouncing off the trees. I'd become accustomed to those sounds over the last few minutes, so when I heard something different in the trees off to my right, I recognized it immediately as worth noting, and I stopped in my tracks. Subbarayan came to a halt beside me, and I was grateful that he seemed to immediately understand that he should keep silent rather than ask what I'd heard.

I heard the sound again. It was definitely footsteps coming through the thick grove of trees, but whether it was human or animal, it was impossible to say. Could it be the maharajah? I couldn't see why he would have left the path, though.

The sound of hoofbeats came from ahead of us, and Thirunal on his horse rounded the bend. Dirt flew up from the horse's feet as it came to an abrupt stop. Even before the maharajah appeared, I was waving my hand and motioning for him to be quiet. He leapt from the horse, rifle in hand, and came to stand beside us.

There were no more sounds from the trees, only the horse snorting and breathing heavily a few yards away. I looked at the maharajah and indicated the woods beyond, and he nodded his understanding. He lifted the rifle and indicated that we should follow him. Since he was the one carrying a gun, I was happy to let him take the lead. In a small column formation, we stepped off the path and into the woods, each of us picking our way carefully among the grass and debris in an attempt to keep as quiet as possible. For once, the trees above us were silent, the usual cacophony of birds hushed as though in anticipation of what would come next.

The sounds I'd heard had not resumed. Who or whatever had been there clearly knew we were coming. I nearly cursed but swallowed it back. For a brief moment, I was hopeful that it was Redvers, but I couldn't think of a reasonable explanation why he would be skulking through the woods. No, this had to be Smith.

Everything was quiet for so long that my skin began to pull tight, as though I would leap from my own body.

After what felt like a lifetime, the maharajah raised his rifle. I was afraid he was going to shoot, and I stepped forward and put a hand on his arm, shaking my head. What if it was Redvers? He shook his head, giving me a look that was unreadable in the near-dark. The only light we had was filtering through the trees, heavy shadows falling across Thirunal's features.

He pointed the rifle toward the treetops, and I let my hand fall to my side. He pulled off a shot, which echoed loudly through the trees and caused me to cover my ears. "Come out. I have plenty of ammunition."

A figure stepped from behind a tree, much closer than I'd expected him to be. The maharajah immediately leveled his rifle at the man, who slowly raised his hands. I took a step to the left of Thirunal, squinting in the darkness to be sure I was correct about the identity of the man who stood before us.

The man was Feodore Smith, who was the person I'd expected to see. What I hadn't expected, though, was that his hands and clothing were covered in something that looked an awful lot like blood.

CHAPTER THIRTY-FIVE

"What did you do with my husband?" I screamed at the man. Subbarayan stepped forward and put a restraining hand on my arm. I tried to shake him off, but he held on, trying to keep me from stepping in front of the maharajah's rifle, which had not wavered from its target. Later I would appreciate his quick thinking, but in that moment, I wanted nothing more than to leap forward and get my hands around Smith's fat neck.

Smith chuckled. "Your husband is fine. For now, I would imagine." He held up his hands, covered with blood that was beginning to dry. "This isn't his. It belonged to a poor unsuspecting goat, which had no idea what was coming for it."

"Where is he?" I choked out.

He shrugged, clearly not interested in answering. "You'll never make it in time." Thirunal pointed the rifle at the ground and cleared off another shot, directly in front of Smith, which made the rest of us jump noticeably, including Smith. I wished Thirunal would give me notice each time he shot the thing; there was a ringing in my right ear now. The maharajah quickly reloaded before Smith could fully recover from the shot that had nearly hit his foot. Thirunal had quite good aim—I had no doubt that if he wanted to shoot Smith straight through the heart he could.

"Shoot him for real," I implored. I meant it mostly as a threat, but a small piece of me would have been happy to see the man bleeding on the forest floor. Well, perhaps a large part of me. He'd caused so much pain, killing two innocent people, and now he'd done something with my husband involving goat's blood.

The maharajah ignored my bloodthirsty request and tipped his head from Subbarayan to Smith. "Subdue him."

Subbarayan stepped forward, and Smith took off to the right, darting through the trees. The maharajah raced after the man, Subbarayan only a beat behind him. I heard a shot in the near distance and flinched, ducking down into a crouch. It made sense that Smith had a pistol. How else would he have gotten Redvers out into the woods?

I was torn. Did I follow the men who were now unarmed, or did I continue on the path to find Redvers? It wasn't much of a question: I was going to try to rescue my husband, wherever he was. I hoped the maharajah and Subbarayan would both be okay, but Redvers was and always would be my first priority. I was glad Thirunal had passed me the rifle, although I had no idea how to use it. I would do my best not to shoot myself, but I needed to hurry.

I made my way back to the path as quickly as I could in the dark, finding the horse standing nervously. I wasn't certain if I could mount the thing while holding a rifle, but without pausing to think, I decided to try. I managed to slow my pace, approaching the horse with as much calm as I had available, gathering the reins from where they dragged in the dirt. The animal, a beautiful black stallion, shifted nervously, and I steeled my resolve. This was the fastest way to get to Redvers, and even though it had been more than twenty years since I'd gotten onto a horse, I had to try.

The rifle had a leather strap, and I slung it over my shoulder, nestling the weapon against my back and flinching. I did not like the feel of that, but I needed both hands to get onto this horse. My left hand still holding the reins, I managed to get one foot in the stirrup and after a few false starts, during which the horse danced in place, I was able to swing my other leg up over the saddle. It was incredibly inelegant, but after some struggle I got myself fully onto the saddle. I took a deep breath and, gathering the reins in both hands, gave the horse a nudge down the path in the direction Thirunal had come from.

Once we were moving, I was relieved to find that the horse was well-behaved. I knew that horses could sense when a rider was inexperienced, and I worried that this stallion would unseat me after a few feet once it realized that I was not a good horsewoman. It galloped down the path, though, as I braced myself and did my best to stay on top of it. I mentally tried to judge how far the maharajah could have searched on horseback before returning to us but quickly gave it up as a ridiculous cause and started shouting Redvers' name instead. I was getting closer to where they had found Gretchen's body and was still shouting my husband's name, over and over.

"Jane?" I finally heard a weak response. I pulled back on the reins, grimacing in surprise when the horse actually stopped, and glanced about wildly.

"Redvers? Where are you?"

"Over here. In the woods."

I got off the horse in an ungainly display and left it standing there, breathing heavily once more from the ride, and started to run toward where I'd heard Redvers' voice. The gun pounded uncomfortably against my back.

Redvers' voice was weak, and we continued the call and response, leading me deeper into the woods until I finally caught sight of him. He was tied to a tree, his head leaning back against it, eyes half-closed. It looked as though his body had been doused in blood—most likely the blood of the unfortunate goat that Smith had mentioned. But there was also a trickle of something dark running down the side of Redvers' face—I wondered if that was why his voice sounded so weak. Had Smith shot him as well? How injured was he? I hurried toward my husband, nearly tripping on a tree root in my haste. I got my feet under me without tumbling to the ground and approached more carefully, spotting a bucket that had most likely held the goat's blood and wrinkling my nose. I pulled the rifle around from my back and slung the strap over my head. I didn't want it touching me anymore, and I thought it would be easier to help Redvers without it banging against my back whenever I moved.

"Where did you get that rifle?" Redvers asked.

"The maharajah. They went after Smith," I said.

"They?"

"Thirunal and Subbarayan." I was impatient with the questions; I needed to get Redvers loose and then tend to any injuries he had. "Did he shoot you?" I leaned the rifle against the side of the tree that Redvers had been secured to. It was hard to see, and I was cursing the fact that I hadn't thought to bring a flashlight along with me.

"No, he pistol-whipped me," Redvers said. "I suppose I should count myself lucky he didn't simply shoot me. But he said tigers prefer live prey."

That was a horrifying thought. "How did he tie you to this?" I asked, trying to find knots in the multiple lengths of rope that held Redvers in place. Panic was making my fingers uncoordinated as they searched along. This couldn't possibly be an unending length of rope, there had to be a knot somewhere. Should I just work on getting his hands free?

"Jane," Redvers said, his voice low but steadier than it had been a moment before.

"What? I'm working as fast as I can, but I can't seem to find the ends." I had nearly circumnavigated the entire tree—a large one, with a girthy trunk.

"Get the rifle," Redvers said again, urgency making his voice harsh.

I froze, turning my head slowly to follow Redvers' fixed gaze.

All the time we had been in Ooty, I'd been terrified of coming face to face with a predatory cat. Well, my fears had finally come true.

It was still at a distance, but I had just locked eyes with an enormous tiger.

CHAPTER THIRTY-SIX

If I hadn't been in so much fear for my life, I might have reflected on what a beautiful creature this tiger was. It was big, much bigger than one imagined a cat to be, even knowing that tigers were large animals. In the near-dark, its orange and black stripes were striking. Slanted, hypnotic eyes reflected what little light there was. It made a noise in its throat that made every hair on my body stand straight on end.

I'd been in danger many times over the last year or so, but I'd never been so convinced that Redvers and I would die. The tiger had stopped moving, regarding both Redvers and me. I took a slow step toward the rifle, tiger eyes tracking the movement. I swallowed hard.

"I want you to slowly back away and leave," Redvers said. "Don't run, though."

"I'm not leaving you here," I said. I could almost reach the rifle. I hoped it wasn't difficult to use, since now was not the time for a lesson in firearms.

"Please, Jane." Redvers' voice was pleading and tear-filled, but I ignored him. The tiger had obviously been attracted by the scent of blood—the blood that Redvers was liberally covered with. It might stay and kill him if I left, and there was simply not a chance that I would do that.

The tiger made another growling noise deep in its throat. It rumbled through my body, and I thought I might pass out from fright. But I managed to get my fingers on the rifle, slowly pulling it to me. "I've got it," I said quietly, my eyes not leaving the deadly creature in front of us.

The tiger took a few slow steps parallel to us, tail twitching. I couldn't understand why it hadn't already attacked us. Perhaps it wasn't hungry? I could only hope that was the case and it wasn't looking for dinner. Because I was certain that Redvers smelled like a tasty meal.

Then the animal stopped and appeared to sniff the wind.

"Put the stock in your shoulder, or it will blast you off your feet."

I had no idea what the stock was, but I assumed he meant the end of the rifle. I did as he said, praying to whatever higher power might exist that we would both come out of this alive. I threw in an extra thought for the tiger, too. I didn't want to kill this animal, although I would do my best to if it came down to it. I held the gun with one end in my shoulder, but the bullet end still pointing down toward the ground, waiting to see what the tiger would do next.

The tiger watched me, not moving. It felt as though we were locked in limbo, each waiting to see what the other did. Could it possibly know that I held a rifle and what one was used for? There were so many stories of the British coming here to shoot tigers for sport; could a tiger understand what this weapon did?

I was probably giving the creature too much credit, but it did seem preternaturally intelligent. I couldn't explain how I came to that conclusion; I simply knew it to be true. The tiger continued its regard of us, dropping down to its stomach but never taking its eyes off me and my rifle. I didn't dare think this meant that we were out of danger, just that we weren't about to be eaten at this very second. I had no doubts that it could leave that crouch and be on top of me in the time it took me to breathe out once.

"You aren't going to shoot it?" Redvers whispered.

My only response was a single shake of my head. I hadn't taken my eyes off the creature, and my body felt electric, nerve endings pulled tighter than piano wire, taut, ready to sing or break, depending only on how they were struck.

I couldn't explain to my husband what I knew. But I knew that if I brought that gun up, it would leap straight for us, and I would be dead before I hit the ground. There was no chance I could shoot it in that time, and even less chance that I could shoot it in a place that would drop the animal dead instead of making it angry.

This went on for either an eternity or mere minutes. Just when I thought I could stand no more suspense, arms trembling with the weight of the rifle, the animal left its crouch, raked its gaze over us one last time, and sniffed the wind to the west. Something there caught its interest, and it turned, moving noiselessly off into the foliage, disappearing nearly immediately. What had it smelled? A cow? The horse that I'd left on the path? One of the small deer that bounded through these woods?

Why leave us and hunt an animal that would be entirely more work to kill?

I stood as I was, frozen in place long past when I could see the tiger or hear its movement through the brush. I wasn't sure how much time passed, but Redvers finally spoke. "I think you can untie me now."

"Why didn't it kill us?" I asked, voice shaking as badly as the rest of my body.

"It seemed to smell something," he said. I was shocked that his voice wasn't shaking as badly as mine was. How was that even possible? I could barely hold my hands still enough to put the rifle down, even though my arms longed to be free of the weight. I finally managed to drop the weapon to the ground, although I kept a close eye on it in case I needed to grab it again.

"I think the knots are to the left here," Redvers said, tipping his head, then grimacing. I frowned, setting aside thoughts of the tiger and wondering how badly his head had been injured. I'd take a look at it once we got him free and into better light.

It felt like an eternity, but with Redvers' help I found the knots, cleverly concealed beneath the rope itself, and managed to undo them despite the continued tremor in my hands. My nails were practically bleeding by the time I finished, but I nearly wept with relief when Redvers was able to shake free and gingerly get to his feet. I moved forward to hug him, but he held me at arm's length.

"I'm covered in blood," he said.

I wrinkled my nose. "Fair play. I'll squeeze you once you've had a bath."

He looked over my shoulder at the trees, clearly searching for the tiger.

"Do you see anything?" I asked.

He shook his head. "I think it's gone."

Even so, I grabbed the rifle and handed it to him. "I suppose you'll have to teach me how to shoot one of these as well. I don't believe it would have stopped the tiger, but I should probably know how to use one all the same." I was much better with a pistol, which Redvers had both showed me how to use and practiced with me. I was getting to be a fairly crack shot, but that was with a twenty-two. Not a rifle that was nearly a third the size of me.

"I suppose I will. Good thing it didn't come to that."

Not yet, anyway. I wouldn't be able to breathe in a full breath until we were safely back in our quarters, windows closed and doors locked against anything else that might want to kill us.

CHAPTER THIRTY-SEVEN

Redvers was moving slowly as we retraced our steps back toward Ooty, so I was relieved when we came upon Thirunal's horse grazing next to the trail. With some effort we got Redvers into the saddle, and though he assured me that he was fine, I wouldn't feel confident about that until we were able to examine him in the light. The wound on his head seemed to have stopped bleeding, but that didn't mean he was anything near okay.

I was, however, still quite shaken and started asking questions to cover my continuing fear. Whether I would remember the answers remained to be seen. "Did Smith say anything to you?"

"He did indeed. What happened to him?" Redvers asked.

"I don't know," I said. I was walking alongside the horse, with one hand on Redvers' leg. It was the contact that was keeping me sane about both this dark forest and his well-being. "Last I saw him, he was being chased through the woods by Thirunal and Subbarayan. There was a shot, but I didn't stick around to see if anyone was hit."

"But you had the gun," Redvers said, slowing the horse, forcing me to slow with them.

"Yes, and I came to rescue you instead of seeing what happened to them." I considered taking the reins to urge them forward. The sooner we were out of the dark woods, the better.

His voice had had a teasing tone, but it sobered now. "And I'm very grateful that you did, my dear."

That short delay in our progress had been long enough for us to realize there were voices coming from the forest directly to our left. I stiffened, but then recognized Maharajah Thirunal's voice.

"Thirunal?" Redvers called out.

"Here we are!" was the cheerful reply. Redvers stopped the horse and we waited a few moments until a trio of men emerged from the shadowy trees onto the path. Thirunal was pointing a small black pistol at Smith's back as Smith walked ahead of the other two men. I was happy to see that Thirunal and Subbarayan both seemed unharmed, although in the moonlight peeking through the trees it looked like Smith had incurred some damage to his face. I was secretly pleased to see it, since I would have liked to cause his face some damage myself. At least someone had gotten a good shot in—his eye would likely be black before morning.

"I'm glad neither of you was shot," I said.

"Smith hit a tree," Thirunal said. "With both that wild shot and then with his body."

"It knocked him off his feet, and we were able to wrestle the gun from him," Subbarayan said. He looked me up and down and frowned up at Redvers. "Are both of you okay?" I could only imagine what he was seeing—Redvers covered in drying blood, slumped over a horse, and me, dirt-covered and carrying a rifle. We were probably quite the sight.

"We are, even though we came face to face with the tiger."

Smith made a noise, but the other men simply looked at us, wide-eyed. "We'll explain everything once we get to the governor's mansion," Redvers said.

*   *   *

By the time we reached the governor's private quarters, Subbarayan was holding the rifle I'd been carrying so there were now two weapons trained on Feodore Smith. I thought it was the safest course of action in case Smith decided to make a break for it, and I wasn't interested in handling a weapon like that again in quite some time. The lessons I'd mentioned to Redvers would have to wait.

Our ragtag group trooped to the governor's quarters, adjacent to but separate from his wife's. I'd always found that to be a strange arrangement—I couldn't imagine wanting a room separate from Redvers. But then again, I thought that I had been extraordinarily lucky in my choice of husband—the second time around, anyway—and not everyone was so fortunate as to find their ideal match.

The servant who answered our knock quickly assessed the situation and called for the governor. Governor Goshen was shocked to find us at his door, with the secretary of state being held at gunpoint by a member of Indian royalty, but he admitted us and ushered us into his sitting room.

"What is happening here?" he demanded even before everyone had found a seat. I noticed that Thirunal had opted to stand behind Smith, pistol at the ready. I thought it was a wise course of action, considering everything that Smith was responsible for and capable of.

"Good evening, Governor Goshen," Redvers started to say.

The governor's eyes flicked to my husband and then widened noticeably at the sight of him. "What the hell happened to you?"

"Smith here removed me from the building at gunpoint, tied me to a tree, and dumped a bucket of goat's blood on me. Tiger bait, you see." Redvers' voice was casual, but I could feel the intensity radiating off him as he sat next to me. I reached over and took his hand. Down the hall, a door opened, and soft footsteps approached, although I wasn't sure anyone else heard them.

"Why would Smith do that?" The governor turned to Smith, expecting an answer.

"This is all foolishness, Goshen. I'm being set up here. It's a conspiracy against the commission."

"All these men—and one woman—are conspiring against you? And a maharajah?" The governor's voice was skeptical, but my stomach bubbled with sudden anxiety. Would the governor, or even the Crown, believe Smith over the rest of us?

"Feodore, you know very well that isn't true." Lady Goshen's voice from the doorway was soft but firm. "It's time to stop lying."

Maharajah Thirunal took that opportunity to give Smith a little poke in the back with the barrel of his pistol. I couldn't say whether it was Lady Goshen's appeal or the threat of a gun that made Smith start talking, but talk he did.

"I did what I did for the good of the commission," Smith started to say. "It's in the Crown's best interest that the commission's visit goes well, without some kind of Indian uprising."

Subbarayan's eyes had narrowed. I got the feeling he had thoughts to the contrary, and I mentally put a pin in that— I would ask him about it once Smith got through spinning whatever tale was about to come. It wasn't going to hold more than an ounce of the truth.

Lady Goshen came fully into the room, taking a seat next to her husband. "I'm sorry, George," she said to him. "You're going to learn some things that are distasteful." Governor Goshen merely raised his eyebrows, and his wife continued. "I've been . . . carrying on with Feodore for several years now. But enough is enough. You've killed two people and nearly two more." This she directed at Smith, who reacted with nothing more than a blink.

"You knew he killed them?" I asked.

She shook her head. "I didn't for a long time. I only put it together recently. Once you left, actually."

I wasn't sure I believed that, but I decided to let it go. My instincts told me Lady Goshen was only guilty of being racist and having terrible taste in men.

"Who did he kill?" Governor Goshen's voice was incredulous, and I truly believed that he didn't know that both Gretchen and his secretary had been murdered.

"He killed Gretchen Beetner, and then he murdered your secretary, Kandiyar," I said.

"But why?" Governor Goshen asked.

"For votes," Subbarayan said.

"Votes?" Goshen's deep frown creased his forehead. "Whatever do you mean?"

Subbarayan looked thoughtful. "I wondered why Goshen was supportive of my holding on to my seat in the government, since he was so adamant about our people not participating in the commission. I realized it was because he thought he could manipulate me more easily than Mudaliar."

Smith grunted. We all looked at him expectantly, but he sat stoically, refusing to admit to the charges against him. I was surprised he'd made any noise at all. But then Smith shocked me and began to speak. "If natives were given voting rights on the commission or in any part of the occupying rule, we would lose power."

"By 'we' I'm assuming you mean the Conservative Party," Goshen said.

"Yes, obviously, George. You and I both know the natives would vote Labour, and they would be able to take power in government. I couldn't have that happen."

"So this was all about keeping Indian people from voting?" I asked. "Why kill Gretchen?" I thought I had an idea of why, but I wanted my suspicions confirmed.

"Because the damned woman was blackmailing me. She

had evidence of my affair with Virginia and was threatening to use it against me unless I altered the commission and allowed natives onto it. I wasn't about to let that happen."

I wondered if his affair coming out was a powerful enough threat for Gretchen to use as blackmail, but it had obviously been enough to get Gretchen killed. "Why not let her simply expose the affair, then?"

"It might weaken my position within my party," Smith said.

Lady Goshen rolled her eyes. I looked at Governor Goshen to gauge his reaction; he seemed to have none. I wondered if he'd known that his wife was occupying herself with someone else while he did the same, or if he was simply quite skilled at hiding his feelings. I didn't bother to ask, since it wasn't any of my concern.

But Smith's motives *were* my concern, and what he'd given us wasn't enough. "No," I said. "There's more. You wouldn't have killed Gretchen over that." What I left unsaid was that the governor was having his own affair and it was a well-known secret. Smith's affair was hardly enough to hurt him politically.

Thirunal poked Smith in the back with the pistol again, hard. Smith jerked forward a bit and grimaced, then spoke through gritted teeth. "Fine, she may have had some information about my business dealings that were . . . less than savory."

That was more like it—a far more convincing reason why Smith had eliminated Gretchen.

The governor appeared to have put something else together, though, and stepped in. "That's why you suggested that I reassign Inspector Thornycrest. I thought it was to reward the man's services, but it was to reward his services to *you*."

Smith shrugged. "He didn't know it was me orchestrating the whole thing."

"Who did you get to deliver all those notes?" I asked. "Or type them?"

Lady Goshen grunted. "That would be me." She shook her head. "I should have opened one of them to see what it was about. But Feodore insisted that they were simply meeting requests, and I didn't think twice about giving them to my staff to have them delivered."

"So you didn't type the notes?" I asked. I wasn't quite able to keep the anger from my voice, and Lady Goshen flinched slightly.

"I did not. But I'm sorry that I had any part in this mess, small as it was."

I opened my mouth to disagree—strongly—with that sentiment, but Redvers squeezed my hand, and I shut my mouth with an audible snap. Some effective curses were on the tip of my tongue, but I swallowed those as well, studying the ceiling for a long moment to gather my composure.

"Did you steal Gretchen's body as well, Smith?" Goshen asked.

Redvers stepped in to field that question, explaining Lala Rai's involvement with Gretchen going missing.

The governor studied Redvers for a long moment. "You seem to know everything that is going on here, son. I assume you and your wife have been looking into things, which is why you're now covered in blood."

Redvers gave a shrug and the governor shook his head. "It will not be unrecognized," he said before turning his attention back to Smith. "You'll hang for this, Feodore."

Smith snorted. "They wouldn't dare. I'll be back in my post within a fortnight."

I could only pray that wouldn't be the case.

It was a long night sorting out the facts, and I was nearly asleep before everything had been answered to the governor's satisfaction. At least Smith had been taken in hand—

cuffs to the local jail. There was not yet an inspector at the station, since Thornycrest was already long gone, but a few uniformed officers came and took Smith away with them. I was never so happy to see the back of someone.

As we were leaving the governor's quarters, he stopped me with a final statement. "It's too bad you didn't kill that tiger, Mrs. Wunderly."

I shivered in horror. "We were very lucky. It didn't seem hungry."

"I haven't had time for my own hunt. If there's one in the area, perhaps it's time to get out there. I could get lucky in a short time."

I left without answering. I would never understand the British taste for such bloodthirsty sport, and despite coming face to face with death at the tiger's paws, I hoped the creature managed to escape being killed. It had left us alone, after all.

Redvers and I supported each other back to our quarters. I was so exhausted I didn't bother looking for danger on the walk there, knowing that we still needed to get my husband cleaned up and take a look at the wound on his head.

I sat on the edge of our tub, running the taps and trying to get a perfect balance of hot and cold while my husband stripped off his ruined linen suit. I frowned at the pile on the tile floor. "We'll throw that out."

He lowered himself gingerly into the tub, the water immediately turning red and my stomach with it. We emptied and refilled the bath several times before the water stayed clean. The wound on his head wasn't as bad as I had feared. There was an egg-sized lump, but we agreed it would go down in time.

We were both quiet. "You were wonderful out there," Redvers said, breaking the silence.

I shook my head. "I didn't really do anything. I thought

we were dead for sure this time."

"You kept your head. Although I think it's time that we get you that gun we discussed."

I shuddered. We'd previously talked about getting me a small pistol, which had seemed like an excellent idea after our last adventure, but a pistol wouldn't have done any good against a leaping tiger. I also wasn't sure I wanted to handle a gun ever again. I was relieved that I hadn't had to kill a living creature and didn't know what I would have done had it decided to come for us.

Redvers was watching me closely. "We can talk about it some other time."

I smiled and agreed.

"Some honeymoon this has been," Redvers said, voice lighter now as he reclined against the back of the tub.

I tipped my head back and laughed. "This was a terrible honeymoon."

He chuckled as well. "Let's see if I can make it up to you. Once I'm back on my feet and out of this bath."

I gave him a wink. "I have a few ideas about how you can do that."

EPILOGUE

We had taken a few days to recover from our exploits, but we were finally packing our things and getting ready to leave India. I wished that I was sorry to go. The country was beautiful, the food extraordinary, and the people wonderful, but we'd been stalked and threatened, and both of us had very nearly died during this trip. I was ready for calmer waters.

Not to mention we had both been suffering from nightmares. I was hopeful that once we'd had a change of scenery we could leave those behind as well. We were in dire need of a good night's sleep and had the dark circles beneath our eyes to show for it. Redvers had been reticent about exactly what his dreams entailed, but mine were wholly centered around our encounter with the tiger. I could see the creature clearly every time I closed my eyes, but in my nightmares the beast came for us in one powerful leap, intent on killing us instead of leaving us be. More than once, I'd been jolted awake, screaming, only to find that Redvers was already awake, suffering from his own night terrors.

Yet despite all my interrupted nights, I was pleased that the tiger was still alive. Last I'd heard, the governor hadn't been able to find it on his recent hunting expeditions, and I was relieved that it hadn't been tracked down and killed—perhaps because, against all odds, it had let us live.

I'd decided to actually rest and recuperate for once, instead of venturing out, so I hadn't had any further interactions with the people that I'd encountered on this trip, with the exception of our porter, of course. I'd been tempted to seek out Savithri but in the end had decided to let things lie. The same went for Lady Goshen and the maharajah. We'd said farewell that fateful night, and I saw no reason to do so again—not only because I disliked goodbyes but also because I didn't care to rehash anything that had happened that night or in the days leading up to it. I wanted to move forward instead of examining the past. For his part, Redvers had finished up his business at the governor's mansion and carried back tidbits of information, and that was enough for me.

I was, however, pleased to hear that Feodore Smith would actually stand trial. Redvers and I had shared concerns that the man would escape prosecution because of his political position—and he still might—but at least he would see his day in court. I could only hope that whoever was chosen to replace him was more magnanimous toward the local people and less obsessed with his own power.

It was unlikely, but I could hope.

As for our next destination, Redvers assured me that this time we would be taking a proper honeymoon, somewhere romantic, with no assignments to interrupt our time together. I was looking forward to it—wherever it was, since he insisted on surprising me—but I also found that after a few days of rest, I was feeling ready to face whatever came our way once more. Regardless of where our travels took us, I felt confident that we would be fine, better than fine, since this time around my choice of husband had been the right one. We would face whatever life brought us—together.

And as for settling down, staying in one place, and forgoing adventure, I was confident that I wasn't ready for that yet.

Or possibly ever.

Acknowledgments

Huge thanks to John Scognamiglio, my editor extraordinaire, as well as to Larissa Ackerman and Jesse Cruz, my outstanding publicists. Thank you to Robin Cook, Lauren Jernigan, and Sarah Gibb. Further thanks to the rest of the Kensington team who work so hard to get books into your hands.

Thank you and all my love to Ann Collette. I wouldn't be here without you. I'm so grateful for you and for our continued friendship—you bring me joy.

Much love and thanks to Zoe Quinton King, my dear friend and editor. I'm so lucky to have you on my team in both my life and my career.

Big love and thanks to Jessie Lourey, Susie Calkins, and Shannon Baker for being my cheerleading squad.

Special thanks to Megan Kantara for checking out the facts about Ooty and for being such an extraordinary and supportive friend. You believe in me when I don't.

Immeasurable thanks for the friendship, love, and support to Tasha Alexander, Ed Aymar, Gretchen Beetner, Lou Berney, Mike Blanchard, Keith Brubacher, Kate Conrad, Hilary Davidson, Dan Distler, Steph Gayle, Daniel Goldin, Juliet Grames, Andrew Grant, Glen Erik Hamilton, Carrie Hennessy, Tim Hennessy, Chris Holm, Katrina Niidas Holm, Megan Kantara, Steph Kilen, Elizabeth Little, Jenny Lohr, Erin MacMillan, Joel MacMillan, Dan Malmon, Kate Malmon, Marjorie McCown, Mike McCrary, Catriona McPherson, Katie Meyer, Trevor Meyer, Lauren O'Brien, Roxanne Patruznick, Margret Petrie, Nick Petrie, Bryan Pryor, Lori Rader-Day, Andy Rash, Jane Rheineck, Kyle Jo Schmidt, Dan Schwalbach, Marie Schwalbach, Johnny Shaw, Jay

Shepherd, Becky Tesch, Tess Tyrrell, Bryan Van Meter, Luis Velez, and Tim Ward.

Thank you to the amazing booksellers and librarians who've supported this book and especially to the folks who hosted me for a real-life tour. Special shout-outs to Daniel, Chris, and Rachel at Boswell Books; Barbara, Patrick, and John at the Poisoned Pen; Devin at Once Upon a Crime; and Jayne and Joanne at Mystery to Me.

Thank you and big love to my amazing family: Rachel and AJ Neubauer, Dorothy Neubauer, Sandra Olsen, Susan Catral, Sara Kierzek, Jeff and Annie Kierzek, Justin and Christine Kierzek, Josh Kierzek, Ignacio Catral, Sam and Ariana Catral, Mandi Neumann, Andie, and Alex and Angel Neumann.

Love and thanks to John and Gayle McIntyre.

Special thanks and love to my dear friend Gunther Neumann, who is truly a rock.

So much love, gratitude, and thanks to Mike Blanchard for being the amazing person that he is. To the bones, babe.

And all the love and thanks to Beth McIntyre. Peach emoji to infinity.

Turn the page for a special bonus novella,

MURDER UNDER THE MISTLETOE!

CHAPTER ONE

The closer our train came to the little English town of Barnard Castle, the quieter Redvers became. It was rather at odds with the otherwise festive atmosphere felt by the other passengers, many of whom were laden down with paper-wrapped packages they were bringing home for Christmas.

"Will someone meet us at the station?" I asked my fiancé.

"Who knows. Hopefully someone will think to fetch us." Redvers' face betrayed little, but tension radiated from him in waves. Coming back to his ancestral home for the holiday had been his idea, albeit a reluctant one. The invitation had been extended by his father—his mother having passed years earlier—and Redvers' first instinct had been to decline. But after some thought he'd reconsidered and accepted for both of us, citing some mysterious reason he needed to speak with his father in person.

I had my suspicions as to why that was, but had kept my nose out of things for once—he would tell me in his own time. And frankly, I was delighted to see where Redvers had grown up. Not to mention I was also more than a little curious to meet his father. Their relationship seemed cordial but hardly close, and I looked forward to seeing their interactions in real life. I hoped it would give me some deeper insight into this man I had agreed to marry.

I still couldn't quite believe I had agreed to marry again. But I had, although so far it was only a verbal agreement—no plans had been set and no rings exchanged.

Despite Redvers' quiet, I was enjoying the beautiful English countryside from our compartment window. The rolling hills had a light dusting of snow already, which I was surprised to see, but we were far north near the North Pennines, a gorgeous range of hills that saw more snow than most other parts of the country. Or so I was told. I was hopeful for a snowy Christmas.

The railroad stop for Barnard Castle was little more than a small covered roof between two tracks—not a building or stationmaster in sight. Redvers and I disembarked, and looking down the train I could see that only two other passengers were getting off here. We fetched our own luggage from the platform, and I was grateful we were traveling light for this trip, just a suitcase for each of us. Redvers had assured me that I wouldn't need anything formal—we would not be expected to dress for dinner, so I had packed sparingly.

At the end of the platform stood a man in a long wool coat, hands clasped before him. He was tall and spare and his face was nearly unlined despite the fact that he had to be well into his forties, causing me to wonder if the man ever smiled. We might have walked past him altogether except that he spoke as we pulled near.

"Mr. Dibble?"

Redvers stopped before him. "That's right." I was startled by the greeting. I'd become quite accustomed to Redvers' habit of using only his given name—it was unusual to hear anyone using his surname.

"I'm your father's chauffeur," the man replied, barely moving. "Carlisle."

"You must be new," Redvers said.

Carlisle gave him a brief nod before he turned to me, the

late-afternoon light glinting off his golden hair. "May I take your case, ma'am?"

"Certainly, thank you," I said, getting my own brief nod of the head in return. We were led to a black sedan where Carlisle stowed my suitcase in the trunk before turning and taking Redvers' suitcase as well, placing it alongside mine. Redvers went around to the other side of the vehicle while Carlisle opened the door for me, waiting until I had slid into the back seat to close the door behind me.

Carlisle pulled onto the road and Redvers broke the silence. "Is my father at home, Carlisle?"

"He is, sir."

Redvers nodded, and it seemed as though that was all that would be said, both men settling back into an uncomfortable silence. I wondered at the tension—was this how it would be with all of the staff in the Dibble household? Carlisle was obviously new, but he didn't seem chatty or even terribly welcoming. Or was the silence simply because Redvers wasn't familiar with this member of his father's staff?

Barnard Castle was a charming little village, what was apparently referred to as a market town, and named after the castle that had once stood here, in ruins now. The shops on the main street were decorated gaily for Christmas—greenery and wreaths and ribbons abounded. Shop windows had their wares on display, and I couldn't help but smile and hope that I would have an opportunity during our stay to do a little shopping. I had yet to find a gift for Redvers, but I had the feeling that the perfect thing would reveal itself to me when I saw it. Or perhaps that was what I was hoping would happen—it was our first holiday together and I was feeling quite a bit of pressure to get it right, even though I was certain Redvers wouldn't really care. It would be the thought that counted as far as he was concerned.

We passed through the town and found ourselves on a narrow country road. I was about to comment on the beautiful countryside, when we took a right turn into what at first glance looked like nothing but a hedgerow, but proved to be an actual road leading somewhere. Two deep, well-traveled ruts were worn into the dirt and we bumped along.

Redvers glanced at me. "Just a bit farther."

I smiled at him, but he was already gazing out the front with what seemed a little like dread. I wondered, not for the first time, if I should be bracing myself for an unpleasant visit.

But this musing was interrupted when the trees opened up and the house revealed itself. It was a charming stone manor house. Nothing nearly the size and grandeur of Wedgefield Manor, the estate belonging to my aunt Millie's fiancé, but a large and gracious home nonetheless. I looked at Redvers, but his expression remained the same—completely neutral and impassive. This was nothing new; he was really quite skilled at controlling his facial expressions, and it was probably only that I knew him so well that I could sense his unease.

Carlisle stopped the car, and I had my door open before the poor man could open it himself. His face didn't change, but I could see his shoulders stiffen. I would have to remember to be a little less American while I was here. Things were obviously more formal at the Dibble home than they were at the last manor I'd stayed at.

"I'm sorry, Carlisle," I said, and the man gave me another small incline of the head. I wondered if he was ever rattled and just what that might take.

Carlisle closed my door behind me. "Your bags will be delivered to your rooms," Carlisle told us. I thanked him and followed Redvers to the front door, which was opened by an older man with salt-and-pepper hair wearing an impeccably kept dark suit. I glanced around the foyer—beautiful parquet floors and a suit of armor standing sentry greeted us, although the décor was otherwise sparse.

"Mr. Youngblood," Redvers greeted the butler. "I trust you're well."

"I am, thank you, Mr. Dibble." Youngblood was currently helping me off with my coat. He reached out and took Redvers' gray wool coat as well. "Your father is in the library."

"Thank you, Youngblood," Redvers said.

I perked up at the mention of a library. At least I might be able to find some new reading material—I hadn't brought any with me since luggage space was at a bit of a premium. Redvers took a deep breath and a look around before turning to me. "Nothing has changed," he said. Then he gave me a completely unconvincing smile. I cocked my head and touched his arm in a show of solidarity. This time his smile was more sincere, and he held out his arm for me to take before leading me down the hallway.

The decorations throughout the place were staid and somewhat stuffy—not a lot of warmth to be found here. The temperature inside the house was even a bit chilly—I was tempted to rub my arms and might have done so if I didn't have the warmth from Redvers' arm. That changed, however, once we stepped through the doorway to the library where a bright fire crackled merrily. Within moments I began to sweat—it went from one extreme to the other at the Dibble home, it would appear. A quick glance around showed the usual bookcases stretching across the walls from floor to ceiling, but it didn't appear that there were going to be a lot of novels for my perusing—all I could see were heavy leather-bound volumes that appeared strictly academic in nature. I would have to make a more thorough inspection later, but I wasn't holding out much hope.

Two figures were seated in the armchairs before the fireplace, although there was no conversation. It didn't appear as though either individual had heard us approach, so Redvers cleared his throat. "Father?"

The figure on the left jerked slightly, then turned. "Redvers. You made it." The man stood and came around his chair, but stopped, resting his hand on the tall back. I knew the British were not necessarily an affectionate people, but I was taken aback. Not even a handshake for the son he hadn't seen in nearly a year?

"Your trip was uneventful, I trust?" Humphrey Dibble asked. I took the man in while he engaged in banal conversation with his son. I felt as though I was seeing Redvers in a few decades—there was no denying the resemblance between the two, and his father with his thick silver hair was still quite a handsome man.

Just then the figure seated in the other chair stood and came around her own chair.

I managed to keep my eyebrows steady, but they were quite tempted to leap up in surprise. I wasn't aware that Redvers' father had a female companion, and one who was obviously some years younger than himself. She had a sharp face, almost foxlike, with a prominent bump on her nose and dark eyes. But even for all her hard edges, she was an attractive woman, dressed in a navy day dress that showed off her petite figure, her hair pulled into a conservative updo.

Redvers wasn't quite so successful with his own eyebrows—I saw one of them shoot up at the woman's appearance. It would seem Redvers hadn't known about this woman either.

"Evelyn Hesse," Redvers said. "I didn't know you would be visiting. I heard your husband passed away. I'm very sorry."

She inclined her head. "Thank you." She looked at Humphrey. "Of course, I mourn his loss, but it has allowed for other opportunities." Evelyn put her hand on Humphrey's arm.

Humphrey Dibble nodded. "Yes, we're engaged to be married."

CHAPTER TWO

Normally I was the one whose mouth was left flapping open like a fish, but this time it was Redvers, which I found to be an interesting change of pace. I decided it was time to take charge of the conversation.

"What a coincidence. I'm Redvers' fiancée, Jane." This time it was Redvers' father who was struck dumb. It was obvious that the Dibble men didn't communicate regularly, or in great detail.

When Humphrey regained himself, he managed to come forward and shake my hand, then his son's. "I thought you said you would never marry, Redvers."

"And I thought you would never marry again. It looks as though we were both wrong," Redvers said, one hand casually resting on the small of my back.

"We should have a drink to celebrate," Humphrey said. He excused himself from the room for a moment, and I turned to Evelyn.

"Have you set a date?" I asked.

"We have. We'll be getting married Christmas Day." Evelyn's eyes were bright—she looked genuinely pleased.

But Redvers and I were both a bit taken aback at the date. "This Christmas Day? As in a few days from now?" Redvers asked.

"Oh, yes. It's to be at St. Mary's. Everything is all set." Evelyn smiled and I thought to myself that she looked a little like a shark that had found its lunch. "We're so glad you could be here for it, Redvers. And of course, you as well, Jane."

"Wonderful," I said. This was shaping up to be quite an interesting holiday indeed.

Redvers' father returned to the room. "I sent Youngblood for a bottle of champagne. I also sent word to your aunts that you have arrived. I'm sure they will be pleased to see you." Evelyn's face darkened at this announcement, but she busied herself with smoothing her skirts.

If I had to guess, Evelyn wasn't a fan of the aunts Humphrey just mentioned. Of course, I didn't know who any of them were—Evelyn or these aunts that Redvers had never spoken of. It brought up some other questions as well, such as had Redvers told his father he would be bringing me home? He'd obviously not told Humphrey we were engaged. So what *had* he told his father? I'd always been aware that Redvers wasn't close with his family, but it was hitting home just how true that was. It made me grateful for my close relationship with my own father.

As Youngblood came into the room bearing a tray of champagne and glasses, Redvers leaned in to whisper into my ear, sending a delicious shiver down my spine. "I can tell you're dying of curiosity. You'll get your chance later."

I grinned and gave him a gentle elbow to the ribs. Just then Youngblood's foot tripped on the carpet and his body jerked forward. He managed to grab the bottle of champagne, but the glasses went flying from the tray, falling to the rug. Three of them appeared to have made the fall unharmed, but the fourth shattered. Evelyn hurried forward and bent down to collect the glasses that had survived.

"I'm so sorry, sir, madam." Youngblood was clearly mortified as he bent to collect broken pieces of glass.

"Accidents happen, Youngblood. I've tripped on this rug myself," Evelyn said.

I was quite surprised that Evelyn was assisting the butler in cleaning up the glass. Normally when events like this occurred, the lady of the house sent for a maid instead of bending down to the task herself. Of course, she wasn't lady of the house quite yet. But even still.

"I'll get new glasses," Youngblood said once the largest pieces of glass had been collected.

"That's fine, Youngblood. And really, you don't need one for me, as you know," Humphrey told his butler. "Or perhaps you can bring me some cold cider instead." Youngblood nodded and went from the room again.

Did Redvers' father not drink? That was certainly an interesting development. We stood around a bit awkwardly until Youngblood returned with fresh glasses, including one already filled with cider for Humphrey. Youngblood made it across the carpet this time, setting his tray onto a small table before opening the bottle of champagne and pouring three glasses of it. Humphrey stood at his butler's elbow and distributed the glasses, taking his glass of cider last. Once each of us had one, we clinked glasses.

"Here's to the future," Humphrey said, and we all murmured agreements.

A few sips in, we heard the sound of the doorbell. Moments later there was a general hubbub as the sound of two women's voices—loud voices—could be heard coming down the hall.

"It would appear your aunts have arrived," Humphrey said.

I shot Evelyn a surreptitious glance, and her face had taken on a vaguely sour look. Confirmation that these aunts were not favorites of hers. I wondered if that street went both ways.

I didn't have long to wonder.

"Well, look who finally decided to come home." The first woman who stepped through the doorway had snapping brown eyes and naturally curly hair that had nearly gone entirely gray. She was joined moments later by a slightly shorter woman with friendly dark eyes and a cheerful smile. Her tongue turned out to be just as sharp, however.

"You can't blame him when you look at the state of the place," the second woman said.

I was already utterly delighted by these two.

Redvers set his champagne on a small table and moved forward, and I quickly followed suit. He hugged the taller woman with curly hair. "This is Carolyn Hennessy. My mother's sister," Redvers told me. Then he turned to the woman with rosy cheeks, her straight salt-and-pepper hair pulled into a low bun, and bent down to hug her also. "And this is *her* sister-in-law, Marie Schwalbach. Aunt Carolyn, Aunt Marie, this is my fiancée, Jane Wunderly." It took no more than that introduction for the women to bustle in and try to elbow each other out of the way in order to hug me first.

"It's about time you got married, young man," Aunt Carolyn said. "Enough of this gallivanting about the world."

"Oh, I think the gallivanting is romantic," said Aunt Marie. "And what if Jane wants to gallivant as well?" They both turned and looked at me expectantly, Redvers' father and his own fiancée completely forgotten for the moment. "Well?"

"I do enjoy traveling," I said. "It's how we met."

"See? There you have it," Aunt Marie said. "That sounds very romantic."

I suspected the two would have happily continued their argument well into the night if Redvers' father hadn't finally stepped forward to interrupt them. "I'm glad you could stop by. I hope you will join us for supper."

"How kind of you," Marie said.

"Perhaps. What are you having?" Carolyn asked.

I picked my drink back up and hid my smile behind it. Christmas might be more complicated than we'd expected, but it was also going to be much more entertaining than I'd dared hope.

After a brief discussion, Redvers' aunts decided to stay for supper. I found that I was pleased that our party was larger than just the four of us. It was obvious from his body language that Redvers was much more comfortable with his two aunts than with his father, and I was delighted for the chance to get to know them better. The women were also a font of information. Or gossip, rather.

"You know this will be Evelyn's third marriage," Aunt Carolyn said to me in a low voice on our way in to dinner. Humphrey had already escorted his fiancée ahead of us.

"Her last two husbands died suddenly," Aunt Marie whispered. "Perhaps *too* suddenly."

"You're not suggesting . . ." I whispered back. They both gave elegant little shrugs before passing into the dining room and taking their seats at the long, very formal wooden table. I was rooted to the spot for a moment before Redvers tugged me forward. He hadn't said anything, but I could see a little furrow between his brows. Put there, I imagined, by his aunts' comments.

The housekeeper served our meal, roast duck with root vegetables and sautéed potatoes. Evelyn cut into her vegetables, stabbing a carrot and looking at it critically. "I'll need to speak with the cook once you and I are married, Humphrey. These are a bit undercooked."

Aunt Carolyn barely paused what she was doing to spear Evelyn with a look. "Mary never had a problem with the cook. Mrs. Bosworth does a lovely job—my carrots are just fine."

Evelyn pursed her lips. "I prefer if we don't bring up the subject of Mary."

Now Carolyn put her fork down. "And why is that, Evelyn?"

"It makes Humphrey upset."

Carolyn looked at her brother-in-law who was busy cutting his meat. "He looks fine to me. I don't think the mention of my late sister's name is going to give him the vapors."

Evelyn's gaze met Carolyn's in an obvious war of wills before Evelyn finally reached for her glass of wine and broke eye contact between the two. Both women had dark eyes, but it occurred to me that while Carolyn's were a warm brown, Evelyn's eyes were nearly black.

The tension stretched until Aunt Marie finally cleared her throat. "Jane, have you and Redvers set a date for your wedding?"

It was my turn to feel uncomfortable. I was hoping for a long engagement so I could adjust to the idea of being married again. Redvers was fine with this, but it was difficult to explain to others because I had no desire to reveal my personal reasons for wanting to wait. "We have not."

"You modern women," Marie said with a shake of her head, but there was no venom in her words. Just mild admonishment.

Carolyn finally dragged her attention away from Evelyn to look at me. "You should get Mother's ring." She turned to Humphrey who'd gone a bit pink. "Where is Mother's ring now? I'm assuming you didn't bury Mary with it."

Humphrey coughed behind his fist. "No, no, of course not. But Evelyn will be wearing the ring." Evelyn beamed down the long table at her fiancé and it took her a moment to realize that everyone at the table was now staring at the ring finger of her left hand.

Evelyn sniffed at the attention being given her. "It's being fitted for me. I have delicate hands." Her hands were indeed quite doll-like.

Carolyn looked fit to be tied, but she continued in a reasonable voice. "That ring belonged to *my* family, Humphrey. Not yours."

Humphrey's face had darkened. "We can discuss this later, Carolyn."

She nodded once. "You can be certain that we will."

Across from me I could see Redvers' face was thunderous as well, and I was curious how similar the two men's temperaments would prove to be. Because it looked to me like Redvers was just as displeased about Evelyn receiving his grandmother's ring as his aunt was. I'd suspected for some time that the reason Redvers had agreed to return for the holiday was to ask his father for something, and since I didn't yet have an engagement ring . . . well, I'd rather assumed Redvers wanted to procure a family ring for our engagement. Based on the look on his face, I would wager a large sum of money it was the very same ring he'd intended to ask his father for.

Evelyn had been pushing her food around her plate rather than eating it, and now she reached for her wineglass, taking a healthy sip. "Tomorrow afternoon we will take the sledge out and choose a tree to put in the sitting room. Redvers, I expect you and Jane will join us, of course."

"If you like," Redvers replied.

"What is a sledge?" I whispered to my fiancé from behind my own wineglass.

"It's a sleigh," he whispered back.

I could see Carolyn and Marie exchange a look across the table, but it had nothing to do with our whispered conversation. "It's early to be putting up the tree, isn't it, Evelyn? Normally it doesn't go up until Christmas Eve," Aunt Marie said.

"We're putting it up a day early because we plan to be wed on Christmas Day. I will have other preparations that will be keeping me too busy to put up the tree then." Evelyn punctuated her statement with a nod.

"In that case, there's not nearly enough room for all of you plus a tree in that old sledge of yours, Humphrey. We'll bring ours as well. Say around one?" Marie said.

Evelyn's lips flattened, but there was no way she could refuse to let this pair join the fun without being incredibly rude. "Certainly," she ground out. "Should we send Carlisle to help you hitch up your horses?"

Carolyn snorted. "I've spent my entire life around horses. Not to mention we have our own help, Evelyn. I have things well in hand."

"It's a bit of a risk, isn't it?" Evelyn asked. "Handling large animals."

"More of a risk to be married to you," Carolyn said under her breath. I was the only one who could hear her since she was seated next to me, and I nearly choked on a sip of my own wine, quickly turning it into a cough.

"What was that?" Evelyn was indignant.

"I said the exercise is healthy. I'm sorry you couldn't hear me."

The two women were back to glaring at each other while the rest of us ignored their silent battle and turned our attention to the chocolate soufflé that had just been served for dessert.

I had so many questions for Redvers by now, I was worried I wouldn't be able to remember them all.

CHAPTER THREE

It wasn't long after our desserts were consumed that Redvers' aunts left for the evening with a promise to see us the following afternoon. Evelyn readied herself to leave for the evening as well, instructing Carlisle to fetch the car and take her home. She and Humphrey were engaged, but it was still considered improper for her to stay the night at his home before they were married, so she returned to her own home close to the center of town every evening. Although I could see she had no trouble ordering Humphrey's staff around as though she was already mistress of the household.

Once it was just the three of us, the conversation became even more stilted. It didn't take long for Redvers and I to claim exhaustion from travel and request to turn in for the evening. Humphrey looked relieved, and we bid each other good night. The housekeeper, a quiet woman named Mrs. Potter, showed me to my room. It was a mid-size bedroom with a heavy four-poster bed and thick wool rug but otherwise spare furnishings. My things had already been put away, and I set about getting ready for bed when I heard a knock on my door.

Redvers. I'd rather been expecting him after he'd been shown to his own room down the hall. He looked delicious in a thick dressing gown of dark red silk.

I opened the door to him, quickly ushering him inside with a quick glance up and down the hallway, before shutting the door and leaning back against it and giving him a wink. "Scandalous. Visiting me in my boudoir this time of night."

He leaned forward to give me a quick kiss before rolling his eyes. "Ridiculous that we've been given separate rooms. As though I'm some green boy instead of an engaged man."

"Well, Evelyn goes home at the end of every evening. We should feel fortunate I'm not staying at the local inn, I suppose."

At the mention of Evelyn's name, Redvers' brows pulled together. He moved deeper into my room, finding only one stiff armchair near the fireplace with its banked fire. With a sigh he looked around, then dragged the wooden chair from the small desk over next to it, before sitting down on the tiny chair. I shook my head and shooed him into the armchair. "I have so many questions, you're going to need to be more comfortable. Besides, you look as though you'll break that wooden chair. And then where will we be?"

Redvers shook his head but did as I asked and moved to the larger chair. I sat down and faced him. "I don't even know where to start, really."

"How about with Evelyn?" Redvers suggested.

"Excellent point. What do we know about her?"

"She is widowed, just as my aunts told you, although I think it's already been two years or more. But they're correct that her husband's death was pretty sudden." Redvers shook his head. "I didn't realize that Evelyn had been married before that. It must have been before she came to the area."

"Do you think your aunts are correct? About the deaths being suspicious?" I didn't want to suggest that they were making things up, but perhaps it was just rumors they'd heard.

Redvers shrugged. "It could just be rumors. In fact, I wouldn't give it a second thought except that she showed up here. I hadn't even heard that my father was courting her, let alone that they were engaged."

"Would he have told you that? It doesn't seem as though you and your father . . . share a lot of information with one another."

One of Redvers' eyebrows lifted. "Yes, I suppose one could say that we're not exactly close. I guess that's not difficult to see."

"Mmm," I said.

He sighed. "I wouldn't have even come here but I wanted . . ." He trailed off, then seemed to make a decision. "I wanted to get my grandmother's ring to give to you."

"I suspected as much."

He snorted. "There's no keeping secrets from you, is there? How can I surprise you if you insist on figuring everything out ahead of time?"

I shrugged. "Are you upset about the ring going to Evelyn?"

Redvers thought about that for a moment. "I am, actually. Even if I didn't want you to wear it, I wouldn't want Evelyn to have it. Aunt Carolyn is correct. The ring was from her family. If anything, it should have gone back to her."

"Do your aunts have children?" It was a little off topic, but I was curious about the women.

"Aunt Carolyn has one son. He lives in London and comes home once or twice a year to visit. Aunt Marie has two children, and at least one of them is still in the area. Last I heard anyway." His face softened. "I was intimidated by them as a child—they've always been thick as thieves—sitting in the back of every gathering and spearing everyone who came too close with their wit. Although they were always really quite kind to me, despite that. They would slip me books that my father deemed 'frivolous.' Basically, anything fictional." I let out a sigh—the library downstairs would have little to interest me then.

Redvers continued. "As I've gotten older, I've gained an even greater appreciation for them. They seem to enjoy thumbing their noses at conventional society."

"They're both widows?"

He nodded. "They live together on the other side of town. Their husbands died several years apart, but of wholly natural causes."

Which brought us back to Evelyn. "Which we're thinking might not be the case with Evelyn's last two husbands." It was a statement more than a question. "But how do we learn more about that?"

"I think we should speak with the doctor in the morning. He attended the last death and perhaps he'll know something about the husband before that. Hopefully he will be able to clear it up quickly. It's entirely possible that it's just a rumor and there's nothing suspicious about it at all."

Perhaps. And I was hopeful for the sake of his father that that was the case. But it was better to be safe than sorry. I didn't want Redvers' father meeting an unexpectedly sudden end, even if the two men weren't close. Besides his two aunts, Humphrey was the only immediate family Redvers had left.

"Will your father be upset if he learns we're looking into this?"

Redvers gave that a moment's thought. "I think if we're careful it shouldn't get back to him."

A yawn nearly split my face in two and Redvers chuckled. "I think the rest of your questions—and I know you have many—will have to wait, my dear."

It was true. I was quite tired from both the travel and the excitement of the day. "But you'll help me warm my bed first?" I'd had reservations about men and intimacy in the past, but since our trip across the Atlantic, I found I was once again looking forward to such things.

"Scandalous," Redvers gasped before giving me a wink. "Of course, I will."

An hour or so later Redvers disappeared back down the hall to his own room for propriety's sake, and I lay down to sleep. It took a while for sleep to actually come—even though my body was tired, my mind was still wound up. I'd met Redvers' father, and even after spending only a very short period of time with the man, I believed that I understood Redvers better. His childhood had not been warm, and he'd been intimidated by the family members who had been kind to him. No wonder he was closed off and private.

I couldn't stop thinking about Evelyn Hesse either. She was a complicated woman. She'd been kind to Youngblood, uncommonly kind, really, but then proved herself to be unpleasant to Redvers' aunts as well. Yet it seemed highly unlikely that she was a killer. It was easy to want her to be responsible for her previous two husbands' deaths, but if you'd killed one husband and gotten away with it—why risk it a second time? Or even a third, with Humphrey? My guess was that her unpleasant personality had sparked the rumors, and we would hear from the doctor in the morning that her deceased husbands had simply passed from natural causes.

Although, I could very much understand why Redvers might not want Humphrey to marry the woman. It was likely that future family gatherings would prove equally as uncomfortable as this one had started out to be.

The only sounds at breakfast, besides quietly murmured "good mornings," were the clinking of silverware against plates. Breakfast was set up on the sideboard for everyone to help themselves, and I'd filled a plate with eggs, fried vegetables, and some toast. I still wasn't prepared to try everything involved in a full English breakfast—anything with the word *black* in the name was suspect to me, especially since I'd learned it often meant blood. There were two pots of tea for the table, but Redvers had had the cook make a pot of coffee especially for me. It had earned a pointed look from Evelyn, but I was not bothered in the slightest. No one was going to stand between me and my coffee.

Evelyn had been at the breakfast table before either I or Redvers, making me wonder what the point of her going home at night was if she was going to be back again before the sun rose. She wore a becoming forest-green day dress of thick wool, ready for our afternoon in the woods. But we had other matters to attend to first.

"We thought we would head into town this morning," Redvers said into the silence. His father had been reading the morning newspaper and jumped slightly at the sound of his son's voice.

"Whatever for?" Evelyn asked.

Redvers answered but addressed it to his father. "Jane would like to stop in a few of the shops downtown."

I gave his foot a little kick under the table for blaming the outing entirely on me.

"You make such a lovely scapegoat," he whispered to me.

I wrinkled my nose at him.

His father and Evelyn ignored all this. "Very well. Ask Carlisle for the keys to the car, unless you'd rather he drove you." Humphrey paused, thinking. "Could you stop by Berman Jewelers while you're in town? The ring should be ready."

I felt Redvers stiffen next to me—he obviously hadn't spoken to his father about the ring, and I wondered if he would even bother. It had already been adjusted for Evelyn;

it seemed a lost cause at this point. And I truly didn't care what I wore—if I wore a ring at all.

"Certainly," Redvers answered evenly.

"Are you certain that's wise, Humphrey?" Evelyn asked.

Humphrey chuckled, although neither Redvers nor I were amused in the slightest. "He's not a lad, Evelyn. He's unlikely to lose the thing between here and there." Humphrey looked up from his paper at his son. "Right, son?"

Redvers gave his father a somewhat feral smile and agreed before glancing at me. I could tell we were thinking the same thing—losing the ring didn't seem to be what Evelyn was insinuating. She seemed worried he might take it.

CHAPTER FOUR

"That was unpleasant," I said once we were in the car and safely on our way into town. It was a short drive, but with the lanes as narrow as they were, I was glad for the safety of a vehicle instead of trying to walk into the town center.

"Indeed," he said.

I was also thinking about how reluctant Carlisle had been to give up control of the car. It was hard to say whether it was because he felt driving members of the family around was his sole purpose on the estate, or because we were taking away his own mode of transportation. Redvers and I were quiet for the rest of the drive—only a few short minutes really, until Redvers found Market Street and pulled into a parking space in front of the Kingshead Arms.

"Let's walk to the doctor's office," Redvers suggested. Despite the chill in the air and the feeling that it might snow again at any moment, I happily agreed, clasping one gloved hand over his arm. Both of us were wearing thick wool coats and were further bundled up with scarves and gloves; I also had a thick wool cloche pulled down over my ears. I was grateful for all of it, especially when the first few snowflakes fell from the overcast sky. I was tempted to catch one on my tongue, but restrained myself.

We walked the several blocks to the doctor's office, located on the first floor of a cream-colored brick building. The front door was decorated with a green wreath, festive with its pine cones, red berries, and large red bow. Redvers held the door for me and I stepped inside, finding a small waiting room with several chairs and a matronly woman behind a small wooden desk.

"Can I help you?" She was very polite, but I suspected no one got past that desk if she didn't want them to.

Redvers stepped forward. "We would like to see the doctor, when he has a moment."

She looked us both over with a practiced eye. "Are you feeling ill?"

Redvers gave her his most winning smile, although it didn't put the slightest crack in her professional demeanor. "We just have some questions for him." He paused. "I'm Humphrey Dibble's son."

The woman unbent slightly. "How is Humphrey? We haven't seen him in some time."

"He appears to be in the height of health." It was an evasive answer, but she didn't seem to notice.

"That's good to hear." She was definitely more friendly now that Humphrey's name had been used. "Please tell him that Mary sends her regards."

"I'll be sure to do that. Do you think we could see Dr. Taylor for just a few moments?"

Mary peered around Redvers at the one other person waiting in the room, an elderly woman who appeared to have fallen fast asleep with her head against the wall. "I don't think it will hurt Doris to have a little extra sleep. You two go on ahead." She wagged a finger. "But don't keep him too long."

We both smiled politely and passed through to the doctor's examining room, knocking on the doorframe to alert the man that we'd arrived. He was a small, trim man, probably only a few years younger than Redvers' own father. This was a small town, and Humphrey had grown up here; it was probable that the two men had known each other for many years.

Introductions were made, and Dr. Taylor took his seat once again. "How can I help you?"

Redvers and I remained standing. The only other option for sitting was the examining table, and I wasn't about to hop onto that just for a place to sit.

"We'd like to ask you some questions about Evelyn Hesse's former husbands," Redvers said.

The jovial, welcoming demeanor was gone in an instant. "And why would you be concerned with that?" Dr. Taylor asked. Then he answered his own question. "Ah, because your father is marrying Evelyn." Redvers nodded, and Taylor was quiet for a long moment while he shifted in his chair, the wood creaking in the silence.

"I think you'd best go," the doctor finally said. "I have actual patients I need to see."

I was taken aback at the abrupt request, but Redvers' expression never changed and he went straight to the heart of the matter. "Do I have reason to be concerned? Did Evelyn's husbands die of natural causes?"

Now the doctor was outraged. "I only signed off on one of those death certificates and I have no idea whether or not she was married before. But more importantly, I don't like what you're implying, young man. It's time for you to leave." Dr. Taylor stood and opened the door pointedly. Redvers and I slowly made our way out of the room.

"Mary, send in Doris please," he called to the receptionist past our retreating backs.

The doctor had been upset by the question, but I noticed that he hadn't exactly denied Redvers' implied accusation either. Taylor had signed off on the last certificate, certifying it as natural, but if there was no reason for suspicion, why had the question upset him so much? It wasn't surprising that the doctor didn't know about Evelyn's first husband, since she hadn't lived here at the time. But his reaction had me wondering if the doctor knew—or at least suspected—something he wasn't willing to admit.

It had begun snowing more earnestly when we stepped out onto the walkway in front of Taylor's office. We made our way back to Market Street, picking our footing carefully on the damp walkways and watching for slippery spots.

"He knows something," Redvers said once we were out of view of Taylor's building.

"My thoughts exactly. Do you think we'll get another chance to speak with him?"

Redvers frowned. "I'm not sure."

"Breaking into his office won't help, will it?"

Now Redvers raised an eyebrow at me. "Is breaking and entering always your first instinct?"

"You can't tell me you don't have your lockpicks with you."

He chuckled. "Very well. You have me there." His face grew serious. "But no, I don't think his files will be any help to us. If he did have suspicions about those deaths, I doubt he recorded those thoughts anywhere. Not after he signed off on the certificate—he wouldn't want to implicate himself in any way." Redvers shook his head. "We'll have to come at this from another angle."

We'd reached the main street. I knew Redvers needed to stop by the jewelry store for his father, but I was hoping for a chance to look in a few of the shops. I hadn't forgotten that I still needed a gift for Redvers. And it occurred to me that I might need to do some further gift-giving.

"Do we need to find gifts for your father and Evelyn?"

Redvers looked as though he'd swallowed something unpleasant. "I have something for Father from the both of us, but not for Evelyn, obviously. Since I didn't know she'd insinuated herself into my father's life."

I nodded. "I'll look for something for her then."

"I suppose. If you must."

I gave him a wry look. "How about you run your errand and I'll look around. We can meet back here in an hour or so?" Redvers agreed, and strolled down the street, hands in pockets. I watched him go for a moment before hurrying into the first gaily decorated shop, boughs of greenery framing the doorway.

I had an hour to find the perfect gift for the man. No pressure. No pressure at all.

At the end of the hour, I'd managed to acquire a gift for Evelyn—a pair of leather gloves in a child's size—but I'd still come up short with an idea for my own fiancé. Nothing seemed quite right. I'd rather begun to doubt whether I knew the man well enough to choose a gift, but I reassured myself that that was a silly idea. I knew him well. The right present just hadn't . . . well, presented itself. I still had a couple days to figure it out.

Redvers was leaning against the car when I returned. "Have you been waiting long?" I asked.

"Not at all," he said, leaning forward and giving me a quick kiss. "Things took longer at the jeweler's than I'd thought they would."

"Oh!" I was surprised. "I thought you were just picking up the ring."

"It wasn't ready yet." Redvers gave me a smile and I wondered if he was up to something but decided to leave it be. Perhaps he was trying to arrange a surprise for me—and for once, I would try not to ruin it.

*   *   *

We were back at the Dibble house in time for lunch, another somber affair. I found myself wishing that Redvers' aunts had come for the meal since they significantly livened things up, even if that included stirring up conflict. I also wondered if the atmosphere had been different in the Dibble family when Redvers' mother and brother—who'd been killed in the war—had still been alive, or if things had always felt so stuffy. It was a far cry from my own family, which was much less than perfect, but at least there was always some kind of lively discussion going on. Truth be told, I was quite bored. Not to mention it was so quiet I could hear everyone sipping at their soup.

I tried to break the silence. "The shops on Market Street are quite charming—they've all done a lovely job decorating for Christmas."

Everyone looked up at me. "Yes, they usually do," Humphrey replied.

"Miss Wunderly, we usually like to dine in silence," Evelyn said. "It aids in digestion."

"Does it?" I asked. "Did you read that somewhere? I'm always curious about current research in medicine."

She stared at me. The irony wasn't lost on me that she wanted me to be quiet and I wanted to discuss the quiet. But the dam had been broken and now Humphrey turned to his son. "Any trouble at Berman's?"

Redvers' face remained completely neutral. "I stopped in. The ring wasn't quite ready yet. Something about a rush job they were working on."

Humphrey shrugged and went back to his soup, but Evelyn's eyes had narrowed. She didn't say anything, however.

"Did you grow up here, Mr. Dibble?" I refused to go back to sitting in silence, regardless of what Evelyn wanted. She shot me an evil look, which I ignored.

"I did, as did my parents before me. And my son Percival

would have eventually taken over the house if he'd survived the war. I'm not sure what will happen to it now." This was said with a pointed look at Redvers, which Redvers ignored by concentrating on the main course that had been placed in front of him by Mrs. Potter.

He'd never mentioned to me that his father wanted him to take over the house and grounds, but I supposed it wasn't much of a surprise. I just couldn't imagine Redvers settling here in this tiny village so far to the north. In fact, I hadn't really thought much at all about where we might live once we were married. Another question I needed to add to my growing list of questions to ask the man.

Lunch was finally over and we all went to collect our winter things for the sleigh ride. I mentally kept my fingers crossed that Aunt Carolyn and Aunt Marie remembered to join us, and that they would be invited to stay for dinner as well. But I needn't have worried—as soon as we stepped outside, I could see their sleigh coming up the drive pulled by two beautiful black horses. Both women were covered head to foot in fur and snuggled under several heavy blankets besides. Carolyn was deftly handling the reins and pulled to a stop behind Humphrey's own sleigh.

"Jane! Redvers! Get in back—there are some blankets and hot water bottles there for you. Hopefully they're still warm," Aunt Marie called. I greeted both women and stepped up into the sleigh, settling myself on the cold leather seat. I was grateful for the still-warm hot water bottle and for Redvers' additional warmth once he got in as well, pulling the blankets over both our legs. Beneath the blanket, he took my hand, entwining our fingers, and I smiled.

I heard what sounded like the stamping of feet behind us. Turning, I noticed a man on horseback who appeared to be waiting for us to leave. "Who is that?"

Redvers shifted to see what I was looking at, still holding tight to my hand. "Oh, that's the groundskeeper, Mr. Jackson. I assume he's coming along to assist with the tree." Content once more, I settled back into my seat.

Humphrey and Evelyn were driven by Carlisle, who seemed as adept with a pair of reins as the steering wheel of a car. Their sleigh wasn't much smaller than the one we were in, and I knew Carolyn's assertions had been simply so that they had an excuse to join us. Carolyn snapped her reins and the four of us followed Humphrey and Evelyn's sleigh out onto the grounds and into the nearby forest. There was enough snow here to make the journey relatively smooth even as it continued to snow lightly.

"We could have fit easily in their sleigh," I said to Redvers in a low voice. Although not low enough, apparently.

"Oh, you certainly could have," Carolyn called over her shoulder. Nothing wrong with the hearing on these ladies. "But why would you have wanted to?"

"Much better this way," Aunt Marie agreed. She rifled under her blanket for a moment and turned around slightly in her seat, holding a silver flask aloft. "A warmer?"

I laughed and shook my head, and she shrugged before unscrewing the top and taking a small swig. "Suit yourself." Carolyn also took a draft before the flask disappeared once more. Moments later the sleigh ahead of us slowed to a stop and we pulled up behind them. Carolyn fiddled with the reins before draping them over the front of the sleigh.

"Now"—Evelyn clapped her hands together—"we need a tree that's well rounded, nicely filled out, but only about eight feet tall. I don't like it when they cut the top off the tree to make it fit in a space."

"Anything else?" Carolyn muttered under her breath.

"Maybe it should be able to walk itself home as well," Marie replied equally as quietly. Evelyn gave them a look but didn't say anything—she couldn't have heard what they'd said, but it was obvious she knew they'd said *something*. The aunts ignored her, which I thought was for the best. It was then that I noticed each woman was carrying a pair of garden shears.

Carolyn saw me looking at their sharp garden implements. "We're here for some mistletoe. And greens for our mantel."

It was decided that Carolyn and Marie would venture one way while the rest of our party would venture the other. We left the sleighs and horses right where they stood under Carlisle's watchful guard.

I was grateful for my sturdy boots as we tromped through the snow. Evelyn and Humphrey were ahead of us—as short as Evelyn was, I was surprised by how quickly the woman could move.

"Did you do this growing up?"

"What part? Turning into an icicle in the forest?"

I gave his arm a light thump. "No, choosing a Christmas tree."

Redvers cocked his head. "We actually did not. My mother would just tell the groundskeeper what she wanted, and he would go out and bring back a tree matching her specifications."

"Oh." I didn't want to disparage the memory of his mother, but I found going into the woods to choose a tree entirely more charming. Despite my chilled feet.

"I have to give Evelyn credit, though. This is more fun." Redvers looked up at the fat snowflakes falling from the sky. "Even if we are cold."

I smiled and touched his arm.

Jackson was doing an excellent job of staying out of sight, but I could hear the occasional sound of a horse's soft whicker amongst the trees. I hoped the poor creature wasn't too cold—and that went for the horses attached to the sleighs as well. But I was soon distracted from my thoughts about horses by Redvers pulling me behind a large pine tree to warm me up.

"Jane? Redvers? Where did you go? We need you to decide about this tree." Evelyn's voice broke the crisp air and we pulled apart reluctantly. With a sigh from each of us, we rejoined Redvers' father and his fiancée.

I eyed the tree Evelyn stood before. It seemed to meet all her requirements—it was round and full and seemed quite tall. "I think it looks wonderful."

Evelyn turned to Humphrey. "Please go stand next to it, dear." Humphrey did as he was told, standing awkwardly next to the large conifer. She shook her head. "I think it's only seven feet. We need one that is taller."

I pressed my lips together so that no unkind observations would fall from them.

My feet were frozen nearly solid by the time Evelyn approved a tree for cutting down. Jackson came forward from where he'd been staying out of sight, looked around, and nodded before getting off his horse. He tied a red ribbon to a branch, then went back to his horse for a handsaw, while the rest of us started the walk back to our sleighs. I had expected that we would cut the tree down and take it with us—it was a little disappointing to do all that hunting and come away without our prize immediately, but I'd enjoyed our time in the woods despite Evelyn being so particular. I'd lost count of the number of trees that had been eliminated for one small reason or another, but Redvers' company and his penchant for warming me up whenever we had a moment alone had more than made up for Evelyn's being difficult to please.

We returned to the sleighs and found Carolyn and Marie ready to go, but no sign of Carlisle. Evelyn looked especially worried, shouting his name between tiny gloved hands. After a few minutes the man came out from a stand of trees holding a handkerchief to his head. "Apologies, ma'am," he said, although he didn't explain further.

"What happened?" Evelyn looked quite concerned, starting to move forward but stopping abruptly.

Carlisle brought the white handkerchief away from his scalp and we could see a splotch of red. "I went into the woods . . ." He stopped whatever he'd been about to say and considered his next words. "For a call of nature." A nod and he continued. "Something hit me from behind and I went down. Must have knocked me out."

Redvers and I exchanged a look. I turned to look at his aunts who each gave me a shrug—they obviously hadn't seen anything unusual.

"Was it a tree branch? They're deuced heavy—could easily knock a man out," Humphrey said.

Carlisle shook his head. "I didn't see anything." After a quick, worried glance at Evelyn, the chauffeur changed the subject. "Are we ready to go now, sir?"

"We are," Humphrey said. "But I can drive if you're not feeling up to the task."

"Oh, no, sir. I'm fine." He folded his handkerchief and tucked it away in his pocket, then climbed into the sleigh, gathering the reins. Humphrey and Evelyn got in slowly behind him.

Redvers and I made our way back to the second sleigh, looking around for unusual footprints. There was nothing to see—it had snowed enough while we were gone that any tracks had been filled except for the ones we were currently making. I could feel a frown furrowing my brow.

"Hop in! Let's go—we're freezing out here." Aunt Carolyn was enunciating quite carefully as she shouted, and I suspected the ladies had been warming themselves from the inside while they waited. Redvers and I did as we were asked and were barely beneath our blankets before Carolyn had the horses moving. We were moving at quite a clip this time, the wind brisk on my face, and I leaned forward to ask Carolyn and Marie how long they'd been waiting for us, when we came around a tight corner. A cracking noise tore through the crisp air and then we were flying.

CHAPTER FIVE

We'd all been thrown from the sleigh as it came loose from its traces. I'd come to rest in the snow, Redvers not far from me. I pushed myself up to sitting and glanced around in a panic, trying to decipher what had happened. Our sleigh was resting on its side, the traces attaching it to the horses having come detached. The pair of horses had come to a stop up ahead and stood patiently, shifting from foot to foot.

Redvers checked that I was fine before pushing himself to his feet, calling, "Aunt Carolyn! Aunt Marie!" Redvers had already reached the two women where they'd landed before I was able to get unsteadily to my feet. Behind us, Carlisle was pulling the horses to a stop; they'd been moving much slower than we had been, so he was able to stop the sleigh easily.

I heard a groan from Carolyn where she lay on the ground. "I knew I shouldn't have had that much brandy."

Redvers was helping Marie to her feet. "It might have helped you both, actually." Redvers checked Marie over and, seeing that she was okay, helped Carolyn to her feet as well.

"Are you all right?" I asked anxiously, reaching Aunt Marie's side. She grabbed on to my arm and held it tightly. She was still quite strong for a woman of her age.

"We're fine. Just some bumps. Right, Carolyn?"

Carolyn nodded then started slowly toward her sleigh, brushing snow off her coat as she went. Humphrey was already there, examining the leather traces, although I noticed that Evelyn hadn't left her seat. Humphrey held one end of leather in his gloved hand.

"Looks like it broke," Humphrey said. Redvers had come to stand beside his father and gestured for him to pass it over, which Humphrey did. Redvers examined the piece of leather then gave a reassuring nod.

"He's right. These things happen, and at least no one was hurt."

Carolyn was taking her own look at the wreckage. "We'll need a ride back, Humphrey." She didn't say anything about the traces.

Of course, Evelyn had plenty to say as Carolyn and Marie climbed into the back seat of Humphrey's sleigh. "Your sleigh is quite old. I'm sure it's just that you haven't maintained the leather properly. It should have been inspected before starting out today, Carolyn. Having spent your life around horses, you really should have known better." Evelyn paused in her lecture but had one final thing to say on the matter. "Perhaps you should have watched your speed as well."

Carolyn didn't reply, but I could tell it was costing her quite a lot to hold her tongue. Redvers and I carried the blankets from the tipped-over sleigh to his aunts and tucked them in. "We'll walk back," Redvers told his father. His aunts protested that we could all fit, but Redvers insisted and I agreed with him—it would have been far too uncomfortable for all of us to squeeze into the sleigh.

"We need to bring the horses back," Redvers said, finally silencing his aunts' protests, although it was obvious that they weren't pleased.

Redvers had kept back one blanket which he draped over my shoulders as his father pulled away.

"You'll be all right?" he asked.

I nodded. Walking would help warm me up and the blanket certainly helped. Although I was going to need a warm bath when we got back if I was ever going to feel my feet again.

Redvers grabbed the reins of the horse on the left and gave a small tug. With a soft whicker, the horses slowly plodded along beside us. "Do you want to get on one?" Redvers asked. "Instead of walking back?"

"Moving will help keep me warm," I said. "Now, do you really think it was just an issue of the equipment being old? I can't imagine Carolyn wouldn't have kept these things well maintained." Although she was getting on in years—maybe she hadn't noticed that the leather was worn.

"It was a clean break," Redvers said. "It's more likely that it was cut. And combined with Carlisle being hit on the head . . ." He didn't need to finish that thought. I knew exactly where he was going.

"Someone cut the traces after knocking Carlisle out."

Redvers nodded. "And who knows how long he was out for? We'll have to speak with him later and ask if he heard or saw anything." He kicked a bit at the snow. "Although anyone could have come along and given the traces a quick slice, figuring that they would snap on our return trip. And the fresh snow covered any sign of them."

"Jackson was with us the entire time."

Redvers nodded. "I'll still speak with him and see if he heard anything."

"*We'll* speak with him."

"Of course, my dear." Redvers was quiet for a moment. "It looks as though someone doesn't like that we've been asking questions."

By the time we returned to the house, horses in tow, Redvers' aunts had been taken home with a promise that someone would be sent to retrieve their sleigh. Their horses were put in the stable behind Humphrey's house where his own horses stayed and were cared for by the groundskeeper.

Evelyn was fussing when we came inside. "I suppose Jackson will be even longer bringing the tree in since he has extra horses to tend to."

"Should we have him bring the tree in first?" Humphrey asked.

She looked around. "No. Those animals need to be cared for. The tree can wait a bit." I was more than a little surprised at this attitude, especially since the horses belonged to a pair of women Evelyn obviously didn't care for, but I silently praised her for this attitude. Meanwhile, Evelyn took a deep breath. "Are the both of you okay?"

Redvers and I both nodded. "We're fine," Redvers told her.

Evelyn clapped her hands together. "Excellent. Then we can get the other decorations up."

Humphrey patted her shoulder. "Certainly, dear. Certainly."

"I'll be happy to help once I've had a quick soak in the tub," I volunteered. "I'm afraid my feet are frozen through." Not to mention I could scarcely feel my face from the wind.

Evelyn gave me a sympathetic look. "Of course, Jane. Take your time."

I went upstairs and did just that—had a warm soak in the tub. When I could feel all my parts again, I returned to my room and dressed as quickly as possible, finding that I was eager to assist with putting up Christmas decorations. As I came down the stairs, I saw that much of it had already been done—boughs of holly and pine covered the railings and hung from doorways. Redvers was just hanging a sprig of mistletoe in the doorway to the sitting room when I reached him. Without missing a beat, he pulled me close and pressed his lips to mine, sending a streak of electricity through my veins. If my bath hadn't warmed me, that certainly would have done the trick.

Evelyn cleared her throat. "Really," she said.

Redvers pulled away from me, his eyes smiling into mine as he shrugged. "The mistletoe made me do it."

I giggled and turned to offer Evelyn my help with whatever tasks she had left, but was interrupted by the arrival of the tree. Carlisle and Jackson were struggling to bring the tall, fat pine through the front door. It was indeed a full tree, and the hall was immediately filled with the lovely scent of pine.

"Should Carlisle be doing this? With that bump on his head?" I muttered to Redvers.

"He seems okay now." But Redvers moved forward to help the men, Humphrey quickly joining him. Between the four of them they managed to get the tree through to the sitting room and into place—right where Evelyn wanted it. I could almost hear Carolyn's voice muttering that Evelyn certainly liked things a particular way. As long as that way was *her* way.

"I think we have enough time to get the tree decorated before we need to dress and head over to the Watsons' house," Evelyn announced once the tree was secured.

"Are we going to the Watsons' this evening?" Redvers asked mildly.

"Yes, we are expected at eight," Evelyn said with a touch of impatience, as though we were the ones who'd forgotten the itinerary instead of being informed just now that we were going anywhere.

I had a moment of panic since I hadn't packed anything suitable for a formal gathering, then mentally shrugged. I had a wool dress in a dark shade of red with me. I'd planned to wear it on Christmas Day, but it would have to do—at least it would look festive, colorwise.

Youngblood had ordered the boxes of decorations to be

retrieved from the attic where they were stored, and Redvers and I began opening cardboard boxes filled with glass ornaments. They'd obviously been collected over many years, and I enjoyed seeing some of the things that Redvers remembered from his boyhood hung on the tree—glass fruit, pine cones, and figures of Santa himself alongside unevenly cut paper stars and small wooden toys on strings. Redvers got up on the ladder to decorate the top half of the tree and cheerfully hung the ornaments handed to him by both myself and his father. It was the happiest I'd seen him so far in this house, and I wondered if it was his enjoyment of the holiday or because he had warm memories associated with decorating the tree. His nerves about the visit had subsided after our arrival, but he was still terribly stiff and formal around his father overall, and I didn't anticipate that changing anytime soon.

The tinsel went on last, and we all stepped back to admire our handiwork. It had turned out beautifully, and even Evelyn had unbent enough during the decorating to enjoy herself. I looked forward to seeing it with the candles lit, but that would be saved until Christmas Eve when we were home and could enjoy the lights. As well as keep an eye on the open flames.

All the same, we congratulated ourselves on a job well done, before Evelyn glanced at the mantel clock. "Excellent. We have enough time to dress and make it to the Watsons'."

We each went our separate ways in order to do that. Evelyn had brought a change of clothing along with her that morning so she didn't have to return to her townhome. I had to wonder if she wrote out a daily itinerary—she seemed to have things scheduled down to the minute.

I changed into the red wool dress and smoothed my hair as much as I could before heading back downstairs to meet the others. The scent of fresh greenery and pine greeted me at the top of the stairs and I smiled. It had been a pleasant afternoon despite the sleigh mishap and Carlisle's bump on the head, and even though I didn't know the Watsons, I looked forward to sharing some holiday cheer rather than sitting through another silent meal.

Humphrey and Evelyn hadn't arrived downstairs yet, and I found Redvers in the library. I glanced around. "No bar cart," I observed.

He shook his head sadly. "Father believes in only a glass of wine with dinner. No cocktails for Humphrey."

"I'm surprised he had champagne on hand, in that case."

"I am too, frankly."

"Hopefully the Watsons don't feel the same way."

"I live in hope."

I took a moment to peruse the bookshelves—the first time I'd had the opportunity since I arrived—and found that they were much as I suspected, void of any fun or fictional tomes. Instead there were lots of books on politics, history, and agriculture.

"This collection is . . . impressive." I was taking a stab at politeness.

"It's boring, is what it is," Redvers said.

"It is. I was being polite."

"You're starting now?"

I gave him a little elbow to the side and we shared a smile. It was about to turn into something more when Humphrey came into the room.

"You're both ready? Excellent. Evelyn will be pleased."

And that was true. Evelyn was quite pleased that we were ready at the appointed time. After giving me an up and down look, she gave a single nod. Before I'd even come down the stairs I had decided not to let any reaction from the woman bother me, but I was a little relieved at her nod of approval despite my lack of more formal attire.

I still felt a bit like the poor relation they would have to make excuses for that evening, but I had already focused my hopes on the possibility of cocktails at the Watsons' gathering. Perhaps there would be some wassail and the singing of carols, which always sounded better with a large group of people. "Do you know how many people will be at the Watsons'?" I asked hopefully.

Evelyn wrinkled her nose. "They're quite well-known in the area; their family has been here for nearly a century, so their gatherings are always well attended. Especially the Christmas dinner."

That boded well for some robust caroling, and I happily followed Redvers and company out to the car.

Carlisle was waiting next to the dark sedan, his uniform restored to good order after assisting with the Christmas tree. But Humphrey had other ideas. "We won't be needing you this evening, Carlisle. I'll drive."

"It's no trouble, sir." Carlisle looked slightly intense. I found his reaction to be a strange one—driving the Dibbles was his job, so of course it shouldn't be trouble.

"You may have the evening off, Carlisle." Humphrey held out his hand for the car keys. "Get some rest after that bump on the head today." Carlisle looked to Evelyn for assistance, but she gave her head a tiny shake. Carlisle slowly pulled the keys from his pants pocket and put them in Humphrey's hand, then turned and disappeared around the side of the house.

"What was that about?" I whispered to Redvers. "He doesn't want to admit that he was hurt this afternoon? Your father wouldn't dismiss him over something that wasn't his fault."

"He would not. But that did seem strange—even more reason to talk with the fellow later."

A short ride later we arrived at the Watsons' estate home, which was considerably larger than the Dibbles'. I had the brief and uncharitable thought that if Mr. Watson was a widower, Evelyn might be otherwise engaged, but chided myself for being unkind. Even if it might be true, the woman would be wed to Redvers' father in two days' time. And she'd been quite pleasant while we trimmed the tree, affectionate with Humphrey, and very polite about my dress. Perhaps there were hidden depths to the woman that we simply weren't seeing.

Mr. and Mrs. Watson greeted us at the door—I was relieved that they appeared to know that Redvers and I would be joining them. And if they didn't know in advance that we were coming along, they covered for it remarkably well.

"Your brother is already here, Evelyn. You'll find him in the drawing room with the rest."

Both Redvers and I did a remarkable job keeping our faces neutral since this was the first we'd heard that Evelyn had a brother, let alone one that was in Barnard Castle.

After exchanging holiday greetings, our group crossed the foyer into the spacious formal drawing room where a rather large crowd was already assembled. The Watsons had also decorated a day early—it was customary to put up the Christmas tree and all the decorations on Christmas Eve, but everything was in place and brightly lit. I spotted Aunt Carolyn and Aunt Marie across the room and gave them a wave. They beckoned for me to join them—they'd commandeered a pair of comfortable-looking armchairs and seemed to be watching the crowd. I could only imagine the commentary they were providing, and I looked forward to hearing it up close. I was about to make my excuses to Redvers and his family when I heard an all-too-familiar voice come from my right.

"Jane! It's about time you arrived. What is that you're wearing?"

CHAPTER SIX

I closed my eyes. How on earth had my aunt Millie come to be at this party? Which is precisely what I asked her—more politely, of course.

Millie and Lord Hughes, her fiancé, had come to join our small group. "We have been in the hills to do some skiing." My eyebrows shot right up at the idea of Millie on a pair of skis. She acknowledged this by adding, "I should say that Lillian and Edward have been skiing. I've been occupying myself otherwise."

I glanced at the highball in her hand. It was easy to guess how she was occupying herself while her fiancé and daughter hit the slopes.

"Of course, Edward is acquainted with the Watsons, and so we were invited for dinner. I knew that you and Redvers were staying nearby for the holiday, and I assumed—correctly—that you would be here tonight." Millie looked pleased with herself for her bit of deduction. "Lillian stayed behind at the lodge. She thought her time would be better served resting since she developed something of a headache, and we agreed. She sends her greetings to you and Redvers, of course."

During this tidal wave of information, Redvers' father and Evelyn stood to the side, observing—Humphrey looked bemused, but Evelyn's face was completely unreadable. Once Millie wound down, I made the introductions between them. It was a strange moment, having my aunt meet Redvers' father. I wondered briefly what it would have been like if my mother had still been alive, making the acquaintance of my fiancé's family. Probably less overwhelming for Humphrey—Millie and my mother had been nearly complete opposites in personality although they'd got on quite well.

As everyone exchanged pleasantries, I could see that Millie was sizing up Evelyn. I had to admit that I was rather looking forward to hearing what she had to say about the woman. But Evelyn must have noticed also and made her excuses.

"I see my brother James. If you'll excuse me." Without waiting for a response from anyone, she broke away from our party and crossed the room, stopping next to a man who was rather on the short side. He had a strong jawline and his dark hair had gone mostly gray, leading me to think that James was likely her older brother.

"The doctor is here," Redvers whispered into my ear, breaking me out of my quiet observation. I looked around the room—as casually as possible—spotting Dr. Taylor as he stood near the fireplace, drinking what looked like a glass of red wine. "Will you excuse us?" Redvers asked. "We need to get some refreshments."

"Of course, of course," Humphrey said. I felt a little badly leaving Humphrey alone with my aunt and her fiancé, but I suspected he and Lord Hughes would find something to chat about. Millie tipped her glass to the side slightly before she asked for a refill, despite hers being half-full.

Redvers and I moved across the room, snagging a few glasses of mulled wine from one of the numerous footmen moving around the room. In an attempt to appear casual, we threaded through the crowd in the direction of the doctor but stayed out of his direct line of sight. It worked out quite nicely that we could stop and talk to Redvers' aunts while keeping a close eye on the doctor.

"Who was that you were speaking with?" Carolyn opened with a question instead of a greeting, which amused me greatly.

"That's my aunt and her fiancé."

"A lot of that going around," Aunt Marie said. "Not a lot of family resemblance between you though."

I shrugged. That much was true. "I was surprised to see them here."

"Everyone turns up for this," Aunt Carolyn said. "The dinner is pretty decent, too."

"Who's that Evelyn is talking to?" Aunt Marie asked.

"I believe that's her brother," Redvers said.

"Interesting," Marie said, letting the word roll about on her tongue as though she was savoring it. "We didn't know she had any family."

"We did not," Carolyn chimed in. "There does seem to be a resemblance there, though."

Was there? I didn't see it, although perhaps they had similar cheekbones. I decided to change the subject, after sneaking another quick look at the doctor. "How are you both feeling after this afternoon?"

"Oh, we're fine. Just a few bumps. We'll take it easy for a few days and be right as rain in no time," Marie said.

I could feel my eyebrows pull together in worry. Even a small spill could be dangerous for women at their age. We'd been cushioned by the snow, but still—I was concerned for their health.

As though reading my thoughts, Carolyn waved a hand at me. "Stop your worrying. We're fine. Now"—she raised an eyebrow—"why are you watching the doctor?"

Sharp hearing and sharp eyes. Perhaps they weren't quite

as elderly as I'd thought. All the same, I decided to let Redvers field this one.

"We stopped by this morning to ask a few questions and
he wasn't . . . enthusiastic about answering them. I was
hoping he might be more amenable after a few drinks,"
Redvers told them.

Both women's eyes lit up, and I wondered how much
trouble we'd opened the door to. "What kind of questions?" Marie asked.

I could see Redvers trying to decide how much to tell
them, and he waited a beat too long to come up with a sat-
isfactory answer.

"They were asking about Evelyn and her dead husbands," Carolyn told her companion quietly. "I'll bet my
spring hat on it."

"Not surprising he wouldn't tell you much," Marie told
us, then turned back to Carolyn. "They should break into
his office. Check his records."

"That's not a bad idea," Carolyn said as Redvers and I
both stiffened. I looked around quickly to see if anyone was
listening to our conversation. As far as I could tell, no one
was. We were lucky so far, but a change of topic was in
order. Fast.

Luckily—for once—Millie chose that moment to join our
little group. "Jane, Redvers. Will you introduce us?"

Redvers made the introductions, then sent a glance of his
own around the room.

Millie noticed and made her own assumptions about
who he was looking for. "Your father excused himself from
us to find a non-alcoholic drink. And that woman never did
come back. Her brother must be quite the conversational-
ist." Everything about Millie's statement was coated with
disdain. It was obvious she hadn't taken to Evelyn Hesse; I
looked forward to finding out exactly why.

"Humphrey always was a wet blanket when it came to drinking," Carolyn said. "In fact, Redvers, would you fetch us a few more glasses of cheer?" I could see from Millie's expression that Carolyn already met with her approval.

Redvers' lips tugged into a small smile. "Of course," he said, moving off to find a footman. I almost told him that he might as well come back with a tray.

Carolyn and Millie struck up a lively conversation about the best Christmas drinks—it seemed to come down to an argument between mulled wine or wassail. I decided to take advantage of Redvers' absence and ask Marie a question.

"Aunt Marie, do you happen to remember what Redvers' favorite books were as a child? I'm desperate to find the perfect Christmas gift for him. Something meaningful."

Marie's face broke into a wide smile in reminiscence. "He did love to read adventure stories as a boy. I suspect that's why he's always on the go now—looking for adventure." I couldn't help but smile as well. "Humphrey and Mary, they were so strict with Redvers. Didn't approve of fictional novels." Marie rolled her eyes. "Absolute foolishness. I do recall that he especially loved *Treasure Island*. He read that one many times. In secret, of course. We always had to sneak novels to the lad."

"Perfect. Thank you so much." I would look in the bookshop the next morning and see if I could find a nice, illustrated copy of the book.

Marie nodded, her eyes warm. "It's a thoughtful gift, Jane."

I certainly hoped Redvers would think so. Then I remembered that we had some questions for Redvers' aunts about that afternoon. "Aunt Marie, how long were you both waiting in the sleigh before we came back?"

Aunt Marie considered this. "We went through what was in my flask and then Carolyn's before you arrived." I hadn't known that Carolyn was packing her own and I suppressed a smile. "So about thirty minutes, I would think." I didn't even need to ask my next question before Marie answered it for me. "We didn't see or hear anyone, but we were away from the sledges for quite a while—which is probably when Carlisle was knocked out and the leather cut. That is what you think happened, isn't it?"

Marie's eyes were shrewd and I didn't even bother sugar-coating my answer. There was simply no point. "It is, actually." Marie nodded and turned back to the others.

Redvers returned with half a tray of both mulled wine and wassail and distributed the drinks to everyone, before turning and handing the empty tray to the nearest member of the staff. He put a hand on my arm. "If you'll excuse us, I see someone Jane and I need to speak with." Millie waved us off but both Carolyn and Marie had a crafty look in their eyes as they watched us go. I hoped they would stay right where they were.

I was a little surprised Millie had hit it off so well with Redvers' aunts, since they all had such strong personalities, but from the last snatches of conversation I'd heard, it seemed they were sharing their mutual dislike of Evelyn Hesse. Sometimes a common enemy was all that was needed to bond people together.

Redvers and I made our way toward the doctor, who had moved from his position near the fireplace to talk to a group of people gathered near the brightly decorated Christmas tree. The flickering of candles shone from many branches and the smell of pine grew stronger the closer we came.

Redvers introduced me to the group, and I smiled and nodded even though I wasn't taking in any of their names. I was more concerned with Dr. Taylor who was now standing to my right. His cheeks were ruddy, which I surmised was from drinking. Perhaps Redvers was correct and we would have more luck with the man than we had this morning.

After the introductions were finished, I turned to the doctor. "It's nice to see you again, Dr. Taylor. Are you enjoying yourself?"

The man shrugged. "As much as anyone, I suppose." He eyed me suspiciously. "I really should be going soon, though."

I nearly reached out to put a restraining hand on his arm. "Oh, you couldn't possibly leave before supper, could you? You must stay."

The doctor looked at me for a moment. "I'm not going to tell you anything else, young lady." He turned away from me, taking a large swig from the mug in his hand. He began to cough, and I wondered if he had swallowed wrong. But his face was soon turning an alarming shade of red as he hunched over into his fit, clutching his chest.

"Dr. Taylor, are you all right?" I asked.

That's when he slumped to the ground.

CHAPTER SEVEN

The doctor's mug of mulled wine spilled from his hand onto the carpet, and it was quite obvious that he was not going to be answering my question. Someone in our group shrieked as Redvers and I both bent down over the man. Redvers felt for a pulse, holding his hand on the doctor's wrist for a long time before grimly shaking his head. "We need to get everyone out of here."

I nodded and stood quickly, standing in front of the scene in an attempt to block it from view. Nearly everyone in the room was already staring at us, so I spoke loudly. "The doctor has just fainted and needs some air. Perhaps we could all go into the dining room now?" It was rude to suggest such a thing without consulting either of our hosts, but I didn't see any other options. I caught the eye of Mr. Watson, who was already making his way to us, and gave him a beseeching look. He saw me and with a quick nod, turned and began ushering people toward the door.

"She's right. We just need to give the man some air. It's quite hot in here. Does everyone have what they need? Excellent. Let's head on in to the dining room. I'm certain supper is nearly ready." Mr. Watson kept up a running dialogue as he ushered his guests from the room. His wife only took a few beats before she began doing the same, leading the pack of guests to their meal.

I made a mental note to thank our hosts profusely later. Then I turned back to the scene behind me. Redvers had managed to convince the people who had been standing with us to head out of the room with the rest, and now it was just the two of us—as well as Aunt Millie, Lord Hughes, and Redvers' two aunts. I should have known they wouldn't be persuaded to leave with the rest.

"He looks pretty dead to me," Aunt Carolyn said. I half expected the woman to nudge the body with her shoe to make sure.

"I agree," Marie replied. "I think they were lying about him fainting."

"I wonder who killed him?" Carolyn mused.

"I'm sure it doesn't have to be murder," Millie chimed in. Marie and Carolyn rounded on her and I stepped in before an argument could break out. I didn't want to see who would come out ahead.

"Perhaps he had a health condition no one knew about." I bent down to look at the spilled wine on the rug, then gingerly picked up the mug the doctor had been holding. I brought it up to my nose and sniffed at it. "Although this smells bitter." I reached for my own mug of mulled wine and did a comparison sniff. Mine smelled sweet and of warm spices—very different from what the doctor's mug smelled like. I said this to Redvers.

He sighed. "I think we should call the police."

Mr. Watson returned, and once we told him that we felt the police should be called, he went quickly from the room once more. While we waited for them to arrive, Redvers managed to convince Millie and company to head in for supper as well. This was no small feat, and we had to promise to give them a detailed rundown of everything that happened in their absence.

In the meantime, Mr. Watson returned once more. He was a pleasant man, of average height and getting plump around the middle. His moustache twitched in consternation. "Normally I would say we should call the doctor, but . . ." He checked his gold pocket watch. "The police sergeant should be here shortly."

"How well do you know the doctor?" I asked our host.

"Well enough, I suppose. This is a rather small community. Why do you ask?"

"I was wondering if he was taking anything. For a health condition perhaps?" Perhaps there was another explanation for the bitter smell.

Mr. Watson shook his head. "I thought the man was in the peak of health. He'd even lost quite a few pounds recently. He was complaining that he'd had to buy all new clothes, but I told him there were worse problems to have." Watson had started to smile, but it faded as he glanced past us to the doctor lying on the floor. "Poor man."

Watson soon excused himself to attend to his guests, promising to have a couple plates of food set aside for us. There had been no questions as to why we'd decided to stay with the body—presumably because folks in the village understood that Redvers worked for the government in some capacity? I knew why we were there—to make certain no one interfered with the body. But what did other people think?

"What do the people in town think you do for a living?" I asked.

Redvers raised one eyebrow at me. "They think I have a desk job in the government."

I snorted. "Your aunts certainly don't think that's the case."

"They've always been much more difficult to fool."

That was easy to believe.

I was about to ask why everyone, including the Watsons, had left us here minding the body, when the police arrived. We were quickly escorted out by the constable, with thanks for keeping an eye on things.

I couldn't resist tossing the sergeant a question over my shoulder as we were being herded out of the room. "But how will you determine what happened? Since he was the town doctor?"

Sergeant Thomas didn't even look up at me. "We called a doctor from the next village over. He'll be here as soon as he can."

I was relieved that someone had been called in to take a look at whether Dr. Taylor had died of natural causes. Because I had more than a sneaking suspicion that he had not.

The other guests had not been informed about Dr. Taylor's demise, so the atmosphere in the dining room was quite cheerful. Redvers and I opted to take our plates into a quiet sitting room, however. I wasn't ready to join in the general merriment—I just hoped that no one had noticed us come into the room and leave once again.

"Any initial thoughts?" I speared a bite of ham with my fork.

"Hard to say," Redvers said. "It's certainly suspicious that we asked Dr. Taylor about Evelyn just this morning and by the evening he's dead."

"Agreed. The trouble is that Evelyn arrived with us. So even if she had decided to remove him from the picture, she wasn't here to slip anything into that drink."

"An accomplice?" Redvers suggested.

"It would be the only way. Who could that possibly be, though? Certainly not your father."

"Her brother? We haven't had a chance to interact with him yet."

"That's true," I said. "We could go back to the party and talk with him. Or . . ." I had an idea.

Redvers looked concerned. "You have a plan, don't you?"

"We could leave now and search her house before she or your father even know we're gone. It's the perfect opportunity—we know where everyone else is and they're otherwise occupied."

It only took him a beat to decide this wasn't a terrible idea. "I'll get our coats."

After convincing a footman to show us where the coats were being kept, locating said coats, and lifting the car keys from his father's pocket, Redvers and I quietly left the Watsons'. I could hear the sounds of singing, and was disappointed that we wouldn't be joining in, but we had more pressing things to attend to.

It took us a little longer than anticipated to get to Evelyn's because we had to stop back at the Dibble home first—Redvers hadn't brought his lockpick set with him to supper. I told him that was silly because at the rate we were going, he should simply keep it on him. Once he procured his kit, we raced back into town.

"How do you know where she lives?" I asked.

"I did some looking around in my father's office last night. I found some correspondence."

"I hate it when you snoop without me."

Redvers shot me an amused look, then pulled the car to the curb. "We're here."

"Here" was a row of brick townhomes in the same creamy color seen throughout the village of Barnard Castle. Lights glowed from the windows of the houses on either side of the one we were parked in front of, but Evelyn's was completely dark. We got out of the car and walked up to the front door where it took Redvers the work of only a few seconds to get the door open. Once inside, we quickly shut the door behind us in the pitch dark.

"I was a little concerned her staff might be here, but it's obvious that there is no one home," Redvers said. "Let's see if we can find some lights."

The two of us felt around in the dark until we found a switch, clicked it on, and illuminated the foyer where we stood. But there was nothing to see—the town house was strangely empty. No furniture, no knickknacks, nothing. We moved from room to room, finding the same everywhere we went. It was a lovely building, although being a townhome there weren't many windows. During the day there would be limited natural light in the interior rooms, but the walls had been brightly painted to compensate. We turned on and switched off lights as we moved through the house.

"This is very strange," I said. "Even though she's presumably moving in with your father after the wedding, it seems incredible that there is nothing here. She hasn't sent crates of things to his house already, has she?"

Redvers shook his head. "I asked Youngblood about Evelyn after we arrived, and according to him, she hasn't sent anything over yet. You're right. This is very odd."

We moved into the hallway and went up the stairs, finding the same emptiness in all but the master bedroom. There was an open trunk that appeared to be half-packed with dresses and other accessories standing in one corner. I walked across the room to the wardrobe and pulled it open, finding more clothing there. A small vanity and a large bed were the only pieces of furniture in the room, although there were still some personal items on the vanity—a set of brushes, a jewelry case, and a glass bottle of perfume.

"At least we know she's actually living here." I gestured at the vanity top. "What do you think this means?"

"I have a few ideas," Redvers said. "Most of them have to do with money."

"You think she was forced to sell everything off?"

"Given the state of things here, it's a reasonable explanation." Redvers opened the drawers on the small vanity, rifling through but finding nothing of interest.

I nodded. "If she's in dire financial straits, she most likely has no staff. It would also explain why she's attached herself to your father so quickly."

Redvers moved over to the trunk, carefully searching through its contents. "I asked Father the other night, and it has indeed been a bit of a whirlwind romance."

"I assumed as much since you hadn't known about it." I didn't point out that the Dibble men didn't speak to each other very often and this was another reason why Redvers hadn't known about his father's engagement. Every once in a while, I *was* able to stop myself from stating the obvious.

Redvers had paused his search of the trunk. "I think I found something." From where I was standing, I could see him move piles of clothing aside as he pulled a packet of papers from the bottom of the trunk. He set the papers next to him on the floor, then set to work straightening everything in the trunk.

I was eager to take a look at what he'd found, but I also knew we needed to head back to the party before we were missed—we'd already been gone a long time. Redvers handed the packet of papers to me and I followed him back downstairs, shutting off lights as we went. We closed the front door and hurried back to the car.

"What happens when Evelyn notices these are gone?"

"It's likely that she will, but we'll have an alibi—we can say we've been speaking with the police." Redvers was already pulling the car away from the curb and speeding back toward the party. "It's unlikely anyone will question that."

I looked at the papers in my hand. "Should we stop back at your father's house to hide these?" It seemed risky to keep them in the car if we were going to drive back with the woman.

Redvers shook his head. "We don't have time. We'll put them in the boot when we stop."

CHAPTER EIGHT

It turned out we didn't need any kind of alibi—no one seemed to notice that we'd been gone even though it had been an awfully long time. I wondered what the Watsons had told their guests about Dr. Taylor since everyone seemed to have forgotten about the episode and was having a delightful time in the ballroom. Although, watching the footmen circulate with their trays of Christmas cheer, I thought perhaps it was the alcohol that had led everyone to forget about the poor doctor.

Chairs had been set up in the large room since the guests couldn't return to the drawing room. And even though there was no Christmas tree here, boughs of greenery were strung about, as well as red paper bells and looped paper chains, so the festive holiday feeling was still apparent. Redvers and I quietly joined the nearest group of townsfolk after snagging some drinks. We exchanged pleasantries, then moved to the next little grouping of people. By the time we made our way to Humphrey and Evelyn, it seemed that we'd never been gone at all.

"I think we're about ready to leave," Humphrey told Redvers when we joined them. "Have you made the rounds and spoken with everyone you should?"

"Indeed, we have," Redvers said. "And we're ready to go when you are. Although I think we should say good night to Carolyn and Marie."

Evelyn's nose wrinkled slightly, but she stayed silent.

"I didn't get to meet your brother, Evelyn." I glanced around but didn't see him in the crowd.

"Oh, he had to leave a bit ago." Evelyn sounded vague. "I'll be certain to introduce you next time."

I murmured something polite about looking forward to it, but it piqued my suspicion. Was the man avoiding us? It seemed awfully convenient that he'd missed meeting us. I was tempted to ask Humphrey how well he knew Evelyn's brother, but instead Redvers and I moved off to find his aunts. They were across the room, seated in a small group with my aunt Millie and Lord Hughes. I rather dreaded what these women could get up to when banded together.

But instead of a sharp comment about where we'd been all evening, my aunt Millie wished us a very pleasant good evening. "I hope we'll see you tomorrow. Along with Carolyn and Marie, of course." Millie beamed at the older women.

"Of course," Redvers said. "You're all welcome to join us for supper tomorrow evening."

I was still suspicious about having these three women in cahoots, but I wished them all a warm good evening, and Redvers and I took our leave. We met Humphrey and Evelyn in the hall, where they were already collecting their coats. The butler had our things ready for us as well and we put them on.

Humphrey patted his pocket. "I can't seem to find the key to the car."

Redvers checked his own coat, pulling the key from a pocket and handing it to his father. "How strange. It seems to have ended up in my coat."

I held my breath for a second. In our hurry to get back to the party, we'd missed that detail. Would Humphrey find it suspicious? Would he put it together that we'd taken his car and left the party? If Evelyn noticed that her things had been searched, we might be outed as the trespassers.

"Must have fallen out of mine and was replaced into yours. Good thing." Humphrey gave his arm to Evelyn and led us out into the night.

Redvers turned to me and winked.

We let Evelyn off at her house since we were passing through town and waited until she was through her front door. If Humphrey noticed anything unusual about the fact that there were no lights on in her town house and no staff awaiting her, he didn't say anything. I watched anxiously as Evelyn used her key in the front door, since we'd left it unlocked after our search. She hesitated after turning the key, gave her head a little shake, then went inside without any further ado. I hoped she would assume that she simply forgot to lock it, not that anyone had been through the place in her absence.

Arriving back at the Dibble estate, Humphrey got out of the car quickly, although both Redvers and I got out more slowly. I looked to Redvers to see if he was going to open the trunk and retrieve the papers, but he gave his head a little shake and we followed his father inside. Once we'd shed our coats, we all bid one another good night, and headed to our quarters. But instead of preparing for bed, I paced my room, waiting for a knock at my bedroom door. If Redvers didn't bring those papers to my room shortly, I would go knocking on *his* door. There was no way I was going to let him look at them without me.

I waited fifteen excruciating minutes before the knock came, and I nearly ran to the door to open it.

"I was beginning to think you were going to go through those papers on your own."

"I wouldn't dream of it." His face was the picture of innocence. "I had to go back out to retrieve them."

I narrowed my eyes at him, since he actually would not only dream of it but had gone ahead and done it in the past, but I ushered him over to the two seats near the fireplace. "Let's see what we have."

Redvers opened the large brown envelope, pulling a sheaf of papers from inside. I was nearly dancing in my seat with anticipation, but I let him look over the first few pages before he handed them over to me.

"Death certificates," Redvers said.

I noticed he'd used the plural. "So she *was* married before. Your aunts were right." I quickly looked them both over myself. "According to these, both of her husbands died of heart issues." I thought about that. "Which would be natural causes, but what are the odds both husbands died of the same issue?"

"It's feasible, I suppose," Redvers said. "They also may have been misdiagnosed. It's almost impossible to tell without digging them up."

I shuddered. That wasn't a pleasant thought.

"This is interesting." Redvers passed over another paper. "It's an appraisal. For my grandmother's ring. Done about a month ago."

My eyes were wide. "Why on earth would she have done that? And how would she have gotten ahold of the ring to have it done?"

"I don't know," Redvers said grimly. "My father kept the ring in his safe, as far as I know."

I couldn't help but wonder what else Humphrey Dibble kept in his safe and whether those contents were still there.

"Who did the appraisal?"

"It wasn't the local jeweler. She's too clever for that," Redvers said.

I had to agree with him there—Evelyn Hesse was far too clever and controlling to get caught that easily.

Redvers passed over the appraisal, but I only glanced at it. I didn't feel the need to find out what the ring was worth. It was none of my affair.

"And here's the summary of her auction from this summer," Redvers said. "We were right about that as well. And it looks as though she walked away with quite a hefty sum."

"If she made a significant amount of money, then why would she have the ring appraised? What would it matter what it was worth?" It didn't make sense to me.

"It's possible that she had debts to pay off with the proceeds from the auction. That would be my best guess."

"Which could be why she's marrying your father so quickly—for financial security." Or for another estate's worth of money if she could dispose of Humphrey quickly and quietly, but I didn't voice this fear out loud. We had no real proof she'd done any such thing to her last two husbands— just suspicion and rumors.

Redvers nodded and I was quiet for a moment. "Will you tell your father any of this?"

He sighed. "It's not precisely the sort of thing we talk about."

Since they didn't talk about much at all, I gave him a long look.

"Point taken," he said.

Another question occurred to me. "Evelyn seems to run quite hot and cold. What do you think your father sees in her?"

"My mother was rather the same way. I suspect it's comfortable for him to slip into the same sort of relationship."

That made quite a bit of sense, especially for someone

who had been married for so many years before his first wife's passing. He was probably also accustomed to a woman running his household and generally taking care of things. Which meant Humphrey might not be interested in hearing our concerns about his wife-to-be.

Especially so close to the wedding itself.

CHAPTER NINE

Christmas Eve dawned overcast and with the feeling of snow in the air. I kept my fingers crossed that we would actually see some flakes, since it always felt more like Christmas with fresh snow on the ground.

Redvers waited to escort me to breakfast, and it was obvious as we entered the room that we'd interrupted a serious conversation between Evelyn and Humphrey. I caught only a few snatches, but it seemed that Evelyn was concerned that someone had been in her town house. I didn't say anything to Redvers, but my hand tightened on his arm.

Evelyn stopped talking when we walked in, but Humphrey had no such reservations. "We could always call the police, my dear. Especially if you think anything was taken."

With a quick glance at us and a shake of her head, Evelyn murmured her dismissal of the idea. "I don't think it's necessary."

"Only if you're certain. The good news is that you'll be staying here after tonight."

Evelyn gave him a genuine smile, which gave me pause. Perhaps she really did care for Redvers' father. Weddings were stressful, and coordinating such affairs was a great deal of work. Could that be why she was so uptight and controlling? On the other hand, Redvers' aunts weren't fans of the woman and obviously never had been. It was all something to consider.

"We should invite your brother James to stay as well," Humphrey said after a moment. It was clearly an afterthought, but he meant well.

Evelyn shook her head. "He's far more comfortable at the Kingshead. He told me so himself when I offered him my town house."

I glanced at Redvers who was calmly sipping his tea during Evelyn's telling of this obvious lie. There was no way anyone could stay with her since there was no furniture in the place. But her story told me that Humphrey probably wasn't aware of the state of her town house.

Throughout the rest of breakfast, I watched carefully to see if she acted any differently toward myself or Redvers, since I was concerned that she might suspect we were the ones who broke into her house. But everything appeared perfectly normal and she didn't seem to be casting any suspicion our way. I was able to relax and enjoy my breakfast, silent though it was.

Directly after we finished eating, Redvers and I excused ourselves to head into town once more. Redvers assured his father that the ring should be ready today and he would fetch it. I mentioned vaguely that I wanted to take a look in the bookshop.

"That's fine. I'll be meeting with Cook and the staff today." Evelyn had an intimidating list lying next to her breakfast plate. "I need to make certain everything is ready for tomorrow's wedding luncheon."

I found myself feeling quite sorry for Cook and the staff, especially if there was the slightest hitch. Some things were out of human control, but I doubted you could tell Evelyn Hesse that.

Redvers and I bundled up once again and took the car

into town just as the first few snowflakes began fluttering to the ground. He found parking on Market Street once again, and we parted ways. I headed to the small bookstore, and he returned to the jewelry shop to fetch his grandmother's ring.

A small bell dinged overhead as I pushed open the door to Brown's Books, and a bespectacled man, tall and lanky, greeted me. "Let me know if I can help you find anything," he said.

"I'm actually looking for a copy of *Treasure Island*," I told him.

The man nodded and put down the leather volume he'd been wrapping in brown paper. "I think we have a copy or two of that. Follow me." He led me down a narrow path between high shelves—the entire place was close and narrow and packed with books, but somehow avoided feeling claustrophobic. I took a deep breath, inhaling the smell of paper, both old and new. It was a delicious, comforting smell.

"Here we are," the clerk said, pulling two books from the shelf. One was a standard hardcover, but the other was a much nicer leather-bound volume in camel with a decorative spine.

"I'll take this one." I plucked the book from his hand and briefly paged through it before holding it close to my chest. I hoped Redvers would like it. "It's a Christmas gift."

The man's eyes smiled at me. "Then we must wrap it as one. Can I help you find anything else?"

I was tempted to ask for the latest mystery novel—perhaps an Agatha Christie or a Dorothy Sayers, but I didn't think I would have time to read it, since there was a wedding the following day and we would be returning to London the day after that. The plan all along was to spend New Year's at Wedgefield Manor with Lord Hughes and my aunt Millie, and Lord Hughes always stocked the latest novels in his library, so I would find plenty of reading material once we arrived there. I was slightly suspicious that Millie and Lord Hughes had turned up here for Christmas when we had already made plans to see them at the New Year, but I wasn't going to ask my aunt if she was following me around the country. I didn't honestly want the answer to that.

"I think that will be all. Thank you for your help," I said.

The clerk nodded and led me to the front of the store where he set to work wrapping the book in brown paper. "I have some red ribbon here too. We'll put a nice bow on it." He glanced up at me from his work. "You're staying with the Dibbles for Christmas?"

"I am. Do you know them?"

"This is a small town. Everyone knows everyone. And my family has owned this store for two generations." I deduced that this was Mr. Brown, then—the owner and not just a clerk. He slowed what he was doing for a moment. "Funny thing about Evelyn Hesse, though." Mr. Brown was obviously choosing his words carefully.

"What do you mean?"

"We all thought she was moving away after her last husband died. She let all her staff go and auctioned off all her things. Well, almost all her staff—she kept her chauffeur."

It was precisely as we'd thought, then, except for the news about the chauffeur. I wondered if that was Carlisle. "When was this?"

"Oh, it was a few months ago now." He shrugged. "But then she was seen around town with Mr. Dibble, and she never did leave."

"What about her chauffeur? Do you know what happened to him?"

"Of course. He's now working for Mr. Dibble."

I nodded. I was curious why Redvers' aunts hadn't mentioned any of this. It seemed as though it would have been common knowledge, both that she'd let her staff go and that she'd brought her chauffeur to work at the Dibble estate. And if the aunts had heard about Evelyn auctioning off her things, there was little chance they wouldn't have brought that up. I tried to think of a way to ask about the auction when Mr. Brown took care of it for me.

"Of course, the auction was very hush-hush—everything was hauled away to Newcastle to be sold. Not many folks in town knew about it, and she let her staff go one at a time. I only know because my cousin's sister used to be employed there. Mrs. Hesse was careful, I'll say that for her. And of course, I'm not a gossip, so I never let word get out. But I was hired to appraise the books in her library."

I couldn't help my amusement at Brown's claim that he wasn't a gossip since that was precisely what he was doing at this very moment. He seemed to realize this and hurried to finish wrapping the book.

"I like Mr. Dibble, is all I'm saying." Mr. Brown handed over my book, complete with a beautifully tied red ribbon, all ready for gifting. "He's been a regular patron of the store over the years."

"I only just met him, but I like him." I paid Mr. Brown, but decided I had another question since it wasn't exactly difficult to prod Brown into gossiping about his neighbors. "It seemed rather sudden to us as well." I smiled and leaned forward a bit as though offering a confidence. "I'm engaged to his son, Redvers."

"Redvers is a fine young man, although we haven't seen him around these parts hardly at all in the last few years. Especially not since his mother passed." Brown shook his head. "A shame about his brother, too."

I nodded. I knew that Redvers' older brother, Percival,

had been killed in the war, but he'd been a traitor and his own men had killed him before he could go to trial. Redvers barely spoke about him, with good reason. "Was Evelyn close with anyone else around town?" I realized that sounded a bit abrupt and hurried to explain. "It just seems as though it will be a small wedding party."

Mr. Brown shook his head. "Mrs. Hesse has always been quite the loner. Not many friends, not much socializing, except for parties at the right houses, if you know what I mean." I nodded knowingly and was rewarded with a smile. "But to each their own. In fact, no one even knew she had a brother until he turned up last week. Bell, I think his last name is. He's staying at the Kingshead Arms, just down the street."

"That's what I've heard," I said, then held the book up. "Thank you so much for your help with this."

Brown smiled and gave a little wave, turning back to the wrapping job he'd been doing when I entered his store. "Hope to see you again."

Back on the sidewalk, I gave some thought to what Mr. Brown had told me. Since we'd already searched her house, it wasn't exactly news that Evelyn had let her staff go and gotten rid of all her things—we'd seen that firsthand, and had seen the auction report besides. And the fact that she'd been a loner wasn't terribly surprising, but if she'd had an accomplice in poisoning Dr. Taylor—assuming he'd been poisoned—who was it, then? Her brother? It was interesting that no one in town had seemed to know that the woman even had a brother. So why had he just appeared now? And were they close enough that her brother might have done the poisoning before we arrived?

The only other option seemed to be Carlisle the chauffeur. But just how close was Evelyn to her driver? Close enough to commit murder together? It seemed to be quite a stretch, even if Evelyn did bring the man along to be employed at the Dibble estate. And we'd left Carlisle behind when we went to the Watsons. It seemed unlikely that he'd have managed to rush there ahead of us in order to slip the doctor some poison. Not to mention the bump he'd taken to the head—had he hit himself with a branch hard enough to draw blood? It was unlikely—Evelyn's brother James was a far more likely suspect.

I was still mulling everything over when Redvers met me back at the car. "Get what you needed?" he asked.

"I did, thank you. And did you manage to complete your task this time?"

Redvers patted his coat. "All ready for tomorrow morning." We got into the car and Redvers pulled onto the road but going in the opposite direction from his father's estate.

"And where are you taking me now?"

"You'll be delighted to know that we're going to talk with Sergeant Thomas."

I *was* pleased. I just hoped the sergeant would be forthcoming with anything he'd learned about Dr. Taylor's death.

The station was a small brick building, with several wooden desks crammed into an open space. There appeared to be an office beyond, but it obviously wasn't assigned to the sergeant since he was seated at one of the worn wooden desks in the open area beyond the front counter. He didn't look thrilled to see us but waved us over before the constable who greeted us could even ask what we were there for.

"I suppose you're here about Dr. Taylor," Sergeant Thomas said.

"You're right about that." Redvers settled himself into a wooden chair opposite the sergeant, and I did the same. "Do you have any idea what happened to the man?"

"And what's your interest, Mr. Dibble?"

Redvers didn't even hesitate. "We're concerned that someone might have had reason to hurt Dr. Taylor."

Thomas sat back in his chair, hands folded over his burgeoning belly. "And what makes you think that?"

"We'd spoken to him that morning about another matter." Redvers stopped there, unwilling to give the sergeant any further information. This resulted in Redvers and the sergeant simply staring at each other, both unwilling to give way to the other. I sighed. We weren't going to get anywhere without revealing some of our worries.

"Sergeant, what do you know about Evelyn Hesse?"

Thomas looked a bit startled at my voice, as though he'd entirely forgotten I was there. But he answered my question all the same. "Not much. She's been widowed twice." He gave a shrug. "Bad luck there."

"Do you believe it was only bad luck?" I asked.

To the sergeant's credit he actually gave that some thought. "At the time her second husband died, there were some rumors. But they were just that—rumors." He looked between the two of us. "Do you have any information to the contrary?"

"Not especially. We're just looking into those rumors since the woman is marrying my father next," Redvers said.

Thomas nodded. "Fair enough. And I suppose you spoke to the doctor that morning about those rumors."

I jumped in. "We did. And he didn't seem especially interested in answering our questions."

"That is unusual," the sergeant said slowly. "Dr. Taylor was a helpful and friendly man."

"He seemed very defensive," I added.

"Hmm." But the sergeant didn't say any more. I couldn't tell if he thought this was a potential lead or just interesting information we were sharing with him.

"You called in a doctor from Copley to examine Dr. Taylor, correct?" Thomas nodded in response to Redvers' question. "Have you heard what might have happened to Dr. Taylor?"

The sergeant considered for a moment, then nodded. "I have. The doctor who examined him performed the autopsy immediately."

We both waited expectantly, and the sergeant finally tipped his head to the side, then gave a nod. "It appears to have been an overdose of mistletoe."

Chapter Ten

M y mouth might have dropped open a bit before I shut it again, and the sergeant held up a hand. "Now, before you go jumping to conclusions, the man was taking mistletoe."

"*Taking* mistletoe? What on earth for? Isn't it poisonous?" I was incredulous.

"It is, but apparently it's used as an herbal remedy for some conditions. Including heart conditions and cancer. The European variety, at least."

I had never heard this before. I glanced at Redvers, and he gave a little shake of his head, telling me that he hadn't either. Of course, I wasn't in the habit of reading up on potential uses for poisonous plants. Perhaps I needed to fix that.

But there was another issue. "Why would he bring it to a party and take it? That doesn't seem likely." People didn't tend to bring their medications to neighborhood gatherings. Which made it far more likely that someone knew he was taking the herb and put it in his drink.

Thomas didn't have a good answer for that.

We took our leave not long after that revelation, thanking the sergeant for his time. He didn't know anything more about the doctor's history of health, but he said he would be looking into it right away. I told him that I hoped he would share whatever it was that he learned, and he smiled noncommittally. It seemed that Sergeant Thomas already had his answer about what had happened to Dr. Taylor. But I wasn't quite so convinced.

Back on the sidewalk I realized it had begun snowing with a bit more enthusiasm, and despite the seriousness of our investigation into Evelyn Hesse, I couldn't help but smile at the fat flakes falling from the sky.

"I cannot believe you're so delighted by snow. It's such a bother." Redvers shook his head, but his lips had quirked into a fond smile all the same.

I grinned, then sobered. "We learned more than I thought we would from Sergeant Thomas."

"We did. Now we know it's likely someone slipped the mistletoe into his drink."

"Someone like James Bell. Evelyn's brother."

"Exactly."

"And if someone like James did slip it to him, could it have been on the orders of your future stepmother?" I asked.

"Please let's not call her that."

I patted his arm and we got into the car. "Where to? Back to the estate? I think we need to speak with Carlisle."

"I agree. But I think we should make one stop first," Redvers said.

That stop proved to be the small cottage of his two aunts. It was a standalone home, unlike the numerous town houses on the surrounding streets. It was utterly charming, built of stone, with a small yard—I imagined that the garden was pretty spectacular in the spring and summer. We knocked on the front door and waited a few minutes before Aunt Carolyn came to answer it.

"It's you!" she crowed in delight. "Forgive me for taking so long to get to the door. We gave the staff the next two days off." She shrugged. "We were planning on being at your house for meals anyway, Redvers."

"Of course. We're actually here to give you a ride. The snow is still coming down quite hard—I wanted to make sure you both could get there."

Carolyn patted his arm. "You're a good boy, Redvers." Then she turned and shouted into the hall behind her. "Marie! They're here to fetch us!"

Aunt Marie emerged from a doorway, bustling forward. "Excellent. I wasn't looking forward to getting back into the sledge just yet. And I think we would have needed it with this weather."

Carolyn rolled her eyes. "It would have been fine. The new traces have already been attached."

"Well, I'm still sore from the last time." Marie's arms were crossed over her ample bosom.

Redvers and I were both smiling at this exchange. "Can you be ready to go soon?" Redvers asked again.

"Certainly, young man. Gracious," Marie huffed before both she and Carolyn disappeared down the hall.

I was wondering just how long we were going to have to stand awkwardly in the small foyer when both women returned wearing long fur coats with accompanying hats. Marie's were white and Carolyn's were silvery gray. I didn't particularly want to know what animal was which—I was just pleased that the ladies would be warm.

"I'm sorry we can't give you a tour right now, Jane," Carolyn said as we went back outside and headed to the car. "I'm afraid things are in a bit of disarray."

Marie agreed. "We lost our maid, and we need to hire a new one after the holiday. The state of things is disgraceful."

I murmured something polite instead of arguing that I wouldn't have cared what the state of things was. It looked like a very charming home, simply but warmly decorated, and I hoped that I would have the chance to see it some other time. Which is what I told them.

"Of course, dear. You're always welcome with us," Carolyn said. "Now, what have you learned about the demise of Dr. Taylor?"

I almost laughed out loud—these ladies didn't waste any time getting to the heart of things.

"Had you heard if Dr. Taylor was sick?" I asked. I turned slightly in my seat so I could see them both tucked into the back seat of the car.

Carolyn and Marie glanced at each other, Marie's lips pursing. "He'd lost quite a bit of weight in recent months." It was hard for me to imagine since he'd looked so naturally trim when we'd spoken to him. But this matched with what Mr. Watson had told us about his friend.

"He enjoyed his sweets, and it caught up to him," Carolyn added. "But then that gut suddenly came off." Carolyn's eyes narrowed. "Do *you* think he was ill?"

I tried to sound casual. "It's something we're trying to figure out." It was more that I wanted to give them a different excuse for his death rather than admit that we did indeed think he was poisoned.

"Poison," Carolyn said to Marie.

Marie nodded. "I don't think he was sick, and there's not much else that would have killed him so quickly. And he really just dropped dead. Right there on that expensive rug."

"It was probably in his wine, since we hadn't been served anything else by that point," Carolyn pointed out. "Although I'm not sure that rug was as expensive as they would like us to think. It might not have been entirely authentic."

I turned back around in my seat to hide my smile. Redvers glanced at me before turning back to the road and I could see that he was fighting a smile of his own.

We were nearly home when Carolyn piped up from the back, "You know, I forgot to tell you something about Evelyn. When I was talking with Millie, I remembered that Evelyn had been seen with another man for a few weeks before she moved on to Humphrey."

"Her brother, do you mean?" I turned to look at Carolyn and saw her shake her head.

"No, this was well before that brother of hers arrived in town. This was a *romantic* interest."

Redvers slowed the car and took the next turn into an even smaller lane. We slid to a stop, and I was thankful Redvers had such good driving skills.

"There was no need to stop the car, young man. I don't think it's that exciting," Marie said.

Redvers raised an eyebrow. "Let me be the judge of that."

Marie pursed her lips and let Carolyn continue. "It was Harold Winters. He lives in that Georgian house in the southwest part of town."

Redvers looked grimly at the street before us where snow was quietly accumulating.

"Are you thinking we should try to talk to him? On Christmas Eve?" I asked. I had no idea how we were going to show up at a man's door the day before Christmas and ask him questions about a woman he used to be involved with.

"I am, in fact. The wedding is tomorrow and we have very little time left to figure things out."

Redvers slowly got the car turned around using a neighbor's driveway while I kept my fingers crossed that we wouldn't become stuck. Our luck held, and Redvers pointed the car back toward town.

"Do you know the words to 'Here We Come A-Caroling'?" Carolyn asked.

I thought for a moment. "Most of them at least. Why?"

"I have a plan."

Carolyn's plan was for the four of us to line up—carefully, since the walkway was slippery—outside Winters' front door.

When he answered it, we broke into cheerful song. Redvers had a lovely baritone singing voice that I'd never heard before—it was so lovely that I nearly stopped singing myself. Marie and I carried the alto line while Carolyn took the soprano. She had the high wavery voice of an older woman, but I could tell that she had been quite a good singer in her day. Harold Winters stood in his open doorway, looking quite charmed by our appearance on his doorstep. Once we finished, he clapped a few times.

"Wonderful. You know, I wish more people would do caroling this time of year. Can I interest you in something warm to drink?" Harold had bright blue eyes and a ring of gray hair around his scalp with some liver spots decorating the rest. He was wearing a thick cardigan sweater and looked as though we might have caught him napping.

Carolyn and Marie exchanged looks as though they thought a warm drink—spiked with something strong, of course—might be just the thing, but I knew that we needed to get back on the road if we were going to make it back to the Dibble estate without becoming stuck in a snowdrift somewhere.

"That's such a lovely offer, but we just wanted to share some Christmas cheer," Redvers said. "I'll help you ladies back to the car now." Marie looked mutinous but took Redvers' offered arm and he helped her down the walk. Carolyn and I stayed behind to chat with Winters, exactly as Redvers had planned.

"Harold"—Carolyn started right in—"you saw a little bit of Evelyn Hesse earlier this year, didn't you?"

A frown passed over Harold's face but was gone again. "I did. Why do you ask?"

"Well, she and Humphrey are getting married tomorrow."

Both Carolyn and I were watching Harold's face for his reaction, but he seemed nothing but pleasantly surprised.

"I'm pleased for them," Harold said with a nod. "Evelyn needs someone to look after her."

I wasn't sure that was the slightest bit true, but I kept that opinion to myself.

Carolyn was barely able to do the same. "Hmm," she said. "Why didn't things continue with the two of you?"

It was starting to become personal, but Harold didn't seem to mind the question. He gave a shrug. "I became pretty sick not long after we'd starting seeing something of each other. I think it panicked her, because she broke things off. But there are no hard feelings."

Redvers had returned for his aunt Carolyn. "Well, that's good to know. I'm glad you're all right now, Harold. Have a Merry Christmas." Carolyn took her nephew's arm and let him lead her away, but not before giving me a pointed look.

I knew what she was getting at. "I'm sorry to hear you were unwell. Do you know what it was?"

Harold tilted his head at me. "I'm sorry, have we met before?"

I gave him my most winning smile. "I'm Redvers' fiancée." It still felt a little strange to say that, but it was coming in quite handy in this small village.

This time Harold came forward and offered his hand. "Congratulations, young lady." Redvers had returned and Harold shook his hand as well. "Lovely to see two young people settling down."

I kept a smile pasted on my face even though I was quite tempted to disabuse him of the notion of my "settling down." "I heard you were sick not long ago, Mr. Winters."

"I was, I was. Strangest thing—it really seemed to come out of the blue. But after a few days in the hospital, I was in fighting shape again."

"And they don't know what it was?" Redvers asked.

Harold smiled, hands clasped behind him. "Between you and me, they thought it was simply a severe case of indigestion. And I'm quite fine now." He looked off in the distance. "Evelyn's chauffeur drove me actually, since the nearest hospital is quite a ways out from here. Dr. Taylor insisted, and I'm awfully glad that he did." Winters focused on us again. "Evelyn really was fond of that chauffeur." We both murmured polite acknowledgments that we were glad he was feeling better now.

I wanted to follow up on Evelyn's relationship with the chauffeur, but Winters looked up at the sky. "The snow doesn't seem to be letting up."

"It surely doesn't. We must be heading back," Redvers said. He and Winters exchanged a few other pleasantries before we headed back to the waiting car. I could see Marie and Carolyn's eyes were burning with interest, but they had the sense to wait until we'd pulled away from Winters' house to start their interrogation.

"What did he say?" Carolyn demanded. "Dammit, I hate that I had to be walked off from the conversation."

Redvers didn't address that, but he did fill his aunts in on what Winters had told us. The only thing that was truly news was that Winters had also mysteriously fallen ill. Could poisoning look like severe indigestion? It seemed likely, and that didn't look good for Evelyn Hesse. Although, she had stopped seeing him once he'd fallen ill—if she'd been poisoning him, it seemed more likely that she would stick around to follow through. As well as the fact that Winters' death wouldn't have benefited her in any way since they weren't married at the time.

"It's possible he really did just fall ill and then get better. It might have nothing to do with her at all," I mused aloud. No one answered me, but I could tell that they were all mulling over the very same thing.

CHAPTER ELEVEN

It was rather slow going back to the estate since, as Redvers predicted, the roads were slippery and becoming more so the longer it snowed—our detours truly hadn't helped, necessary though they'd been. We pulled up to the Dibble manor and Redvers and I each opened a door for one of his aunts and carefully walked them up to the front door, despite their complaints that they weren't as old as we were making them out to be. Protests aside, I noticed that Marie was holding quite tightly to my arm so that she didn't slip. We deposited the women safely inside where Youngblood began collecting their things.

"Have you seen Carlisle this morning, Youngblood?" Redvers asked.

The butler frowned slightly. "I believe he's in the garage, sir." Redvers made our excuses to his aunts and whisked me back out the front door before we could divest ourselves of our winter things.

We walked around to the side of the house where the garage stood. It had obviously been added as an afterthought, well after the rest of the house was constructed, but the builders had done a fairly neat job of blending it with the rest. The barn-style door was closed already—Carlisle had wasted no time in fetching the car from the front of the house and pulling it into the garage for the evening. Redvers opened a standard door on the side of the building and we went in.

It was a small space, with room for the Dibbles' sedan and little else besides. I was a little surprised that there wasn't a second vehicle, but then again, with Humphrey's thrift in other places, perhaps it wasn't such a surprise after all. Carlisle was wiping snow from the front of the vehicle.

"Carlisle," Redvers said as we approached, "may we have a word?"

"Certainly, sir." The answer was all politeness, but I noticed that he didn't stop what he was doing in order to talk with us.

"How's your head?"

Carlisle did pause at that, then continued using his garage rag to tidy the car. "It's better, sir, thank you."

"That was quite a nasty hit you took," I offered. There had been a lot of blood, but I also knew that head wounds tended to bleed quite a lot, making them seem worse than they were. "Did you happen to see or hear anything?"

Carlisle stood, examining his handiwork then turned to us. "No, ma'am. As I said before, I had to"—he looked embarrassed—"answer a call of nature, if you'll excuse me. Next thing I knew, I woke up on the ground." He shook his head. "Never heard a thing."

"And it couldn't have been a branch that snapped and hit you? We've had an unusual amount of snow this year." Redvers didn't sound as if he thought it was really a possibility, but he was covering all the bases.

"No, nothing like that. I would have noticed if there was a big branch lying next to me."

"True enough."

None of this was terribly helpful. If it wasn't a branch, it was likely Carlisle had been attacked from behind. If Carlisle hadn't seen or heard anything to identify them . . . well, it could have been nearly anyone.

"How long have you worked for Evelyn?" Redvers changed course.

Carlisle thought for a moment. "It must be around eight years or so now. I went to work for her first husband, Mr. Palmatier, and I just stayed on after that."

"You must like working for her then," I said.

"She's as good as any other."

Hardly a glowing recommendation. But then, having gotten more than a taste of Evelyn Hesse myself, I supposed it was fairly positive. It was a little surprising that he'd stayed with her so long, though. And it certainly didn't sound like the devotion of a servant who would do anything for their employer.

"She didn't bring any of the rest of her staff here?" I asked.

"No, ma'am." Carlisle set his jaw and smiled. It was obvious he wasn't going to be expounding on that.

"How about her brother? Do you know anything about James?" I tried again.

"Not much. I know he only just arrived in town last week," Carlisle said.

"Do you know where he came from? London perhaps?"

"You'd have to ask her that, ma'am. I'm only her driver."

He was answering politely enough, but we were being stymied at every turn. I sincerely doubted that Carlisle didn't know the answers to at least some of these questions, but short of pinning him against a wall and threatening the man, there wasn't much we could do to get anything different out of him. I sensed that Redvers felt the same way.

"Thank you for your time, Carlisle," Redvers said.

We were about to walk back out the door we'd come in when I noticed what appeared to be a motorbike beneath a drop cloth parked along the wall. One tire was peeking out of the back.

"Is that your motorbike, Carlisle?"

He paused for a long moment. "It is, ma'am."

"It's too bad you can't get it out and ride in this weather."

"It is at that, ma'am."

I looked at the man for a beat longer, then Redvers and I left.

Instead of heading immediately back into the house, Redvers convinced me to take a quick walk around the grounds, in the snow, which was nearly past my ankles by this point.

"I'm going to drown in snow because you fancy a walk," I said.

"I was just hoping to get a moment alone with my own fiancée before we go back inside. Once we're in there, there will be no privacy. Or private conversations." Redvers pulled me into a kiss, which warmed me for the next few minutes. "Besides, I thought you liked the snow."

I ignored that particular jab. "I don't believe a word Carlisle said." I paused and thought about that for a moment. "Except perhaps for the part where he said she was as good as any to work for. That part I believe."

"I agree. I don't believe the man was telling even a fraction of what he knows." Redvers was frowning. "He and Evelyn seem much closer than he was letting on."

"No one saw who attacked him or cut the traces on the sleigh. We don't know who could have slipped Dr. Taylor an overdose of mistletoe, although we do know it couldn't have been Evelyn because she was with us. It was unlikely to be Carlisle because we had the car and I think it's unlikely he went there by motorbike in this weather. It could have been her brother James, because we don't know when he arrived at the Watsons'."

"If someone did slip something to Dr. Taylor, James is our most likely suspect."

I agreed. "But Sergeant Thomas seems to think it wasn't murder at all since it appears the doctor was taking mistletoe for a health condition." I frowned. "But I still doubt the man would take medicine at a party. And we still don't know if Evelyn killed her former husbands or if they died of natural causes as well."

"You're good at making lists of things we don't know. You can add this: we don't know whether Carlisle thinks Evelyn killed her previous husbands."

"You're right. We don't know that, but he was never going to tell us even if we had asked the question."

"No, he was not." Redvers looked at my feet. "Are you all right to go a bit farther?" We were walking in the back of the house in what was most likely a lovely garden in the spring and summer. Now all we could see were snow-covered lumps dotting the landscape.

"I am." The hem of my coat and dress were gathering snow and my boots would be a nightmare to remove, caked as they were with the white stuff, but they were sturdy and resistant against water. My feet were merely cold, not wet, and I could survive a pair of cold feet.

"It was an interesting question you asked him," Redvers said, taking my gloved hand in his. "About Evelyn's brother."

"Do you have any idea where the man is from?"

"I do not."

"It would be helpful to speak with James—do you think he'll come to the house today?"

"If James isn't here already, he's unlikely to make it here now," Redvers said. The snow appeared to be slowing, but he was right. It was going to be difficult to get to the estate now—we'd made it back in the nick of time.

"The wedding is tomorrow." There had been so much

going on that I hadn't had time to think about the upcoming wedding—or my own wedding years earlier that had been the start of a disastrous marriage. I knew I wasn't making the same mistake, but the pomp of a wedding and all the planning—I was certain I didn't want to do the same thing again. I wanted everything to be different this time.

"Don't remind me." Unaware of my thoughts, Redvers pulled me close, gave me another warming kiss, then tugged me in the direction of the front of the house. "I suppose we'd best go in. I can't have you turning into an icicle the day before Christmas."

"I do appreciate that," I said with a smile. I was fortunate that the man beside me did an excellent job of erasing any nerves I had about the past or future.

By the time we trudged through the snow to the front door, a new vehicle had taken up residence in the driveway. I had no doubts as to who it would be, and neither did my fiancé.

Redvers and I looked at each other. "Aunt Millie," we said at the same time.

CHAPTER TWELVE

We were correct, of course. Millie and Lord Hughes, along with her daughter, Lillian, had made the trek over from Copley before the snow could stop them. It appeared that they had arrived just before we came inside, since Youngblood had an armful of coats that he was walking away with.

"You look a fright, Jane." Millie's greeting rang through the foyer.

"Thank you, Aunt Millie." My impertinence earned me a hard look from my aunt, which I was able to ignore because my cousin Lillian came forward to give me a warm hug.

"Cousin Jane. It's so nice to see you." Lillian looked well—healthy and strong, like the sportswoman she was.

"You as well, Lillian. I missed you at the dinner last night."

"I didn't want to spend time with a bunch of strangers," Lillian said with a shrug. "And I knew I would be seeing you today."

I smiled. I enjoyed how straightforward Lillian always was. "I'm glad to see you now." I glanced around at the three of them. "I see you've only just arrived—right in time, too."

Lord Hughes nodded. "If we'd waited much longer, I don't think we'd have gotten through. Not with this snow."

It occurred to me that they probably wouldn't be getting out this evening either. But it looked as though Millie had accounted for that already.

"We brought overnight bags, just in case," Millie informed me.

Youngblood had returned and was gathering Redvers' and my things. I sat on a bench to work my frozen laces from my boots. "It's a good thing," Redvers replied. "I think we'll all be staying here tonight."

"I do hope your father has enough rooms," Millie said.

Youngblood's formal veneer cracked for a second before he smoothed it back over and left with his armload. I could tell he was offended at the very suggestion that the Dibble estate wasn't up to snuff for visitors. Despite Evelyn's fussing about the staff, Youngblood and Mrs. Potter ran a fairly tight ship.

Redvers assured my aunt that there was plenty of room for everyone as Evelyn and Humphrey joined us in the foyer, attracted by all the noise. Humphrey looked pleased at the additional company, greeting Millie and Lord Hughes warmly. Evelyn's face was unreadable—it was impossible to tell if she was put out about the additional bodies in the house or whether she was taking it in stride.

"Come join us in the sitting room. We have a lovely fire going." Humphrey ushered everyone down the hall, Redvers and I bringing up the rear. Entering the room, I could see that Carolyn and Marie had taken up residence in a pair of armchairs near the fire, soaking up the heat. Both their faces lit up at the sight of Millie and company, and I found myself pleased that Redvers' family members and my own liked each other so well, although it gave my heart a little pang that my father wasn't here—and of course, my mother.

A solitary figure sat in a chair some distance from the fire, apparently reading and paying the rest of us absolutely no mind. I immediately recognized him as Evelyn's brother

James Bell. His legs were crossed, showing off a brightly patterned pair of socks, completely at odds with the rest of his demure tweed suit. He looked up when we entered and closed his book, setting it aside and coming forward to greet us.

"I'm sorry, I was just finishing that chapter before I joined the festivities. James Bell," he said, shaking our hands vigorously. I was unexpectedly charmed by his warmth as we joined the others. I'd expected him to be standoffish, especially since he'd been sitting alone, yet he was anything but.

After exchanging greetings with us, Carolyn turned to Evelyn. "Now, Evelyn. You were just telling us about your family before everyone arrived."

Evelyn's lips pursed. "I'm certain we can find another topic to discuss. One far more interesting."

James tsked. "Now, Evelyn, you're about to become part of the family. I'm sure they just want to know more about us."

Millie looked at James approvingly before turning back to his sister. "Exactly, Evelyn. We need to know more if we are to properly welcome you to the family."

I nearly let a laugh escape at the irony of my aunt—a near-perfect stranger—welcoming Evelyn into the family. No one else seemed to find this as amusing as I did, although I did see Redvers give his head a little shake.

It was obvious Evelyn was battling with herself, all eyes in the room concentrated on her. "There's not much to tell," she finally said. "I have the one brother, James." She gestured to her brother. He nodded encouragingly, so Evelyn continued. "Our parents died when we were young. I met my first husband in London, we married not long after. I moved here for a fresh start after he passed away." She gave a little shrug then clapped her hands together. "Now, perhaps we should play a parlor game, since there are so many of us."

It wasn't an elegant transition, but it did the trick to divert attention away from herself. Evelyn soon had the room divided up into two teams and was soliciting ideas for a game of charades, when I saw her glance in the direction of her brother and turn a bit pale. No one else seemed to notice since they were concentrating on writing ideas on the slips of paper they'd been given, and when I looked, James was cheerfully doing the same. I hadn't seen him so much as look at his sister, but perhaps I'd missed something between Evelyn's reaction and my looking at James.

Turning my attention to the rest of the party, I was surprised to see Millie enthusiastically filling out her own slips of paper. She'd never been one for more than a game of cards, so it was unusual to see her going along with things, especially when it came to playing parlor games while sober. It seemed that her engagement to Lord Hughes was softening her up. Although I *was* dreading finding out what her attitude would be once she discovered that Humphrey was a near teetotaler. A glass of wine with dinner wasn't going to suffice for Aunt Millie, and I doubted she was going to be shy about that fact.

After another surreptitious glance at James, Evelyn murmured something to Humphrey and excused herself from the room. Redvers and I locked eyes. Should one of us follow?

"I'll grab something to put these in, Father." Redvers held his folded slips of paper aloft before passing them to me with a wink and following Evelyn from the room. They both returned minutes later—Evelyn first and Redvers only just behind her, now carrying a man's bowler hat.

I raised one eyebrow at my fiancé, but he simply gave me a nod in return, which wasn't in the slightest bit enlightening. Men were entirely too frustrating for words at times. But when he came to my side with the hat in order to collect my slips of paper, he leaned down to whisper in my ear, "She went to the library, pulled a book from the shelf, reached behind it, and put something in her pocket. I couldn't see what it was."

"Come now, Redvers. What are you two whispering about?" Millie demanded to know.

"Just sweet endearments, Aunt Millie. You know how it is with engaged couples."

Millie coughed and turned a bit red, while both Aunt Carolyn and Aunt Marie grinned. A glance at Lillian told me that she was barely restraining herself from rolling her eyes at the lot of us—my cousin was not one for any sort of sentimentality.

Evelyn had seemed a bit nervous when she entered the room, fussing with the decorations on the mantel above the fireplace and then with the skirt of her dress as though she didn't want to make eye contact with anyone, but she soon seemed collected once again and kicked off the game, electing Marie to start us off by choosing a clue from the hat.

I was barely paying attention, however. I was trying to figure out a way to get whatever Evelyn had pulled from behind that book and hidden in her pocket.

CHAPTER THIRTEEN

I hadn't come up with any brilliant ideas for searching Evelyn's pockets by the time the game finally wound down, and I'd earned myself some admonishments from my aunt for not putting my best effort forward when it was my turn to act out the cue on the slip of paper I pulled. To be fair, however, I'd gotten Cleopatra, and there were only so many times one could pretend to be bitten by a snake and die with no one guessing correctly before you gave up.

But whatever Evelyn had retrieved from the library, it seemed to be something that unsettled her. More than once during the game I caught her looking around nervously, glancing out the windows as though she expected something or someone to appear on the snow-covered landscape. Everyone had already gathered in the house so I couldn't imagine who or what it could be.

Once the game had ended, and finding that the time had slipped into late afternoon, Millie looked around for a bar cart. I winced inwardly, not looking forward to how this conversation was going to go. "Isn't it time for a cocktail?" Millie asked.

"We should escape now," I whispered to Redvers.

"Escape where? We're practically snowed in," he whispered back.

For once Millie didn't admonish us for whispering amongst ourselves, mostly because she was waiting for an answer to her question.

"Humphrey doesn't drink," Aunt Carolyn informed her.

"Bit of a fuddy-duddy," Marie added, earning her an offended look from Humphrey.

"But never fear, Millie." Carolyn pushed herself up from her chair and went over to the couch, bending down and pulling a bag from behind it. "We came with supplies." Opening the bag, she pulled a large bottle of brandy from it.

"Where did she have that in the car?" I asked Redvers quietly. I was somehow astonished and not at all surprised at the same time.

Redvers was unsuccessfully trying to hide a smile. "Where there's a will."

Judging by the look on his face, Humphrey was shocked—at first, it looked as though he was going to object, but then he obviously thought better of it and shook his head instead. "But I'm not fetching any glasses," I heard the man mutter. I looked over at Evelyn, expecting a similar reaction, but found that she was once again fiddling with her skirts.

Millie examined the bottle that Carolyn brought over. "Brandy. It's not whiskey, but I suppose it will have to do." She looked at Humphrey, who was observing them with folded arms and, realizing she would get no help there, turned to his son. "Redvers, be a dear and call for some glasses."

"Of course, Aunt Millie." Redvers went to do as he was asked.

"He really is a good boy," I heard Aunt Marie tell the other women, and they all agreed. Lillian excused herself to go back to her room, pleading a headache, although from the sly smile she gave me on her way out, I knew she just wanted some time to herself, most likely to read or practice her putting.

If I was a betting woman, I would have put money on the latter. My cousin was never far from a bag of golf clubs, no matter the weather. All she needed was a ball and a cup, and she would make do.

Our collective aunts decided a game of cards was just the thing to accompany their glasses of brandy now that they were poured, and they roped in Lord Hughes to join them. Humphrey excused himself with some "business he needed to attend to," giving Evelyn a buss on the cheek as he did so.

"I'll just see to the guests then," Evelyn said.

"Thank you. That would be lovely," Humphrey told her on his way out of the room, either ignoring the tone of her voice or misreading her completely. Evelyn was obviously not thrilled to be left tending to the guests, and sent Humphrey's retreating back a cutting look, but she did help them get their game started and even took a chair nearby. I noticed she also took a small glass of brandy now that Humphrey wasn't in the room.

James stood and quietly left the room. No one else seemed to notice, except for his sister who watched his retreating back with an unreadable look while sipping her brandy. Redvers and I took the opportunity to take his place—it was the farthest part of the room away from the rest of the party, making it possible to have a quiet word to ourselves.

"I see Evelyn isn't the teetotaler your father is."

"Apparently not, but I can hardly blame the woman."

"I can't either. She's been saddled with far more company than she anticipated." I would have been put out myself, in her shoes. "And the night before her wedding to boot." But it seemed unlikely that pre-wedding jitters were the sole reason for Evelyn's odd behavior. "She's seemed nervous all afternoon, though. Very unlike herself. Could it be whatever she found?"

"It could be," Redvers said. "Any thoughts on what it might have been?"

"Plenty, but nothing I can prove."

"You let your imagination run wild, creating ridiculous and far-fetched scenarios, did you?"

I stuck my tongue out at him. "It seems likely that it was a note from her brother."

"What makes you say that?"

"I saw her look at him and go a bit pale before she went and retrieved it."

Redvers considered that. "Did you see him give her any kind of signal?"

I shook my head. "I didn't see him so much as look at her."

"Neither did I. Which in itself is interesting."

"We know nothing about the man. But he's more sociable than I expected."

"Yes, I expected him to be much less pleasant," Redvers agreed.

I changed the subject. "We know it was mistletoe that did Dr. Taylor in. Should we be concerned that the poisoner is here in the house?"

"They might well be, but the good news is that Father doesn't drink."

"Except wine. It was in Dr. Taylor's wine."

Redvers frowned. "Good point. I'll make a few phone calls. I'm curious to see what they've found about James Bell."

"You already have your people looking into him?" I wasn't even certain why I was asking the question—of course he had. The wry look Redvers gave me instead of an answer said he wondered the same.

The phone calls to the mysterious agency that Redvers worked for—I always imagined men hiding in shadows and popping from phone booth to phone booth to avoid detection—wasn't much use either. Someone *had* started looking into James Bell, but so far had come up with a big blank.

"It's not usually a good sign when they come up with nothing," Redvers said.

I agreed. In my experience so far, it meant the person wasn't who they seemed. So who was James Bell?

In the meantime, the best we could do was keep an eye on Evelyn Hesse, so we took a seat in the pair of armchairs near the fire close to where our relations were playing cards. I was considering letting myself doze off for a moment, when I heard Aunt Carolyn start some interrogating of her own.

"Millie," Carolyn said while examining her hand of cards, "do you happen to know anything about herbs? And herbal remedies?"

A quick frown crossed Millie's face, but she answered as though this was an entirely normal question to ask while playing a game of bridge. "No, I don't know much about herbal remedies. Were you thinking of trying one?"

"I was just curious. How about you, Evelyn?" Carolyn speared the woman with a direct look as she asked the question. "Any experience with herbal tinctures?"

Evelyn's face remained impassive although she blinked several times. "What type of herbal remedies are you referring to, Carolyn?"

"The use of common plants for treating medical issues. I heard recently that mistletoe could be used for some heart ailments. Can you imagine?" Carolyn hadn't taken her eyes from Evelyn the entire time she spoke, cards pressed against her chest for safekeeping so that no one else might peek at them. Millie and Lord Hughes looked only mildly interested in the topic, but Marie's eyes were also bright. "It being poisonous and all, it seems extraordinary that it would be used for anything medicinal."

I nearly sighed out loud. I had come to love Redvers' aunts dearly, but they certainly lacked subtlety. Our aunts had that in common, for certain.

"Other poisonous plants are used for medical reasons as

well. Such as foxglove—it's used as digitalis to treat heart conditions," Evelyn said. "I don't think it's so extraordinary."

"I suppose you're right," Carolyn said. "Looks like you know something about plants, Evelyn." Her tone was mild, but I knew Aunt Carolyn felt that Evelyn had fallen right into her trap. Redvers and I exchanged a look, and he simply shook his head. We both knew that nothing had been proven.

Evening approached and the card game was wrapping up—as was the bottle of brandy that Aunt Carolyn had magically produced. Evelyn announced that she was going to dress for supper but that the rest of us shouldn't feel the need to. The generosity of her statement was undercut by the fact that none of the rest of us really had anything to change into. As soon as Evelyn left the room, Millie bustled over to me.

"Is there something going on in this house?" Millie demanded to know.

"What makes you ask that, Aunt Millie?" I tried to look as innocent as possible since I thought the last thing we needed was yet another aunt trying to "assist" in the investigation.

"Because that woman has been acting strangely all afternoon, and her brother has been entirely too friendly." Millie was keeping her voice low, and I could see Carolyn and Marie behind her craning their necks in our direction in an attempt to hear what was being said. "I also saw him speaking with the chauffeur when we arrived and neither of them looked happy."

My eyebrows shot up at this. It made sense that James and Carlisle knew one another, but this was the first time I'd considered whether the two men could be working together. If Millie really did see them together when they arrived, that meant that Carlisle and James spoke to one another right after we'd questioned the chauffeur. Was it because Carlisle was reporting what we'd asked about? Could we have been looking at the wrong connections all along?

It still left a lot of questions about who knew what. As well as what had made Evelyn so nervous all afternoon. The woman hadn't acted any differently toward either Redvers or myself, but there was definitely something suspicious going on.

"You're certain it was the chauffeur?" I asked.

Millie gave me a pointed look then frowned. "And I could swear I saw him somewhere else recently as well." She shook her head. "I never forget a face, but apparently I can forget *where* I saw it. Never mind, it will come to me."

"Was it at the Watsons' house?" I asked. If Carlisle was there, he might have been the one to slip mistletoe into the doctor's drink instead of James. Although it didn't solve the issue of how the chauffeur had gotten there since we'd taken the car. Could Carlisle have taken his motorbike after all? Was it possible to ride one on the snowy streets fast enough to have beat us there? It somehow seemed unlikely, but I didn't want to rule it out completely. But if James and Carlisle were working together, it was unlikely that James was the one who hit Carlisle in the head while we were in the woods.

"You can't rush these things, Jane. I told you it would come to me. Now, you haven't told me if there's something going on here or not."

Redvers put a hand on Millie's arm. "Nothing going on at all, Aunt Millie. The doctor had his little episode at the Watsons' party, but nothing to do with us."

"Little episode? The man died."

Redvers coughed. "Yes, well. I didn't want to put it quite like that." He patted her shoulder once and looked sincere. "But the poor man's death still isn't related to anything here."

Millie narrowed her eyes at Redvers but after a moment decided to accept his answer. I could see him shooting his own aunts warning looks over Millie's head. The two women gave him little nods in return—they would keep what they knew to themselves. Through all of this, Lord Hughes simply looked amused as he collected the playing cards together—he really was the most even-tempered man. I supposed it was the only way he was able to live with Millie—they seemed to balance each other out.

Humphrey came back into the room looking for Evelyn. "Has she gone to change?"

An idea came to me. "She has. I'll just go see if she's coming down soon."

"Thank you, Jane. I have something I want to give her before tomorrow morning."

With a quick nod and a glance at Redvers, I hurried up the stairs. I was nearly down the hall when Evelyn came out of her room.

"Humphrey is looking for you," I said. "I told him you were getting dressed for supper."

"Thank you, Jane." Evelyn stood where she was. "I'll walk down with you."

I stalled. I needed her to go back downstairs so I could search both her room and the dress she'd just taken off. "That's not necessary. I just need to grab something from my room."

"I'll wait. It's no trouble," Evelyn said, hands clasped in front of her. She seemed quite determined for us to go downstairs together. I considered telling her that I needed to use the lavatory, but I suspected she would simply wait for me to do that as well. Was she suspicious that I wanted to search her room? It certainly seemed that way.

Chapter Fourteen

In the end I went into my room and grabbed the gift that I'd bought for Redvers. I couldn't think of anything else that I would have come upstairs for. I decided that I would put the gift next to the tree for him to open later.

Evelyn had indeed waited for me and the two of us went downstairs to rejoin the others. Humphrey looked pleased to see us. "Evelyn! I have something for you."

Her dark eyes lit up and she came forward. Humphrey reached into his pocket and pulled out a small box, opening it and removing the ring that Redvers had fetched from the jeweler that morning. He took Evelyn's hand and slipped it onto her finger.

"Fits perfectly," Humphrey said.

"And it looks as good as new." Evelyn turned her hand back and forth to admire the way the sapphire caught the light. "They really can work wonders."

I recalled that Carolyn had wanted to have a word with Humphrey about this ring, and I wondered if that conversation had ever taken place. Carolyn's lips were pursed, but she didn't otherwise seem upset that her mother's ring was being given away to someone outside her family. Perhaps she and Humphrey had worked things out between themselves.

Redvers looked rather resigned as well. I felt for the man—

the ring he'd wanted to give me had just been given to a woman he didn't particularly like. It was a rather hard pill to swallow.

Humphrey ushered everyone out of the drawing room and into the dining room while I stayed behind to put the neatly wrapped gift beneath the tree. When I turned around, I saw that Redvers had waited for me, leaning against the doorframe. "And what is that? A gift for me?"

"Not only is it *not* for you, it is decidedly none of your business."

His eyes twinkled. "You'll have to wait until tomorrow for your gift."

I sauntered across the room then reached up to kiss him. He was standing beneath a sprig of mistletoe after all. I looked up at the parasitic plant with its dark leaves and white berries. "I'll never look at it quite the same after this week."

Redvers glanced at it as well then offered me his arm. "I'm not sure how it came to compel kissing in the first place."

"Are you complaining?"

"Not in the slightest."

With the additional guests, I could already sense that supper was going to be a lively affair. And thank heavens for that—sitting in silence and listening to each other eat had become a new nightmare for me. Although I noticed that James hadn't come down for dinner. I was about to ask if he was taking dinner in his room when Youngblood came around with a bottle of wine and poured a portion out for Humphrey to taste.

Humphrey sniffed at his glass. "This smells a bit bitter."

Evelyn's eyes widened. "Does it? Let me smell." Humphrey opened his mouth to say something, but Evelyn had already leaned toward him and with a wave of her hand knocked the glass out of Humphrey's. Wine splashed onto the carpet while Youngblood took a large step back and out of the way.

"How clumsy of me. I'm sorry, dear." Evelyn sat back into her chair. "Youngblood, I think we should have a different bottle. That one must have gone bad. Perhaps you could open the next one here in the dining room."

Youngblood stiffened at the orders. He was obviously offended at the suggestion that he couldn't tell when a wine had gone bad and at the direction to open the next bottle within their viewing, but like the professional he was, he maintained his composure and agreed. "Very well, ma'am. And I'll send someone to clean this up."

"Yes. Do that." Evelyn looked around at everyone staring openly at her, squared her shoulders, and changed the topic. "Do you ski often, Lord Hughes?"

Lord Hughes gave a little cough but answered the question. "When I get the chance. Too many years there simply isn't enough snow, even this far north."

Everyone else appeared to move on from the episode as well, but Redvers and I locked eyes. We would need to take a look at that bottle of wine to see if it had been tampered with. But how could we ensure it wouldn't be poured out now that Youngblood left the room?

"Excuse me," Redvers said abruptly before he stood and left the room.

"Where does he think he's going?" Millie asked me. I could only shrug. I hadn't come up with a good excuse, and obviously neither had he since he didn't offer one as he left. Luckily, further questions were prevented by the first course being served. We had just set our spoons to our soups when Redvers returned, taking his seat as if nothing had happened. Everyone's eyes were on him, but he happily ignored them and set in on his own bowl. "Cook always does a marvelous job with the soup. I'll have to tell her that."

Humphrey nodded, and after a few beats chatter started up again. I half expected Evelyn to tell everyone that they preferred to eat in silence as she'd done to us, but she was concentrating solely on the food before her and ignoring everything else around her.

When I could see that everyone else was otherwise engaged, I turned to Redvers. "You secured it?" I asked in a low voice.

"Of course. Now enjoy your soup."

After supper, the party—still minus James—retired to the drawing room once more. While everyone was getting themselves settled and deciding on entertainment for the evening, Redvers and I slipped from the room. We went down the hall and through a door into the servants' area, earning us a dark look from the housekeeper as she bustled by, but she said nothing. Redvers showed me into the butler's pantry where he had stashed the bottle of wine.

Redvers picked it up and sniffed at the top, frowning. "I don't smell anything unusual." He passed it over to me and I did the same, shaking my head.

"I don't either. Could your father have been mistaken?"

"It's possible, I suppose." Redvers reached up and took a glass down from a shelf and poured some of the wine into it. We both leaned close to examine the red liquid as Redvers tipped the glass from side to side.

"I don't see anything either," I said. "It seemed like there was residue in the bottom of Dr. Taylor's mug."

"Of course, that was mulled wine. There's usually some residue from the spices."

"True. But the bitter smell is absent as well. Besides, why poison your father before they're even married?"

"Unless it's a warning?"

"To whom?" It seemed that a note would be a better way to administer a warning—like the one Evelyn had slipped into her pocket earlier. Assuming it was a note, of course, but I'd become increasingly convinced that it was, the longer I thought about it. "Unless the poisoning takes place over a period of time and this is just the start." It was the only other reason I could come up with.

Redvers just shook his head before putting the glass down on the wooden counter next to the bottle. We both stood there regarding them. "I'm trying to decide if we should pour it away or if we should hold on to it for evidence. Just in case."

I sighed. "I think we should hold on to it. If we pour it away, you know we'll need it later."

Redvers nodded. "I'll find an old cork to stopper the top and then I'll hide it in my bedroom. In the meantime, you should join the others. Before they become too suspicious about where we've disappeared to."

I raised an eyebrow, but did as he suggested, making my way back to the drawing room. Nothing had yet been sorted about how to spend the rest of the evening, but I did notice that another bottle of wine had followed the group into the room.

It turned out that that bottle of wine had prevented any sort of organized entertainment, and it also meant that everyone turned in at a reasonably early time. All the aunts tottered up to their rooms, a little worse for wear, as well as Lord Hughes. Humphrey and Evelyn lingered for a few more minutes.

"You'll see to the fire, Redvers?" Humphrey asked.

"Of course, Father."

"Well. Big day tomorrow—have to be up early." Humphrey looked at Evelyn, who smiled and nodded. "And Evelyn will obviously have to stay here tonight because of the snow." Humphrey looked at both of us to see how we were taking this news.

"Yes, of course," Redvers said, and I nodded my agreement.

Humphrey cleared his throat. "Well, good night, then."

"Good night," Redvers and I said at the same time, watching Humphrey lead Evelyn from the room. We could hear their footsteps down the hall and up the stairs before I finally let out a breath.

"Alone at last."

Redvers' eyes twinkled. "Are you going to give me my Christmas present now?"

I laughed. "It's not Christmas morning yet. And you assume I even got you anything."

"Well, my dear. I have to explain to you that when we were children, we always opened gifts the evening of Christmas Eve. So it's entirely appropriate that you let me open that gift sitting beneath the tree."

He was like a little boy, and I couldn't resist his enthusiasm. I stood, bent over, and kissed the man before going over and retrieving his gift. "Very well," I said as I handed it to him. He started in immediately by carefully removing the ribbon and beginning to unwrap the ends. As enthusiastic as he'd been, I was a little surprised he didn't tear right into the paper, but he was careful and methodical, as he was in most things in life. When he finally pulled the book from its wrapping, he held it for a moment, passing a hand over the beautiful leather binding.

"*Treasure Island*," Redvers whispered before looking up at me. If I hadn't known better, I might have thought that his eyes were a bit damp. "I loved this book as a boy."

"I know you did."

"One of my aunts told on me, did they?" He smiled but became quickly serious again. "It's perfect, Jane. Thank you."

I cleared my throat and told him he was welcome. He leaned forward and kissed me, then gave me an impish smile. "I was serious when I said you'll have to wait until tomorrow evening for your gift."

I laughed and gave his knee a little slap. "You made me give you yours now, and you mean to tell me I can't open mine until tomorrow night?"

"Exactly. You really do catch on quickly."

The sound of my laughter muffled the sound of the footsteps coming into the room, so we were both surprised when Evelyn cleared her throat behind us. I jumped a bit in my chair, but Redvers simply turned to look.

"I'm glad you both are enjoying yourselves." Evelyn's voice was a little sour and it was difficult to tell exactly how she meant that.

"We thought you'd gone to bed," Redvers said.

Evelyn ignored that. "Did you find anything in the wine?"

"How do you know we looked at the wine?"

She rolled her eyes. "Do I seem stupid? Just answer the question."

Redvers and I looked at each other and back at her. "No, we didn't," Redvers finally said. "I didn't smell anything strange, nor did there seem to be any residue."

Evelyn stared into the low-burning fire for a moment. "Interesting. That's not what I expected. But I also expect that you know what you're about." She looked between the two of us, her dark eyes burning. "No matter what the two of you might think, I do love your father."

"I don't think I ever suggested otherwise," Redvers said, but Evelyn waved this off with a quick swipe of her hand.

"Just remember that." She looked between the two of us once again before sweeping back out of the room.

Chapter Fifteen

My mouth was still agape when we heard Evelyn's footsteps going back up the stairs. "What do you think that was about?" I asked.

"I haven't the foggiest idea."

"Do you think we should be worried about your father?" I asked.

Redvers gave that a moment's thought. "She was obviously worried that there was something in the wine because she knocked it out of his hand, and then came to ask us about it. But really, it doesn't do her any good to harm my father before they're actually wed."

"Has he changed his will?" This had only just occurred to me.

But Redvers shook his head. "He didn't. I'm still listed as his sole heir. It's in the safe."

"The same safe that she obviously broke into at some point? When she took the ring to have it appraised?"

"That very one."

We were both quiet for a long moment. "Why take the ring but not the will? It seems like she could have easily taken it and destroyed it."

"She could have. But she didn't."

"Do you think she was telling the truth just now?"

Redvers nodded slowly. "Do you know, I think she was. She seemed sincere."

"And intense."

"That, too. I think she really does care for Father and seems worried that someone will hurt him."

I thought about that. From what I could see, it did seem to be true. "It seems strange that she would poison her previous husbands but marry your father for love."

"That's true," Redvers said. "It's difficult to reconcile."

"And her concern would lead us to believe that someone else is trying to poison him."

"We don't actually know if someone is, since we didn't find anything in the wine. But it's enough that Evelyn seems worried someone might try."

"Which leaves us with our two main suspects: Carlisle and James." I thought about the two men. "Who were seen speaking to each other this afternoon. I know we think James attacked Carlisle, but is it possible that they're working together? And that's why Evelyn is so nervous?"

"Anything is possible."

"Why bring Carlisle with her to this estate if he's involved, though?" I asked.

Redvers just shook his head. He didn't have an answer to that.

I sighed. "It really seems to boil down to money."

"It does at that," Redvers agreed. "It's just a matter of who is getting what."

"Do we know where James disappeared to before dinner?"

"His room." Redvers' voice was filled with certainty.

"And you know this how?"

"Because I checked on him when I went to get the wine. He was in his room, and Mrs. Potter said she'd taken a tray up to him."

That made sense, and I wasn't surprised that Redvers had checked on James' whereabouts while he was out of the room.

"If there was something in the wine, either he or Carlisle could easily have put it there."

"Exactly. The bottle likely had been uncorked and was sitting in the butler's pantry for some time before Young-blood served it."

"Do you think it's worth trying to talk to either James or Carlisle?"

"We might as well try."

We decided to speak with Carlisle first, but that turned out to be impossible to do because we could not find the man anywhere. The hour had grown late and everyone else in the house had turned in for the evening, so we didn't check behind any closed bedroom doors, but we certainly searched the rest of the house, including the room where Carlisle was quartered. He was nowhere to be found.

"How could he have just disappeared? It's not as though he could have taken a car to get somewhere—there's too much snow." I was baffled.

"And yet it seems unlikely that he would have left on foot either, for the same reason. Where would he have got to before he was absolutely freezing?"

He was right—I could tell the temperature outside had dropped because the house had become awfully frigid. I was shivering in my dress and longed for the comfort of the fire in the drawing room. Or my bedroom, for that matter. Redvers noticed how cold I was and pulled me close, rubbing my arms. "Let's get you back to your room."

"Shouldn't we try to talk with James first?"

"It can wait until morning."

I decided not to argue.

Back in my room, Redvers took the time to warm me up thoroughly, but I was still grateful that a maid had left a low fire in the fireplace.

"Shouldn't you get back to your room?"

Redvers shook his head. "I'm staying right where I am."

"Your father will be scandalized."

"Let him be. I'm not taking any chances tonight."

I didn't have to ask what kind of chances he meant. We couldn't find Carlisle anywhere. I wasn't certain that there had been anything in Humphrey's wine tonight, but I did feel certain that something strange was going on. Not only that, but it seemed more and more likely that Evelyn's husbands *hadn't* died of natural causes. Especially given her reaction at dinner to the bitter smell Humphrey thought he detected in the wine.

My door was securely locked, but we had rattled some chains with our inquiries. I decided I would let Redvers indulge his protective nature. Just this once.

I had a restless night's sleep, dreaming that I heard footsteps in the hall and the distant sound of the front door closing. I was definitely looking a bit worse for wear but was still up at the appropriate time to get ready for the wedding. Redvers, being the thoughtful man that he is, went down to the kitchen and brought me back an entire pot of coffee.

"I could kiss you," I said.

"Why don't you?"

"Because I'm having a love affair with this coffee just now."

"I should know I always come second to coffee." He chuckled, then left me to get ready while he did the same.

Thirty minutes later we met again downstairs where we had a light breakfast. Millie and Lord Hughes were already finished eating, but no one else appeared to be up and about yet.

Redvers frowned. "Have you seen my father or Evelyn yet?"

Millie shook her head. "There's been no one down all morning. I imagine they're getting ready."

Redvers looked at his pocket watch then toward the stairs. "You know, I think I'll just go check and see if anyone needs anything."

I looked sadly at the buttered toast on my plate and snuck a large bite before following Redvers from the room. Millie rolled her eyes at me but kept further admonishments to herself.

I caught up with him on the stairs. "I'll go to Evelyn's room, and you'll talk to your father?"

He nodded, but when we reached the upstairs landing, we could see Humphrey in the hallway knocking on Evelyn's door already.

"She's not answering. I know it's customary not to see the bride the morning of the wedding, but this is ridiculous."

I hurried to his side. "Let me try." I knocked and called out for Evelyn, announcing myself, but there was no sound from within. I reached for the doorknob and when it turned easily in my hand, I looked at Redvers. This didn't bode well. The men stood back as I pushed open the door and put my head around the side of it, but there was nothing to see. I pushed it all the way open and stepped inside, the Dibble men right behind me.

"The bed hasn't been slept in," Redvers said. It had been turned down by one of the maids but obviously hadn't been touched since that point.

I opened the door to the large wardrobe, showing nothing but a few empty hangers. "Did she keep anything here?" Even if she didn't keep personal things at the house yet, it was likely that she would have hung up the garments she brought in her overnight bag. A quick glance around the room showed me that was missing as well. In fact, there was nothing in the room to suggest that a guest had been there at all.

"This is very strange. Where could she have gone?" Humphrey looked confused, but not overly concerned. "Perhaps she forgot something at her town house and will meet us at the church."

I didn't have to look at Redvers to know that he didn't believe this theory in the slightest either. But neither of us wanted to destroy Humphrey's hope that the day might still go as planned.

"We can head to the church and see if she's there. And then perhaps check at her home," Redvers said. He walked to the window and pulled the curtain aside. "It's stopped snowing and we should be able to get there in the sledge."

"Excellent idea, Redvers. I'll have Jackson get it ready." Humphrey left the room and Redvers and I waited until he was well out of earshot before we spoke.

"How could she have left?" I asked. "There's no way she could have taken the car. One of the horses maybe?"

"We should check the stables. Although Jackson will find out soon enough if all the horses are accounted for." He thought for a moment, then motioned for me to follow him. We went to the end of the hall where there was a narrow doorway leading to the servants' quarters on the upper floor. He opened it and climbed the stairs with me following close behind him.

"Where are we going?" I whispered.

"The attic."

I thought it unlikely that Evelyn would be hiding in the attic, but I trailed behind my fiancé all the same. We traveled the length of the hallway and I noticed that it was even colder on this floor. "The poor servants. It's an icebox up here."

"It is, although Humphrey is generous with the coal and each room has its own fireplace. Which is unusual, to be certain."

That made me feel better. Otherwise, it would be intolerable to live up here.

We came to a door at the end of the hallway and climbed the stairs to the attic space. Redvers had to duck his head slightly—the ceiling was quite low.

"What are we looking for? Evelyn?"

"No, we're looking for old sports equipment," Redvers said.

"I don't think this is the time of year to look for tennis rackets, dear."

"You're correct there. It's a good thing we're looking for a pair of skis. I think there may have also been a pair or two of snowshoes." He rounded a set of old trunks and came to a stop. "Yes, here we are."

I stood next to him with my hands on my hips. I could see what was there—a broken set of snowshoes, an old cricket bat, and some balls along with some other pieces of sporting equipment, but I had no idea what was missing.

"Both the skis and the other pair of snowshoes have gone walkabout."

"You think Evelyn took a pair to snowshoe out of here?"

Redvers nodded. "And someone followed her with the skis. Or vice versa."

I thought for a minute. "I suppose it was still snowing after they'd left, too, so we won't find any tracks."

"Exactly."

"Who do you suppose followed her? And what did they intend to do once they caught up with her?"

Chapter Sixteen

On the way back from the attic, we stopped by Carlisle's room and knocked on the door. When there was no answer, Redvers tried the knob, and we let ourselves in. It was hard to tell whether or not the bed had been slept in last night since it was in total disarray. But looking through the small chest of drawers, it appeared as though the man had cleared out as well, because there was nothing there.

"Judging by the fact that his things are gone, it would appear that Carlisle went after her. Taking either the snowshoes or the skis," I said.

"It would appear that way."

"But what about James? Is he still in the house?"

We went back down to the floor where the guests were quartered and knocked on James' door. There was no answer, so we tried the doorknob. This time we met with resistance—it was locked.

"How inconvenient of him to have not left this open for us like the others," I said.

"Indeed." Redvers' voice was wry. He checked his watch and sighed. "And we don't have time to deal with this now. We need to find Evelyn and figure out whether we're going to have this wedding."

* * *

We didn't want to alarm Redvers' father unnecessarily, so we kept our concerns about Evelyn to ourselves, as well as our questions about the whereabouts of the missing chauffeur and Evelyn's brother. We did insist that Jackson drive us to the church first, however, assuring Humphrey that we would ensure everything was ready for them. Humphrey thanked us for our help and waved us off.

I was a little nervous getting into the contraption after having been thrown out of the last one, but Jackson assured me that the traces were in perfect shape. A few minutes into our ride I was able to take a deep breath and relax—nothing seemed wrong and Jackson was an excellent and cautious driver. Still, I was relieved when we pulled up in front of St. Mary's church. We'd had no issues navigating the streets since it appeared everyone was still hunkered down—there wasn't a soul out and about yet.

As we got out of the sleigh and Jackson turned around to head back to the Dibble estate, the priest opened the door to the church holding a broom and wearing a thick coat with a fur hat on his head.

"Are you here for the wedding?"

"We are, although we have something to see to first," Redvers said. "The bride isn't here yet by any chance, is she?"

The priest shook his head, propping the door open and setting his broom into the snow. I thought it would be entirely more efficient to use a shovel, but I kept this opinion to myself. "No one is here yet, but it's still early. A few hours before the ceremony begins." He looked at the sky. "I hope it's stopped snowing and that people are able to get here."

"I'm sure they will," Redvers said. "We'll see you shortly." He took my arm and led me down the sidewalk. I was more grateful than ever that my boots were thick and sturdy since the snow had drifted quite deep in places. Luckily we didn't have far to walk to Evelyn's town house.

"Did you remember your lockpicks?" I asked. We'd reached her front gate, and Redvers opened it, leading the way up the walk.

"I'm offended that you even need to ask."

"I just want to make sure we don't have to go back for them. Like last time."

Redvers lifted an eyebrow but didn't otherwise respond, reaching out and testing the doorknob on the front door instead. It turned and he pushed it open. "Looks like Evelyn is leaving doors unlocked all over town."

The downstairs was just as echoing and empty as it had been the first time we'd visited, so we immediately went upstairs to the bedroom Evelyn had been staying in. This time, we found a different scenario entirely—she had obviously cleared out completely. There was nothing left except a silver key lying on the vanity where her brushes and personal things had once sat. "I assume this is for the front door." Redvers picked up the key and pocketed it. "We'll try it on the way out." He looked around. "Nothing. Not even a note."

Or a ring. I noticed that if Evelyn had disappeared, she'd done so with Redvers' grandmother's ring since there was no sign of it here or back at Humphrey's house. I decided this wasn't the best time to bring that up, however.

"How could she have cleared out so quickly in this weather? With that large trunk?" I asked.

Redvers shook his head. "I don't know. But I wonder if we can still catch her."

"Where?"

"The train station. It's the only way out of town at this point."

I'd had more than my fill of snow by the time we slogged through the stuff on our way to the train station. The only bit of luck we had was that the stationmaster—a loose term, really—was still there. "You just missed the train."

"I see that. Was Evelyn Hesse on board?"

"Do you know, she was," the man said. He was dressed informally, much different than what one found in the larger towns and cities. I supposed that the Barnard Castle stop was small enough that it almost wasn't necessary to have the position, let alone formal attire.

"Did she happen to have a trunk with her?"

"She had that sent over the day before. Old George fetched it from her place yesterday and then delivered it this morning. Between you and me, she paid him a pretty penny for the service, but George can always use the extra coin."

I almost asked how George managed to get the trunk here so early in the morning with all the snow, but decided it didn't really matter. What mattered was that Evelyn was not only gone, but it appeared that she'd intended to leave well before she had.

"Did anyone else from town get on the train?" Redvers asked.

The stationmaster shook his head. "Just Evelyn."

That was positive news at least. Our other two suspects were at least still in the general vicinity. It was now just a matter of determining *where* exactly.

We thanked the man and began the walk back to the church. "I'm not sure how I'm going to break the news to Father."

I patted the arm I was holding. I wasn't sure how he was going to do that either.

The front walk to the church had been brushed clear by the time we returned, and a few guests had trickled in—I assumed most of them had arrived on foot. Lillian, Lord Hughes, and Millie had come in the sleigh with Jackson and were waiting for us in the back of the church.

"Your man went back to get Carolyn, Marie, and Humphrey," Millie informed us. "Where have you been?"

I wasn't sure what exactly we should say at this point, since it was obvious that a wedding wasn't going to take place this morning. I was relieved when Redvers answered the question instead.

"We were looking for Evelyn."

Millie's eyes narrowed shrewdly. "Let me guess. She's scarpered."

"She has in fact. Took the first train out this morning."

Millie ruminated on this for a moment before turning and looking through the carved wooden doors leading into the church proper. Everything was beautifully decorated for Christmas, greenery and bows adorning the pews leading to the altar, and candles glowing. Lord Hughes turned and looked as well, then turned to my aunt.

"Are you thinking what I'm thinking, my dear?"

"I am, but let's wait to see what Humphrey has to say first." She looked at Redvers. "Break it to him gently."

"I'll do my best."

I wanted to know what Millie and Lord Hughes were thinking, but didn't get the chance to ask since Carolyn and Marie came through the doors at that moment, Humphrey right behind them.

Aunt Carolyn sidled up to me. "I heard Evelyn has gone missing." I think she meant to say it quietly, but everyone heard her quite clearly.

"You still haven't found her?" Humphrey looked between me and Redvers. I shook my head.

"Father, her things were gone from her house. And we spoke to the stationmaster and she got on the train with her trunk this morning," Redvers said, his voice gentle.

Humphrey chewed this news over for a moment. "I suppose I'm not getting married today, in that case. Wish I'd known that before I went to the trouble of getting dressed in my best suit." Despite this casual statement, I could see that his shoulders were tense, and he was clenching and un-clenching his jaw.

Redvers stepped forward and paused, putting a hand on his father's shoulder. "I am sorry. Is there anything I can do?"

Humphrey was as still as a statue for a moment before reaching up and awkwardly patting his son's hand. "I appreciate it, son." He looked at Redvers for a long moment. "I'm . . . sorry that we don't speak more often. It's been difficult since your mother died."

Redvers nodded. "I'm sorry, too."

"I thought Evelyn would be able to take her place. She couldn't quite though."

I could tell that Redvers didn't know what to say to that. He patted his father's shoulder and cleared his throat. There was still plenty unresolved between the men, but I was glad that they had made this start at least.

I looked over and saw Millie and Lord Hughes exchange another look. Then Lord Hughes stepped forward. "Bad luck, Humphrey. Truly. But if you don't mind, might we . . . well, borrow your wedding? It seems a shame for it to go to waste."

Humphrey took his turn looking through the wooden doors at the scattered assembled guests. "That's a good point, Hughes. I say go ahead. But what about the license?"

Lord Hughes patted his breast pocket. "I've been carrying one around. Millie couldn't decide just where she wanted to get married, so I thought I'd keep one with me, just in case."

Millie shot her fiancé an annoyed look at that, but then suddenly looked a bit nervous, fussing with smoothing down her hair. She already looked lovely, dressed in a simple pastel blue suit that made her eyes shine brightly. And she'd obviously taken time with her hair and makeup that morning since it was a special occasion to begin with. All she really needed was a bouquet. I looked around the outer room we stood in but didn't see anything appropriate. Sticking my head inside the church itself, I spotted a small vase with lilies on a table off to the side. That would do nicely.

I made my way around the side of the church pews, checked to see if anyone was watching, then quietly pulled the flowers from their vase. I gave the stems a little shake then hurried back to the outer vestibule.

"Do you have a handkerchief?" I asked Redvers.

"Where did you get those?" He looked amused, and pulled a clean handkerchief from his pocket, handing it over to me. I wrapped it around the stems, then smiled at my own handiwork.

Lord Hughes had already gone to speak with the priest and tell him about the slight change in plan. I wondered if the priest would even agree to the plan since this was a Catholic church and neither Millie nor Lord Hughes were members. I actually had no idea if either of them was even Catholic, but I suspected some money might change hands to make things happen. I gave Aunt Millie the small bouquet I'd arranged.

"Where did you get these?" she demanded.

"Don't worry. I'll put them back later."

"Like hell you will." Millie looked at them. "They're lovely." She looked up at me, eyes shining. I'd never seen my aunt look so happy, and my heart felt light. "You'll stand up with me, of course, Jane."

It wasn't a request so much as an order, but I was honored at her directive. It was her way, after all. "You don't want Lillian to?"

Millie shook her head. "I want her in the front row to see it all."

Within minutes Lord Hughes came back to let us know everything was set, then went back to the front of the church to take his place. Lillian had already seated herself at the front, and from where I stood, I could see that she was turned in her seat, waiting for her mother to come down the aisle. The organ started up, and Redvers offered me his arm.

"What are you doing?" I whispered.

"Escorting you."

I threaded my arm through his and we walked down the aisle, splitting off at the altar to take our places in front. Looking at the few faces assembled, there was some confusion at the change of groom, but after a few shrugs to each other, the guests seemed ready to take it in stride. Humphrey was now seated on the groom's side of the aisle, and looking at him, one might never know he was the one that was supposed to be getting married.

The music changed, and Aunt Millie came down the aisle, looking lovely. She walked by herself, which felt entirely appropriate, knowing the woman. She didn't need anyone to give her away. On the bride's side, Aunt Carolyn and Aunt Marie were positively beaming with delight—although I thought it likely they were even more delighted that Humphrey wasn't going to be marrying Evelyn Hesse after all. Even my cousin Lillian wiped away a few stray tears as Millie took her place and the ceremony began.

"That was a lovely wedding," I said. We'd all gone back to the Dibble estate—in shifts, in the sleigh—for the luncheon that Evelyn had so carefully planned then abandoned. I noticed that Aunt Millie still had the pilfered bouquet of lilies, and I was unexpectedly touched by her sentimentality. Of course, that also could have been the champagne that Humphrey had so graciously provided.

"It was." Redvers smiled and we locked eyes for a moment before his face grew serious. "But now we need to find a possible murderer."

He was right. We'd put our investigation on hold to enjoy the wedding, but it was time to get back to work. The trouble was, I hadn't the foggiest idea what our next steps should be. Evelyn had gone, as had our other two suspects. But where?

"Let's start with James' room, since we have the time to do a proper search. Let's hope he's left us something to find," Redvers said. We quietly left the room without being noticed by any of the family and headed upstairs. Redvers bent down and went to work on the door—I watched him closely to see if I could pick up any techniques, which was a nice change of pace since I was usually serving as lookout while he performed this operation. Luckily there was no need for him to hide his lock-picking activities in his father's house.

"Here we go." Redvers clicked the lock over and pushed the door open, blocking my view as he entered first. I went up on tiptoes to see over his shoulder, but was disappointed to realize there was nothing much to take in.

"Has he done a runner as well?" I sighed. "At least he had the decency to leave his things behind for us to search." Redvers had already applied himself to the small piece of hand luggage he'd found, placing it on the bed and removing the contents. While he did that, I poked around the rest of the room, finding nothing of real interest.

"Anything?" I asked.

"Perhaps." Redvers was opening an envelope he'd found beneath the mattress. Not a clever hiding spot, but perhaps James had wanted it where he could grab it quickly.

"What is it?"

Redvers raised an amused eyebrow at me. "Your patience continues to astound me."

"It should. I haven't snatched that from you yet."

Redvers ignored that, passing over the paper while he lightly slapped the envelope against his palm. "It's a marriage license."

I could now see that this was the case. The license had been issued many years earlier and was between James Bell and Evelyn Montgomery. My mind was blank for a long moment as I tried to put the pieces together. "James isn't her brother at all," I said.

"It would appear not."

"And if they're still married . . ."

"Then her other marriages weren't legal either."

"Do you think this is what she was afraid of?" I asked. "And why she left?"

"I'd wager it's a large part of it."

"Then how does Carlisle fit in?"

"That, my dear, is the question. And a difficult one to answer since they all seem to have disappeared." Redvers tucked the license back into its envelope and into his pocket.

CHAPTER SEVENTEEN

I was ruminating on the fact that it was probably for the best that the morning's events had gone the way that they had since Evelyn was already married, when Youngblood came to fetch us.

"Sir, there's someone here to see you."

"Who is it?" Redvers asked.

"The stationmaster."

A curious development. Redvers and I hurried down the stairs, closing James' door behind us. The man we'd seen just that morning was standing in the foyer, wringing his soft wool cap in his hands.

Redvers took one look at him, then looked to Youngblood who'd followed us down the stairs. "Is the library available?"

"It is."

"Let's go in there." The three of us proceeded into the library, which was otherwise deserted. As soon as we crossed the threshold, the stationmaster started talking.

"I lied to you this morning, Mr. Dibble. I was paid a fair amount to do it, but I couldn't live with myself. So I came here straightaway." Having made this confession, the man's shoulders straightened and he stopped mangling his cap. It had obviously weighed on him.

"Who paid you?" I asked, although I already suspected I knew the answer.

"That tall man, the chauffeur who drives for your family. He paid me to tell anyone who asked that Mrs. Hesse had left on the train."

I was wrong then. Because I would have bet money that it had been James Bell who had paid off the stationmaster. Why would Carlisle have done it?

"Do you know where he is now?" Redvers asked, and the man shook his head. "Have you actually seen Mrs. Hesse?"

Now that he'd broken his silence, he was entirely eager to assist us. "I did not, but Old George really did deliver her trunk to the station, and that went on the train. It came with a message that it was to be left at the luggage room once it arrives in London."

"How did you get here?" I asked this more out of curiosity.

He shrugged. "I have a horse."

We thanked him and sent him on his way before Redvers asked Jackson to hitch up the sleigh once again.

"Jackson will drive us, won't he?" I asked as I put on my winter things and mentally prepared myself to venture out into the cold once more.

"I'm perfectly capable." Redvers wound a red scarf around his neck, and I gave him my most skeptical look. I'd been comfortable with Jackson driving that morning, but I was a little more concerned about Redvers taking the reins, capable though he was at so many things. "It's just like driving a camel." His eyes twinkled and I knew he was teasing me. And as it turned out, I had nothing to worry about since he drove quite carefully—perhaps out of deference to the fact that I was still a little skittish about sleighs in general.

We immediately headed to Evelyn's town house, since it was the most logical place for any of them to take refuge until the snow melted enough for them to leave town. Because of the snow, it was easy to tell that at least one person had been here recently—there were numerous tracks leading to and from the front door that hadn't been there when we'd stopped that morning.

Redvers eyed the footprints in the snow. "Let's go around back and through the kitchen."

"Good idea."

We left our sleigh and horses tied up just down the street from the town house and walked all the way down the street and around the back of the block of homes. A large stone wall mostly blocked our view, but we counted gates until we came to the house we thought belonged to Evelyn. Letting ourselves into the small backyard, we could see that there were footprints here as well, but they were much older and had nearly been filled by drifting snow.

"Could they have been here this morning when we searched the place?" I asked quietly as I studied the walkway, doing my best to guess when the prints might have been made.

"It's possible. We didn't search the cellar." Redvers' voice was grim.

"That was foolish of us. On the other hand, they probably won't expect us to return. So now we have the element of surprise."

"How very optimistic of you," Redvers was already pulling his lockpicks from his pocket. I found myself hoping he also had a weapon stashed away in there—a gun rattling around in his coat pocket would be nice right about now. Especially since we had no idea what we were walking into.

The house was still quiet when we got through the door and let ourselves into the kitchen, listening for any movement in the house. There was none. Redvers indicated that we should check the cellar, and we found the door at the far side of the kitchen. He reached into his pocket and pulled out a pistol—I was delighted to see that my wishes had come true and we were armed.

The old wooden stairs were creaky, and it was nearly impossible to walk down them without making noise. Redvers went first, and even though he'd indicated that he wanted me to stay in the kitchen, I stayed right behind him. We hit the dirt floor and looked around, but there was nothing to see. From where we stood, we could see every corner of the small space, and while it was obviously used as something of a dumping ground for junk, there were no people hiding here.

"Where else could they be?" I whispered.

Redvers' brows were pulled together in thought, and he shrugged. "Let's check upstairs again. But more thoroughly this time."

We started our search of Evelyn's empty town house over, but this time checking every cupboard and nook we could find. Still there was nothing. Redvers and I looked at each other, completely perplexed. "Where else could they have gone?"

A thump from above answered that question. We both looked at the ceiling and back at each other.

"There must be a loft." He scanned the room and walked to the next, searching the ceiling. We hadn't seen a staircase, so there obviously wasn't an attic, and I wasn't entirely certain what a loft was. I followed him into the second room.

"Here it is." Redvers pointed, and I saw a section of the ceiling that looked the same as the rest, but if you concentrated you could see a faint square in the plaster. "It's a hatch—a well-concealed one."

But there was no obvious way to get to it. Redvers went back into Evelyn's room and returned with the wooden chair that had been in the corner. Standing on it, he reached up and felt along the square. I could see when his fingers hit a small latch that had been painted to match the rest. Tugging on it, the hatch came away and a wooden ladder descended. Redvers gestured for me to stay where I was, and for once I wasn't going to argue. Besides, there wasn't exactly room for both of us to crawl up that ladder. His pistol in one hand, Redvers gingerly climbed up and I watched nervously as the rickety thing swayed. He popped his head up into the space quickly and back down, then tucked his gun into his pocket and proceeded up the stairs. I desperately wanted to know what was going on since I could hear thumping noises—I positioned myself beneath the hatch but couldn't see anything but wooden rafters in the space above.

Then I heard another voice, obviously female. A few moments later I saw a skirt descending the wooden ladder. By the time she reached the chair, I knew it was Evelyn Hesse.

"Where are the others?" I asked.

She turned her dark eyes on me and then stepped to the floor, rubbing red marks on her wrists, the ring Humphrey had given her flashing in the light. "I'm fine, thank you for asking." It was obvious she'd been bound, and I was surprised at her calm demeanor.

"I assumed as much since you're standing here," I said.

Evelyn didn't have a response for that, so I asked again about where James and Carlisle had gone.

"We need to go after them." Her face was pinched with worry and her voice was rushed. "James is going to do something rash."

Redvers came down the stairs as well and pushed the hatch back into place before stepping to the floor. "Do you know where they would have gone?"

Evelyn nodded. "I think I do."

Chapter Eighteen

We got back into the sleigh, although I had Evelyn sit next to Redvers on the front bench so that I could keep an eye on her from the back. I didn't trust the woman, regardless of whether or not she'd been trussed up like a turkey and stuffed into a crawl space.

"How much of a head start do you think they have?" Redvers asked.

"Not much. I'd say only about twenty or thirty minutes," Evelyn said.

"And just where do you think they've gone to?"

"I heard James say that he was going to take Carlisle into the woods and that he wouldn't be coming back." Evelyn's voice was worried.

Redvers had the reins in hand, ready to direct the horses—he just needed a direction. "There are a lot of woods, Evelyn. We're going to need something a little more specific."

Evelyn leaned over the side of the sleigh, and I was about to ask what she was doing, when she answered my question for me. "Well, how about we follow the snowshoe tracks they made."

I scooted to that side of the bench and leaned out myself. They were faint, but still there. It was difficult to tell much besides the direction they'd gone since there was quite a bit of overlap. But at least it was something to work with. Redvers turned slightly to look at me and we communicated without speaking. I would watch both Evelyn and the tracks to make sure she was up to no tricks.

We lost and picked up the snowshoe tracks several times as we passed areas in town where there was overlap with other footprints or snow had been cleared away, but we managed to follow them to the edge of town where they led over a field and directly into a grove of pines. We were able to stay with them for a while, but soon the trees were too close together for the sleigh to continue.

"We'll have to go the rest on foot." Redvers got out of the sleigh and secured the horses to a nearby tree. Evelyn and I also dismounted, and I eyed the snow warily. It was going to be tough going through the deep snow—hopefully James didn't feel it necessary to go deep into the forest to carry out whatever he had planned for Evelyn's chauffeur.

Speaking of which, I had questions for Evelyn as we trudged in the cold, still following the tracks. "You're married to James." It was more of a statement than a question. At first, I didn't think that she would answer, but after a few minutes she did.

"I am."

"Which means your other marriages weren't legal," Redvers said.

"Strictly speaking, they were not." She sighed, a puff of white in the cold air. "It was James' idea for me to marry wealthier men for their estates. I was not interested in the scheme, but he had methods of . . . persuasion."

I knew firsthand about a husband's methods of persuasion and the kind of damage they could do, and I felt myself soften toward the woman. It also explained where the proceeds from her husbands' estates had gone—directly into James' pockets.

"After the last one he promised he was finished and I wouldn't see him again. It seemed like the proceeds would be enough to set him up nicely somewhere—he mentioned going somewhere warm, like the Caribbean. And he was gone for long enough that I foolishly believed he had actually left and I could risk going after my own happiness with Humphrey. Clearly I was wrong, because he turned up again."

And here we were.

"And their deaths?" Redvers asked. I could see he had one hand in his pocket, and I knew he had his pistol at the ready.

"My first husband was significantly older than I was and not in the best of health. James chose him specifically, hoping that nature would soon take its course." Evelyn paused. "Unfortunately it wasn't quite fast enough and James . . . hurried things along."

We both let that sink in for a minute before asking the next question.

"And your second husband?"

Evelyn's lips were pursed as she watched her footing on the uneven ground, narrowly avoiding tripping on a root concealed by the snow. I was listening to her story but I was also keeping an ear out for the men we were looking for.

"Dr. Taylor believed in herbal remedies and put him on mistletoe for a heart murmur, but James altered the dosage. Taylor signed off on the death as angina because he thought he was covering his own mistake."

That was quite clever, really, setting it up so that the doctor felt he was the one who had made a mistake.

"Why didn't you leave town?" I asked.

Evelyn shrugged, lifting her skirt a bit. "He would have found me. And he'd taken everything I had—starting over is not inexpensive."

"What did you have hidden in the library?" The question had been bothering me for hours.

Evelyn gave a single laugh. "Booze. I needed a snort to deal with everything. I wish I'd known Carolyn was going to be useful."

That was not at all what I'd expected her answer to be, although I could see why she might have hidden some alcohol from her teetotaling fiancé. I was about to ask about how Carlisle fit into the equation, when Redvers suddenly stopped and put his finger to his lips. Evelyn and I both stopped in our tracks, listening for what he heard. The faint traces of male voices carried to us, and we started moving again, but with more focus on keeping quiet.

We came near to a small clearing where James was holding Carlisle at gunpoint. We could hear the conversation more clearly now, although it didn't appear that we'd been spotted by either man yet.

"I'm going to toss this flask to you, and I want you to drink it."

"Why would I do that?" Carlisle asked.

"Because it will be less painful than me shooting you. Either way you're going to die, so you may as well make it easy on yourself."

"I'm not going to make this easy for you," Carlisle said. "And why didn't you kill me when you had the chance before?"

James sighed, although his gun never once wavered. "I had rather hoped that I'd hit you hard enough." He shrugged. "We'll call it a trial run. Now I know I need more thorough means."

"And you'll try to make it look like I died of natural causes," Carlisle said. "No one is going to believe that."

"I think they will, but really it doesn't matter. I simply can't leave any loose ends. I'm taking Evelyn and fleeing somewhere where we can make a fresh start." He cocked his head. "Might actually head to the islands this time."

"What makes you think she wants a fresh start with you?"

"I'm not interested in what she wants. I'm interested in the rich men she can attract. She still has a few good years left in her, I think."

It was hard not to make a noise of disgust at that. But Carlisle did it for me. "How many men do you think you can take out this way before you're caught?"

James didn't answer that because Evelyn burst from behind the tree she'd taken cover behind and ran to Carlisle, kicking up clumps of snow in her wake. I waited for her to slip and fall but she made it to the man without incident, putting herself between the chauffeur and her husband.

"Don't do this."

James looked surprised to see Evelyn, but recovered in only a moment. "I'll shoot both of you, you know." James' voice was chillingly casual, and I wondered just what Evelyn's marriage to this man had been like.

"And then what about your scheme? The money from the auction is gone. Where will you get more?" Evelyn was keeping James distracted, and looking at Redvers I could see that he was going to take advantage of the man's distraction. Unfortunately, just before he crossed into the clearing, a gust of wind blew through, causing several trees to dump their loaded branches of snow.

James turned and saw Redvers coming out of the tree line before Redvers could get close enough to make a move. "I see you came with friends," James said. "I'm assuming this is who freed you." He gestured with his gun for Redvers to join the others. "Where's your fiancée?"

"She's at the house," Redvers said firmly. "I'm not the type of man who puts my fiancée in danger."

"How noble." James watched Redvers cross the white

expanse to join the other two. "Well, I'll just make sure." I'd been hiding the entire time behind a large pine tree, praying that my skirt wasn't showing around the edges, when I heard the first shot ping off a nearby tree. I steeled myself, my entire body tightening with fear but also with the knowledge that I could not make a sound to give myself away. Another shot pinged several trees off to my left, and I covered my mouth with my gloved hand, bracing myself for more.

"Looks like you're telling the truth," James said. "That should have flushed her out."

I wasn't sure the reasoning behind this was sound, but then I didn't think James' mind was entirely sound. No further shots seemed to be coming so I cautiously peered around my tree to see what I could. James had turned back around and was once again focused on his prisoners.

I was cursing the fact that I didn't have a pistol of my own. This wasn't the first time the issue had come up, and I decided it was something that needed to be rectified as soon as was physically possible. I was tired of winding up in situations where I was unarmed. But looking around I realized I could resort to a different kind of weapon. I crept away from the group, hoping that Redvers could keep James from shooting anyone long enough for me to locate something hard and easily swung. It was hard to do with so much snow covering the landscape, but I finally managed to locate a large rock—one I couldn't lift. I whispered a curse to myself and kept hunting, moving the snow away from the base of a tree with my boot. Aha! The rock had a smaller companion. I lifted it easily and then tested its weight in my hand. I said a little prayer that it was heavy enough to do what I needed it to.

I crept back to my original hiding place, then checked to see what James was doing. He was still holding his pistol steady, although his other hand was digging in his pocket for something.

Redvers was speaking to the man, deliberately not looking at me, only at the man holding a gun on him. "I hope you still have enough bullets. You'll need several, you know."

"I should still have three, which is precisely how many you need."

"That pistol holds five rounds, correct? You shot off three, which means you'll be one short."

James showed the first sign of emotion—frustration. "I only shot two into the woods. That leaves me three."

Redvers shrugged. "If you're certain." He looked casual enough, but I could tell that his shoulders were tense with stress. I took a deep breath and moved out of the protection of trees, praying that there would be no sudden gusts of wind and that the others wouldn't inadvertently give me away.

I'd nearly made it to James when a murder of crows somewhere in the woods behind me chose that moment to fly up out of the forest. James started to turn in my direction and I started to drop to my knees when Redvers made a sudden movement forward and James brought his gun back to aim directly at Redvers' chest. My heart stopped in my own and I nearly cried out, but managed to restrain myself. Evelyn shrieked and Carlisle gasped as well, drawing attention away from me once again. I managed to stand back up out of my crouch on shaking knees and closed the distance between myself and James while I had the chance. I raised my weapon, closed my eyes briefly, and then swung down with all the strength I could muster.

CHAPTER NINETEEN

James fell like a bag of rocks, and I did the same, this time dropping to my knees in relief. The other three rushed forward, Redvers reaching James first and retrieving the gun that had fallen only inches from the man's hand. He pocketed the weapon before checking to see if the man was still breathing.

"Is he dead?" I didn't want to be responsible for taking a man's life, but I also knew that I would do anything to stop Redvers from being shot.

"He's breathing." Redvers looked at me, then stepped over James' prone body to help me to my feet. "Nice swing though."

"Thank you. Although I think it's about time I get a pistol of my own, don't you think?"

"You might be right. I do hate finding either of us at the end of a gun, though."

"It's not a favorite pastime of mine either, but it does seem to happen with increasing frequency."

"Enough!" Evelyn shouted. Redvers and I stopped our nervous banter—adrenaline still coursing through our systems made us chatty—and looked at the woman who was standing over her husband with her hands on her hips. "What are we going to do with him?"

Redvers cocked his head at the prone form in the snow. "Drag him?"

"Nothing less than he deserves," Evelyn said before turning to her chauffeur and wrapping the man in a tight hug, surprising both Redvers and myself. "I'm so glad he didn't hurt you. I thought for certain you were dead."

Carlisle returned her embrace, awkward though it was due to their height difference, and I was struck again that it was an awfully close relationship for a woman and her chauffeur. I narrowed my eyes and spoke a thought out loud. "He's not simply your chauffeur, is he?"

The two broke apart and looked at me then at one another. "Of course not. He's my brother."

Redvers chuckled. "So your brother is your husband and your chauffeur is your brother."

"Precisely."

"Makes perfect sense." Redvers was still amused.

In the end no dragging was necessary since James came around enough to walk back to the sleigh under his own steam. Once that was done, we delivered him directly to the police sergeant who seemed delighted to have someone to lock away in his cell.

"Doesn't get enough use, really," Sergeant Thomas said. "You'll have to give statements, of course."

There was a collective nod, Evelyn electing to go first. I was curious about how the woman would talk her way out of being held responsible for any part of what had occurred. Although given how clever the woman was, I had little doubt she'd be able to talk herself clear of things.

While we waited for our turn to speak to the police constable, I took the opportunity to ask Redvers the question that had been on my mind since we'd all gotten back in the sleigh and turned toward town.

"Will you tell your father about any of this?"

Redvers thought for a second. "I don't think so. I'll let Evelyn make that decision."

"And if she still wants to marry him?"

"I don't think that will be a problem."

"What if she really loves him?" It struck me that she might want to go through with the marriage once she could untangle herself from James.

"I think it's in Evelyn's best interests to disappear for a while." Redvers sounded terribly certain of himself.

"Or what?" I asked. "You're not going to threaten her, are you?"

He looked offended. "I would never. No, I think regardless of what she convinces Thomas of, there are still plenty of questions about what her actual involvement was. She's smart—she knows she is better off being well on her way, and quickly. Besides, there's still the fraud she was involved in since she was never legally married to those men. The extended families might have something to say about that, especially their estates."

Carlisle had been watching us this entire time but couldn't hear our quiet conversation from where he sat. "I don't know what you're discussing, but if you're worried about Mr. Dibble, don't be." His jaw tightened. "We'll be leaving directly."

I nodded. At least everyone seemed to be on the same page as far as that was concerned.

An hour later Redvers was giving his statement and Evelyn and Carlisle were readying themselves to leave.

"I'd say it's been a pleasure, Miss Wunderly, but it hasn't, not really." Evelyn pulled her gloves back on, but not before I caught a flash of the family ring still on her finger. She reached into her jacket and pulled out a letter. "Please give this to Humphrey, will you? It explains everything."

I took the letter and nodded; then a final thought occurred to me. "What about Dr. Taylor?"

Evelyn stopped and turned back to look at me. "What about him?"

"Did James kill him?" What I really wanted to ask was whether any of the three of them had killed the man, but my tongue didn't form the question.

Evelyn must have seen it in my face though, and she gave me a grim smile and a shrug. With that, she and Carlisle disappeared into the night. It was an answer that left me wondering whether we should be letting Evelyn and her brother leave after all.

They were well and truly gone when it occurred to me that I'd forgotten to ask if she was going to bother returning the family ring.

CHAPTER TWENTY

It was quite dark and even colder than before when Redvers and I finally got back into the sleigh and headed back to his father's house, so I snuggled close to my fiancé in the sleigh. Purely for body warmth, of course. He tucked me safely under his arm, and despite the cold and the events of the last few hours, I felt myself relax.

We didn't talk much on the way back—both of us were too weary and had too much to think about. Instead, we kept our own counsel until we pulled the sleigh up in front of the house and went inside, notifying Youngblood that Jackson should take extra care of the horses—they'd been worked hard today.

"Where have you two been all day?" Millie was still wearing her blue dress from that morning, although it was slightly creased from the long day. She looked tired but was still glowing with pleasure.

Redvers and I exchanged a glance as we divested ourselves of our coats and gloves. "Sorry we missed the afternoon, Aunt Millie. But I'm so delighted for you and Lord Hughes." I went forward and bussed her cheek, effectively stopping her questions for the moment.

"Well, come in and join us." She led us into the sitting room where the rest of the family had gathered.

*   *   *

We spent a quiet evening chatting with our family, and one by one they all finally drifted off to bed. Humphrey was one of the last, and Redvers gave him the letter that Evelyn had given to me.

He looked at it. "Where did you get this?"

"We found it in her town house," Redvers lied smoothly.

Humphrey looked at it for a long moment before tucking it into his pocket. "Thank you," he said. "Good night to you both. Have a pleasant night's sleep."

We wished him good evening, and when we were finally alone in the room, I let out a long sigh. Nothing about the day had gone as we'd planned, and I was glad it was finally over. But I still had a few stray questions.

"We never did find out if James had anything to do with Mr. Winters getting sick."

"I had someone look into that—I believe it was nothing more than a coincidence. He legitimately fell ill."

"But then Evelyn panicked that James was back, and broke things off," I said.

"And then relaxed again when a few months passed and she thought that she was in the clear. That's when she began spending time with my father."

I was too tired to chastise him for not telling me this information sooner. There had been an awful lot happening after all.

I was quiet for a moment. "Do you think your father will be all right?"

"I do. He'll be just fine." Redvers seemed convinced of it. I hoped he and his father could talk more, but I thought it was best to push the issue again later. So I moved on to a topic that I suspected was a little less difficult, although I wasn't sure by how much.

"Evelyn still had the ring." I paused. "Your grandmother's ring. She left with it."

"I know," Redvers said. "Which reminds me . . . I need to give you your Christmas gift." He rummaged in his pocket before pulling out something small. He stood from his chair and knelt before me, holding out a ring. I immediately recognized it as his grandmother's—the beautiful sapphire surrounded by tiny diamonds.

"Wait. Where did you get that?"

He looked amused and took my hand, slipping it on. It fit perfectly.

I leaned forward and kissed him before repeating my question.

"I'm delighted that I finally managed to surprise you," he said.

"But how?" If the man didn't tell me soon . . . well, I didn't know what I was going to do.

Redvers got to his feet and sat back in his seat, looking smug. "When I was at the jeweler's I had him make a paste copy. That's what Evelyn has."

"Did you suspect all along that she would do this?"

"No, I didn't expect any of what happened. I just didn't want her to have Grandmother's ring." He shrugged. "Aunt Carolyn was right. It should stay in the family."

I laughed. "And what did you think would happen when we came back for a visit and they saw I had the real ring?"

He shrugged. "I figured I would cross that bridge when we got there. And as it turns out, it all worked out for the best." Redvers smiled. "Now we just have to set our own wedding date."

The ring felt good on my finger, not heavy or like a chain needing to be broken. So I nodded. "You're right. We do."